THE CASE OF THE GOLDEN GREEKS

THE MASKED MAN OF CAIRO

BOOK THREE

By Sean McLachlan

To Almudena, my wife
And Julián, my son

THE CASE OF THE GOLDEN GREEKS

THE MASKED MAN OF CAIRO

CHAPTER ONE

Cairo, Autumn 1919

The talk at the Geographical Association of Egypt would have been perfect except for the presence of an unwelcome husband and a hidden murderer.

Sir Augustus Wall had settled into his red velvet seat in the society's main lecture hall, a grand auditorium seating several hundred people facing a stage. The ceiling was decorated with elaborately painted Arabic designs of stars and rosettes. Egyptian ushers in spotless white djellabas and red fezzes showed the members to their places.

Augustus, of course, was at the center and near the front, although not too near the front. His standing in the antiquities trade demanded a prominent place. His general lack of sympathetic demeanor demanded the mild rebuke of having to look over a few rows of more prominent, and much more personable, heads.

Sitting next to Augustus was Zehra Hanzade, a breathtakingly beautiful Ottoman woman who was a good friend, profitable business partner, and—to Augustus's endless frustration—nothing else.

Nevertheless, she was enchanting. She wore a shimmering emerald green caftan embroidered with gold thread, and let her luxuriant black tresses hang loose over her shoulders. Zehra chatted amiably with him about the upcoming lecture.

"I've always wanted to hear Professor Harrell speak," she said. "I've been following his work for many years. Who would have thought he'd make such an important discovery in such a remote place as Bahariya Oasis?"

"Virgin territory, I suppose," Augustus replied. "Not much work has been done except with the temple of Alexander the Great. I have a site report from the British expedition, if you'd like to borrow it."

Zehra's big brown eyes flashed. "Oh, that would be lovely. I'll come over tomorrow and fetch it."

Augustus felt his heart skip a beat.

"It might give me some good ideas for work."

That came from Suleiman, Zehra's husband. He sat on Zehra's other side and Augustus had angled himself perfectly so that the thin man was entirely hidden behind Zehra's plump, wonderfully curved frame.

And now Suleiman had to go and ruin the illusion.

"If you come up with anything good, be sure to give me first pick," Augustus said, trying to maintain a courteous tone.

Suleiman leaned forward, further destroying Augustus' fantasy of being out alone with Zehra, and nodded. His eyes were bloodshot and hooded from his perpetual smoking of Indian hemp, but his unassuming exterior hid the fact that he was the best antiquities forger in Cairo. He was also a major supplier to Augustus' antiquities shop. Augustus sold real antiquities only to those worthy of owning them. The tourists got fakes.

"Ah! It's starting," Moustafa said.

Moustafa, Augustus' assistant, sat on his other side. His brawny frame barely fit in the seat. He was the only Soudanese in the audience. Zehra was one of the few women. Augustus tried to convince himself that was why the pair of Americans sitting two rows in front of him kept turning around, but he knew they were actually staring at the mask that hid his war wound.

"It won't start quite yet," said Heinrich Schäfer, a German Egyptologist sitting next to Moustafa, and one of the few Europeans in Cairo Augustus thought worthy of friendship. "We have a dull introductory speech to get through first."

"Indeed we do," Augustus grumbled, for who came onto the stage but the creaking mummy that ran the society, Sir Archibald Windell, who everyone at the club called "Sir Windbag" for his endless speeches that were renowned from Alexandria to Khartoum as a sure cure for insomnia.

Augustus' own insomnia underwent rapid treatment.

Sir Windell gave a long, rambling talk about the importance of studying all aspects of the protectorate of Egypt, as if the assembled crowd didn't already know that, and then launched into an anecdote about his own travels to Bahariya Oasis that was supposed to be funny and might indeed have been if anyone had gotten the joke. Finally, after a torturous half hour, Sir Windell brought himself around to introducing the speaker.

"Dr. Thornton Harrell of Oxford University will no doubt be known to many of you as the excavator of tombs 34 and 35 at Abusir, but in recent years he's been exploring the remains at the oases of the Western Desert. You may find preliminary accounts of these findings in the latest two numbers of *The Journal of Egyptian Archaeology*. What he will speak of tonight is a startling discovery he made in Bahariya Oasis, one that has not yet been published in any form. The members of the society will be the first to hear it, and we have taken the liberty of not inviting the gentlemen of the press."

Laughter rippled through the audience. Several people applauded, Augustus included.

"Finally," Augustus muttered. "Old Windbag said something worth hearing."

"So without further ado—"

"Thank God!"

"—it is my honor to introduce to you, Professor Thornton Harrell of Balliol College, Oxford."

A slim, middle-aged man with a deep tan rose from the front row and sprang onto the stage. Shaking Sir Windell's hand, he immediately got between the head of the society and the lectern, thereby stopping him from coming back to say anything more. The crowd thundered its applause.

To everyone's relief, Professor Harrell got straight to the point.

"I've come to speak to you about a most fortunate and astonishing discovery of a tomb of the Greco-Roman period near the temple of Alexander in Bahariya Oasis. The temple was built most likely in the year 332 BC, when Alexander the Great stopped in Bahariya in order to consolidate control over the hinterland of his newly conquered territory before heading down to Memphis to consult with the oracles there. Then he returned to the oasis, and it was from Bahariya that he journeyed further on to Siwa Oasis, almost to the border with present-day Italian Cyrenaica, the land of the ancient Libyans. At Siwa the priest of Amun-Re revealed, or was made to reveal—" this brought chuckles from the audience "—that Alexander was the living embodiment of the sun god, and thus pharaoh. It was mostly likely on his way back from this famous meeting that he commissioned the temple in his own honor at Bahariya, it being unique among pharaonic temples in that it was built in honor of a living pharaoh rather than in honor of one deceased. The interior decoration shows Alexander offering to Amun-Re. Alexander's cartouche is on a portion of the wall nearby.

"It was while surveying this temple that I made the most interesting discovery of my career, or should I say our water boy did. Young Hamza was leading a donkey to the nearest well in order to top up our supplies when the animal's leg broke through the surface. Hamza had some trouble extricating the poor donkey, and when he did, he saw that the hole led down into a sizeable underground chamber. He immediately ran back with the news.

"Upon investigating the hole, I discovered that it broke through the ceiling of a tomb. A rectangular chamber measured twenty feet by eight, and contained three shelves on each of the walls, all filled with mummies. The mummy wrappings, while of unusual manufacture, were immediately recognizable as dating to the Greco-Roman period thanks to their style."

The professor motioned to someone standing at the slide projector in front of him. The lights were dimmed and the assistant placed a candle behind the projector. Immediately a glass photographic plate was projected onto a screen hanging behind Professor Harrell. Augustus leaned forward with interest. It showed a stone shelf, thickly covered in dust. Three mummies lay side by side on the shelf. The dust had been cleared away from the nearest mummy to reveal a cartonnage mummy casing with a gilded head and chest. Funerary scenes featuring various Egyptian deities were embossed on the chest, while the face showed a serene smile and wide eyes. Augustus nodded. This was, indeed, in the Greco-Roman style. It was simplistic, almost cartoonish, an odd melding of ancient Egyptian styles and an earthier Classical style typical of artifacts of the common people.

But this mummy was for no common person. The face and chest were gilded. All the previous Greco-Roman funerary masks he had seen in this style were of brightly painted plaster.

Professor Harrell went on to explain how of a total of 82 mummies found in the tomb, twelve had gilding in this style. There were three other styles of mummy: the more familiar coffins with plaster masks like those found in numerous other sites, ceramic anthropomorphic coffins that looked eerily like human beings when still covered with dust, and bodies simply wrapped in linen, often with crude features painted on the face and a few scenes from the *Book of the Dead* painted on the chest. These were obviously for the poorest of the dead, although they had been well preserved because they had been wrapped in reeds.

"We also found a great number of associated artifacts in this undisturbed tomb, including pottery dating from the third century BC to the first century AD, as well as bits of jewelry and a number of Ptolemaic coins including, most intriguingly, a coin of Cleopatra VII."

"A fascinating woman," Zehra whispered to Augustus. "And a most unique manner of death, don't you think?"

Augustus could only nod, not trusting himself to speak. Cleopatra, after the fateful battle of Actium against the Roman legions and knowing all was lost, killed herself by clutching a poisonous asp to her breast. Any mention of breasts in the presence of such a beautiful woman as Zehra was highly disordering to the intellect. Augustus struggled to focus on the lecture. Why did Zehra torture him so?

The slideshow lasted for about half an hour, with several more images of the tomb, an undecorated rectangular chamber with several shelves full of mummies. Close-ups of the best preserved mummies made Suleiman lean forward and study every detail with his bloodshot eyes. Augustus smiled. There would be more Greco-Roman mummies before long. Professor Harrell theorized that this tomb was not directly associated with the temple, there being no evidence of priestly burials. Rather these were notable people from the lay community—men, women, and children who wanted to gain extra favor in the afterlife by being buried close to the temple of the great Alexander.

When the talk concluded, there was a long round of applause. Professor Harrell had made an obviously important discovery. Augustus could see Heinrich Schäfer furiously scribbling notes. He leaned over to his German friend.

"A new chapter for your *Principles of Egyptian Art*?"

"Indeed," Schäfer replied, his pen still dancing across his notebook. "Every time I think I'm about to finish, new material gets unearthed."

The professor now called for questions.

A gentleman stood, rocking slightly to and fro. The society was famous for its cocktail hours before the lectures.

"Professor, why would the Greeks and Romans see fit to live in such a remote place?"

"Bahariya Oasis was less remote in antiquity than it is today. It was famous for its dates and grapes, both of which were used to make wine. Also, it was an important source of iron. The next nearest source was in Meroë in present day Soudan. The settlement was quite prosperous and I estimate that it had a population of some 30,000, roughly half again the size it is today."

The next person to stand was an Egyptian, who asked several technical questions about the construction of the gilded mummies, such as the treatment of the gold itself, its thickness, and the materials used in the lower layers.

Augustus glanced at Suleiman and saw that his usually glazed eyes were focused and alert.

"Does that man work for you?" he murmured to Zehra. It gave him a good excuse to lean in close to her.

She smiled at him. "For tonight at least."

"One or two of those gilded sarcophagi would look good in my showroom."

"I was thinking the same thing."

Once the Egyptian was done, an Englishman stood.

"Professor, I was wondering if you found evidence of other tombs, and if you have an estimate of how extensive this necropolis might be."

Professor Harrell nodded and said. "A most interesting question. We found—AH!"

The professor went stiff, slapped the back of his neck, and put his other hand to his chest. As a murmur went through the crowd he swayed back and forth, his face going pale, and then fell face first with a bang on the lectern.

CHAPTER TWO

Moustafa Ghani El Souwaim acted on instinct. He leaped out of his seat, nearly knocking Herr Schäfer to the floor, and bounded down the aisle.

"The murderer is behind the curtain!" he shouted, pointing to the curtains that hid the right side of the stage.

It had been pure luck that Moustafa had spotted him. While the member of the audience had been asking his question, Moustafa's gaze had strayed from the lectern and for no particular reason settled on the heavy red curtains that screened the stage's right-hand exit.

He'd seen the curtains part, and a vague shape behind the narrow gap. Then a blur of motion and the Egyptologist slumped on the lectern.

Within moments Moustafa was at the front of the room and jumping onto the stage. Everyone was in an uproar. Most of the crowd was on its feet but besides a few gentlemen helping an elderly lady who had fainted, not a single one of them was doing anything useful.

Except for his boss. Mr. Wall was just a few steps behind him.

Moustafa glanced at the dead lecturer as he ran past. A slim metal dart with bright green feathers on the end was stuck in Professor Harrell's neck. The man was rigid, fingers clenched on the edge of the lectern.

That's all Moustafa had time to see as he ran to the curtains and, taking a step to the side, opened them.

Beyond he saw a room empty of anything other than a few chairs and a schedule tacked to the wall. No one was in sight. To the left, narrow stairs ran downward.

Moustafa angled to the left as he crossed the room to stay out of the line of fire of whoever might be at the bottom of that stairway.

Mr. Wall took a different tactic. He angled right, drawing a compact automatic pistol from his jacket pocket and leveling it as he crossed the line of fire.

He stopped midway and then ran straight for the stairs.

"He's bolted," Mr. Wall said.

"You bring a gun to Egyptology lectures, boss?" Moustafa asked as they got to the top of the stairs.

"As you can see, we need it."

Moustafa felt like saying that normal people don't have this happen to them often enough to take such precautions, but he decided now was not the time.

They went down the stairs, Mr. Wall leading with his gun, and came to a large storage cellar. Lit by only a single weak electric bulb at the far end above a partially obscured door, the cellar was nearly filled with stacks of chairs, old display cases, wooden crates, and what looked like the background scenery for the Christmas pantomime.

Moustafa glimpsed a shadow move behind a stack of old desks.

He heard a puffing sound, and jerked to the right, ducking and almost ending up on the floor. Something shot past and thunked into a chair behind him.

Mr. Wall's pistol barked, the flash bright in the dim room. Moustafa grabbed a table leg sitting on a work bench and threw it at the far door, which was just opening.

He timed it perfectly and it hit the killer flat in the back as he was rushing out.

Something clattered on the floor. The man staggered, and the door closed behind him.

"Don't let him get away!" Mr. Wall shouted.

Did his boss think he needed to be told? They got to the door and yanked it open. Just at the last moment they remembered themselves and ducked out of sight. Moustafa took a quick peek and saw the killer disappearing beyond a second door at the end of a short hallway.

In two long strides they were to the far door. They opened it and Mr. Wall almost fired at the first thing he saw in the alley beyond.

Faisal.

He was sitting on the ground at the far side of the alley.

"Where did he—" Moustafa saved his breath. The street urchin was already pointing to the left.

The alley led to a busy sidewalk. A large evening crowd walked each direction while street vendors cried their wares.

Moustafa pushed out into the throng and looked both ways. He hadn't seen the killer's face, only that he was of medium height, with a dirty white turban and simple djellaba of the same color. He thought he had glimpsed a black beard but couldn't be sure.

He saw dozens of men passing by who matched that description.

He stormed past Mr. Wall, who was still gazing baffled at the crowd, and strode up to Faisal, who jumped to his feet and backed off.

"Did you see his face?"

"I don't know him. What has he done?"

"Did you see his face!"

"Yes."

Mr. Wall came up. "He just killed a man. Get into the street!"

Faisal brightened. "Don't worry, Englishman, I'll find him."

Faisal ran out the alley and scampered up the nearest lamppost, leaning far out, one foot planted on one side of the post with his hand gripping the other side. He studied the crowd, looking slowly in all directions as a fat corn seller shouted at him to get down.

After a minute he dropped to the pavement, ducked a swipe from the corn seller's broad hand, and ran up to them.

"Sorry. He's gone."

"Would you remember him?" Mr. Wall asked.

"Sure."

"What are you doing here?" Moustafa demanded. This boy was no end of trouble, always tagging along and begging Mr. Wall for money.

"I saw you taking the motorcar. You always go somewhere interesting when you take the motorcar."

"You couldn't have hidden in the back seat this time," Moustafa said, his suspicion growing. "I was sitting in it with the Hanzades."

"Oh, I, um, ran along behind you."

Moustafa clipped him on the side of the head.

"Don't lie!"

"Ow! It's the truth."

"You wouldn't know the truth if it bit you on the ass! Now tell me what happened before I pull off your fingers one by one and feed them to the jackals."

Faisal gulped. "I saw you come in here and looked for a back way in. The only one I found was this one, but the door was locked. So I sat in the alley hoping for it to open. What's going on inside? Did you see some moving pictures?"

"Just answer the question, Faisal," Mr. Wall said patiently. Too patiently. Just because Faisal had helped out on one or two cases, Mr. Wall had become far too indulgent with the little beggar.

"I was sitting there and that flute player came to the door and unlocked it."

"Flute player?" Moustafa asked. The lice must have dug into the boy's skull and eaten his brain.

"Sure, he was carrying a long reed flute. He unlocked the door and went in. Then I snuck in behind him. I didn't like that room, though. Too many places for the djinn to hide. So I went back to the alley."

"Then what?" Mr. Wall asked.

"The flute player came running out a few minutes later, with you two chasing him. He didn't have his flute, though."

"What's this about a flute?" Moustafa demanded. "We were chasing a killer, not a member of some band!"

"I think I know," Mr. Wall said. "Faisal, you stay here. We'll be back."

"Did I help? That's got to be worth something. I only need—" Faisal's voice was cut off as Mr. Wall closed the door on him. Moustafa gave a sigh of relief. That boy was more annoying than a swarm of mosquitos.

They reentered the storage cellar. By now another light had been switched on and several men were searching the room.

"He's gone," Mr. Wall told them. "He had a key to this back door and he left through it."

"We'll call the police," one of the men said.

"And the professor?" Moustafa asked.

"Dead."

Moustafa grimaced. That's what he had suspected.

Mr. Wall did not grimace. The side of his face not covered by his mask was open and eager. He squatted near the back door and peered around him.

"Ah! There it is."

He bent under an old desk and pulled out a reed tube about a meter long.

"This is the murder weapon," Mr. Wall announced. "What Faisal mistook for a flute."

Moustafa looked at it uncertainly. "How did it shoot the dart?"

"It's a blow tube. You place the dart in, daubed with poison of course, and blow. The dart shoots out. Effective enough at short distances. They're common in many jungle cultures around the world. Not known in this region at all. Our killer is obviously a traveler."

Mr. Wall's knowledge of Egyptology was only surpassed by his expertise in different and unusual ways to kill people.

"Why didn't he just shoot the professor?" Moustafa asked. "Wouldn't it have been more certain?"

"Perhaps. It's one of the many questions we have yet to answer."

Moustafa suppressed a groan. Mr. Wall had found another case.

CHAPTER THREE

Faisal didn't know what to think. He had followed the Englishman to this place hoping to have some fun and instead someone got killed. People got killed around the Englishman a lot. Maybe someone had put a curse on him.

While that would be bad, this curse sure did make Faisal a lot of money. He always found ways to help the Englishman and that earned him some really big tips, plus lots of good food and even some rides in the motorcar. Once it had even gotten him into the place where they showed moving pictures.

It had nearly gotten him killed a few times too. Plus he had seen all sorts of terrible things like severed heads. He hoped whoever was dead inside this big English building didn't have a severed head. He never wanted to see another one of those as long as he lived.

Faisal paced back and forth in the alley, thinking of the possibilities. What could he ask for this time? Money, of course. He always needed money. Maybe another trip to the moving pictures? Oh, and some sandals. The ones he had gotten as part of his disguise last time were almost worn out.

What was taking them so long? He stopped and stared at the door. They weren't going to forget him, were they? Moustafa was always telling him to go away, but the Englishman knew better. He knew how useful Faisal was.

Maybe they had caught another killer inside? Maybe the whole band were killers and not just the flute player. The Englishman could be fighting for his life with a murderous drummer right this minute while Faisal cooled his heels outside.

It was up to Faisal to save him again.

Just as he made it to the door, the Englishman flung it open, knocking Faisal onto the ground.

"Faisal, where are you?" The Englishman looked around, then down at his feet. "Oh, there you are. What are you doing lying down at a time like this?"

"Ouch. Nothing. Did you catch anyone else?"

"No, the man worked alone. Did you get a good look at his face?"

Faisal nodded. He really had, and this would mean all sorts of good things if he could point the man out.

"What did he look like?" Moustafa demanded, appearing at the door.

Faisal hesitated. If he told them, they wouldn't need him anymore.

"Oh, he's hard to describe, but kind of unusual looking. I'd recognize him for sure."

"Bah! The Little Infidel doesn't know a thing," Moustafa scoffed. "He's just hoping for a handout."

"I'm not!" Faisal whined.

"You say you saw him, but did he see you?" the Englishman asked.

Faisal shook his head. "No one sees me."

"Just like we don't want to see you," Moustafa barked. "Now go away."

The Englishman held up a hand. "Wait. If he says he saw the murderer's face, I believe him. You better stay with us."

Faisal stuck out his tongue at Moustafa, then had to scamper back as the Nubian tried to clout him.

"Behave," the Englishman said, and held up the flute. "Have you seen this before?"

"Yes, it's the flute the man was carrying."

"If this is a flute, then it plays pretty deadly music."

"How can music kill someone, you silly Englishman?"

The Englishman reached into his pocket. Faisal perked up. He was getting his reward so soon?

He deflated a little to see the Englishman only hand over a piastre.

"I deserve more than that if I help you catch the musician!" Faisal whined.

"You'll get more if you catch him," the Englishman said. "Go get yourself something to eat and bring it back here. Then stay put. We'll need you later."

The Englishman and Moustafa closed the door on him again.

Faisal shook his head in frustration. They were always leaving him behind when something interesting was going on. He bet something really interesting was happening in that big English building, and he didn't get to see it. Maybe he could sneak in without them noticing him. There were a lot of Englishmen in that building, so it would be hard, but he could manage it.

His stomach grumbled.

He looked at the door, then looked at the piastre in his hand. His stomach grumbled again.

Food first.

He ran off to find the nearest falafel stand.

By the time he got back, several motorcars from the Colonial Police had parked in front of the building. He avoided them and went to the back alley, sitting against the wall and eating his dinner. The Englishman, like all Englishmen, didn't know the prices of things and so he had given him too much. That was all right. He had only spent half a piastre on the falafels and so had another half piastre left over for breakfast. He could go the *ful* stand where Mina worked and tell her he was working on a mystery for the Englishman again.

Faisal had to wait a long time. Once Moustafa popped his head out the door, shouted "Wait there!", and then slammed it shut again before Faisal could say anything. Faisal shrugged. He was ten years old. Or maybe twelve. No, more like ten. Or eleven. Anyway, he had learned a lot in however long he had been alive, and one of the things that he had learned was that patience paid off. It sure paid off when you were waiting for everyone in a house to fall asleep before you snuck inside, or for a market stall owner who thought he was on to you to finally stop paying attention just long enough for you to swipe something.

At last Moustafa and the Englishman appeared. Faisal's heart skipped a beat. They were not alone.

With them was the worst and most important Englishman in Cairo.

Sir Thomas Russell Pasha ran the Colonial Police. Faisal had snuck into his office once. That had been the scariest break-in he had ever done, and he didn't even get anything out of it.

Well, he got a new djellaba and sandals to play the part. That was nice.

But those hadn't been worth the danger. No.

The policeman said something in English to the Englishman, who turned to Faisal and asked him in Arabic,

"He wants a complete description of the man you saw."

Faisal gulped. He could hold out on the Englishman, but he couldn't hold out on Sir Thomas Russell Pasha. It looked like that piastre was all he was going to get.

"He was older. Not old, though. His hair was black, and he had a tanned face like a farmer or a road worker. Kind of a flat face. Lots of lines in it. He had a scar here on the left cheek and a short beard that was a bit messy and needed a trim."

The Englishman translated this and the policeman laughed.

"Sir Thomas says you just described ten thousand people here in Cairo and probably a hundred thousand in all of Egypt."

"I'd know him if I saw him again. Honest!"

"Was he with anybody?"

"No. Oh, I forgot to tell you. He was about as tall as Youssef."

"Who?"

"The barber on our street."

"You mean my street? You don't live on my street. The neighborhood watchman would have beaten you flat by now."

Karim? Ha! That old goat was so slow and stupid he couldn't catch a blind donkey with a broken leg.

"That's right, Englishman. I live on another street."

The Englishman was very smart but also very easy to fool, which didn't make any sense but that sure was lucky for Faisal, who had made a comfy home for himself in an abandoned shed on the Englishman's roof. The Englishman never came up there. He always hid inside his house, hardly seeing anyone.

"We might need you again, Faisal, if we catch a suspect and want him identified. Come around to the house tomorrow."

"I will. But what am I going to eat until then?" Faisal said clutching his stomach.

"You can eat garbage!" Moustafa shouted. "Stop asking for money every time you open your mouth."

"Here," the Englishman said, giving him another piastre while Moustafa grumbled. "Show up around sunset. We might have more on this case by then."

Faisal jumped up and spun in the air.

"Thanks, Englishman! I'll see you tomorrow. Maybe I'll find out something more for you."

He sure hoped so. The Englishman always paid well for information. Faisal needed to figure out where he could find the flute player who had killed someone.

CHAPTER FOUR

Augustus met with the chief of police at his favorite lunch spot, the front terrace of Shepheard's Hotel. That is to say, it was Sir Thomas's favorite spot. Augustus had no favorite spot, or rather his favorite spot was as far away from people as one could get.

But the chief of police had invited him because of the previous night's murder. That piqued Augustus' interest enough to show up. He assumed that because they would discuss police business, Sir Thomas wouldn't bring any unwanted companions along. When Augustus arrived, he let out a sigh of relief to see he was right.

They sat as usual at a small table close to the end of the terrace. The terrace was set above and a bit back from the street, further protected by a railing of ornate ironwork. Lined up on the opposite side was a crowd of Egyptians selling tours, live animals, and fake antiquities. One fellow in a dirty yellow djellaba and matching skullcap had a tired-looking monkey in a small wire cage. A parrot perched on another man's shoulder nearby screeched at the monkey. The monkey banged on the wire cage, baring its teeth at the parrot. Vendors shouted at the Europeans having breakfast. Traffic blared. The hotel guests carried on with their conversations.

"Do you pick this table because it's so loud here it's impossible for people to eavesdrop?" Augustus asked.

"Of course, my good man. The only more private spot is my office on the Citadel, only that's a long way off. The crime happens down here in the city, so this is where I prefer to be."

Augustus nodded. Sir Thomas was a conscientious and hardworking enforcer of the law, although a tad unimaginative. The stranger aspects of the more unusual cases tended to elude him. Augustus suspected that was why he was here eating lunch with him.

He did not expect what the police chief said next, however.

"You've come in on the final stages of an extensive investigation, old chap."

"Have I?"

"Indeed. We have been investigating a series of crimes connected with members of the Geographical Association of Egypt for some time."

Sir Thomas dug into his eggs Benedict as he let this sink in. Augustus took a sip of his coffee, waiting to hear more. He had often helped the police chief on various affairs. This was the first time he was being asked in so late in the game, however. That murder taking place right in front of him proved fortuitous.

"We received a complaint from a clerk at the society a few months ago, saying that the assistant director, one Carl Riding, was embezzling money by funding expeditions that never materialized. Poor old Sir Archibald Windell is very much a figurehead, you see. A bit too long in the tooth to pay attention to affairs, so Riding is the man really running the show. The clerk said the money would be itemized and doled out to private parties for work all up and down the Nile, but no results ever came back. This has been happening for years and the supposed recipients of the funds came up with various excuses for their failures—sickness among the party, a boat capsizing and losing all the artifacts and photographic plates, that sort of thing. These were all relatively modest expeditions spread out over the course of several years, so no one noticed at first. It was only after some time in Riding's office that the clerk realized what was happening. Fearing his position if he spoke out at the society, since he didn't know who else might be in on the game, he came to us."

"An honest man. Your clerk is a rarity."

"Indeed. It would make my job quite a bit easier if there were more of his ilk. At first we thought this to be a routine affair. We had a man watch Riding and discovered something rather surprising. He was funding expeditions, just not the ones he said he was. It appears that the recipients of the money did buy the equipment they said they would, and did set out from Cairo. So far their destination and purpose is unknown to us."

"Do you have the dates and personnel for these expeditions?"

"I'll send you a list, but it won't do you much good, I'm afraid. As far as we can tell all the names and institutional affiliations are fake."

"Was Professor Harrell funded by the society?"

"Yes, but here's the interesting part. His was a legitimate operation. Riding also doled out funds to real expeditions using real scholars that came back with real results. Harrell's was one of them."

"I suppose the society couldn't fund only false expeditions without being revealed," Augustus mused.

"What's more, the good professor had requested a meeting with me."

"Did he now?"

"Yes, he sent me a note the other day. We were supposed to meet this morning. A pity he didn't tell me what he wanted to see me about."

"You should have met him earlier."

"Indeed."

"You seem to have found a most interesting puzzle."

Sir Thomas grinned and popped the last bit of egg into his mouth. He wiped his mouth with a napkin and said, "A puzzle that is all but complete, my friend. Our man watching Riding, along with the assistance of the clerk, has discovered at least three respected members of the society who have knowledge of what Riding has been doing. They are all listed as donors to various false expeditions. Other donations are listed as anonymous."

"And Riding wouldn't solicit donations from people who weren't in on the game, because he'd have difficulty explaining why none of these expeditions ever succeed."

"Precisely. And the clerk took a peek at the donation records and found these three individuals only contributed to the false expeditions. I'll write down their names, and the name of the clerk. A most enterprising fellow, but don't contact him unless absolutely necessary. He quite rightly fears for his position and doesn't want his work for us to be revealed."

"I'm sure you've gotten all you can out of him," Augustus said, while adding silently, *and anything more interesting I'll have to dig up myself.*

"What we really want to know are the identities of those anonymous donors," Sir Thomas said. "We're thinking they were in the audience, and that Harrell was mixed up in it somehow, and that he was killed not only to keep him quiet, or to keep him from learning something, but also to keep others quiet."

"So Harrell's very public killing was to send a warning of some sort."

"That's it, yes."

"Have you any idea of the nature of this warning, or who might have been its intended recipients?"

"None whatsoever."

"Hmm, sounds interesting, but why call me in?"

Sir Thomas laughed. "Do you think you're such a man of mystery? I can read you like the morning newspaper. Witnesses tell me that as soon as the poor professor fell over with that dart in his neck, you and your assistant were bounding on stage to run after the murderer. You're as much in this case as I am now, regardless of whether I bring you aboard or not. I might as well have you sharing information rather than going your own way and causing all sorts of trouble. You know, for a moment many in the audience thought you were the killers. A good thing no one else present was armed like you were."

"Indeed," Augustus said, somewhat nettled by the police chief's easy manner.

Sir Thomas studied him. "Do you always go armed?"

"Always."

"Cairo isn't as dangerous as all that."

"It is for me."

Sir Thomas laughed, then checked his watch. "Oh, you had best be going. I'll get the bill. If you tarry much longer, you'll be roped into conversation for another hour at least."

Augustus thought he knew what the officer was hinting at and sprang from his seat.

"Very well. I'll get to work on …"

His words trailed off as he saw his greatest fear had been realized.

Sir Thomas's sister Cordelia and their aunt Pearl approached the table. Cordelia was a pretty girl with blue eyes and cornflower hair, well into her twenties and still unattached. She had come with what local Englishmen called "the fishing fleet," unmarried women staying for the season to find a suitable match among the colonial officers or in the ranks of management among the various commercial enterprises. Cordelia had stayed through three seasons, with only a break to France during the worst of the summer heat, and still had not landed the right fish.

That was because she was fishing for Augustus, and he wasn't biting.

Her eyes lit up when she saw him.

"Oh, Augustus, such a pleasant surprise!"

"How very nice to see you," Augustus said, eyeing the door. "And you too, Aunt Pearl."

Everyone except the servants referred to Aunt Pearl as if she was some spinster relative. She had a familiar manner—aided no doubt by a regular and abundant supply of alcohol—that put everyone at ease. Aunt Pearl wanted nothing if not to see her last unmarried niece find a good match, and she and Augustus were in silent agreement that he was not a suitable candidate.

Augustus pulled out chairs for both of them and they sat. After a moment's hesitation, Augustus sat too. He cursed himself for not having fully vanquished the social niceties.

"Well then," Aunt Pearl said once she had settled her plump body into the wicker chair and smoothed out a brightly colored dress more appropriate for a woman of Cordelia's age. "I think it's time for my morning constitutional."

Augustus checked his watch. 12:45. Nearly an hour late. The poor dear must be beside herself. Indeed, he could detect a slight trembling in Aunt Pearl's hands.

An Egyptian waiter appeared, dressed in an immaculate red fez with matching vest and slippers, plus billowing white pantaloons. The tourists all oohed and aahed over the supposedly authentic native costumes at the hotel, although in reality the chap couldn't have been any more inauthentic if he had been wearing a deerstalker cap and a pair of plus fours.

"I'll have a double gin and tonic and the girl will have a mango juice," Aunt Pearl declared.

"Right away, madam," the waiter said with a bow. "And the good sirs?"

Sir Thomas lit a cigarette. "Another coffee for me. I'm on duty and it looks to be a long day."

"Nothing for me, thank you," Augustus added. "I must be leaving shortly."

Cordelia's face fell. "But we just got here."

"Ah, yes, well as much as it pains me, I do have quite a bit to do today."

"At your shop?" Cordelia asked.

"Oh, I'll be out and about town most of the day," Augustus said. Actually he did have work to do at his shop, but Cordelia knew where that was and might make an unannounced, and unwelcome, appearance.

When would this woman understand that he wasn't interested? Never, most likely. She saw him as a charity case. She had worked as a nurse all through the war and taking care of broken men had gotten into her blood. Now that the battles had stopped, she wanted to take care of one of the enduring casualties.

Augustus had moved to Cairo looking for anonymity and peace. The last thing he needed was some starry-eyed woman following him around.

It was his fault, really. He had saved her life from a French criminal gang. Now she looked at him as some sort of tragic hero. He'd never get rid of her at this rate.

Perhaps he should pop off his mask and give her a glance of the ruin hidden beneath. That would be sure to shatter any girlish illusions. Sadly, he was too much of a gentleman to do such a horrid thing to a lady, even one as annoying as her.

He stood, bowed, and said his goodbyes.

"That was a bit rude, old chap," Augustus said to himself as he stepped onto the street and pushed through the gauntlet of souvenir sellers. "But sad to say, courtesy hasn't gotten the message through."

Within half a block, Augustus had forgotten about her and was on his way to his second appointment for the day.

Dr. James Wood of the Royal Institute of Tropical Medicine received Augustus in his sunny office on the top floor of the institute. Lined with bookshelves of medical texts, it was immaculately clean and well ordered, as was Dr. Wood himself, a trim man in his middle years. When they shook hands, Augustus caught a faint whiff of antiseptic.

Dr. Wood offered him a drink and they both settled down to a short portion of Scotch.

"My assistant tells me the chief of police has sent you to get the blood results on Professor Harrell," the physician said, an unspoken question in his tone.

"I sometimes work as a private investigator, and I was present at the murder. Plus, I am a bit of an expert on exotic weapons. The blow gun used a poison dart of the curare variety, I take it?"

Dr. Wood nodded. "Indeed. To be precise, the poison was from the Amazonian vine known to science as *Chondrodendron tomentosum*. The natives there extract the toxin from the leaves and create a sort of paste they put on darts and arrows. The dart hit the jugular vein, sending the poison straight through the heart, causing it to palpitate and inducing a heart attack. The venom would have paralyzed his entire voluntary nervous system and killed him within a few minutes through asphyxiation, but the professor's apparently weak heart made death all but instantaneous."

Augustus took a sip of his Scotch and thought about this.

"Is death always certain with this type of poison?"

"In medical science nothing is certain. But the poison was highly concentrated and virtually pure. Plus, there was a direct hit on a major vein. Whoever did this knows their business."

"Do you happen to have a picture of this vine?"

The doctor fetched a volume from his library, flipped through it, and handed it to Augustus open to a page showing a long, leafy vine.

"There it is, although I don't know how they managed to get the poison. No such vine could grow naturally in this climate. From what I've read, the toxins must be extracted from freshly picked plants. If the plant dries out, the toxins lose their efficacy. They must be growing the vine locally somehow."

Augustus finished his Scotch and stood. "Thank you very much for your help, doctor."

Dr. Wood studied him for a moment. "I notice your skin is irritated around your mask."

"Life here keeps me in an almost perpetual state of irritation."

The doctor chuckled. "Try teaching the natives about basic sanitation and the germ theory of disease."

"A Sisyphean task, no doubt."

"Shall I examine you?"

Augustus tensed. He did not like anyone, even members of the medical fraternity, to look at his wound.

Sensing his hesitation, Dr. Wood said, "I served on the Western Front, my good man. There is nothing I haven't seen."

Reluctantly Augustus removed the tin mask. It had been made for him, as for many others in his state of mutilation, by a group of French artists based on old photographs of when the soldiers had been whole.

Dr. Wood paled a little and tightened his lips.

Seen it all, eh? Augustus thought. *That may be so, but no one gets used to seeing this.*

"There is a light redness and inflammation to the skin all around where the mask rests," Dr. Wood said, having regained his composure. "It would be best not to wear it at all times."

"I beg your pardon?" Augustus couldn't think of any other reply to this ridiculous statement.

"You live alone?" It came out more as a statement than a question. Augustus resented the assumption.

"I do."

"Then it would be best to leave it off while you are indoors. I will also prescribe you a salve to help reduce the irritation. The skin can get quite sensitive around wounds of this nature."

And what would you know firsthand of "wounds of this nature?"

The doctor wrote out a scrip.

"Apply a small amount of this to the affected area every evening before bed. If there's anything else I can do, do not hesitate to ask."

"Can you build me a new face?" Augustus heard himself snap. He had not intended on saying it out loud.

Dr. Wood looked embarrassed. "Surely this has been explained to you."

Augustus cleared his throat. "I apologize for my outburst."

"Think nothing of it. Did you notice there is a small crack on the edge of your mask?" The doctor offered it to him. Augustus put it back on.

"A street urchin thought it would be funny to knock it off."

"I hoped you gave him a good thrashing."

"No, but my assistant has on numerous occasions."

"Oh, I forgot to mention that this particular plant compound is rather unstable. Once made, it will not keep its poisonous qualities past a few weeks."

"Meaning it was made locally."

"With plants found only in South America, yes."

Augustus scratched his chin. "Hmmm. That's interesting. Yes, very interesting indeed."

CHAPTER FIVE

Working for a European had many advantages, but serving their caprices was not one of them.

Moustafa had opened the antiquities shop on Ibn al-Nafis Street that morning as usual, but as soon as Mr. Wall came downstairs he told him that he had a different task for him today.

He handed Moustafa the blowgun.

"Could you find out who sells these?"

"In Cairo, boss? I've never even heard of this weapon before."

"There must be someone who knows something about it. I'll watch the shop. You go see what you can find out."

So now he was exploring the weapons shops in Khan el-Khalili, Cairo's largest and oldest market. Or rather, he was exploring the shops that displayed legal items, but also sold weapons.

Except for ceremonial weapons like the swords and muskets used in weddings, weapons were strictly illegal. The ceremonial weapons were all made to be useless, the blades dull and brittle, the musket barrels too weak to fire. Shopping for real weapons would land you several years of hard labor, especially after the Colonial Police had clamped down on the independence protests.

And now Moustafa had to do it.

Or course Mr. Wall was right in assigning him the job of going from shop to shop dropping broad hints. Mr. Wall, as a foreigner, would have gotten nowhere. But in five hours of constant searching, he had been offered hashish, women, a punch in the nose for trying to buy illegal goods, threats to call the police, a mountain of evasive answers, and finally one good lead.

It came after giving a bit of money to a cutlery store owner who looked like he had something to say.

"Go to Abd-el-Salam's on Antique Street. Don't tell anyone you heard it from me."

Abd-el-Salam's looked like every other shop on the street—a narrow storefront set on the ground floor of an old stone building. Three stories rose above it, the blank stone walls punctuated by dark wooden meshrabiyya. Moustafa wondered if any women were watching him enter the shop from behind those ornate screens, and what they might say to their husbands.

The interior was all but filled with rusting bric-a-brac. Metal chairs, railings ripped from old houses, brass lamps, boxes full of bent nails, busts of dead European leaders … if it was old, battered, useless, and made of metal, Abd-el-Salam had it.

He also had a couple of interesting items in his dusty display window. On the left as he came in the door was a metal platter painted with a scene of red-coated British soldiers in pith helmets fighting Egyptian troops wearing white uniforms and red fezzes. In faded letters above the scene it said, "Battle of Tel-el-Kebir, 13 September 1882, 3rd Battalion Kings Royal Rifle Corps." To the right of the entrance was a genuine Mamluk scabbard made of brass with verses of the Koran etched on it. No sword, just the scabbard. While these two items didn't actually say "Weapons sold here," they gave Moustafa confidence in the cutlery seller's word.

A hunched man in a heavy brown djellaba shuffled out of the gloom. He had the easy smile of a shopkeeper who is about to start a sales pitch.

"How are you, honorable sir? Welcome to my humble shop. We have many things to interest you."

Moustafa bided his time. He made a slow passage through the shop, and any time he found something of a military nature—some old shell casings etched with scenes of drinking Englishmen, a faded uniform of the Egyptian army from the time of Mohammad Ali, a German Pickelhaube—he would handle them and nod appreciatively. Abd-el-Salam was beside himself. Here was a customer actually showing interest! He was sure to buy something.

Moustafa gave the man a searching look, then walked over to the Mamluk scabbard.

"This is beautiful," he said, genuinely admiring the craftsmanship. "Pity it's missing its most important part."

Then he moved over to the regimental tray. "Ah, the Battle of Tel-el-Kebir. When the great Ahmed Ourabi stood up against the British. The Egyptians were sadly outgunned. They only had American-made Remingtons while the British had the Martini-Henry. A fine gun, the Martini-Henry, although one has to take care to aim a bit low since the kick is so strong. Unless one is firing at a target of more than 400 yards. The bullet is relatively slow, you see, and begins to drop sooner than the average rifle."

More of Mr. Wall's knowledge. Working for him, Moustafa was learning as much about weapons as he was about Egyptology.

He gave Abd-el-Salam another significant look and put a fifty piastre note on the tray.

Moustafa and the shop owner stared at each other for a minute. Moustafa could tell what was going on in his mind. Abd-el-Salam was weighing the odds. In front of him stood a Nubian asking to see whatever illegal goods he sold here. Many of the Colonial Police were Nubians. But this man did not act like a policeman. He did not bully or threaten. Instead he bribed. Bribes always went to the police, not away from them.

At last the shopkeeper pocketed the money and nodded toward the back of the room.

"Come this way," he said softly. "I think I might have more items to interest you."

Abd-el-Salam led Moustafa to the back of the shop and down a staircase so narrow that Moustafa had to turn to the side to fit. It led to a small domed cellar.

Moustafa gaped. All around him was an impressive array of weaponry. Spears, swords, clubs, and axes from a dozen different armies and tribes were arrayed in tidy racks. A shelf held a collection of knives. He moved over to it and picked up a dagger in a silver scabbard so tarnished as to be almost black.

"Ah! You have a good eye, artistic sir. This is a rare item, more than seven hundred years old, from the time of the Ayyubids."

Moustafa drew the knife and held it to the light.

"The Ayyubids did not have forged steel of such quality. This is a fake."

"Oh no! Not at all! You see, it was made by my great-grandfather more than a hundred years ago to sell to tourists. He made hundreds of them. This is the last. It is not a fake antique, knowledgeable sir, but an antique fake."

Moustafa snorted and put the dagger down. He scanned the room and noticed there were no guns. Perhaps there was another room he hadn't seen, and would not see if he didn't buy anything here.

It didn't matter. He wasn't looking for guns. His boss had too many of them already. He would probably have to buy something if he wanted to get anything from this man about the blowgun, though.

Then he saw it.

He hung in a scabbard of crocodile skin next to a row of spears.

A sword from the army of the Mahdi.

He pulled it off the rack. The leather binding around the hilt was still in good condition. With a feeling of reverence, he drew it.

The blade was straight and more than three feet long, keen on both edges and coming to a fine point.

Moustafa's eyes lit up. These were the swords wielded by the followers of the Mahdi in his great revolt that had pushed the British out of the Soudan in his father's time. Epic battles had been fought and won with swords like these as the Mahdist Empire, thrilled at following the promised final prophet, conquered the southern tribes and the Somalis and the Abyssinians. They had even pushed into southern Egypt itself.

The Mahdi had been a false prophet, and his rule had been a disastrous one. He had been the scourge of the land, burning any village that resisted. When famine came, he declared it God's will and let his own people starve. And then the terrible vengeance of the British came.

But for a few glorious years, the Soudanese had held their heads high.

Moustafa turned the blade this way and that, admiring the shine from the oil lamp on the steel.

Abd-el-Salam bowed and smiled. "If I were a tailor, generous sir, I would say it looks good on you."

"How much for this?"

The shopkeeper named an inflated price. Moustafa didn't haggle too much. He wanted the shopkeeper happy, and Mr. Wall had already promised to repay any "reasonable expenses." Moustafa wasn't sure a sword that might have once drank British blood counted as a reasonable expense, but he didn't care.

Once a deal had been made on the sword and the shopkeeper had wrapped it up in an old carpet so Moustafa could take it home without being arrested, the shopkeeper sent a boy to fetch some tea from the nearest cafe.

They settled down to their tea and after a few minutes of chatting about nothing important, Moustafa got to the point.

He pulled the blowgun from a bag he had with him.

"Have you ever seen a weapon like this?"

"Ah, this is very interesting," the shopkeeper said, taking it and turning it over in his hands.

"Do you know what it is?"

"There is no word for it in Arabic, I believe. It is a tube in which you put a dart and blow it out. The darts are covered in poison. They are used in the great Amazon jungle, as well as the jungles of India and further east."

"You sound like you know quite a lot."

Abd-el-Salam bowed. "I am but a poor shopkeeper, but as they say, 'education is the greatest treasure.'"

"And how much treasure is your education going to cost me?"

"Oh, we are good friends, my Soudanese swordsman. I would not dream of overcharging you for just a bit of information. But tell me, what exactly do you want to know?"

"Who in Cairo uses one of these? The man was Egyptian, not a foreigner."

That caught Abd-el-Salam by surprise. "An Egyptian?"

Moustafa handed over a fifty piastre note, which Abd-el-Salam looked at with ill-disguised contempt. Moustafa handed over another fifty.

"I know of only one man who uses such a device, and he was a foreigner. A strange man, quite short and broad. Not a European. He had the skin of an Egyptian but his black hair was straight, his eyes brown. He spoke very little Arabic, and he spoke it with a strange accent."

"Did he say where he was from?"

Abd-el-Salam shook his head. "He named a place but I had never heard of it and it passed from my mind. He was here with his master and another man, making purchases."

"Making purchases?"

Abd-el-Salam looked at him. Moustafa gave him a hundred piastre note.

"With his master, a European. The other man was Egyptian. I cannot tell you any more about my customers. I am only telling you this because I heard about the murder with the tube that blows darts. Everyone is talking about it. I believe a man has the right to protect his house and family, and should be able to go armed, but to kill a man giving a speech?" Abd-el-Salam tut-tutted.

"Tell me more about this Egyptian."

"He talked with both the European and the other foreigner. The European spoke the other foreigner's language and translated for him. The Egyptian had the air of a student learning from two respected teachers."

"What did they talk about?"

Abd-el-Salam looked away. "They spoke in low tones so that I could not hear."

"What did the Egyptian look like?"

"I am sorry, but that is all I can say."

Moustafa held up another hundred piastre note. Abd-el-Salam shook his head.

"That is all I can tell you."

Moustafa thanked him, rolled the sword up securely in the carpet, and headed back to the house on Ibn al-Nafis Street.

As he arrived, Mr. Wall was just wrapping up a small ebony statue of Anubis for a customer. Once the man had left, his boss turned to him.

"Any luck?"

Moustafa relayed what he had learned.

"Excellent! I'll ring Sir Thomas with the information. It shouldn't be too hard to track down someone growing Amazonian plants in Cairo."

When he came back he pulled out his wallet.

"I suppose you had to pay a few bribes and buy whatever is in that musty old carpet?"

Moustafa named what he had paid in bribes and then, smiling with pride, unwrapped the Mahdist sword.

"Good Lord! I wouldn't want to face you if you were wielding that!"

Moustafa gave it a few experimental swings.

"Careful you don't decapitate any statues," Mr. Wall said.

"I might just be able to with a fine sword like this! My uncle fought at Omdurman and several of the other battles. He taught me how to fight with one of these when I was barely out of boyhood."

"A fine piece. I daresay it might come in handy before this whole thing is through. I seem to recall I wanted to buy you one of those. Well, now I have. How much was it?"

Moustafa paused and looked at it. The sword had been expensive, but he did not want Mr. Wall to repay him. No, this sword should not be bought with English money.

"That's all right, boss. I bought it for myself."

"Are you quite certain?"

"Yes, boss."

"Very well then. Put it away for the time being and help me with this stock I'm taking. We won't be able to do much more with the case until I hear back from Sir Thomas." The phone rang from the back room. "Ah! I suspect that's him now."

Mr. Wall went to the back room and talked for a few minutes while Moustafa busied himself around the shop.

As last Mr. Wall returned, and said the thing Moustafa least wanted to hear.

"We'll have to wait until evening when Faisal arrives. We'll need him for this job."

CHAPTER SIX

Shortly after sunset, Faisal knocked on the Englishman's door, aware that the eyes of all the men in the Sultan El Moyyad Café across the street were on him. Like everyone else on the street, they assumed he was just a useless street boy. They probably thought he was knocking on the Englishman's door to ask for alms. They didn't have any idea he worked for the Englishman. No one did. Even the other street urchins thought he was lying.

"He didn't give you that piastre," they would say. "You just picked his pocket."

Pick the Englishman's pocket? Never! The Englishman was good to him. He would never rob him. Oh, sure, he took some food from the pantry sometimes. Just a little. Just enough so he could eat. He couldn't help the Englishman if he was hungry all the time, could he? So he just took enough to eat. And a little extra. Just a little. Just enough to give to some of the other boys. Then they would do things for him, like be lookouts.

Moustafa answered the door. Just his luck.

"Well?" the Nubian asked.

"Well what?"

"Spit it out. Did you find out anything?"

"About what?"

"About the murder, you blockhead!"

"What do I know about it?"

"Bah! You're useless. Go away."

He heard the Englishman's voice from inside.

The Englishman must have said to let him in, because Moustafa turned to face inside, scowled, then turned to Faisal.

"Wipe your feet."

Faisal had been begging so he had left his sandals in his shed. You didn't want to look like you had any money if you were out begging. He wiped his feet on the rush mat in front of the door, and that got one of his toes itching. He stood on one leg and ground that toe into the mat, then rubbed hard back and forth, but that didn't get it. He tried flicking his toes together. That made his toe itch more, and got the toe next to it started too. He tried rubbing his foot against the mat again. It didn't help.

So there was only one thing left to do. He sat down on the threshold, picked up the edge of the mat and started rubbing it in the space between his toes.

"What are you doing!" Moustafa bellowed.

"Ah, what a relief! I had—"

Faisal yelped as he got picked up, plopped on his feet, smacked upside the head, and told to go inside.

Faisal walked into the front room of the Englishman's home. It was his least favorite room because this was where the Englishman kept most of his ancient things. Standing here and there were statues of men and women and strange creatures with animal heads and human bodies. He knew for a fact that some of these were actually djinn turned to stone thanks to a charm he had bought from the old widow Khadija umm Mohammed. Her charms always worked. The house was safe from djinn, but the stone djinn still made him nervous. Then there were all the strange objects on the shelves, and the crocodile wrapped in linen hanging from the ceiling, and the big stone box where he had found a human head, and …

"Stop gawking and go to the courtyard!"

Faisal stuck out his tongue at Moustafa, scurried around a statue to avoid getting smacked, and ran into the courtyard.

This was a better place, with a nice fountain and shady trees. There were a few stone creatures here, but Faisal was pretty sure they were only statues. A couple of lamps lit the scene.

The Englishman sat at a small table with a teapot and two cups and a plate piled high with pastries. Faisal's stomach growled loud enough to echo off the walls.

"Hello to you too," the Englishman said. He poured himself some tea and took a bite out of a pastry.

"Hello, Englishman," Faisal replied, not taking his eyes off the pastries.

"How would you like to make some money tonight?"

"Do I have to see any heads without their bodies?"

"I doubt it."

"Good. I didn't like that."

"Living on the street I assumed you would have long since become accustomed to any brutal sights."

"Not heads without bodies."

Faisal turned, expecting Moustafa to say something like, "Stand up straight and stop scratching your armpit or I'll make your body have no head!" but the Nubian had left.

He turned back to the pastries.

"It might be a little dangerous," the Englishman warned.

"It always is when you ask for me. Why don't you ask for me during the safe times?"

The Englishman laughed. "Because I don't need someone with your specific talents when all I'm doing is running the shop and trying to avoid Cordelia."

Faisal smiled. Cordelia was the Englishwoman who wanted to marry the Englishman. She never would, though. Khadija umm Mohammed had put a spell on her to make sure of that. Faisal's little house on the roof would never be disturbed by some woman hanging laundry.

"I will give you ten piastres and make sure you eat well today. Fair enough?"

Faisal's stomach grumbled again.

"What do I have to do?"

"Just break into a house."

"Oh, that's easy!"

"Then perhaps I should pay you less."

Faisal plopped down in the other chair and grabbed a pastry. "Too late, Englishman! You already named your price." His next words were muffled by the pastry he had stuffed into his mouth. "These are good. What are they called?"

"Scones. We generally have them at tea time, which is long past, but I need some refreshment for tonight's activities. You'll taste them better if you don't spit crumbs all over the table. Would you like some tea?"

That night, Faisal found himself with Moustafa and the Englishman outside a house in a good neighborhood not far from that big hotel the Englishman liked to eat at with Sir Thomas Russell Pasha. Faisal had watched them sometimes, sitting up there like sultans as they were served food and drink, and wondered what they talked about.

The house looked like most in this neighborhood—three stories high with shuttered windows. The walls had been recently plastered and were annoyingly smooth. Why did house owners do that? Didn't they know he could fall?

Luckily there remained a way up. A tall palm tree, growing out of an open space in the cobblestone road right next to the house, reached almost as high as the house itself.

"Can you get up it?" the Englishman asked as they strolled by, pretending to go somewhere else. Faisal walked beside them, hand outstretched as if he was begging. There were a few people in the distance so it was best to make everything look natural.

"I can go right up that tree and jump to the windowsill of the second story window."

"Good. Now the owner is out at the moment. He is at a meeting at the building where you saw the killer. He's going to be arrested there, but I want to take a look in his house."

"There will be servants."

"Sneak past them and unlock the front door. We'll handle the rest."

"Give me a piastre," Faisal said, his hand still extended.

"I thought you wanted ten piastres."

"No, I mean right now. You see, I'm pretending to beg, so you have to give me a coin to make me go away. Otherwise I'd just keep following you. Going away without getting something first wouldn't look real."

Moustafa muttered something. The Englishman fished into his pocket.

"Here's a piastre. Now go do your job."

Faisal leapt into the air and spun around.

"No problem, Englishman. I'll see you in a few minutes."

Faisal sauntered off, his eyes darting to and fro as he tracked all the people within view. Most were walking away or focused on various tasks, like the syrup seller who had taken the brass tank off his back and was cleaning the taps. A husband and wife walked his way, and he paused to beg from them, pestering them and following them until they were far enough away from the palm tree that he didn't need to worry about them.

The only other person looking his direction was a shoeshine boy a little younger than he was, sitting at the corner and watching his every move.

Was he a lookout for the people of the house? Faisal didn't think so. The boy was being too obvious. He was probably just a street boy like him who could tell Faisal was casing the house.

Well, let him watch. Maybe he would learn something.

With a grin and a wink to the boy at the end of the street, Faisal grasped the narrow but strong trunk of the palm, planted his feet on the rough bark, and within moments had scampered up to the height of the second story window.

Now came the tricky part. The shutter was closed. That would be easy enough to pick. He had a thin piece of metal he had scrounged that would slip right between the shutters and lift the catch. The real challenge was leaping the few feet from the tree to the windowsill, which was barely wide enough to hold him, without bashing into the shutters and alerting anyone in the house.

And there was someone in the house. He could see a faint light filtering

45

through the shutters. Someone had a lamp burning in another room not far from the room he would enter.

He had to be quiet and he had to be careful.

Positioning himself, Faisal took a deep breath and jumped. His foot landed perfectly, but his hands didn't get a good grip and slipped. He scrabbled at the stone, feeling himself tipping over, and then a firm grip against a crack in the stone stopped him.

Faisal breathed again.

Maybe I should ask for twenty piastres next time.

He pulled the bit of metal from his pocket and eased open the catch.

The window opened onto a sitting room. Divans and cushions were arranged around a low table. The room was dark, but he could see a light burning beyond an open doorway. He heard a laugh, muffled by a door and some distance.

Faisal eased himself inside, peeked out the window to see the shoeshine boy grinning at him, gave him a wave, and closed the shutters.

Tiptoeing across the sitting room, he peeked into the hallway. At the far end, a light shone through a partially open door. He heard at least two voices talking and the clatter of dice rolling. One voice made a triumphant cry. It sounded like the servants were playing backgammon instead of doing whatever they were supposed to be doing while their master was away.

At the other end of the hallway a staircase led downward. No lights were on below, but there was enough light in the hallway for him to see his way to the stairs.

Faisal didn't like this hallway. There were a lot of strange things hanging from the walls, like spears and clubs and masks fringed with feathers that stared at him with their blank eyes as he snuck past. This was almost as bad as the Englishman's house. Why did Europeans put all this stuff in their homes?

He got to the head of the stairs and paused. The steps descended into complete darkness. What else might be down there?

He glanced over his shoulder. The light from the servants' room seemed faint and distant now, like the fishermen's lamps when they fished at night far out on the Nile.

He pulled a stub of candle and a match from his pocket. Besides all the old things, the Englishman had lots of useful things in his house too, so many that he never missed them if Faisal took a few. It didn't really count as stealing if the Englishman didn't miss them, and he was working for the Englishman anyway so they were almost practically his things too.

Faisal summoned the courage to descend the stairs far enough that he would be out of sight of the hallway, then struck the match against the stone step.

The light flared, and Faisal almost shrieked with terror. A huge face with bugged-out eyes and jagged teeth stared right at him from so close it just needed to lean forward a little to eat him.

Faisal pressed his back against the wall, a scream choked in his throat.

A second later, Faisal saw it was a mask.

Only a mask, he told himself. *Masks can't hurt you.*

Unless they had djinn hiding in them.

Faisal hurried down the stairs.

He came to a front hall with more masks and spears on the walls. In the center of the room stood a stone base with a strange wooden statue on it. It had a fat belly and stubby legs and long, thin arms. Its face was as flat and pointed as a digging stick, with big oval eyes.

That was a djinni for sure. It seemed to be asleep, though. Perhaps it had gone to haunt another house.

That was lucky. He was really going to need to get a charm against djinn if the Englishman wanted him to break into more European houses.

The front door stood just beyond it. The Englishman and Moustafa would be hiding in the shadows across the street, waiting for him to let them in.

And he would, but he wanted to explore a bit first while the djinn were away. It was a nice night, cool with no wind. A pleasant night to be out, as the Englishman said. They wouldn't mind waiting for a couple of minutes.

Faisal tiptoed down the front hall, his candle casting a feeble light ahead of him. There were no more statues or masks here and he felt better.

To his right, an open doorway led to a dining room. Silver cutlery gleamed in the light of his candle, and Faisal's eyes gleamed too. He could sell those for a lot. The European who owned this house was a killer, the Englishman and Moustafa said so. That meant that all his possessions would be confiscated by the government. But what did the government need with some extra knives, forks, and spoons? They had plenty, and he didn't have any.

He started going around the table, putting the cutlery in his pockets.

Then the sweet smell of roasted meat wafted to his nostrils. His stomach grumbled.

A small door led away from the dining room. It stood partially open. No doubt it led to the kitchen.

He studied the door, then looked at the table, which still had half its silverware.

This is one of those situations where the Englishman had told him he should use logic. The Englishman always talked about logic any time Faisal brought up djinn and magic, but logic could be used in any situation where you were faced with something you couldn't quite figure out.

Faisal's main job was to open the front door. So logic said he should go straight to the front door and open it. But he was already halfway through stealing the cutlery, and it would be against logic not to finish. That would be lazy too, and Faisal wasn't lazy. He worked very hard at begging and stealing. Most people didn't realize what a hard job that was.

But his stomach kept growling, and he needed to keep quiet so those servants upstairs didn't hear him, so logic said he should go into the kitchen and take a few bites of that rich, juicy, wonderful-smelling meat. Just a few bites. Because he had a job to do. And silverware to steal.

And didn't logic also say that he could open the door just as easily five minutes from now as he could right away?

His stomach grumbled again. Yes, best take care of that first.

He tiptoed into the kitchen, the silverware rattling in his pockets. A dim light came from the coals inside the cast iron stove. Grabbing a cloth off the counter, he wrapped his hand and opened the stove door.

Just as he thought, there was a big chicken in there, roasted with lots of juice and potatoes.

The Englishman was right. Faisal should use logic more often.

CHAPTER SEVEN

Faisal opened the door right on schedule. Faisal's schedule.

"Well, you certainly took your time," Augustus said.

Faisal burped.

"The servants are upstairs."

Augustus and Moustafa moved into the front hall. Faisal handed him a candle and hurried out the front door, clinking and clanking as he went.

Moustafa frowned as the boy disappeared around the corner. "What's he stolen this time?"

"Never mind that," Augustus whispered. "Let's overpower the servants and have a look around."

Augustus took a quick glance around the front hall and knew he was in the right house. Spears and masks in the style of the tribes of the Amazon hung on the walls, and there was a statue in the center that looked Malay. Ainsley Fielding, retired solicitor, amateur ethnologist, world traveler, and member in good standing of the Geographical Association of Egypt, was also, according to Sir Thomas's investigations, wanted for murder in France, extortion in Germany, and theft in more nations than Augustus had bothered to read in the report. More importantly, he had spent a great deal of time in the tropical regions, most pertinently Amazonia.

He was, according to all accounts, a retiring man, more a listener than a talker. No one in Cairo had heard of his Amazonian travels.

At least no one they had spoken to yet, but murdering someone with a blowgun sent an abundantly clear message to those in the know.

Mr. Fielding was not to be trifled with. At least he would be in handcuffs before long. In the meantime, Augustus wanted to see what other little twists and turns there might be to this mystery.

He also needed to catch that Egyptian who had been trained in the use of the blowgun. That was not the sort of man to be left free to roam the streets. Then there was that mysterious foreigner the weapons dealer had told Moustafa about. Could he possibly be an Amazonian native, brought all the way here? That stretched credulity, but he couldn't deny the possibility.

Augustus went to the bottom of the stairs and blew out the candle. A faint light came from above, just enough to see by as they crept up and found themselves in a long hall. They could hear conversation and see light from a door that stood open a crack at the end of the hall.

He motioned to Moustafa and they both pulled pistols from their pockets, he the usual compact automatic, and Moustafa a heavy Webley service revolver from the Great War. The floor was stone with a thick carpet of Mexican pattern that muffled their footsteps as they crept to the door, flung it open, and held up the servants …

… at least that was how it was supposed to happen.

When Augustus kicked the door open, they saw three Egyptians sitting on cushions around a low table. Two were playing backgammon while the third, who faced the door on the opposite end of the table, watched.

Their recovery from being surprised would have done credit to a squad of German *Sturmtruppen*. One man grabbed the backgammon set and flung it at the intruders while the other two rose, drawing pistols from the pockets of their djellabas.

Augustus batted away the backgammon set with his free hand and fired three quick shots, but his defensive move put his aim off and only one of the servants went down. Another jerked back an instant later with a shot from Moustafa, but then they both had to dive for opposite sides of the doorway as the third man fired.

Cornered, outnumbered, and unsure of the situation, the servant made a bold move, one for which Augustus gave him enduring respect.

He charged, firing as he went.

He burst out the doorway directly between Augustus and Moustafa, making it too risky for either man to shoot.

So Augustus fired at the man's foot.

The servant toppled over, but not before firing one last time at Augustus, who was already dodging to the side.

That move saved his life, or at least an important part of it. The bullet grazed his upper thigh, cutting a hot trail along the flesh.

Augustus slammed into the wall and stood there for a second, dazed. Moustafa fired again, the servant's head jerking back as he took a bullet to the throat. Then the Nubian peeked around the doorway to see if either of the other two servants remained alive, nearly got his head shot off as an answer, and got back out of the line of fire.

"You all right?" Augustus asked, his own voice sounding distant, unreal.

"Yes, boss. He's behind the table, which he has overturned to make a shield. It looks thick. Now what?"

Augustus paused a moment as his head cleared. He knew how to focus through the shock of a fresh wound, and ignore the pain that came moments later. He had done it all too many times. Augustus pulled a jam tin from his pocket. An igniter was fastened to it.

"Here's a little trench engineering for you," he said with a smile. Moustafa's face wavered and faded, partially replaced by the mud-stained visage of an old comrade.

Augustus blinked, tried to focus. It was happening again. He was slipping.

But he could see the doorway clearly enough. Or the entrance to the German dugout. Whatever it was, he needed to throw a flash grenade into it.

He pulled the igniter and tossed the jam tin into the room. The gun cotton and chemicals inside burst into flame with a loud bang and a shower of sparks. Augustus and his companion popped out from behind their cover, ending up shoulder to shoulder as they fired at the man who was staggering about the room, holding his hands to his eyes as his clothes smoldered.

Augustus leaned on the doorjamb as his companion (*Moustafa. His name is Moustafa and you are in Egypt*) stamped out little fires that had flared up on the furniture and carpet.

"Are they all dead?" Augustus asked.

"Yes, boss," Moustafa said, fetching an ewer of water and pouring it on a particularly stubborn flame. "Are you badly hurt?"

Oh right, his thigh. He parted the tear in his pants and took a look.

"No, only a graze. Hurts like the devil, though, and ruined a brand new set of trousers."

"Then don't dress up when you're going on jobs like this," Moustafa grumbled.

Augustus smiled. His assistant was still cross with him for letting Faisal into the house. He had been in an ill mood ever since. Moustafa hadn't even wanted to bring the boy along. Augustus agreed that Faisal was dirty, grasping, unreliable, and irritating in general, but what Moustafa failed to see was that Faisal was also useful. His assistant needed to realize that Faisal's services would be called upon any time they were needed. He was just as useful as Moustafa, although in a quite different way. That was why he had sat the boy down to tea, something that nearly caused Moustafa to have a fit. Augustus had wanted to prove a point.

Perhaps he had gone a bit far with that, Augustus mused. Seeing the boy gobble scones and slurp tea while holding the cup with both hands was enough to turn a man's stomach. It was a miracle the urchin hadn't broken anything. A tea set was not the sort of thing one should get attached to, but it would have been a damned inconvenience if he had smashed it all.

Moustafa came out of the servant's room, coughing from the smoke.

"None of those three looked like the man with the blowgun," Moustafa choked out. "Two were too stout and the third too tall."

"Pity. Let's find Fielding's office," Augustus said, tying off his wound with some bandages he had brought for the night's outing.

They found it in less than a minute, a large room off the same hallway. The door was locked, but a good kick from Moustafa took care of that. Inside they found a desk, a file cabinet, and two large shelves of books.

As they started to rummage around, Faisal poked his head around the corner.

"You made a lot of noise. The neighbors are shouting for the watchman. Don't worry, they think the noise came from a different house."

"How could they?"

"I paid that shoeshine boy on the street to say he saw some men with guns go into a house a couple of doors down. That won't fool them for long. Oh, you owe me a piastre."

"Shut up and go stand watch!" Moustafa shouted.

"All right, but stop shouting or they'll hear you."

Faisal moved away, still clinking and clanking from whatever he had looted.

"I don't know why you put up with that little thief, boss."

"Because he's proved himself useful in the past," Augustus replied, searching through the desk as Moustafa rummaged through the file cabinet. His thigh burned and blood oozed around the bandage. "He can be our eyes and ears, and nobody suspects him. As he said himself, he is beneath notice. An invisible scout can be quite handy. Besides, you or I could have never climbed that palm tree and gotten in that window."

"You will regret it, sir. He will rob you blind one day."

"Oh, I doubt that. He's getting a steady supply of piastres and free meals. Besides, I don't see any way he could get into my house, even with his abilities."

"He's probably robbed you a dozen times already. Mark my words. Ah!"

Moustafa held up a topographic map bearing the logo of the Geographical Association. It showed the caravan route to Bahariya Oasis.

"Well isn't that interesting," Augustus said.

They searched some more and found a more detailed map of the oasis itself, and a sheaf of notes on the place. They also found a couple of books on the Western Desert and its oases, but they were standard volumes and they didn't bother with them.

"We should go, boss."

"A quick survey of the house and we're off," Augustus said as he limped out the door.

They went through the rest of the upstairs rooms and found nothing of interest except a well-equipped chemistry laboratory. By now the pain was increasing, but Augustus didn't let that slow him down much. He needed to find something more, something that would tell him just what they were up against.

He found it not in the house, but in the courtyard downstairs.

Most Cairene homes of any size have a courtyard with a fountain where the family could rest in the cool shade. This one, however, had been turned into a greenhouse. The heat and humidity were almost overpowering. Strange, unfamiliar plants grew in abundance in orderly rows, each plant provided with a small sign stuck in the earth with its taxonomic designation.

Knowing that haste was essential, Augustus hobbled along the rows until he found what he was looking for—the leafy vine called *Chondrodendron tomentosum*.

Well, it would have been leafy, but nearly all the leaves had been stripped. Augustus felt the edge of one stub of a leaf, and could feel the moisture from inside it.

The leaves had been stripped quite recently.

"Time to go," he said.

"I've been saying that for quite some time now, boss. Even the Little Infidel has been saying it."

"Yes, yes."

Moustafa was growing a bit too bold. Of course, boldness was one of the reasons he had originally hired him. That and his knowledge of Egyptology and his remarkable ability at languages. But the boldness was beginning to wear on him. He disliked the cringing obsequiousness of the colonial servant class, for it generally masked disrespect if not downright hatred, but Moustafa was taking it a bit far in the other direction.

Still, it was best not to be present at the scene of a gunfight when the authorities arrived.

They got to the front door and opened it a crack. A crowd was clustered around the front door of a house two doors down. They could see the neighborhood watchman, recognizable by his long stick, arguing loudly with a man standing at the house entrance, who was obviously the owner and who did not want an excited mob entering the private domain of his wives and daughters. The crowd was beginning to back off, convinced by the owner's protestations of innocence. This was their neighbor, after all, and most likely there had never been the sound of gunfire from his house before.

Beyond the crowd, on the opposite side of the street, stood Faisal, unnoticed as usual. He leaned against some large water pots almost as tall as he was. The boy was looking right at the door behind which Augustus and Moustafa hid.

The crowd began to look around curiously. Augustus tensed as he saw one young man, his headscarf in disarray from having put it on in haste while running out of the house, stare in their direction. His brow furrowed.

"That's torn it," Augustus said. "I think he's noticed the door is a bit ajar."

"Now what do we do?" Moustafa asked.

A resounding crash stopped Augustus from answering.

Faisal had tipped over one of the water pots, shattering it. As water spread out across the street, the boy leaned against another pot and tipped it over. It smashed just like the first, releasing a gush of water.

The entire crowd turned and began shouting. Several men ran for Faisal.

Augustus and Moustafa took that as their cue to leave.

CHAPTER EIGHT

Moustafa glanced nervously over his shoulder as they walked through the darkened streets. No sign of pursuit. Just as well, because it didn't look like Mr. Wall would be able to run. In fact, he was slowing down. They had already stopped to bandage the leg again—Mr. Wall always brought along bandages as well as a small personal arsenal on these little excursions—but the man was obviously in pain. Moustafa felt tempted to carry him but no, let him suffer the consequences of his rashness.

"What was that thing you threw?" he asked. That bomb had been something he hadn't seen before. He thought he was familiar with all his boss's weapons.

"A flash bomb. Easily made with commonly bought materials and stuffed into an ordinary jam tin. The only manufactured part is the igniter, which can be purchased from miners or demolition crews."

"Is it legal to purchase igniters?"

Mr. Wall's laugh was sufficient answer.

"How in the world did you learn to make such a device?" Moustafa asked.

"In the early days of the last war, the army didn't see fit to provide us with grenades, so we had to fashion our own. A few months in the trenches was the equivalent of three years at Oxford reading chemistry and engineering."

"They didn't give you grenades?"

That surprised him. The English were usually so organized and efficient. If only the Egyptians and Soudanese could be like that.

"No they did not. They also didn't give us steel helmets, proper shovels, or anything approaching sufficient quantities of barbed wire, high explosive artillery shells, or machine guns."

"During the war I read about the fighting, boss. All those things were essential."

Mr. Wall sighed. "Essential for trench warfare, my good man. The generals, in their infinite wisdom, thought the war would be one of movement, not position. They envisioned a grand thrust to Berlin and everyone would be home by Christmas. And we were home by Christmas—Christmas 1918!"

Mr. Wall's wild, sarcastic laugh echoed off the darkened buildings.

Moustafa found himself edging away from his boss. The man was a lunatic. In times of danger he thought himself back in the war, and every night he drugged himself free from nightmares by smoking opium until he fell unconscious.

The man was also brilliant, and had given Moustafa a good job, access to his personal library, and more respect than any other European Moustafa had ever met.

If only this job didn't involve getting shot at …

"Hello!" a voice chirped from the other end of the street.

Moustafa's hand thrust into his pocket for his gun, but then he saw it was only Faisal.

The boy paced them on the other side of the street. He still clanked and rattled as he walked.

"Now what are you up to?" Moustafa snapped. "Planning on destroying more property?"

"No, just seeing how you're doing."

"And sniffing around for your payment, I'm sure."

Faisal pretended like he had just remembered that. "Oh, right! I need ten piastres for breaking into the house and another piastre because I had to pay the shoeshine boy."

Mr. Wall reached into his pocket and pulled out some coins. When Faisal remained on the other side of the street, he said, "Well, come on over here and get it."

Faisal glanced at Moustafa. "Can you throw it over here?"

"Whatever for?" Mr. Wall asked.

"Because if I go over there, Moustafa will turn me upside down and shake out everything from my pockets."

Moustafa grunted. The boy may be ignorant, disrespectful, and utterly lacking in religion, but he was not stupid.

Mr. Wall laughed, a true laugh this time, and tossed the coins across the street. Faisal snatched them out of the air.

"Now what are we doing?" the boy asked.

"Going home and going to sleep," Mr. Wall said. "After that, we're meeting with the chief of police. Want to come along?"

"Nope," Faisal said, turning into an alley and disappearing. "I'll check on you later, Englishman," his voice said, fading away. "I know you'll need me."

The next day, Moustafa sat sipping tea in a European cafe with Mr. Wall and the chief of police. He would rather be anywhere than there. Firstly, he was the only Soudanese in the place who wasn't serving drinks, and secondly, he had to sit with a murderer.

Sir Thomas Russell Pasha had a dim view of the independence movement. When there were mass demonstrations earlier in the year protesting the lies the English had told the Egyptian people, the police had replied with truncheons and gunfire.

And what justification was there for that? During the war the English had used Egyptian labor, Egyptian crops, and Egyptian cotton. A million Egyptians had worked in Europe for the war effort, and many had died of diseases or artillery fire. Egypt had been promised a seat at the table at Versailles, and the chance to negotiate for independence. Instead the independence leaders had been arrested and the protestors attacked.

The English always talked about fair play, but they really only meant fair play among themselves.

Moustafa focused on what the killer with the respectable title was saying.

"So we arrested Ainsley Fielding last night. One of my men shadowed him and caught him meeting with three other officers of the Geographical Association. With them was a ledger enumerating their affairs. It turns out they were funding expeditions to perform illegal excavations in out of the way places, then selling the artifacts on the antiquities market and splitting the profits. The expeditions got funding plus access to the society's maps and field reports, making them much more efficient than your usual grave robbers."

"I assure you they didn't sell me anything," Mr. Wall said.

Mr. Wall never bought antiquities that didn't have a proper provenance and he always turned away the many shady dealers who came calling. Mr. Wall frowned on the illegal antiquities trade. He didn't have an issue with selling fakes to the shallower members of the buying public, however.

Neither did Moustafa. The idiots who wanted a New Kingdom sarcophagus as a flowerbed for their garden got what they deserved.

Sir Thomas took a sip of his tea. "I never dreamed that you would do business with such people, my good man. It seems that the late Professor Harrell had learned of this operation and threatened to go to the police. The culprits feared he had already told other members of the society, so they murdered him in public, both to silence him and intimidate the others."

"But the actual killer is still at large," Mr. Wall said.

Sir Thomas shook his head and smiled. "No, and this is where it gets interesting. We caught a man standing guard, and what a strange sentinel he was. A South American native, no doubt brought back by Fielding. And you shall never guess what he had on him."

"A blowgun and poison darts," Mr. Wall said.

"Indeed."

"But the man we're hunting is an Egyptian."

"You and your servant didn't get a good look at him, you said so yourself."

Moustafa rankled at being called a servant, but kept his mouth shut.

There was no use trying to tell this boil on the toe of a camel anything.

"We didn't get a good look at him," Mr. Wall said. "Faisal did."

The policeman's brow furrowed. "Who's Faisal?"

"The beggar boy."

Sir Russell laughed. "Really now, you don't believe him, do you? He was just looking for a handout. Didn't you hear how vague he was? I say, Sir Augustus, I think you're going a bit too native."

"There's more to this gang than you've caught," Mr. Wall replied, an edge to his voice the police chief either didn't notice or chose to ignore.

"That's true enough. At least one of the gang got away. Someone killed three servants in Fielding's house last night and made off with the silverware."

"You just can't get good help these days," Mr. Wall said. "You said Professor Harrell *seems* to have learned about the operation. You don't know that for sure?"

"No. The criminals are keeping their mouths shut and have hired good solicitors. Not good enough to keep them out of prison, but we're going to have a devil of a time finding out who those anonymous donors are. At least we've broken up their operation."

"So it had nothing to do with the professor's excavations in Bahariya Oasis?" Moustafa asked, remembering the maps and notes.

The chief of police laughed and said in a voice dripping with condescension, "Goodness no. Why should it? But you did very well chasing after the murderer and gained us a vital clue. Your master must be very proud of you."

Moustafa missed whatever the son of a dog said next because through a red haze he was having a vision of taking the teapot and shoving it up one of Sir Thomas's orifices and out through another. By the time he recovered his senses, the illegitimate son of a pimple on a baboon's bottom had gotten to his feet.

"So case solved. Thank you for your help, Sir Augustus. A pleasure as always."

And then he was gone.

Mr. Wall turned to Moustafa. "There's more to this than he's seeing."

"Why didn't you tell him about the maps, boss?"

"Should I have?"

"No, boss."

Mr. Wall laughed. "Because we would have to admit how we got them, eh?"

That and we wouldn't get to do whatever it is you're planning.

"So, Moustafa, how would you like to do a little exploring? It requires a bit of a trip, but you'll get danger pay the entire time."

"Would this trip involve going to Bahariya Oasis, boss?"

"It would indeed."

"Those papers do make it look like Fielding and the others were mixed up with Harrell more than they admitted."

"And if they aren't admitting it, that's because there are more conspirators still at large. I'd like to find out what they're hiding."

Moustafa smiled. One of Mr. Wall's best traits was that he liked to show up the chief of police.

Moustafa enjoyed that too.

And he liked seeing parts of Egypt he had never visited, and exploring ancient temples and tombs no one had seen for thousands of years.

Damn that man. He'd yank him out of his comfortable family life without a second thought and drag him halfway across the Western Desert to face an unknown situation that would certainly involve risking his life. And yet Moustafa could never say no. Moustafa had always looked to the horizon. Even when he was a little boy in his village in the Soudan he had always listened to the marabouts when they told tales of their travels. When he had turned sixteen he had left his village to see the world. He had traveled to Khartoum, worked on excavations in the Soudan, and eventually made his way all the way north to Cairo.

But he'd never been deep into the Western Desert.

Just the thought of it stirred his imagination. Unlike the Europeans, he did not romanticize the desert. It wasn't mysterious or alluring, it was harsh and dangerous. But what lay beyond, now that was interesting. The oases were *terra incognita* to most Egyptologists. They dismissed them as peripheral areas lacking in importance. Professor Harrell was the first researcher to do any systematic excavations.

What he had found was enticing—a rich tomb with mummies from the Greco-Roman period. And Alexander the Great himself had probably passed through there. Moustafa wondered about that temple to him, no doubt a grandiose monument to a great leader. He'd like to see it.

He'd like to see something most of those arrogant European researchers had never seen, and learn some things they did not know.

Perhaps he could write another journal article. His first article, written under an English pseudonym since they would not consider an article from a Soudanese, would come out in a month's time in the *Journal of Egyptian Archaeology*.

Yes, another article would be a good idea. What had the editor said in his acceptance letter?

May I congratulate you on such a fine study. You have a most promising career ahead of you.

Those words looked so beautiful they could have been written in gold.

"Penny for your thoughts," Mr. Wall said.

Moustafa looked at him. "It will be a long and dangerous trip. Neither you nor I have ever crossed the Western Desert. Neither of us know what to expect."

He saw a glint in Mr. Wall's eyes. "And that's precisely why you want to go."

Moustafa smiled ruefully. Why had God ordained that the only European who truly understood him had to be a complete madman?

CHAPTER NINE

"You want me to go where?"

The Englishman was out for his usual evening walk, leaning on his cane because he had gotten injured in the leg. Faisal had spotted him and tagged along, hoping he was going somewhere interesting. That was when the Englishman told Faisal he had a new job for him. Faisal didn't know if this Bahariya place was interesting or not, because he had never heard of it.

"It's an oasis in the desert. The killer has probably fled there, along with his associates. I'd like you to come along because you are the only one who saw the killer's face. I need you."

Faisal smiled. The Englishman was one of the only people who really appreciated him. And why shouldn't he? Hadn't he helped him more times than he could count? He even did things for the Englishman that he didn't know about, like protect the house from djinn and robbers and pour his alcohol into the sink when he was sleeping.

But then Faisal thought of something that didn't make him feel so good.

"Is it far?"

"Yes, quite far."

"Will we have to cross the desert?" Faisal asked, looking around at all the houses. He'd only been to the edge of the desert a few times. It had felt strange not being surrounded by buildings.

"I see no other way to get there unless you have a flying carpet."

"Not even you have enough money to buy that kind of magic. The desert is dangerous. There are sandstorms and bandits and djinn and—"

The Englishman stopped and rapped his walking stick on the cobblestones impatiently.

"How many times do I have to tell you that djinn don't exist?"

"I've seen them!"

"Where?"

In your house.

When Faisal didn't answer, the Englishman went on.

"We will travel with a caravan. I'm getting Moustafa to arrange it. They travel between Cairo and Bahariya all the time. We'll be perfectly safe."

"Nothing is perfectly safe with you, Englishman."

The Englishman let out one of his long, strange laughs and started walking again. Faisal paused before following. He didn't like it when the Englishman laughed like that.

He noticed the Englishman was still limping badly, even though the fight had been two days before.

"Does your leg still hurt?"

"It's nothing. Didn't you know I'm immortal? No bullet can kill me. No artillery shell either."

Faisal gulped. It had been a German cannon that had taken half the Englishman's face off.

"What does Moustafa say?" Faisal asked.

"About what?"

"About going to this oasis."

"He is in complete agreement."

Faisal had his doubts about that.

"What does he say about me coming along?"

"I haven't yet told him."

That's what Faisal thought.

Karim the watchman rounded the corner, a grumpy old man with a big cudgel who kept an eye on the neighborhood at night. He liked to give Faisal beatings when he could catch him, which wasn't often.

Karim scowled at Faisal. Faisal scowled at Karim.

"Is this filthy urchin bothering you, sir?"

"Not at all. Have a good evening," the Englishman said as he passed him by.

Karim stopped and turned in astonishment. Faisal thumbed his nose at him, then ran to get the Englishman between him and Karim.

"So how much will you pay me?"

"I was wondering when we'd get to that."

"I'll be very helpful."

"I have no doubt you will be. We still need you to identify the killer, after all. How about a piastre a day?"

"Is that what Moustafa makes?"

"No, of course he makes more."

"Why of course? I'm more helpful than he is!"

"He has a family to support."

"But I do more for you," Faisal whined. "Besides, I need to pay for a—"

Faisal stopped himself. He had almost told him that he needed to pay for a charm to protect himself from the desert djinn. But if he told him that, the Englishman would never hand over the money. Faisal would make good money hawking that silverware, but that was stolen money and couldn't be spent on magic. Khadija umm Mohammed said so and she knew absolutely everything about magic.

"What do you need to buy? If you'd like my recommendation, I'd suggest some soap."

"Why?" Faisal asked, scratching himself.

"Never mind."

"I, um, need to buy some wood for the shelter I live in with the other boys."

"I'm surprised you don't steal some. That's what you do with everything else."

"Oh, there are no houses being built where I live. We'd have to carry it a very long way and someone would take it from us."

"Hm, I suspect Moustafa would say you are lying. But I will consider it a sign-on bonus."

Faisal didn't know what that meant, but it sounded like he'd get the money.

"Wood is very expensive," Faisal said hopefully.

"Of course it is. How about ten piastres?"

"Better make it twenty. The shack is pretty big," Faisal said, checking that Karim was still walking away. If the watchman saw the Englishman handing him money, there was no telling what he might say.

"Twenty it is," the Englishman said, handing it over. Faisal looked at it, surprised. He thought he'd have more of an argument. "Now we have a deal, don't we? You'll come across the desert with us and help us find the man with the blowgun."

"The what?"

"That tube you saw him with that you thought was a flute. He blew into that to shoot a poison dart to kill another Englishman."

"Oh. Will he shoot that at us?"

"He might."

Faisal's young mind tried to think through what he was agreeing to. Twenty piastres felt good in his hand, but how long would this desert trip take? And what about all the dangers on the way? And then at the end of all that there was a killer. Knowing the Englishman, there were probably a lot of killers.

But that was all too far in the future for him to picture clearly. All he could really focus on was the twenty piastres in his hand and something the Englishman had said.

I need you.

Who ever said that to him?

No one, that's who.

"All right," he said at last. He felt a spike of fear as he said it.

"Moustafa is organizing our passage on a caravan. It would help if you didn't look like a complete ragamuffin. Whatever happened to that blue djellaba the French gang gave you? It was brand new and here you are dressed in rags."

"How can I beg in a brand new djellaba?"

"I see your point. But wear that. And the sandals they gave you. You'll need the sandals in the desert. During the day the sand will burn your feet, even through all those layers of dirt. And take a bath."

"A bath? The public bathhouse costs money."

"Then go jump in the Nile. From what I hear the Bedouin look down on city dwellers, so we have to make a good impression."

They walked in silence for a time. Some of the people who passed looked at the Englishman curiously, both because of his mask and because he was the only European who lived in this neighborhood. Nobody took much notice of the beggar boy dogging his footsteps.

"Englishman?"

"What is it, Faisal?"

"Are you still mad at me for helping the Apache gang?"

"You had to. They kidnapped you and threatened you. That wasn't your fault."

"So you're not mad?"

"No, Faisal. I'm not mad."

Those words didn't reassure him as much as they should have. The Englishman didn't know the whole truth. Faisal had been kidnapped, it was true, but then Edmond, the leader of the Apaches, had treated him well. Edmond had protected him from the other gang members and gave him good food and a nice new blue djellaba and even the first pair of sandals he had ever had in his life. Edmond had talked a lot about his son who had died. He always talked about his son when he was giving Faisal things.

Edmond had even called him a good boy. No one, not even the Englishman, ever called him that.

But he had been a criminal. Faisal still hadn't figured out what he thought about the Frenchman. Edmond had treated him better than anyone, better than the Englishman even, but he'd been a bad person. He had tried to kill the Englishman and other good people.

And Faisal had helped Edmond escape.

He knew that had been wrong. He knew many of the things he did were wrong. But stealing was something he did because he had to. Begging wasn't much better. Pointing the police in the wrong direction after all the bad things Edmond had done was the wrong thing to do. Edmond was out there now, hurting more people, and all because Faisal had lied to the police.

So why didn't he feel bad about it? Just because Edmond had treated him nicely? Was it because Edmond was so sad about losing his son?

Sometimes Faisal found himself wishing the Englishman had lost a son.

"Englishman?"

"What is it now, Faisal?"

Faisal was about to ask why he had never taken a wife. But he sensed that the Englishman wouldn't like that question. It was strange, but it had been easier to talk to a bad person like Edmond than a good person like the Englishman. Edmond was a killer, and the Englishman caught killers. So why had he felt safe around Edmond and he always felt a bit afraid around the Englishman?

Afraid? Why should he feel afraid? The Englishman would never hurt him.

No, but being around the Englishman was dangerous. Moustafa had been shot and stabbed and beaten up, and he was the strongest man Faisal had ever met.

And this journey would be dangerous. He didn't have to know anything about the desert or caravans or this Bahariya place to know that.

"Are you sure you need me to come along?"

"Of course. You're essential to our investigations. How else would we find the murderer?"

Faisal smiled. Once again, they couldn't do it without his help.

Maybe he should ask for more money.

He almost did, but couldn't summon up the courage.

Faisal felt the money in his pocket. Twenty piastres would buy a good charm. At least he would be safe from djinn.

If only Khadija umm Mohammed sold charms against bullets and flutes that shot poison darts.

CHAPTER TEN

Despite the continuing pain in his leg, Augustus was in a fine mood. He had an interesting little mystery to solve, one that Sir Thomas didn't seem to be aware of. The chief of police had caught the main culprits, found what he thought was the murder weapon, and was tracking down the various fake archaeologists who had benefitted from the sham expedition scheme.

Sir Thomas had dismissed the idea that an Egyptian had learned to use a blowgun and had already decided that Professor Harrell had nothing more to do with the conspirators than threatening to reveal their crimes.

A study of the papers found in Fielding's home showed otherwise. Among them was an itemized list of equipment necessary for an expedition to Bahariya. Calculating from the amount of food stores, Augustus estimated that at least twenty men had gone on that trip. The map of the oasis was marked with a small dot labeled "Temple of Alexander", and three more dots just south of it.

There were also a few sheets of paper written in Turkish.

That intrigued him. Looking through his collection of archaeological journals, he could find no evidence that Professor Harrell had ever worked in the Turkish-speaking areas of Asia or indeed had ever been there. In their brief survey of Fielding's library, Augustus and Moustafa had not seen any volumes in Turkish. So that meant that in all likelihood that neither the late professor nor the well-traveled criminal spoke the language. Then why did Fielding have these papers in his possession?

Augustus couldn't read Turkish, and neither could Moustafa, although that polyglot could probably learn it in a couple of months.

They didn't have a couple of months, so that meant he got to call on the aid of the most enticing, vivacious woman in all of Cairo—Zehra Hanzade.

They met at her house, that sanctuary of good taste and beauty in a fashionable side of town. A muscular, bare-faced eunuch ushered him into a front hall with a gleaming marble floor and Classical statues. He followed the eunuch, who Augustus knew also worked for the Hanzades as a spy and bodyguard, down a corridor lined with French and Dutch landscapes into a sumptuous sitting room decorated in the Louis XIV style. All of the furnishings were period and not reproduction, and Augustus would have wagered a fair bit of money that some of the more elegant pieces had once been owned by the Sun King himself.

Zehra rose to greet him, taking him by both hands. She wore a burgundy caftan embroidered with gold thread, and her hair was, for once, tied up with a complex array of gold braids.

While Augustus had always been hypnotized by how her tresses flowed down her shoulders, having her hair up allowed him to admire her neck, as well formed and free of blemishes as the marble statues in the front hall.

"So nice to see you, Augustus. Suleiman sends his regrets. He is currently working."

The distant sound of a hammer smashing stone came to his ears. Suleiman must be making one of his creations look old.

"One mustn't interfere with an artist in the crucible of creation," he said, grateful to have this splendid woman all to himself.

"You mentioned on the telephone that you needed help with a translation," she said as they sat, she stretching out on a divan and he sitting primly on a chair opposite. He would have loved to have stretched out on the divan as well, but there were limits to his courage. Charge into machine gun fire? Yes. Get any closer to her than he had already? No man had that amount of courage.

He outlined what they had already discovered and produced the papers, which were three small pages written in an expansive hand.

She read the papers. Augustus used it as an excuse to watch her. He could watch her read all day. Perhaps he should buy her the collected works of Tolstoy.

"It's some sort of code," she said, looking at him with those lovely brown eyes. "Written in plain Turkish but obviously referring to something else. It details supplies for a caravan from Cairo to the Sinai."

"The opposite direction of where we need to go."

"I doubt that's coincidental. It goes into great detail about how much fodder the donkeys will need, including the number of donkeys, and very specific amounts of oats and forage."

"Don't most caravans use camels or have I been greatly mistaken all this time?"

"They do. Some poorer merchants going short distances use donkeys, but no one would use them to go to the Sinai, especially not for a caravan of supposedly this size."

"Some sort of tally for something else?"

"I think so. No one makes such a detailed plan for feeding animals on a caravan. Those with the knowledge to run such a caravan do the numbers in their head. I'll make out a translation for you."

"Could you make it out in French? Fewer people will be able to read it."

"Yes, I speak French."

"I know. You speak most beautifully."

Augustus felt a flush of nerves at his daring, but those eased as he was rewarded with a brilliant smile.

As she got to work, Augustus opened a gold cigarette case on the coffee table—Zehra always kept Woodbines on hand especially for him—lit one, and thought about the significance of the note being in Turkish. Until the last war, Egypt had technically been an Ottoman territory, although it had long since stopped being so in reality. In fact, it had been a de facto British protectorate since 1882, with a puppet khedive nominally in charge and nominally subservient to the Sublime Porte.

All that ended with the war. The Turks made a brief attempt to invade, and then got pushed out of the Sinai, out of Palestine, and out of Jordan and Syria and Iraq. The British Empire ended up with a lot more colonies in the Middle East than it had bargained for.

But Turks still held a great deal of economic power in the city. The Hanzades, although wealthy, were rather petit bourgeois compared to some of the great families. Huge mansions in Zamalek and the Sheikh al-Maarouf district were the centers of great merchant dynasties. The British government looked at them with a wary eye, but they were too influential to root out and, being merchants rather than patriots, were perfectly happy to continue with business as usual—that is, making money under the regime of the moment while ignoring the pleas for pan-Turkish patriotism constantly issuing from Constantinople.

And Augustus was increasingly becoming aware that the British were only the latest "regime of the moment." The Greeks, the Romans, the Libyans, the Nubians, the Persians, the Turks, the French ... all had been sent packing sooner or later. And the British luggage was already out of storage. Earlier that year there had been a wave of independence protests that brought the colony to a standstill. Sir Thomas and his men had crushed it, but nationalist sentiment seethed below the surface.

Even his own assistant Moustafa had gotten in on the game.

Fortunately, that mountain of muscle had a good brain on top, and he hadn't turned his desire for independence into a hatred of foreigners.

Augustus couldn't say the same about some of the natives he passed in the street. From the whitest Greek merchant to the darkest Nubian doorman, there was a new attitude in the air—aloof, reticent. Outward displays of hostility were rare, but the half-glanced glower when they thought you weren't looking, the slowing down of work, the clipped responses, all showed that a large number of Egyptians—not all, but enough—had tired of English dominance.

Unlike of the fools that Sir Thomas dined with and Augustus only tolerated when he had no other choice, he did not think this was a passing phase, a fit of pique as one might get with a petulant child. No, this was deep rooted and would not go away. Sir Thomas thought he could crush it, and failed to see that while his heavy-handed measures could stop the protests and break up strikes, he only ended up encouraging the sentiment he was trying to abolish.

Zehra finished and handed him both the original and the translation.

"So you are going to Bahariya Oasis?" she asked.

"Yes. Care to make the journey?"

"I am not one for long camel rides. I prefer my palanquin."

"I am sure if you asked, your servants would carry you the entire way."

Good Lord, just ask me. I'd be happy to perform the service.

She laughed—a brilliant, musical sound—and then grew serious.

"This could be dangerous. I know a merchant who sends caravans into the Western Desert. He might know a good local contact. Let me telephone him."

She put on a pair of silk slippers and padded away. As Augustus waited, the eunuch came in with some Turkish style coffee. Augustus studied him as he poured, wondering if being unmanned in the presence of such feminine beauty was a blessing or a curse.

Zehra returned a few minutes later.

"He can see us this afternoon. His name is Orhan Bey, one of a dynasty of merchants who have been here for three generations. I only told him that you are interested in conducting an excavation in Bahariya Oasis and that you need local contacts."

"That could prove most useful. Thank you."

Orhan Bey's palace stood on the banks of the Nile, on a little bluff that had a commanding view of the river. It was surrounded by a high crenellated wall that must have dated back centuries. Nothing was visible within but the tops of some palm trees and a minaret of complex brickwork laid in a pattern that spelled out verses of the Koran.

"He has his own mosque?" Augustus asked Zehra as they arrived in a hired coach.

"He only uses it on Fridays, when his entire family and a member of the ulema come. On other days he likes to pray at Al-Azhar. He's a major donor to both the mosque and the religious school."

They came to the arched gate, where a heavy wooden door stood shut. Like in many old houses, including Augustus's own, the large portal had a normal-sized door set into it for more regular use. The larger gate would only be opened for processions or to allow a carriage or motorcar to pass.

They rang an electric buzzer, the simple brass button looking startlingly modern next to the aged wood and medieval arch, and a view slit protected by a heavy iron grill opened in the door.

Before Zehra could speak, the servant who answered cried,

"Ah, Mrs. Hanzade, you grace us with your presence! A thousand pardons for making you wait."

"Really, Abdullah, I have waited less than ten seconds," Zehra said with a smile as the smaller door opened.

"Too long for such an esteemed guest. My master told me to expect you. I should have been waiting outside."

This was said as the servant, a small man with a pencil-thin moustache, fez, green vest and matching pantaloons, bowed deeply. He then welcomed Augustus by name and led them through a vast garden. Palm trees offered shade, a sparkling fountain cooled the breeze, and an explosion of flowers filled the air with perfume.

"I'm surprised our host doesn't have a eunuch guarding the door," Augustus whispered to Zehra in English, giving her a wry smile.

"Oh, he is much more conservative than I am. His wives are kept in the women's quarters. A staff of eunuchs guards them there."

Augustus almost pointed out that if the man was so conservative, that his morals should keep him from inviting a woman like Zehra over for coffee, but he decided discretion was best in this situation.

From the gate a wide graveled driveway led to a large garage, another modern anomaly, as was the chauffeur in full livery polishing a Rover luxury touring car with silver fittings. As the servant took them down a path cutting across the garden, they left these last vestiges of the modern world behind.

Beyond the garden stood an imposing stone palace. The stone itself was plain, but several large windows of dark wood had intricately carved wooden meshrabiyya screens, allowing the women inside to look out without being seen. One corner of the upper story was entirely given over on two sides to these screens, Augustus supposed this was the sitting room for the harem. He wondered how many ladies were looking out of those screens at them.

A pair of burly servants at the front doorway of the palace bowed as they passed. Augustus noticed the telltale bulges of pistols hidden under their shirts.

The front hallway couldn't have been more different than that of the Hanzade home. Instead of cool marble and an array of nude Classical statues, the hallway was one of complex blue and green tiles on both the floor and walls. The ceiling was of wood, carved in a pattern of interconnecting stars sitting atop an arcade of arched windows that let in daylight. A gallery ran around the upper story and a grand staircase swept up to it. On the walls of the ground floor were an array of animal heads—lion, gazelle, Barbary sheep, and hippo.

"Is our host a sportsman?" Augustus asked, switching back to Arabic for the servant's benefit.

"Oh yes," Abdullah said. "I had the honor of reloading my master's spare rifle when he shot that one." The man indicated a particularly large lion. "He shot it from five hundred yards as it was running after a gazelle."

"I'm sure the gazelle was grateful for your master's marksmanship."

Abdullah laughed. "Not for long. That's the gazelle over there."

The servant led them to a small sitting room cast in a strange green light thanks to the stained glass windows to one side. Unlike the native stained glass, which were made up of patterns of small holes cut through marble and filled with tiny colored panes, these were more European in style, having large panes held in place by a network of thin lead *cames*. Their host being a Muslim, the colored glass only showed abstract designs, but they were pleasing to the eye, as were the tile walls that hinted at floral designs without quite crossing the line into depicting living things, and the embroidered silk cushions on the low divans set around a hexagonal wooden table inlaid with mother of pearl.

Given the lavish interior, Augustus had half expected to be kept waiting, but Orhan Bey was no fool. Not amount of wealth would make Zehra Hanzade wait for anything. He came out of a side door, dressed in a fine suit that looked like it had been tailored for him in Paris, a spotless white turban on his head. He went up to Zehra and bowed.

"Zehra, enchanting to see you as always."

This was said in perfect French, Orhan Bey showing Augustus the courtesy of assuming that he knew the language.

Orhan Bey extended his hand. Augustus took it.

"Sir Augustus Wall, I have heard so much about you. Zehra sings your praises on every occasion."

Augustus almost swooned. "Pleased to meet you too, Orhan Bey. Does she really?"

"Oh yes, she says your antiquities shop is second to none. I do not collect such things myself, as they are contrary to my religion, but I always admire a keen businessman."

While these and other pleasantries were exchanged, there was a flurry of activity in the sitting room as servants set out coffee, tea, sweets, cigarettes, and a sheesha. Orhan Bey invited them to sit and the servants withdrew. Zehra sat at the chair provided with the sheesha. Augustus cocked an eyebrow. Conservative Muslims frowned on women who smoked in public, or indeed women mingling with men who were not their close family. Orhan Bey was obviously selective in his conservatisms.

"I took the liberty of having my man fill the sheesha with strawberry flavored tobacco, your favorite," Orhan Bey told his female guest.

Augustus opened the gold cigarette case set in front of him and was not surprised to find Woodbines inside. No doubt the rich Turkish merchant had asked Zehra what he smoked.

There were several more minutes of pleasantries, asking after one another's health and the health of their families. This was standard in all the Muslim world, and Augustus found it as false and irritating as the pleasantries that passed for courtesy in the Western world.

At last they got down to business. Zehra told their host how Augustus was going to Bahariya Oasis in search of antiquities, and given the recent murder of Professor Harrell, which all of Cairo had heard about, he was concerned about his safety and wanted to secure some local contacts he could trust.

Orhan thought for a minute.

"It is late in the season. All of the Bedouin I know who travel that route are either back in their desert homes or are staying for the hot season here in Cairo or along the Nile. Even the Bedouin enjoy a dip in the river in the summer. You will have a very hot journey."

Augustus had expected this, and had already prepared a reply.

"So my assistant tells me, but nevertheless I am anxious to set out at the earliest possible opportunity. Professor Harrell's discoveries have galvanized the Egyptological community. I know of several expeditions being planned for the autumn. I want to get there first."

"Ah, if only more of my people had the energy of you Westerners, the great Ottoman Empire might still be in its glory days. I know just the man who can help you. He lives on the outskirts of the oasis and I think you will find in him a kindred spirit as well as someone with the ability to help you in an official capacity."

"It would be most kind of you to make an introduction. He sounds like just the fellow."

"His name is Captain Claud Williams."

"An officer?" Augustus asked, surprised. He had expected to be introduced to some Bedouin sheik or local merchant.

"Indeed. We met during the late war. He was stationed in Cairo for a time and joined the Cairo Motoring Club, of which I am a founding member. I own, in addition to a Rover touring car, a stripped down Model T Ford that I use for desert journeys. I'm afraid it looks a bit ridiculous," Orhan Bey chuckled, "and not something a man of my station would generally be seen in, but I discovered that by removing excess metalwork such as the running boards and engine housing, and making a few modifications to the tires and engine, one could make a vehicle that could skim over all but the softest sand. Claud, as I came to call him, became a good friend. He was most interested in my alterations and came up with some improvements of his own. These he incorporated into his service with the Light Car Patrols in the Western Desert."

Augustus nodded. During the war, the Germans and Ottomans had riled up the Senussi religious order in Italian Cyrenaica to rebel against the Italian colonists as well as launch an invasion of Egypt. They had taken most of the oases in the Western Desert, Bahariya included, before a British force ejected them. The most effective arm of the force had been the armored cars, modified motorcars covered with metal plating and mounted with a turret and machine gun. There were also lighter scouting vehicles. The desert warriors had nothing with which to fight such technology, and were soundly defeated.

Orhan Bey went on.

"I was amused to see my ideas being used to fight the British Empire's enemies in the Western Desert and then to eject the Ottomans from the Sinai and Gaza. I am sure my esteemed Ottoman ancestors would have never dreamed that I would inadvertently aid in their empire's destruction."

"I must say you don't seem terribly broken up about it."

Orhan Bey shrugged and turned his palm up. "Why should I be? I may be of Turkish extraction, but my family has been living in Egypt for three generations. I am just as much Egyptian as the Armenian who tailors my shirts, the fellahin who till my land, and the Lebanese grocer who supplies my kitchen. Egypt is a nation of many different ethnic groups. It always has been, and we are all in agreement that the Ottomans did nothing to improve this country, not like the British."

That last statement seemed to have been tacked on almost as an afterthought. Augustus got the impression that he had caught the Turk in a slip.

But Orhan Bey's admiration for what the Ottoman Empire had been, and his indifference to what it had become, was all too common among the Turks he had met. Except for the hotheads in the pan-nationalist camp, they knew their glory days were over and sought their fortunes elsewhere.

"Claud is from New Zealand, and a fine gentleman," Orhan Bey said. "His current posting is in Bahariya, where he is stationed as a lookout and cartographer. I am sure he would be most happy to help you in anything you might need, and if you could deliver this for me both of us would be grateful."

Orhan Bey clapped his hands and a servant brought in an embroidered bag, which he handed to Augustus. Inside was a carton of Woodbines, several issues of the *Motoring Journal* and the *Illustrated London News*, as well as a sealed letter.

"I know a bit about lonely postings," Augustus said. "I'd be happy to bring him some reading material."

Orhan Bey leaned forward.

"Take care in Bahariya, my friend. There are British soldiers garrisoned there for a reason. It is not the safest of places."

"No?"

"It is a center for smuggling. The Bedouin move drugs, guns, and even slaves from Libya into Egypt through there. The locals are peaceful enough, but if you run into the wrong caravan, not even God or the British army can help you."

CHAPTER ELEVEN

"God is great!" the camel dealer shouted as he slit the sheep's throat with a long, curved knife. The blood spurted on the sand and the deal was done. The camel dealer and his customer would now sit down, have tea, money would be handed over, and the sheep boiled for supper.

Moustafa walked around the spreading pool of blood. He was at the camel market in Birqash, a village outside Cairo. It was the largest of its kind in all of Egypt, maybe even the world, and a good place to find what he was looking for.

The camels, and herds of other animals for sale, were kept in a vast enclosure ringed by a low stone wall. The dealers had set up their camps within, keeping their animals hobbled by their tents as potential buyers—Bedouin mostly, and a few village headmen—walked up and down examining the merchandise.

The camels came all the way up from the Soudan, in huge herds along the Forty Days Road to the camel market at Deraa near Abu Simbel, and then on boats up the Nile. Others walked the whole way. Moustafa's chest swelled to see so many Soudanese traders, and to hear the dialect of his homeland spoken by so many mouths. He missed home sometimes. Even though he had chosen his path a long time ago, and had never once regretted his decision to head north to seek learning, he did feel a lack in his heart for the village and the family and the friends he had left behind. He would always be half a foreigner in Egypt.

Or would he? The talk in the cafes was mostly of independence, and one of the main questions besides when and how this would take place, was whether or not the Soudan would join an independent Egypt as one nation, or whether it would go its own way.

Moustafa was of two minds about that, just as he was of two minds about independence. The British needed to go, of that there was no question, the tricky part was in the details. When should they go, and what would they leave behind? Like all other colonizers, the British, and the French before them, had ruled Egypt for their own profit. But they had given too. The French had built the Suez Canal, and introduced the printing press, that greatest of all European inventions. The British had laid railroads and bridged the Nile. They had introduced countless improvements. That made the French and British far superior to the Ottomans and Mamluks, who introduced only oppression and extra taxes and gave nothing in return.

Another sheep's throat was slit, and another deal was closed. Yes, this was why they still needed the Europeans, this superstition. Of course one should give thanks to God for good fortune in business, and of course one should sit one's customers down to a good meal after the bargaining was done. That was only proper. But these simple herdsmen and merchants truly thought that if they didn't kill a sheep, God would send misfortune down upon them. More likely God would send misfortune down on them for sharp dealing, for using a thousand tricks to hide illnesses among their stock, for lying about a camel's age or heredity. Far too many Muslims only pretended to be Godly, thinking that a few simple rituals could stand in for clean and honest living.

He examined the camels. Most looked worn out after their long journey. Some of the dealers were running them up and down a broad avenue in the middle of the market to prove their vitality. Others didn't dare try to coax their sorry animals into a run. When you bought a camel from the Soudan at this place, you had to give it at least a month of grazing before trying to get any work out of it, preferably a season.

Still, this was where the Bedouin came, and if he wanted to find a caravan to Bahariya Oasis, this was the place to look.

"This a fine one, good sir," someone beside him said in the Soudanese dialect. He turned to see an older man, his clean white turban in contrast to his dark and seamed face.

Moustafa smiled and put a hand on his shoulder. "I am only idling while I try to find a caravan of Bedouin, countryman."

He had been spreading this news all around the market, hoping it would reach the right ears.

"Ah! The Bedouin are thieves," the camel dealer said in a low voice. "Why trust them when you can buy your own camel and cross the desert yourself? You are Soudanese. Any man from the south knows the desert just as well as a Bedouin. No, better!"

"Not the desert I'm going to."

"Nonsense. I can see you are an intelligent man. Take a look at this one here. A fine neck, eh? It shows good health. And the feet are in good condition despite the great distances it has walked. Why, it simply ate up the miles!"

"It's all right," Moustafa said with a nod. He moved over to another. "This one looks strong."

"Oh yes, you have a good eye. This is the best of the lot."

"I'm sure you will sell him quickly then. Good day."

He stepped out into the avenue, hoping to find some Bedouin on the other side, and to get away from the sales patter.

"Look out!" the camel seller cried.

Moustafa saw a herd of running camels bearing down on him. He leaped aside, only to get knocked down by a donkey coming the other direction.

The camel dealer helped him to his feet. Moustafa looked down at his djellaba and saw the usually pristine white cloth was smeared with unspeakable filth.

"Perhaps you do not have such a good eye after all, my countryman," the camel dealer said.

"Hey Southerner!" someone called. Moustafa turned to see half a dozen Bedouin sitting under the shade of a tarpaulin. "We have water. Come clean yourself and we will fetch more for some tea. I heard you are looking for passage through the Western Desert, yes?"

***

The next day, Moustafa stood at the door of a modest house in the European quarter. He checked his djellaba was clean and his headscarf was on straight. While he had spoken to Herr Schäfer many times and had even borrowed books from him, this was the first time he had been invited to his home.

Taking a deep breath, Moustafa knocked. After a minute, the door was opened by an older Egyptian in servant's livery.

"We are not accepting tradesmen at this time," he said loftily, and started to shut the door.

"I am not a tradesman. Herr Schäfer invited me here."

"Oh, are you here about the drapes?"

"I just told you I am not a tradesman!"

"Is that Moustafa at the door?" Herr Schäfer's voice came from within. "Aziz, let him in!"

Moustafa glared at the servant, who shot back a contemptuous look, and stepped inside.

Herr Schäfer's house was what Moustafa expected—a comfortable European home that had little in the way of adornment other than countless books. Bookshelves lined the front hall and the dining room off to one side of it. The servant led Moustafa into a large study lined on all four walls with floor-to-ceiling bookshelves. The desk and coffee table were also piled high with volumes in several languages.

Herr Schäfer rose from his armchair, putting his down his pipe.

"Moustafa! Good to see you," he said, shaking his hand. "Would you like some coffee? Aziz, get us some coffee. Please sit."

Moustafa sat. He could not help but look around in wonder.

"A lifetime of collecting," Herr Schäfer said with pride. "My wife is quite the reader as well. She's away at friends today. She reads mostly novels, I'm afraid, and complains that my books edge out her own."

"This is the most extensive personal library I have ever seen."

"And this is only a small part. Augustus regularly comes and plunders it. And I want to extend that invitation to you. Feel free to come any time, look through it all, and borrow what you like."

Moustafa's heart skipped a beat.

"That is most generous of you, sir!"

Moustafa looked around again. All that learning …

"Not at all," Herr Schäfer said, the stem of his pipe disappearing under his bushy moustache. "Augustus and I have discussed it at length. You have an obvious talent, and I must say you have made yourself indispensable to him. By allowing you to continue your education, I am helping him as much as I am helping you. But let's get to the matter at hand. Augustus tells me you are heading to Bahariya Oasis, although he told me this in the strictest confidence. He wants to have another of his little adventures. Try to keep him from getting shot this time, eh?"

"It's already too late for that, sir."

Herr Schäfer leaned forward. "Is he badly hurt?"

"Just a graze, sir."

"Ah, good. I'm afraid that man courts danger altogether too much. It's the war, you know." Herr Schäfer's voice grew softer. "I am glad I was too old to go to the front, although even at my age I was called up for the reserves. If the war had lasted another few months, I may very well have found myself in a trench with a gun in my hand. Thank God that didn't happen. I saw how the men looked when they came back …"

Moustafa shifted uneasily in his seat. "It seems a great waste, sir."

Herr Schäfer nodded sadly. "It was indeed. I lost two nephews. Fine young men. One was only seventeen." The Egyptologist sat up straight, visibly shaking off the memories. "But on to the matter at hand. From what Professor Harrell said there is a great Greco-Roman settlement and tomb complex at Bahariya. This period is a neglected one in Egyptological studies. Have you read much about it?"

"I must admit I haven't, sir."

"Don't be embarrassed. Most people haven't. In fact, I myself have been giving it short shrift in my *Principles of Egyptian Art.* Given Professor Harrell's discoveries, I'm going to have to expand that section. You see, scholars have traditionally looked at the period as one of decline. Ancient Egypt had gone through some tumultuous times, and had been occupied by numerous foreign powers for brief periods—the Libyans, your ancestors the Nubians, the Persians. And then Alexander the Great took it from the Persians and his general Ptolemy I Soter founded the Ptolemaic Dynasty after Alexander's death."

"I am familiar with the basics, Herr Schäfer."

The German scholar waved his pipe, sending curls of rich smoke wafting up to the ceiling.

"Of course, of course. I merely state these things as a prelude, a way to point out that Egypt hadn't been run by Egyptians for far too long. There is a similar sentiment on the streets today."

Moustafa tensed. He did not want to discuss politics with a European who was about to offer him access to such an extensive library.

Herr Schäfer went on.

"By this time, Egyptian art had gone into what many people see as a steep decline. Inscriptions and paintings had become cruder, the sarcophagi had become broader, almost squat in appearance, losing the fine proportions of the earlier periods. There were some bright spots, such as those fabulously lifelike mummy portraits, but those were of foreign invention. Native Egyptian art had lost its way."

"One can see that in the mummy decoration," Moustafa said. "Besides the mummy portraits, there were other Greek and Roman influences. Like the plaster masks used on some mummies. They look like poor imitations of Classical busts."

Herr Schäfer smiled. "That they do. A good way of putting it. But I believe we may be looking at it incorrectly, through the wrong set of eyes, if you will. What we see as decadence, the Greeks and Romans saw as a fusion of cultures. After all, the Greeks and Romans who had colonized Egypt did not have to take on Egyptian traditions. They could have continued to be buried in simple graves or marble sarcophagi carved with scenes from Classical mythology. Instead they chose to take on Egyptian ideas of the afterlife, although adding their own style to it."

Herr Schäfer handed over three slim volumes. "You should borrow these. They all cover the period, although I must say they are all lacking. We simply do not have a good comprehensive study of the art of the period. The history, yes, but not the art. How is your draftsmanship?"

The sudden change of subject took Moustafa by surprise.

"I ... have practiced a little, sir, but I would not say I am an expert."

"Can you draw something with scientific accuracy?"

"Yes."

"That will be good enough. If you have the time, I would be greatly in your debt if you could make some illustrations of any significant Greco-Roman artifacts you come across in the Western Desert. It would fill a lacuna in my work, and I would be happy to pay for any illustrations I end up using in my *Principles of Egyptian Art*."

Moustafa's jaw dropped. "I would be honored, sir!"

"It would be a great help for me." The scholar fetched an excavation report. "Now look at these illustrations of the reliefs in the temple of Hatshepsut at Deir el-Bahari. Fine, aren't they? The illustrator not only captures the content and proportions of the original, but also its essence."

"These are excellent," Moustafa said, leafing through the volume. "I cannot match this quality."

"Few can. The illustrator is one Howard Carter, an Englishman and the best archaeological draftsman of this generation. He's wasting his talent, however. Now he's off in the Valley of the Kings thinking he'll discover the undisturbed tomb of Tutankhamun."

"That would be wonderful."

"Fanciful is the better word. All those tombs were plundered centuries ago. He would be better off sticking with illustration. Sadly, the man has contracted gold fever. Be that as it may, I would be very happy if you could find the time to make some sketches for my book. I know that Augustus will be keeping you busy, and no doubt in danger, but if you can it would be beneficial to both of us."

"I will try my best, sir."

"Perhaps you'll find something that will make a good journal article to follow up the success of your first." The scholar tapped the stack of books he was lending Moustafa. "These will be of some help, but you are for the most part entering unknown territory."

"We will be leaving soon. I'll read as much as possible and get them back to you before we go."

"Nonsense! Take them with you."

Moustafa looked at the books uncertainly. "Are you sure, Herr Schäfer?"

"Quite sure, I have plenty of other books to read," he said with a chuckle. "Ah! Here's our coffee."

Aziz entered with a tray. He made a point of pouring Herr Schäfer's coffee first, even though Moustafa was the guest.

Moustafa seethed. This was what colonialism had done to Egypt, made the servants think they were above the scholars. Of course, Moustafa knew that he would have never become a scholar if it wasn't for colonialism. It was the Europeans who had started the investigations into Egypt's past. Most Egyptians didn't care.

As Aziz finally got around to pouring his coffee, Moustafa wondered if, when colonialism ended, they would lose the good things that came with it along with the bad.

CHAPTER TWELVE

Taiyer ibn Akbar would buy anything and never tell a soul who he had bought it from. Big or small, old or new, it made no difference. Carpets, shoes, brass lamps, furniture—as long as it was stolen, Taiyer ibn Akbar would buy it.

Taiyer ibn Akbar was an older man with a paunch pressing against the fabric of his yellow djellaba. He wore a white turban to hide his balding head and although he had no beard, his gray and black stubble was shaved so rarely that he might as well have had one. One eye was milky white, the other sharp and penetrating. Faisal couldn't decide which bothered him more. Still, he had done good business with Taiyer ibn Akbar.

"What do you have for me today, Faisal?" he asked in a voice made friendly by greed.

They sat in the back of his junk shop, piled high with all sorts of goods covered in a deep layer of dust. Chairs, bed stands, side tables, candlestick holders, all lay in a jumble so high it obscured the view from the street outside. Most of this stuff never sold. It had been here from the time when Taiyer ibn Akbar's father had owned the shop. All had been purchased honestly, and acted as a screen to hide the true business that went on in back. Often homeowners who had experienced a robbery would scour the bazaar for shops like this, hoping to spot their stolen property, little knowing that stolen property never went on display.

Taiyer ibn Akbar sat behind a small hexagonal table inlaid with mother of pearl. It had been beautiful once, probably adorning the house of some rich Ottoman merchant from the time of Faisal's great-grandparents, whoever they were. Now it was battered and scratched and stained and many of the bits of inlay had fallen out.

Faisal set down his bundle and slowly unrolled the cloth to reveal the bright silverware inside.

Taiyer ibn Akbar took in a sharp breath.

"Well, well, Faisal. You have outdone yourself this time!"

"I'm a good boy, aren't I?"

"A good boy? Ha! You are an excellent thief, and that's even better."

Faisal wasn't sure why that compliment didn't feel good.

Taiyer ibn Akbar picked up each utensil one by one and studied them in the dim sunlight filtering in from the front.

Faisal swelled with pride. These were the nicest things he had ever brought him.

Taiyer ibn Akbar put down the last utensil, looked at Faisal for a moment, and said, "One hundred piastres."

Faisal almost shot through the ceiling. One hundred piastres! That was more money then he had ever held in his hand!

But then his street cunning took over. One hundred piastres was a lot of money, sure, but this silverware was worth way more than that.

"Two hundred piastres," Faisal said.

Taiyer ibn Akbar scoffed. "Come now. They are used, and look at this design. They are easily recognized. I will have to sell them to a middleman who will ship them to Alexandria to sell there. That cuts into my profits. I'll give you a hundred and ten."

"Are you trying to rob me? I nearly fell out a window getting these, and also—" Faisal caught himself before he let slip about the gunfight, "—also had to run from the servants. I won't sell them to you for less than a hundred and eighty."

"Nonsense. Because you are a good boy I'll give you a hundred and twenty. I cannot go any higher."

Faisal felt anger burn in his skinny chest. Calling him a good boy only so he could rip him off? Faisal felt like taking the silverware back and storming out of the shop.

But Taiyer ibn Akbar was the best fence he knew. The others were even stingier, or if they saw such a nice prize might clout Faisal over the head and take the silverware without paying.

"Enough of this. We both know we're heading for a hundred and sixty," Faisal said.

"Forty."

"Sixty!"

"Fifty."

Faisal paused. A hundred and fifty was probably the best price he could get.

He was about to say yes when he looked down at the silverware and felt a tug of regret. They were so nice. He had never owned something so nice. Why did everyone have nice things except him?

But that was foolish. What would he do with a bunch of European eating utensils? He ate with his hands, like other Egyptians. Well, maybe a knife to cut some meat, when he had meat, or a spoon when he ate soup, but usually with soup he just drank it from the bowl. He didn't even own a spoon. And a fork? What would he do with a fork?

He picked out a knife, a spoon, and a fork.

"I want to keep these," he said.

Taiyer ibn Akbar stared at him, baffled.

"Why?"

Faisal didn't know.

"I just want them."

"Don't be silly. If you break up the set, it's worth a lot less. You know that!"

"Only pay me a hundred and twenty then."

Faisal was shocked by his own words. What was he doing?

"I'll give you ninety," Taiyer ibn Akbar grunted.

"A hundred and ten and not a milleme less. I know every fence in

Cairo."

Taiyer ibn Akbar smiled and put a hand on his shoulder. "Look, Faisal. We have done some good business together, haven't we? I have always given you a good price. Now let me give you some good advice. I see the way you are looking at these things. You're thinking 'I own nothing nice. I should keep these.' But what will you do with them? They'll only get stolen by one of the other street boys. And even if you hide them well, silver gets tarnished after a time. You have to take care of it, and you don't know how to do that. Look, I'll give you a hundred and fifty, and we'll order some falafel from down the street. My treat. What do you say?"

Faisal's stomach grumbled. He hung his head, fiddling with the three shiny, beautiful utensils in his hand.

"No," he said at last. "I want a hundred and ten and I get to keep these."

He couldn't look at Taiyer ibn Akbar when he said it.

"You're a very foolish boy," Taiyer ibn Akbar said with a sigh. Then he threw up his hands. "Very well, a hundred and ten it is! But don't come to me in a week's time trying to sell them. The set will be long gone by then."

The fence paused in the hope that Faisal would reconsider, but he held firm.

Faisal was very busy for the rest of the day. First he snuck into the alley behind the Englishman's house. It was half filled with trash and heaps of cracked bricks and bits of broken old furniture. No one came back here, and that suited Faisal just fine. He climbed the sheer back wall of the Englishman's house, using handholds and toeholds in the cracked old masonry, some of which he had dug out deeper with a little chisel he stole from a carpenter's shop. He was the best climber in Cairo, and going up the wall was as easy as going up a flight of stairs.

Which was just as well, because he made a lot of trips up and down the wall that day.

First he hid away his set of silverware. Then he went down and bought a nice thick cushion, a deep green in color. He bought a bright yellow cloth too, and a new pair of sandals to replace the ones that were wearing out. Edmond had given him his first pair of sandals, and he felt bad that they were wearing out, but there was nothing to do but replace them. At least he still had his nice blue djellaba.

Faisal took all those things up to his little shed on the roof. Then he went back down.

He bought some carrots, and some cucumbers, some bread, and a whole roast chicken.

As he climbed up the wall the final time, the smell of that roast chicken made his stomach growl louder than Mohammed al-Hajji's voice when he gave the call to prayer.

It took all of Faisal's willpower not to gobble the chicken as soon as he got to the roof. Instead he set the food to one side. He took an old box from the junk he had piled up in front of the door of the shed. That pile kept anyone standing on the roof from noticing that he had cleared the inside of the shed of all the other junk. He put the box in the center of the clear space, and laid the yellow cloth over it. Smoothing it out, he placed his new cushion in front of the box. Then he set out his knife and fork and spoon and placed the food at the center of the box.

He unwrapped the newspaper from around the chicken and was about the throw the paper away when he realized that if he did that, he'd stain his nice new yellow cloth.

Silly boy, he could hear Taiyer ibn Akbar saying in his head. *You forgot to buy a plate.*

Faisal groaned. What a stupid mistake!

Oh well, he had some money left over. He could buy a plate tomorrow.

He looked at the chicken, licking his lips. He picked up the knife and fork. The knife was easy, but how did you hold this fork thing? He tried to remember how the Europeans did it at Shepheard's Hotel, and realized he had never paid any attention to that. He just held it in his fist like the knife.

He jabbed his fork at the side of the chicken and it shot off the box and landed on the floor with a splat.

Cursing to himself, he picked the chicken up, dusted it off, and put it back on the box.

No, not a box, he corrected himself. A table.

This time he was more careful and got the fork in the chicken without the chicken getting away from him.

He hacked into the chicken with the knife and tore long strips of it off with the fork, gnawing away at the end until he got to the fork. The last bit he had to bite carefully off the fork so he didn't crack his teeth against the metal. He got the hang of it soon enough. Then he discovered it was easier to spear the chicken with the knife to hold it steady, and rip off chunks of meat with the fork.

The cucumbers were even easier. All you had to do was stab the fork into the middle of the cucumber and chew away at both ends. It was very efficient, because instead of picking up slices of cucumber from the table with your hand, you could have the whole cucumber right next to your mouth and eat it as fast as you wanted.

The Europeans were very clever about some things.

Oh, he nearly forgot!

He stopped hunching over his food and sat up straight. Europeans always sat up straight when they were at a table, and spent as much time smiling at the others around the table as they did eating their food. They also stuck their noses in the air.

Faisal practiced that, pretending the Englishman and some other Europeans sat around the table. Not Sir Thomas Russell Pasha. Faisal didn't like him. Maybe the Englishman's friend with the motorcar. He seemed all right.

And so Faisal ate his food and kept his nose in the air and pretended to talk with the Englishman and the European with the motorcar. They talked about all the things Europeans talked about when they sat at a table eating. Faisal wasn't sure what those things were, but he talked anyway.

"I went in my motorcar to see the moving pictures today," he said to one of his pretend friends.

"I went to the big hotel with the fence around it and ate there. I went in my motorcar, of course," his friend replied.

"Maybe we should go to the moving pictures this afternoon," Faisal said.

"Oh yes. Shall we go in my motorcar or yours?"

It was hard to eat with your nose in the air. Maybe that's why so many Europeans were skinny even though they were all rich.

That was a funny game. A bit silly too. But fun.

And the knife and fork made the food taste better.

***

Even though eating at home was a lot more fun now with his table and his European utensils, Mina's *ful* stand was his favorite place to eat. The beans were always fresh and they always made it with extra vegetables and lemon juice, just the way he liked it. And it was only half a piastre.

And he got to see Mina.

Mina was his best friend. She was the only one of his friends who had a home. Sure, it was just a little lean-to made of reed mats by the side of the street behind their *ful* stand, but there were plenty of children who lived in places just as bad who turned up their noses when he passed. Mina didn't. Even Mina's parents didn't do that.

Mina was also the only one of his friends who believed him when he said he worked for the Englishman. When Mina's father had wrenched his back and couldn't work, Faisal had given up some of his pay to get the Englishman to take him to a doctor. The Englishman himself had come to the *ful* stand to talk with Mina's family. The look on their faces! They had always laughed when he said he worked for the Englishman, and then he and the Englishman had walked up side by side and Faisal introduced them.

The doctor had fixed up Mina's father in no time and the *ful* stand was doing better than ever. Mina didn't have to help out so much anymore and had time to play.

As Faisal strolled up to the stand for breakfast, he saw Mina and a few of the other girls playing pick-up-sticks.

When Mina spotted him, she skipped over.

"Hey Faisal!"

"How's your father's back?"

"Still good," she said. "He's getting more business than ever."

Faisal could see him by the *ful* stand of green and red painted wood, ladling out the seasoned chickpeas to a crowd of workmen. The stand was in front of the tall stone wall of a rich man's house. Just beyond the stand was Mina's house, a lean-to of papyrus reed mats.

"I have another job with the Englishman. I'm going to have to go away for a while."

Mina cocked her head. "Go away? Where?"

"To Bahariya Oasis," Faisal said.

"Where's that?"

"In the Western Desert," he said, gesturing vaguely to the west. "I thought everyone knew."

"Why would he want to go there?"

"He's looking for gold, plus a man who kills Europeans."

Mina giggled.

"It's true!" Faisal said.

"Come on. Where are you really going?"

"To the Western Desert. You know how foreigners love old things. There was another foreigner who dug up old things who got killed and my boss is looking for him. Plus he'll probably dig up old things and sell them in his shop for lots of money."

"There's nothing in the desert except sand and Bedouin."

"That's what I thought too, but the Englishman said there are some old temples and tombs and things there."

Mina looked concerned. "Aren't those places dangerous?"

Faisal puffed out his chest. "Sure, but I went to Khadija umm Mohammed. Look."

From beneath the neckline of his djellaba he pulled out a charm tied on a leather strap around his neck. It was a strange stone of shiny green, with magical writing etched all over it by Khadija umm Mohammed herself.

Mina leaned closer to look at it.

"That looks powerful," she said. "Khadija umm Mohammed is the best sorceress in the neighborhood."

She saved you from getting married to that fat old man, he thought.

"She sure is," Faisal said. "I had to work hard to get enough money to buy it."

Mina raised an eyebrow. "Work?"

"For the Englishman! You can't buy charms with stolen money. Everybody knows that. They won't work if you do."

Faisal's stomach grumbled. Mina laughed.

"Well, I hope you don't buy *ful* with stolen money!"

"Of course not," Faisal replied, wondering if money he tricked out of the Englishman counted as stolen money. They walked over to the stand, where Mina's father greeted him with a smile and a wave. He served Faisal a big portion.

They sat against the wall a little way from the crowd as Faisal ate.

"Mina, aren't you going to play?" one of the other girls called over.

"In a minute!"

The girls gathered into a huddle and whispered among themselves, giggling.

"How long will you be gone?" Mina asked, turning back to Faisal.

"It takes ten days to get there. I guess it takes ten days to get back too. I don't know how long we'll stay."

"He needs you for all that time?"

"I told you, I do stuff for him. Like, um, taking messages."

Faisal had almost let slip about breaking into houses. Mina didn't like that sort of story.

"Ten days each way?" Mina whined. "You'll be gone for weeks!"

Faisal smiled. Mina was the only person in all of Cairo who would miss him. Sure, he had plenty of friends among the street boys, but they were all too busy trying to survive to think much about what he was doing. Mina had a father and a mother and a roof and regular meals. She could afford to think about friends.

"I'll bring you something from Bahariya."

"What do they have in Bahariya that we don't have here?"

Faisal shrugged. He really needed to learn more about this Bahariya place.

"I don't know. Something, anyway. Some desert thing."

"If you tease me by bringing back a handful of sand I'll put it in your *ful*."

"That won't help you get customers!"

They both laughed.

Mina looked at him. "So you're really going?"

"I told you! Yes, I'm going. I won't bring you sand. I promise."

Maybe he could bring her a camel's saddlebag. He'd seen the Bedouin in the market. Their saddlebags were all covered in designs. One had told him that every design meant something, sort of like the old picture writing. Only the Bedouin knew how to read it.

That was a good idea. He'd bring her one of those saddlebags … and fill it with sand! It would be a great trick. And she couldn't get too mad because she'd get a nice gift too. The look on her face when she opened it up!

"What are you laughing about?" Mina asked.

"Nothing. I just thought of something, that's all."

"Be careful."

"I'll be fine," Faisal told her, and quickly started to talk about other things.

Faisal got a bad feeling. He'd never gone so far away and he wouldn't know how to get back. In all his other adventures with the Englishman, he'd been in Cairo. He could make it back on his own. Now he had to rely on the Englishman for everything, and the Englishman wasn't right in the head.

Was it a mistake to think he could rely on the Englishman?

"What are you thinking about, Faisal? You've gone all quiet."

"Oh, nothing. I'm just thinking about how much fun the trip will be."

CHAPTER THIRTEEN

Augustus was hardly an expert on camels or desert caravans, but he did not like the look of this group that Moustafa had hired. They met the caravan at the village of Kirdasah on the edge of the desert west of Cairo, the pyramids visible a couple of miles to the south. The animals looked old, a bit thin, and more than a little foul tempered. One gurgled in resentment as a driver put a load on its back. Another got to its feet and tried to walk away. In its path lay another camel, which calmly ignored the first camel's attempt to pass and ended up getting bitten. The animal sprang up with an outraged roar and soon the two were biting and bellowing as a circle of camel drivers gathered around, beating the pair for all they were worth.

The camel with the pack took the opportunity to stand up, its half-secured load slipping sideways and nearly tipping the beast over. The children and old men of the village, who had gathered a little way off to watch, laughed and cheered.

The men didn't look much better than their camels. The head of the caravan was a one-eyed old hawk named Farouk, who couldn't stop staring at Augustus' mask and only just managed to return his greeting when they first met.

Farouk had six men, mostly older and looking almost as worn out as the camels. They were bringing a load of manufactured goods to the oasis, which they would trade for dates, olives, and camel saddles, which they said the men of Bahariya made better than anyone else in Egypt.

Faisal had been assigned to guard their baggage, which he did by piling the suitcases and crates and bags in a large heap, sitting on top, and throwing stones at anyone who came close. His aim was shockingly accurate and he seemed to be enjoying himself thoroughly. As instructed, the boy wore his new blue djellaba and sandals, and had even managed to clean up enough that he was only dirty rather than filthy.

Dirtier still were the stares a couple of Farouk's henchmen gave Augustus. He did not think these Bedouin would try to rob them and leave them to die of thirst in the desert, but they would almost certainly try to filch a few things and extort more money from him via any number of made up reasons. Augustus was accustomed to dealing with city Egyptians, something he could manage quite well. The Bedouin were a breed apart. They had never felt much effect from colonialism and they did not think of Europeans as people to obey and feel intimidated by. This caravan would bring trouble. He was sure of it.

His doubts must have been written on his face, because Moustafa said, "Sorry, boss, but it is late in the season. Not many caravans are going to the oases."

"We can't wait. Did any of this pirate crew hear of an earlier caravan leaving with our man along for the ride?"

"I asked them, boss, but they said no. You must understand these are Bedouin. They are born smugglers. They would not discuss who they brought to Bahariya with an outsider, and to them I am almost as much an outsider as you are."

"What do you think of these camels?"

Moustafa grunted. "Newly bought. Most camels come up from the Soudan during the winter and are sold in the market just outside of Cairo. They are exhausted by the long journey, and need at least a full season to recover."

"And these have not had a full season."

"No, boss."

"Do you think they can make it to Bahariya?"

"The Bedouin think so, boss."

"That's good enough for me."

"And it will be good enough, as long as we don't get off course or have to make a run from bandits."

The Western Desert was rife with bandits, and the men of this caravan had only three antiquated rifles between them. It was a good thing he had brought along a German submachine gun looted from the battlefield, along with a pair of Lee-Enfield rifles, pistols for each of them, several grenades, and a variety of bladed weapons. Moustafa had even brought along that sword he was so proud of. If any bandits came after them, the two of them would have to hold their own and not expect any help from this shoddy crew.

And Moustafa was always scolding him for having a personal arsenal!

Farouk swaggered up to them. That man had been swaggering all morning.

"We're just about ready to go. If you want us to pack your things, you need to get your brat to stop throwing stones."

"I apologize for his behavior," Augustus said. "My ... servant ... is a bit overly zealous in protecting my things."

This elicited a derisive snort from Moustafa.

Augustus called off Faisal, who looked disappointed at losing his position of authority, and the Bedouin packed the last of the camels. Then they settled down for a final tea and a prayer before leaving. Augustus tried to contain his impatience. The day was already well advanced and here they were dilly-dallying. He didn't say a word, though. Best to have them happy. It was a ten-day trip to Bahariya, with no wells along the route. Tempers would flare soon enough.

Moustafa joined them when they prostrated themselves in the direction of Mecca. Faisal did not. That earned the boy a few hard looks. While children were not actually required to pray, this was not one of the five daily prayers but rather a prayer for blessing before going on a journey. To have a believer stand idly by was not a good omen.

Augustus decided not to enlighten them as to Faisal's beliefs or lack thereof.

At last they packed their prayer rugs away, had a final long drink from the village well, and mounted up.

Augustus had done quite a bit of horse riding in England before the war. That experience did him no good here. He had heard men of the Camel Corps complain that learning to ride a camel was a harder job than trekking through the desert or fighting the Turks. He had yet to meet an Englishman in the Camel Corps who actually liked camels. Most of them said things about the beasts that were unrepeatable in all but the rudest company.

He watched as Moustafa rapped a long stick against his camel's front legs and got the animal to sit, which it did by folding all four of its legs beneath itself. The Nubian then mounted on the saddle, let out a short shout, and rapped his stick against the camel's back flank. It raised first its back legs, then its front.

Moustafa looked at Augustus with triumph.

"It's been a long time, but you don't forget," he said.

"A bit like riding a bicycle, I suppose."

"I've never ridden a bicycle."

"What's a bicycle?" Faisal asked, looking at his own camel nervously. The Bedouin had given him the smallest, but it still towered over him.

"A machine that will not to get us to Bahariya," Augustus said.

One of Farouk's men had given him a long, thin stick. Augustus went up to his camel, which stood there impassively, and rapped it against the animal's ungainly front legs.

The camel didn't even look at him.

"You have to hit him harder," Farouk called out. "And shout 'hai!' as you do so."

"Hai!" he shouted, smacking the animal's legs as hard as he could.

The camel lunged its head forward, baring its teeth. Augustus dodged to the side, narrowly avoiding the snapping teeth, and rapped it on the top of the head.

"That's it," one of the other Bedouin said. "Show him who's boss."

"Hai!" Augustus shouted again, smacking the camel's legs several times.

The beast gurgled, got down, and Augustus climbed aboard.

He had noticed that camels get up with their hindquarters first, so he was ready when he got tilted forward. Augustus leaned far back in the saddle, gripping the saddle horn.

What he was not prepared for was how quickly the camel rose up on its front legs. The force sent him tumbling right off the back of the camel and into the dust.

Immediately he checked his mask was in place, although the raucous laughter from all sides told him it must be. No one would have laughed if they had seen his face. The camel turned its long neck and looked at him with an expression of smug superiority.

Dusting himself off, Augustus squared his shoulders and stalked toward the camel.

"Hai!" Down came the stick on the animal's legs. It bellowed in protest, but obeyed.

The camel tried the same trick again, but this time Augustus was ready for it. He just barely managed to retain his seat and gave the beast a few raps on the head to show it what he thought of it.

"Faisal, be careful when—" Augustus blinked. Faisal sat in his saddle, watching him. "How did you get on your camel without it throwing you?"

"I didn't give it a chance. I jumped onto the saddle from the ground."

"Perhaps I should try that next time."

"You can't. You're too clumsy."

"Let's go," Farouk said with a grin.

He let out a cry, kicked his camel several times with both heels, and trotted off. The Bedouin and Moustafa followed in a regular line, each trailing a pack camel on a rope behind. Augustus and Faisal jammed their heels into their own animals and tried to follow. Augustus' camel didn't budge. Faisal's started walking around in circles.

"These animals are sillier than you, Englishman."

"And they are as dirty as you. I swear I'll have fleas before we get out of sight of the Nile."

"You should be nicer to me, Englishman. I have saved you many times," Faisal said, still going around in circles.

"Then save me from this damned beast!" Augustus said, still whipping his camel to no effect.

In the end it was Moustafa who saved him. He trotted back and instructed them on how to make the camels do their bidding. After giving the village another half hour's entertainment, they finally got underway.

The camels walked sedately along a flat patch of sand for some time, the village dwindling behind them, the Nile glimmering distantly beyond. To the south, the pyramids disappeared behind a sand dune. And then they climbed a dune, and went down the other side, and the village and the Nile went out of view. All around there was nothing but sand, with no sign of life but a few vultures wheeling high above in the pale blue sky. Augustus stared at them for a moment, and adjusted his keffiyeh. Everyone in their little caravan wore one. It was the only practical headgear in the desert because the light cloth not only protected the head and neck, but the part that hung around the neck also caught any slight breeze and helped cool the skin. Even so, the sun felt like a hammer.

He was so distracted by the vultures and the sun that he did not see one of the Bedouin whip his rifle out of its saddle case and fire.

CHAPTER FOURTEEN

The gazelle bounded away as the Bedouin's bullet kicked up some sand near it. The Bedouin racked the bolt back to put another bullet in the chamber and fired again.

And missed again.

The gazelle sprinted over a sand dune and was gone.

Moustafa's heart sank. The Bedouin had a tradition that if the first hunt of the caravan trek was successful, the caravan would ride through good fortune.

If it was unsuccessful, the caravan was trekking into disaster.

He cursed himself for momentarily lapsing into such superstition. That was worthy of the youth he had left behind, the ignorant Soudanese village boy who even back then knew the limits of his horizons and headed north to broaden them.

He hadn't been that ignorant village boy for a long time. Still, he couldn't quite get the unsettling feeling out of his gut.

Moustafa told himself that what he was really worried about was the reaction of the Bedouin. They were as superstitious as Faisal, with their talk of omens and djinn and spells. He had met many in the Soudan and had eagerly asked about their travels. All their tales were half truth, half fantasy. He supposed the Bedouin up here were no different.

Judging from their somber faces, he was right.

Of course they did not blame the man who shot at the gazelle for his bad aim. The fact that he had missed twice had been a sign from God, not of bad marksmanship. Now the Bedouin would be nervous and pessimistic, and that could lead to mistakes.

"Why does everyone look so sad?" Faisal asked. "That gazelle would have been good to eat, but we brought plenty of food along."

"Quiet," Moustafa grumbled. The last thing he needed was to fill the boy's lice-ridden head with even more nonsense.

The caravan continued in glum silence. They were well out in the desert now, with nothing to be seen but sand dunes all around. A faint track led them west and a bit south. Farouk had explained to him that this was the less common caravan route to Bahariya. Most went from Al Minya on the Nile, some 120 miles south of Cairo, straight west to Bahariya in a trip that only took four days. Moustafa got the impression that Farouk hadn't been planning to take his men to Bahariya at all until he showed up with an offer. He had no idea what they had originally been planning.

They certainly were charging an extortionate amount for their services. Moustafa had haggled half the afternoon back at the camel market, and only just managed to get to a somewhat acceptable figure.

But those worries slid out of his mind as more important thoughts occupied it.

Moustafa worried about his family. He had never left them for so long. He'd be gone at least a month, probably more. Nur would have to take care of the five children all by herself. At least the neighbors were respectable people who had promised to check in on them, and Mr. Wall had given him an advance on his salary so they would be cared for in his absence.

Still, it wasn't right for a man to abandon his family for so long just for some fool errand of his boss. It wasn't like he was going to war or on the Hajj. He was simply following the whims of a European who wanted to prove he was more intelligent than another European, something that he had already proven many times before.

And Moustafa wanted to prove he was more intelligent than many Europeans, something he already knew in his heart was true.

But they didn't know it. They would never know it. Oh, how he dreamed of making a name for himself through his journal articles, all written by "George Franklin." He was already planning his second article, and there would be more, one or two a year as he pored over the books in Mr. Wall's and Herr Schäfer's libraries and explored every ancient site he could. Then, after he had made a name for himself, after he had become the talk of Egyptological circles, with every one of those important European researchers wondering who this mystery man was, he would accept a lecture engagement at the Institut d'Egypte. All the great Egyptologists would be there, sitting in an institute that did not allow Africans to become members, and he would show up at the door. The doorman would try to stop him but he would barge through, stride up to the podium, and give forth a lecture of such intelligence and learnedness that the audience would have to accept him as an equal.

God willing, it would happen some day.

He put his hand on one of the saddlebags, feeling the reassuring shape of the books within. Herr Schäfer, at least, respected him, as did Mr. Wall. They did not quite treat him as an equal, and he found himself calling Mr. Wall "boss" and Herr Schäfer "sir." Neither of them ever corrected him on this. There was a gulf both sides recognized.

How could it be any other way when neither man was a Muslim?

If only the Europeans embraced Islam, then they would truly be the greatest race on earth.

For the first half of the day they passed through low dunes before coming to a long stretch of flat nothing. The last village was far behind them, and they saw no one. Farouk had told him that so late in the season there was a good chance they would not see another group before making it to the oasis.

That suited Moustafa fine. They had really no idea what they were heading into, or what might be waiting for them once they got there. Meeting strangers in the middle of this wasteland would do them no good.

At noon Farouk called a stop. There was no shade, so the Bedouin used some blankets and poles to pitch a few lean-tos to hide under away from the sun. As the Bedouin brewed some tea, using dried camel droppings they had gathered along the way as fuel, Faisal looked around in wonder.

"It's just so … empty. All day it's been like this."

"Quite a change after Cairo," Moustafa agreed. "I suppose you have never been this far into the desert before."

The boy shook his head.

"Personally I think it's wonderful," Mr. Wall said. He lay on his back in one of the lean-tos, smoking a cigarette. "No people. No one to bother you. Perhaps I should move here."

"You'd be bored to death within a day!" Faisal laughed.

Moustafa smiled. The little brat wasn't so foolish. For someone who put on the airs of hating all humanity, Mr. Wall certainly had a full social life. If only he wasn't so fixated on Mrs. Hanzade. She was an exquisite woman, to be sure, but a married one. Why did his boss torture himself so?

Accepting a tea from Farouk—strong and thick with sugar the way the Bedouin liked it—he pulled out one of the books that Herr Schäfer had loaned him.

It was a history of the Ptolemaic dynasty, those great descendants of Ptolemy, Alexander the Great's childhood friend and right-hand man. Ptolemy had joined in Alexander's campaign in Egypt and when the conqueror traveled to Siwa Oasis to consult with the oracle of Amun-Re and be named a living god and the new pharaoh, Ptolemy was named as a son of Zeus. After Alexander's death in 323 BC, his vast empire, only a few years old, held together for a time but inevitably split. Ptolemy got Egypt, and used his divine pedigree as proof that he should reign.

And reign he did. For the first time, Egypt began to look outward. The city on the Mediterranean that Alexander had named after himself became a center of Hellenistic culture and learning. People from all over the civilized world came to see it, and it exported not only the vast grain shipments that made Egypt so important, but also science and poetry and literature.

Ptolemy's successors were good rulers, for a time, but like all dynasties it began to deteriorate, with corrupt and profligate kings and much familial infighting. There were a few bright spots, including the brightest spot of all, that of the last ruler Cleopatra VII, who became as much a legend as Alexander himself.

It was an era he knew little about, and yet it spanned three centuries of Egyptian history. Moustafa thrilled to every page. He'd had an insatiable thirst for learning ever since he was as young and as ignorant as Faisal. Leaving his village had been the hardest, and most rewarding, thing he had ever done.

If only this book had more information on the archaeology of the period. Herr Schäfer had been correct when he said it was an era that had been overlooked by generations of Egyptologists. He supposed it was only natural. Those scholars interested in Classical antiquities had half of Europe to explore. Egyptologists, and the institutions that sponsored them, wanted gold mummy cases and alabaster statues. Only the historians appreciated what Ptolemy and his successors had achieved.

The other two books Herr Schäfer had loaned him were equally limited. One described the antiquities of Alexandria, but focused on the more Egyptian monuments such as the Serapeum, that great underground tomb for the sacred Apis bulls. The other summarized many of the stray Greek and Roman finds scattered throughout the country, but gave far more space to the essentially Classical-style statues that had been found in Egypt rather than those artifacts that showed a fusion of Classical and Egyptian styles.

He would change that, Moustafa decided. He would write an article on some aspect of the Greco-Roman period. Professor Harrell's work had been left incomplete after his murder. There was much to be done, and ironically the public killing of the pioneer in the field would spark public interest and enthusiasm.

Those mummies had been fascinating, with a level of craftsmanship hitherto unknown in Greco-Roman burials. Professor Harrell had said they dated from the late Ptolemaic Period into the early years of the Roman occupation. Perhaps he should concentrate his research on those. He wondered what had happened to the examples Professor Harrell had found. No doubt they were in storage somewhere in Cairo, out of reach to an

African like him. He'd have to see if he could find some in Bahariya to bring back. Focusing on the gilded mummies would be pandering to the public taste, something unworthy in a scholar, but it would help him get published, and he could include other finds in his article.

Mohammed al-Biwati leaned over and looked at the book with obvious distaste.

"Why do you read such things?"

"It tells of the history of Egypt. It was a great nation once and can be so again."

Moustafa glanced at his boss as he said this, but the man appeared to be dozing. Faisal was listening, though, sipping his tea and staring at him.

Mohammed al-Biwati pointed at an engraving of a nude statue. "This is forbidden. You shouldn't make images of people, and certainly not shameful images like this. Don't let the boy see."

"See what?" Faisal asked, moving closer.

"Nothing," Moustafa said, snapping the book shut. He turned back to the Bedouin. "These images are not harmful. The Koran says that we should not set up graven images. What God meant by that was putting up idols to worship like the pagans. This is merely a drawing of an old sculpture."

"One of the very same idols the pagans used to worship, and here it is in a book, being read by a Muslim! The only books you should read are the Koran and the Hadith."

Moustafa shook his head and didn't reply. How could he explain to an uneducated man that one could be faithful to one's beliefs and still look at such things with detachment? It wasn't like being a scholar was going to turn Moustafa into a worshipper of Apollo or Thoth!

And yet Mohammed al-Biwati's words still stung. He had heard them many times before from many mouths. Everyone judged him for what he was, Muslim and foreigner alike.

He looked from the book in his hand to the vast desert beyond. Why couldn't he love both?

CHAPTER FIFTEEN

Faisal was already missing his little home on the Englishman's roof. He had fixed it up really nice just a few days ago but now here he was in the middle of the desert.

The money he had made from hawking the silverware had bought him lots of food. He had been feasting ever since.

During his feasts on the roof he fumbled with the unfamiliar fork. He stood in the street in front of Shepheard's Hotel and watched how the Europeans did it, and then tried to imitate them. He still hadn't gotten the hang of it. He knew it was silly to keep these things he didn't need when he could have gotten some money for them, but they made him feel good. After every meal, he used a clean cloth and some water to shine them up, holding them up to the strong sunlight and watching how they gleamed.

They were nice things. He had never owned any nice things before. He had never expected to have any nice things. He had sure never expected to have any nice European things. They made him feel special somehow, holding them in his hands and sitting on the cushion in front of a box like it was a chair and a table in some fine European dining room.

Faisal urged his camel forward to catch up with the Englishman and Moustafa. He was beginning to get better at ordering the camel around. It was a lot easier to handle now that it was out in the desert. It acted calmer here.

"Hey Englishman, why do the Europeans all eat with knives and forks instead of their hands? And why do the Arabs eat with their hands and not with knives and forks?"

"I don't know. That's just how things turned out."

"Are knives and forks better?"

"For eating our kind of food, yes."

"Those pastries were nice. I haven't eaten any other European food."

"They're called scones. Don't you remember eating that chocolate cake in the German house?"

"Oh yes. That was nice too."

He remembered the gunfight in the German house more than the cake. And he remembered seeing for the first time the Englishman go away in his head. That hadn't been so nice.

Remembering that reminded him of why they were out here.

"Do you think the flute player went to the oasis on an earlier caravan?" Faisal asked.

"Most likely," the Englishman said. "There's something there he's after. That's why he killed Professor Harrell, to keep him from divulging the secret."

"Divulging? What does that mean?"

"Giving away the secret."

"Is that an English word?"

"He's speaking Arabic, you blockhead!" Moustafa called over.

"How can he know more Arabic than I do?" Faisal asked.

"Because he's an educated man instead of an ignorant Little Infidel," Moustafa growled.

"I'm not ignorant. I'm the only one who knows what the flute player looks like."

"How many times to I have to tell you he isn't a flute player!" the Nubian shouted. "That wasn't a flute, that was a blowgun that shot poison darts."

"Yes, a blowgun is what a flute is when you use it to shoot darts. Everybody knows that."

"Bah! I give up!" Moustafa kicked his camel to make it trot further up the line.

Faisal giggled. Teasing Moustafa was fun, and it was good for him to think Faisal was ignorant. Of course he knew that killer wasn't really a flute player. The Englishman had explained it all that very same night. Faisal was smart and nobody knew it. That was good because everybody underestimated him, like when he said he had to pay the shoeshine boy a piastre when he really only paid him half a piastre. Faisal got to keep the other half.

"Must you torment him so?" the Englishman asked.

Faisal put on an innocent face. "What did I do wrong?"

"You pretended to be ignorant. You should never do that. There's enough ignorance in the world as it is."

Faisal thought for a moment. Was the Englishman saying he was intelligent? He had never been called that before.

"Hey Englishman, do you think I'm—"

"Good Lord, Faisal, are you going to badger me with questions all the way to Bahariya?"

Faisal slumped. "No."

"What did you want to know?" The Englishman asked in an exasperated voice.

"Nothing."

The Englishman didn't ask again.

Faisal looked at his blue djellaba, still almost new. Edmond had given him it to him. Of course he had only given it to him as a disguise to break into the Citadel, but he had given it to him all the same. He had even bought one that was better than the cheapest.

Edmond had never gotten impatient with him for asking questions. Faisal had asked him about France, and the gang that called themselves Apaches after the tribe in America, and about the strange religion Edmond called anarchism. Edmond had answered all his questions. He never seemed to get tired of answering his questions.

But Edmond had used him to try and hurt people, good people like the Englishman. He tried to hurt Cordelia too. Cordelia wasn't a bad person as long as she stayed away from the Englishman. Edmond was no different than a lot of the thugs who prowled the streets of Cairo, thugs he had learned to avoid.

And if he missed Edmond and thought of him as a friend, what did that make him?

These thoughts went round and round in his head like a swarm of midges, never stopping, never settling down to an answer.

But after a while he found himself thinking less and less of these things, because the vast space and silence of the desert began to get to him. Up one side of a dune, down another. Sand dunes stretching as far as he could see in all directions. The sky overhead. Blue. Brown. Blazing yellow from the sun. No other colors. No other shapes. Faisal found himself looking at his hand, or the saddle or his camel's head, anything that had a bit of texture and coloring to it. Anything that had a bit of life.

This was a scary place. He didn't know how to survive here. If everybody left him he would be dead within a day, that was for sure. When his father disappeared, Faisal had already been living more on the street than at home, so when he had to move to the street all the time he had figured out how to survive. Sure, he had been beaten. He had been robbed. But he had survived. There was no way to do that here. The desert was bigger than every bully in Cairo put together, and had far less pity. You could run from a bully, or bribe them, or flatter them to please their arrogance.

You could do none of those things with the desert.

The sun dipped low to the west and the Bedouin stopped and pitched camp. They unloaded the camels, hobbled them, and stacked the saddles and packs in a big pile. Faisal watched all this, interested. The Englishman made a pile of their own things and Faisal sat on it. He looked for stones but couldn't find any, so he kept a hold of the stick he used to drive the camel.

The Bedouin made a fire out of dried camel dung and started making tea. Faisal had learned that was one of the ways the Bedouin knew they were on the right course, by the dried droppings of the camels that had passed before them.

Moustafa set out some blankets for himself and showed Faisal which pack held more.

"Get several," the Nubian said. "It gets very cold in the desert at night."

"Try sleeping in an alley."

"You wouldn't have to sleep in an alley if you stopped being lazy and got a job! Then you could have a house to live in."

Moustafa stormed off. Faisal stuck out his tongue at him.

I do have a job, Faisal thought. *And I do have a house.*

The Englishman moved a little away from the fire and set up a tent.

"Are we going to sleep in that?" Faisal called over.

"You'll be fine under the stars," the Englishman said, putting his things inside.

Moustafa stormed back over to him. "Why are you bothering him?"

"I'm not!"

"You think you're too good to sleep by the fire with the rest of us?"

"Well, why doesn't he?"

"Because he values his privacy."

Faisal remembered the time he had seen the Englishman without his mask and shuddered.

"It looks terrible," he whispered to the Nubian, "but he shouldn't think we're not his friends just because he's missing half his face."

Moustafa smacked him upside the head.

"He is not your friend."

"He is so! He's your friend too."

"Nonsense. He's my boss."

"He's only your boss at the shop. You came all the way out into the desert because he's your friend. The cleaning lady didn't come, did she?"

"Quiet, you ignorant scamp."

Moustafa walked off, grumbling.

Faisal hung around the fire as the Bedouin made tea. They ignored him, but he knew he'd get some of that tea because they worked for the Englishman, and so did he. When it came it was hot and sweet, heaped with sugar. Faisal slurped his tea, feeling quite content. Moustafa joined them and this time he didn't shout at him. Instead he looked around the desert with a dreamy expression. After a time, the Englishman joined them too. He sat quietly, sipping his tea. Faisal wanted to ask him all sorts of questions about their trip and where they were going, but everyone was so quiet he didn't want to disturb them.

The whole desert was quiet. He had never been someplace so silent. There was always noise in Cairo, even in the middle of the night. You could always hear people talking in the street, or market vendors trundling carts across the cobblestones, or some baby crying or some husband and wife screaming at each other. Then there were the dogs barking and the cats howling. You were never alone in the city. You could always hear lots of things happening around you.

Here all you heard was a strange hissing sound. He looked around and didn't see where it came from. It seemed like it was all around them.

"What's that noise?" he asked.

"Just the wind moving the sands," Moustafa said.

Faisal nodded. That made sense. During the summer windstorms in Cairo the dirt on the street made a noise a bit like that.

The Englishman got up, nodded to Farouk, and went to his tent.

One of the Bedouin, a wizened, thin man with a pointed beard beginning to grow grey, poked Faisal in the ribs.

"Only *some* of that is the sand moving in the wind."

Faisal looked at him. "What do you mean?"

The Bedouin, whose name was Mohammed al-Biwati, leaned in closer. His breath was stinky.

"Some of that noise is the djinn talking to each other."

Faisal trembled. "No!"

Mohammed al-Biwati nodded, his face growing serious. "That's their language, a hissing like a cobra. Hear them? Hsssss. Hsssss."

"Stop it," Moustafa said. "You're putting nonsense into the boy's head."

"It is not nonsense," Mohammed al-Biwati said. "I know the desert better than you, my Nubian friend. The djinn fly in between the grains of sand and swirl up around travelers in the desert." He turned back to Faisal. "They look for people to take away to the City of Brass, far, far away in the middle of the desert. There they make them work as slaves for all time. They especially like city dwellers, because they are easier to catch, and most of all they like young boys."

"Enough!" Moustafa shouted. The Bedouin all laughed.

"I'm not afraid," Faisal said, although his voice trembled as he said it. "I have a charm against djinn."

He pulled out the pendant Khadija umm Mohammed had sold him just before he left. It was a smooth green stone that was bright and shiny like glass, although you couldn't see through it. Strange symbols were etched on its surface.

Mohammed al-Biwati studied it, then turned to Farouk. "What do you think of this?"

Moustafa cut in, "I think it's base superstition and the boy wasted his money."

"I've gotten rid of lots of djinn with Khadija umm Mohammed's charms," Faisal said.

Farouk nodded. "It does look like a good charm. I think if you're lucky you will still be here in the morning ..." he glanced at Mohammed al-Biwati.

"... unless someone takes it from you," Mohammed al-Biwati added.

Faisal couldn't decide whether they were teasing them or bullying him. Living on the streets as long as he had, he had seen how quickly teasing could turn into bullying, and how bullying could turn into violence.

He looked at each man in turn. In as brave of a voice he could muster, he growled,

"If anyone tries to take this charm from me in my sleep, I'll gouge his eyes out."

The Bedouin all laughed again. Mohammed al-Biwati gave him a friendly slap on the back that nearly knocked him face first into the sand.

"Ah, a little fighter! I think maybe you are part Bedouin."

After that the men turned the conversation to other things. Faisal stayed silent, watching the empty sand dunes around them and listening to the djinn hissing their strange language between the grains of sand. He clutched his charm.

Night came quickly. Almost as soon as the sun went below the horizon,

118

the sky turned dark and was carpeted with a million stars. Faisal gaped at the sight, and for a time he forgot about the djinn and their hissing words. The Bedouin began to sing a low song about a man on a caravan far from his oasis home.

After a minute, Farouk cut off from singing, perking up and cocking his head to one side. He sniffed the air.

One by one, the others broke off and sniffed too.

Then Faisal smelled it.

It was a strange, sweet smell, heavy in the air and unlike anything he had smelled in the desert. It smelled familiar.

Then he remembered where he had smelled it before. He sometimes smelled it coming up from the Englishman's house after the Englishman turned the lights off.

And now it was coming from the Englishman's tent.

Faisal stood up. "I think his tent is on fire."

Moustafa pulled him down. "Stay where you are."

"But the Englishman might be in trouble!"

One of the Bedouin, a man named Abbas, said, "Oh, he's not in trouble, and his tent is not on fire. What you're smelling is—"

"Quiet!" Moustafa snapped.

Abbas merely shrugged and went back to stoking the fire.

The smell stopped after a time, and everyone bedded down. Faisal put his blankets next to where Moustafa lay. Moustafa grumbled and turned his back to him. Faisal didn't like the Nubian much, but he'd protect him from the Bedouin if they tried to take his charm.

But if the charm didn't work, who would protect him from the djinn?

The wind blew over the sand dunes, hissing as it went. The djinn blew with it and hissed as well. The hissing almost seemed to make words.

"Hssss. Hssss. Faissssal. We will take you to the City of Brassss."

The fire died down, and the darkness pushed in closer and closer around the little camp. Faisal curled up under his blankets, gripping his charm.

He only fell asleep when exhaustion overtook him.

CHAPTER SIXTEEN

The next morning, Augustus felt sluggish. He had, as usual, smoked some opium before going to bed in order to ward off his nightmares. Back home that wasn't a problem because he could sleep in, but here in the desert the Bedouin awoke before dawn, said their prayers, cooked and ate their breakfast, packed and saddled the camels, and were off before daybreak.

A perfectly reasonable way to enjoy comfortable temperatures for the first couple of hours of travel, but he felt like a lead weight in his saddle. All he wanted to do was lie down on the sand and take a nap.

It didn't help that Faisal kept yawning.

"Do please stop that," Augustus said after Faisal yawned for the tenth time.

"I'm tired," Faisal said, scratching his armpit and yawning again. "Are we there yet?"

"We have nine more days."

"Nine more days!" Faisal looked panicked.

"I told you it was a ten-day journey."

"Oh. I forgot. Do I get my piastre for yesterday?"

"Of course." Augustus reached into his pocket.

"Wait until we get to the oasis. There's nothing to spend it on here," Faisal lowered his voice, "and the Bedouin might take it."

"Have they been bothering you?"

"They threatened to take my charm."

"Good Lord. What charm?"

"Nothing," Faisal mumbled.

Augustus decided not to pursue the matter. He was quite sure it wasn't of the least importance.

After a minute's blessed silence, Faisal piped up again.

"Is it true that you need to clean silver?"

"Yes. Why in the world are you asking me that?"

"How do you clean it?"

"There's a special liquid called silver polish. Faisal, if you're going to ask me a question, at least make it a useful one. It's not like you need to take care of a silver table service."

To his surprise, Faisal burst out laughing.

The hours stretched out. Their camels plodded along and Augustus was lulled by their regular motion and the empty sameness of the landscape. Once he jerked his head back as he almost nodded off.

"Careful," Farouk called over to him. "Your mind can drift here. Keep focusing on different things, like the head of your camel and then the pack on the camel in front of you. If your eyes keep moving, your mind will stay awake. Otherwise you may fall off, and if we don't see you fall, we might leave you behind."

"It's good advice, sir," Moustafa agreed. "I should have told you before. I forgot you have never been on a journey like this before. You keep alert too, Faisal."

"I am," the boy piped up. "I'm on the lookout for djinn."

"Bah!" Moustafa scoffed.

"Hssss," one of the Bedouin whispered.

"Stop!" Faisal whined.

The Bedouin all laughed.

Augustus tried to stay alert and found it difficult. Concentrating when there was nothing to concentrate on required a serious act of will. He began recounting the reigns of pharaohs and adding up sums in his head. His mind grew tired of such pointless work and began to drift again. He shook his head. The tender skin under his mask was sweating and prickly from the heat. At least sitting atop a camel for hours on end rested his leg and allowed his wound to heal.

As their journey continued over the course of days, each one blurring into the next, Augustus began to look forward to stopping, not because he was tired of the journey, but just to have a change of pace. The Bedouin camped each day at about noon and sheltered in the shade of their lean-tos until about four to avoid the heat of the day. He took to pitching his tent, taking off his mask, and putting on some of that salve Dr. Wood had given him.

On the fifth day, he didn't get the chance.

They had just made their midday camp. The caravan had unloaded the packs and hobbled the camels, and Augustus hadn't had time to pitch his tent when a cry from Abbas made them all turn to the west, where he was pointing.

At first all he saw was a strange change on the horizon. Instead of shimmering in the desert heat, it had thickened, grown fuzzy.

"What's that?" he asked. The wind began to pick up.

"Sandstorm!" Farouk said. "Grab a blanket and put it around yourself. It will protect you."

They scrambled to get blankets from the packs. The camels lifted their heads, sniffed the air, and then lay down in a huddle, their backs to the wind.

By the time everyone got their blankets, the storm was almost upon them.

It had rushed up from the horizon with shocking speed, a great brown cloud taller than any building, with a core of impenetrable black. Faisal screamed.

"Sit down with your back to the wind and wrap the blanket around you. Over your head. You will be all right," Farouk said.

Everyone sat.

"Stay close to me," Augustus told Faisal. "My body will shelter you from the worst of the wind."

"Thanks Englishman, but Moustafa is bigger," Faisal said, running over to the Nubian.

"Get away, Little Infidel! I don't want to catch fleas."

"Stop moving, you're letting the wind blow on me!"

That was the last Augustus heard of them, because just then the sandstorm hit with its full force.

Augustus covered himself with the blanket and got buffeted by the wind. The sand made a horrible rasping sound against the blanket, and he could feel it pushing on his back. He hoped Moustafa was making sufficient shelter for Faisal, otherwise the scrawny boy would probably blow away entirely.

He sat, in all-encompassing sound and darkness, and waited for the storm to pass.

It did not.

For hours the wind blew. Sand began to pile up behind him, his body creating a dune, and every now and then he had to push himself back and over it to get away from its weight, otherwise he knew the dune would grow big enough to engulf him. Every time he did so, grains of sand would swirl under his protection, getting in his mouth and eyes. He learned to keep his eyes shut. There was nothing to see but pitch blackness anyway.

A sound came to him from over the incessant hissing of the sand. It sounded like a scream. He sat, helpless, knowing there was nothing he could do.

Time lost all meaning. He began to count the number of times he had to shift to escape the sand dunes he was creating.

But even counting this movement did not help him keep track of time, for he had no idea of the number of minutes or hours between each time he had to move.

He sat, and endured.

His mind cast back to another time when he had sat and endured.

Those who had never been there always assumed that daytime was the worst time to be in a trench. It was then that most attacks occurred, after all, and most of the shelling happened during daylight hours as well. The vast majority of casualties happened during the day. It was also the time when most of the work got done, and there was always work to be done—shoring up trench walls, hauling duckboard and food and ammunition from the rear areas, using periscopes to draw detailed sketches of enemy positions … the officers foisted a thousand and one tasks on the exhausted men.

But that was what made the daytime tolerable. One worked, and worked, and the hours slipped by in an aching fog of fatigue.

At night, time seemed to stop. Unless one was subjected to the terror of a patrol in No Man's Land, one sat in a dugout or on sentry duty, and waited.

Sleep wasn't a refuge because it never lasted long. There was always someone clambering over you to get to their place in the dugout, or rats skittering up your legs, or the Germans throwing a few shells over just out of spite, or a comrade waking you up for your turn standing watch.

Being on sentry duty was even worse. You had to stand in the utter darkness, eyes and ears alert for any sign of the enemy. And you had to stand still, for there were men over on the other side looking for any sign of movement. Every now and then there would be a rattle of machine gun fire as the enemy traversed your line with bullets aimed just above ground level.

This led to a peculiar practice. The instinctive response to this random firing was to hunker down low, only showing your eyes and your helmet over the lip of the trench. That was the wrong thing to do. As the enemy machine guns made their traverses, their bullets spreading out along your line, if one hit you, it either banged off your helmet or got you right between the eyes. A concussion or instant death.

The wiser move was to stand on a box on the firing step so that half your body was exposed. That way when the enemy machine gun traversed, the bullet would get you in the gut, a painful but treatable wound that would earn you a few months back home.

The mental hurdle of actually exposing more of one's body to machine gun fire when there was no officer egging you on was almost insurmountable. Many men new to the trenches hunkered down, and lost their lives to stray bullets as a result.

One also had to keep completely still, for an occasional flare would rise up from one side or the other. In the wavering light, a half exposed man who didn't move looked like a burned-out tree or a blasted bit of equipment, and might escape danger. Once again the natural instinct was to duck down when the night suddenly lit up, but the enemy would be waiting for any such movement and would concentrate their fire on it.

The flares and bursts of random fire happened several times a night, but were only terrifying interludes between the endless aching hours of suspense. You stood, and you waited. You stared into the darkness and listened for even the softest sound as evidence that someone was creeping up to kill you.

The hardest part wasn't actually the fear or the weariness. It was trying to maintain a mental focus. The mind in such a situation will naturally turn to nicer things—home, a fondly remembered cricket match, or simple fantasies of returning to one's dugout and getting a good night's sleep.

But letting the mind wander when stationed at the front could easily be fatal. One had to focus on the danger and the fatigue and shadows that always seemed ready to turn into enemy soldiers. One had to face the terrible truth in order to survive it.

So that's what Augustus did, all through that long storm. He did not let his mind wander. He did not let himself nod off. Instead he listened to the hiss of the sand against his blanket, felt the wind buffeting the fabric and the grittiness of the grains that filtered through, smelled the dead scent of the desert, suffered the ache of his back and legs as they maintained the same position for hours on end, and tried to measure the ever increasing weight of the dune forming at his back before shifting position to escape it.

But despite all this his mind lulled into dreary half sleep. Images flickered in his imagination—dead comrades, scenes from schooldays, and once, all too clear, the face of a woman he had once thought would become his wife.

She had been the daughter of an Oxford don. They had met at a professor's tea party—he the successful former student, she the quiet and somewhat reserved belle of the party. Everyone had been touched by her beauty, and her mother and father beamed with pride at how she quickly became the center of attention. Chaucer and Thucydides were quickly forgotten as the students began to talk to her of lighter things. She, to their surprise and her credit, replied in perfect Latin and began to hold forth on Cato the Younger.

A beautiful young woman countering male flattery with a discussion of Stoicism was a sure way to win Augustus's respect. His heart was won over shortly thereafter. One tea party led to another, and then walks in Christ Church meadow and by the river. The don approved of their friendship and gave them as much freedom as propriety would allow.

Then war came, and promises were made. For the first three years they were kept. Letters went back and forth across the English Channel, and his brief furloughs were spent in Oxford seeing her.

And then a German shell blasted all that apart. He could not remember all the excuses she gave for breaking off their engagement. All he remembered was how hollow and obviously false they sounded.

And he had ended up alone.

Augustus jerked out of his half-sleep, his war-trained ears alerting him that something had changed around him, and change was dangerous.

The wind was dying down. The pressure on his back weakened.

And then, as quickly as it had started, the sandstorm stopped.

Augustus paused a moment, listening and hearing nothing.

Carefully, Augustus shook his blanket, releasing a cascade of sand, and looked around.

He cried out in shock.

He was alone amid the dunes.

CHAPTER SEVENTEEN

A startled cry shook Moustafa out of his doze. He realized the wind had stopped and peeked out from under his blanket …

… and gaped.

He was alone!

A moment later he saw Mr. Wall sitting to his right, half buried in sand. Then he picked out the others, each covered by a blanket, the blankets covered with sand to make them look like little dunes. The camels, already the color of the desert, were all but invisible where they placidly sat. To the east, the sandstorm receded, a boiling mass of wind and darkness.

"It's good to see your face, Moustafa," Mr. Wall said. "For a moment there I thought you had all disappeared."

"For a moment I thought so too, boss."

One by one the Bedouin got up and shook themselves. Moustafa noted the sun was getting low in the west. The sandstorm had been a short one, only about six hours, although it had been fierce and seemed much longer.

"Where's Faisal?" Mr. Wall asked.

A low hump in the sand shifted and rose.

"Here I am, Englishman," said a very sandy Faisal.

"And dirtier than usual, I see," Mr. Wall said with a smile.

Everyone took a minute to shake out their clothes. The Bedouin casually went over to check the camels, who looked as indifferent as they had just before the sandstorm hit.

Mr. Wall cursed, and started searching around him.

"What's the matter, boss?"

"One of my bags is missing. I had just unpacked it when the sandstorm hit. It must have gotten buried."

He began to dig all around, pushing his hands into the sand.

Then Moustafa realized that all of their bags and equipment were buried. Most lay in a large heap near the camels. He cleared that off and found all the bedding and water skins and food. After a while he found Mr. Wall's tent and the guns as well.

"The guns are covered in sand, boss. We'll have to strip and oil them."

"Never mind those, where the devil is my bag?"

"What does it look like, Englishman?" Faisal said, walking over.

"It's a small bag that went in this case here," he said, pointing to a larger portmanteau. "I had just taken it out. I could have sworn I put it right here."

Mr. Wall kept digging around. Faisal helped too.

Farouk came up beside Moustafa. "Did he lose his money?"

"No," Moustafa said. From the desperation with which his boss was searching, he had an idea what it might be.

"I don't see it," Faisal said. "It isn't important, is it?"

"Of course it's bloody important! I wouldn't be searching for it otherwise, would I?"

Faisal slunk away as Mr. Wall continued to search.

The boy came up to Moustafa. "Why did he shout at me? I was only trying to help."

"He's going to be shouting a lot more tonight, I'm afraid."

"Why?"

"Never mind."

Mr. Wall searched until night fell and the desert grew pitch black, but the case was well and truly lost. They had lost a few other things as well—a water skin that was still half full, a length of rope, one of the Bedouin's spare sandals. Nothing too important. Nothing that could drive a man mad.

Or a madman madder.

Moustafa had no clear idea what effect not getting his opium would have on Mr. Wall. He smoked it every night, saying it kept him from having dreams of the war. While that may very well be so, Moustafa heard that the body became dependent on the drug, and that to stop taking it led to sickness and sometimes even death.

And here they were halfway to nowhere.

After Mr. Wall gave up searching in the sand, he systematically went through every piece of his luggage. The Bedouin watched with interest, staring at all the strange European items. Expensive items. Moustafa did not think it was a good idea to display all their wealth to these people, but he wasn't about to try and talk sense to his boss at the moment.

At last Mr. Wall gave up and slumped by the fire. He ate his dinner and didn't say a word. As soon as he was done he went into his tent.

Faisal, for once, kept quiet. Moustafa wondered how much he understood.

They bedded down. It took a long time for Moustafa to fall asleep. No sound came from the tent, however, and at last his weariness pulled him under.

A shout woke him up in the dead of night.

"Gas attack!" a voice screamed in English. "Put on your masks! To your posts!"

The Bedouin all sprang up, grabbing rifles and knives. Faisal poked his head out from under his blankets.

"What's going on?" Faisal asked. "What did he say?"

"It's all right, Mr. Wall!" Moustafa called.

No reply came from the tent.

They settled down to sleep and for a time all was quiet, until an ear-splitting shriek ripped the night.

Once again Moustafa called out a reassurance, and once again he got no reply.

"What's going on?" Faisal asked.

"He's having nightmares about the war," Moustafa explained.

"He doesn't usually shout in the night."

"Never mind that. Go back to sleep."

They were awakened a third time as Mr. Wall shouted orders to his men, men who were probably all dead and buried.

After that their rest was undisturbed. They woke late, with the morning heat already beginning to rise.

Mr. Wall emerged from his tent pale and drawn, with black circles under his eyes. Moustafa guessed that after waking up the third time, he had decided not to try to sleep at all.

"Are you all right, Englishman?" Faisal asked.

Mr. Wall grumbled a response and drank three cups of strong tea in rapid succession.

They set off for another long day, only stopping when the sun had nearly reached its high point, then sheltering in the shade of a tarpaulin of camel's hair fabric set up with a couple of poles. Mr. Wall kept nodding off and jerking awake.

Abbas took Moustafa aside.

"Is he all right?" the Bedouin asked.

"He is ill. He is a strong man, though, and will recover."

"Not soon," Abbas said, shaking his head. "And he will get worse before he gets better. That was opium he was smoking in his tent. He lost it in the sandstorm, didn't he? I have seen what that can do to a man. If he doesn't get any, he will become far more ill than he is now. How are we going to bring him along when he gets like that?"

Moustafa looked at Mr. Wall grimly. His boss lay listless in the shade, Faisal staring at him from the far end of the shelter.

"I don't know. Let's try to make good time while he can still travel."

They broke their midday camp early, setting out in the hot sun, and kept a steady pace until it was almost dark. During the long day Mr. Wall grew worse. Despite the heat he began to shiver, and then he started fanning himself as his face poured with sweat.

By the time they made camp that evening he was on the verge of collapse. Moustafa had to help him put up the tent and he immediately disappeared inside. One of the Bedouin brought him tea, and dinner once it was ready. He could barely get it down.

"He is groaning like a man about to meet death," the Bedouin reported.

"What do we do?" Faisal asked.

"We might have to camp here until his … sickness … passes," Moustafa replied.

Abbas took Moustafa aside again. By silent agreement the Bedouin had kept the truth of the matter from Faisal. "Your boss will not be able to travel tomorrow, and perhaps not the next day either. After that, if he lives, he will be weak but will probably be able to mount a camel."

"You seem to know a lot about it."

Abbas smiled. "There is much money to be made smuggling such things across the desert. The fools who seek oblivion are willing to pay a very high price."

"Know your place!" Moustafa snapped. "Mr. Wall is an educated, respectable gentleman. He takes such things because of the war."

Abbas sneered. "In the village of Qasr, in Bahariya Oasis where I was born, there is an old man who was wounded in a fight with a different tribe. A sword cut took off all the fingers of his right hand. Another cut slashed out both eyes. A spear went through his thigh and left him lame. So he sits, unable to see, unable to work, and only able to walk slowly with the aid of a stick. All day he sits in the shade of the palm trees, telling tales to the children who gather to listen. At night when we gather around the fire he sings songs to entertain us. He has family and he has friends. He is useless for work, and yet he is admired and loved. He does not seek oblivion. He accepts what was written for him like a good Muslim and a strong man."

Moustafa turned away without replying.

A short while later a long, pitiful groan came from the tent. Moustafa went to see Mr. Wall. Abbas, much to his irritation, came along.

Mr. Wall lay inside the narrow tent, his portmanteau empty by his side. All his things lay scattered about the small interior of the tent. He had obviously been ransacking his baggage in search of his opium. Moustafa guessed he had done this many times that day.

"Is there anything we can do, boss?" Moustafa asked.

"No. It's hopeless," Mr. Wall moaned.

"It is not hopeless," Abbas said in a kind voice. "It will feel bad for a time and then the sickness will pass."

"What the devil do you know about it?" Mr. Wall snapped.

"Opium is a—"

"Opium? Who said anything about opium? I'm ill, no doubt from that miserable tea you brew!"

Abbas maintained his composure.

"Englishman, we cannot tarry here for long. As soon as you are better we must—"

"I'll be fine in the morning. Away with you!"

Abbas gave Moustafa a smug, knowing look, and left the tent.

"Boss, what Abbas says is true. He knows such things. He smelled the opium you smoke at night and knew what it was."

"Does Faisal know?" Mr. Wall asked, suddenly worried.

"No boss," Moustafa replied with surprise. "We told him it was a special type of tobacco."

Mr. Wall groaned, gritting his teeth as his entire body shuddered.

Moustafa put a hand on his shoulder. "We all understand, boss. Even Faisal in his own ignorant way. No one is judging you. You just rest and—"

"You understand nothing!" Mr. Wall shrieked, smacking away his hand. "Why do you people plague us so? All this 'yes sir' and 'no sir' and 'right away sir', when you want nothing better than to send us all packing! My God, I hate falseness. Isn't it enough I give you a good job and books to read? Now you want to pretend we're friends! Get out of my sight. It's bad enough being stuck here without you gawking at me."

Moustafa's fists clenched. After all he had done for this stupid, selfish man.

Moustafa had just enough self control to leave the tent without saying or doing anything that would cost him his job. He stalked back to toward the fire the Bedouin were building.

Faisal met him halfway.

"Is he all right?"

"All right? There's nothing about that man that's all right!"

Faisal stood there, confused. "Maybe bring him some water. Did you see how he was sweating? He must be terribly thirsty."

"I'm not going to bring him a single drop! Let his foul mouth dry up like the Sahara!"

Faisal put his fists on his hips and frowned. "How can you say that? He's our friend!"

"That man is no one's friend."

"I'll bring him some water." Faisal ran to fetch one of the water skins.

"Bring him the entire Nile if you want to!" Moustafa shouted after him. "He'll never show an ounce of gratitude!"

CHAPTER EIGHTEEN

Thus began the longest two days of Faisal's life. The Englishman snapped at him when he first entered the tent, but Faisal was used to being snapped at and simply handed him the water skin. The Englishman took a long drink and then turned his back.

He didn't keep his back turned for long. After a while he turned on the other side, then lay on his back, then started shivering and covered himself with blankets. A little while later he threw them off and started to sweat.

Faisal sat in the corner of the tent holding his arms around his legs, his chin resting on his knees, and watched. He had no idea what was wrong with the Englishman. This wasn't like any sickness he had ever seen. It didn't just affect his body; it also affected his mind. The Englishman kept shouting in his own language. Faisal didn't need to know English to know they were curses. You could tell by the way he said them.

As that first night wore on, he seemed to get worse and worse. He flailed around, shouting, then clutched himself and trembled all over. Once Faisal ducked out of the tent to speak to the men, but Moustafa was sulking and the Bedouin disdainful. Faisal went back to the Englishman. He'd have to handle this himself.

But what could he do? He was no doctor. All he could do was give the Englishman water when he was able to drink and try to give him a bit of bread. The Englishman drank greedily when he was in the sweating times, but didn't eat at all.

Then the truth struck him. The Englishman was possessed by djinn!

They must have come at him during the sandstorm. Faisal had heard a whole army of them flying around, hissing their strange djinn words. Faisal had always heard the djinn couldn't attack a European. But maybe that was only city djinn. Maybe the desert djinn were stronger. They must be stronger if they could make a sandstorm like that.

That made sense. They wanted to get Faisal but he had the charm. The Bedouin had charms too. Moustafa was too strong and foul tempered to possess, so they went after the Englishman. Faisal bet there was a whole bunch of djinn inside him now.

Well, he had a cure for that!

He started to pull the charm off from around his neck, then paused. If he took off the charm, would the djinn leave the Englishman and come after him? Or maybe they were too busy attacking the Englishman to notice.

Faisal gulped. He'd have to take that risk.

He pulled the charm from around his neck and tried to put it around the Englishman's neck.

That wasn't so easy. The Englishman kept flailing about, not really seeing Faisal but resisting him at the same time. The djinn tossed the Englishman's head from side to side to keep Faisal from putting on the charm.

"Getting tricky, are you?" Faisal said, angry. "Well, I can get tricky too!"

The Englishman had a pocket in his shirt with a button. He unbuttoned it, stuffed the charm inside, and buttoned it up again.

"Ha! Let's see you get rid of it now."

The djinn sure tried. The Englishman twitched and lashed out, forcing Faisal to back away. His heart leapt as he saw the Englishman sit up and his eyes finally focus. Had the charm worked?

"What are you doing here?" the Englishman growled in Arabic. He had been speaking English up until now. "Get the hell out! Why does everyone think they can just barge in here? Looking for another handout? Don't I give enough to you, you ungrateful little beggar? I said get out and leave me in peace!"

Faisal's eyes filled, but he blinked the tears away. That was the djinn talking, not the Englishman.

The Englishman fell back on his blankets with a gasp. He trembled all over. Then he tossed and turned like he was having a bad dream, although his eyes were open. They were open, but not seeing. They looked all glassy and unfocused. He reached out a trembling hand and Faisal gave him the water skin.

The night wore on, while Faisal, horrified and fascinated, sat in the corner, as far away from the Englishman as the little tent allowed.

The Englishman tossed and turned all night, getting worse with each hour. Faisal grew worried that the charm wasn't going to help at all. Khadija umm Mohammed had made it for him, and maybe that meant it only worked for Egyptian boys and not Englishmen. He should have asked her.

Should he take from the Englishman's pocket and put it around his own neck? The djinn might get tired of torturing the Englishman and come after him.

He decided against it. Maybe it took time for the charm to work. These djinn were sure strong, and there were a lot of them. There was the trembling one, and the shivery one, and the sweaty one, and the groaning one, and the angry screaming one. Some spoke in English and some spoke in Arabic. The ones that spoke Arabic got bored after a while and Faisal only heard the Englishman speak in English, and then those djinn got bored and the Englishman didn't speak at all. The trembling shivery sweaty groaning angry screaming djinn all stayed, taking turns playing with him.

At mealtimes, Abbas would bring Faisal food and ask how the Englishman was doing. He seemed to know a bit about these djinn and said that it would take time for them to leave. Faisal asked for Moustafa to come visit, but the Nubian never did. That made Faisal mad.

At times the djinn grew tired and the Englishman fell quiet, allowing Faisal to catch a bit of sleep. But it wasn't long before they attacked again, and Faisal would be woken up by a groan or the Englishman's teeth chattering. Then he had to take care of him all over again.

At times the djinn would get really strong and the Englishman would scream and thrash about. Once he even knocked his mask off. Faisal winced and turned away, grateful that the low light inside the tent made it hard to see that half his face was missing. It looked awful, the cheek all gone, his teeth showing through, and one eye hanging in a bit of bone and gristle. Faisal tried to put the mask back on him, but the Englishman was moving so much he couldn't. Eventually he gave up and set it to one side.

Many strange thoughts came to Faisal during those long hours. He thought of life when he was small, just him and his father living in a dirty little room at the end of a clammy alley. His mother had died giving birth to him. She had been a good woman despite what everyone said. They were just jealous because she had been the best mother in the world.

His father was a different story.

He was a huge man, with big strong fists and a red face from drinking every day. He worked sometimes as a laborer, but never kept a job very long because he always argued with the bosses. What little he earned he would drink up, and there was very little food at home. Faisal had been living on the streets even when he still had a place to live.

When enough liquor got inside his father, he'd fly into a rage, cursing the bosses who fired him, cursing his mother for not being there to cook and clean and work to make money for his drinking, and most of all cursing Faisal. He blamed Faisal for her death.

"If it wasn't for you," he'd say, breathing his stinky breath over him, "I'd have a woman in the house. She could take in sewing, or clean the homes of rich people. We'd have bread on the table."

Even when he was really small, Faisal knew enough not to point out that if his father worked more and drank less, there would be bread on the table and a lot more besides. But that would have earned him slaps and kicks, even more slaps and kicks than he usually got.

After his rages, his father would fall into a drunken stupor on the bed and moan and thrash about. He'd speak words that made no sense. He'd toss and turn and sweat and groan, just like the Englishman was doing now.

Faisal stopped himself. How could he compare the Englishman to his father? The Englishman was possessed by djinn, while his father's madness was his own fault. His father was a brute who hated everybody and drank because he didn't want to be in this world. The Englishman wasn't like that. The Englishman was his and Moustafa's friend, and the Englishman never, ever hit him.

But even though the thought was unworthy, as Faisal stared at the Englishman suffering in his bed, half his face gone and the other half all twisted in pain, he kept seeing his father lying there, suffering because of his own weakness.

"The djinn are putting that thought in you," Faisal said to himself. "They know you're taking care of him and are trying to set you against him."

"It's not going to work!" He shouted into the air. "I know your tricks!"

So Faisal stayed by the Englishman's side, giving him water when he was able to drink, putting the blankets back on him when he threw them aside, and waited for Khadija umm Mohammed's charm to work its magic.

Then, after two days, the Englishman fell silent for a long time. Faisal feared he was dying, but his breathing was steady. It wasn't long before Faisal fell asleep too.

When he awoke the Englishman was still quiet. Faisal curled up in his corner of the tent, chin resting on his knees, and watched him.

At last he woke up.

The Englishman grunted and got up on one elbow, using the other hand to rub his eyes. Faisal tried not to look at his face.

The Englishman sighed, mumbled something to himself in his own language and then looked at Faisal, noticing him for the first time.

"What the Devil are you doing here?"

"You let me stay."

The Englishman rubbed his eyes again. "So I did."

His hand went to the open wound on his face.

"Good Lord!"

He scrambled around until he found his mask and put it back on.

"Sorry, Faisal."

"It's all right."

"I must have put you off your breakfast. Sorry."

"It's dinnertime."

"Sorry."

The Englishman wouldn't look at him.

"It's all right. The djinn attacked you for two days. Are they gone now?"

"The djinn? Oh … right. Yes, they're gone now."

"Now you believe me! I told you the djinn are real."

"Yes, Faisal, evil spirits are real, just not in the way you think they are."

Faisal didn't know what the Englishman meant by that, but he was used to the Englishman saying strange things. All that mattered was that he was better now.

The Englishman took a long drink from the water skin and rummaged around his bag. He pulled out some money and counted it.

"Thank you for your help," he said, holding out some money.

Faisal hesitated.

"Go on, take it. You have certainly earned it."

Faisal took it and counted it. Fifty piastres.

His eyes bugged. Fifty piastres!

That was a lot of money, so why did it make him feel bad to hold it?

He looked at the Englishman, then at the money in his hand, then back at the Englishman again.

"I can't take this."

"Of course you can."

"No," Faisal said with sudden determination. He set the money down by the Englishman.

"Take the damn money! You're always asking for money, and when I give you some you don't want it?"

"I didn't save you from the djinn for money, you silly Englishman! Why don't you understand anything!"

Crying, Faisal burst out of the tent and ran back to the fire.

CHAPTER NINETEEN

If the desert could have swallowed him up, Augustus would have happily allowed it to rather than face the others. On wobbly legs he staggered out of the tent and went over to the fire. The last light was just fading in the west. The Bedouin were busy preparing their meal. Moustafa didn't look at him. Faisal sat on a distant dune watching the sunset with his back turned.

"Dinner is ready if you are able to eat," Abbas said.

Augustus didn't feel able, but they had to get started early tomorrow and he needed some energy.

"How's the water situation?" he asked as he sat down, landing hard on the sand.

"Bad," Farouk said with a note of accusation in his voice. "You drank much during your illness and there is no water on this route."

"What do you propose we do?"

"It is as far to go forward as it is to go back, so we go forward. There is a detour we can make. It adds a day to our journey but there is a well there. At least, there was a well ten years ago. I do not know if it is dry now or not. None of us has been there since then."

"Do you think we should try it?"

"If we do and there is water, all will be fine. If there is no water, we will have wasted a day and will be in even worse trouble."

Augustus bit his lip.

"It is all in the hands of God," Mohammed al-Biwati said.

The other Bedouin nodded.

Augustus managed to eat a little. The sickness that had wracked his body for the past two days had ebbed into a low ache that permeated every fiber of his being, and every one of those fibers screamed at him to return to Cairo. Only his pride kept him from taking that course. He had to go forward. Perhaps there would be a physician in Bahariya who would have some opiates.

That, he knew, was a slim hope, but he held onto that hope to keep him heading for Bahariya.

He looked around the barren desert and the sullen faces and felt desolate. He had no help here.

"I suggest we try the well," he said after much thought. "We can start early tomorrow."

"Are you sure you are able to travel?" Farouk asked.

Augustus looked at him. "I have to be."

They set out before dawn. Augustus had managed a few hours of fitful sleep. The Bedouin got his camel packed and saddled and he just managed to get mounted without embarrassing himself.

Within an hour the heat felt intolerable. He knew his drug-starved body had become hypersensitive. The day would be hell.

The heat beat down on them and he tried not to think about the five or six days of travel that remained. Augustus pulled at his shirt where it stuck to him with sweat and felt something in his pocket.

"Good Lord," he muttered. "If that's my opium I think I'll have to murder someone."

He unbuttoned his pocket and pulled out a leather strap with a small talisman of glazed green ceramic. It had odd marks carved all over it in vague imitation of ancient demotic, obviously done by someone who had seen the script a few times but had no understanding of it.

He urged his camel forward and caught up with Faisal.

They rode side by side for a minute. The boy didn't look at him. Neither he nor Moustafa had said a word to Augustus since he had woken up.

Augustus cleared his throat. "I … um, I do believe this is yours."

He held out the talisman to him.

"Keep it," Faisal mumbled.

"Oh, the djinn won't come after me again. You scared them off. I wouldn't want you to lose sleep thinking you were unprotected. You've lost enough sleep as it is, eh?"

Augustus chuckled. The joke fell flat. Faisal took the talisman and put it around his neck.

"Thank you for helping me, Faisal. You're a good boy."

Faisal looked at him, shocked.

"Yes," Augustus coughed. "A very good boy."

The boy's face lit up.

"Clever too. You're a great help to me. I couldn't have solved any of these murders without you."

Augustus tousled his hair, trying not to wince as he felt a variety of unidentifiable particles.

"I'll be a big help with this mystery too!" Faisal said, bouncing up and down in his saddle.

"I have no doubt that you shall. And when we return to Cairo I think you deserve to go to the moving pictures again."

"Really? Will we see the man with the funny moustache?"

"Charles Chaplin? I think we might. There are other funny men I think you'd like. Harold Lloyd, Buster Keaton …"

Faisal laughed. "Even their names are funny."

The boy launched into a long description of the Chaplin film they had seen, getting so distracted that Augustus was able to wipe his hand on his saddle without Faisal noticing.

For once, Augustus was grateful for the mite's inane chatter. It kept his mind off things.

Near the end of the day Farouk, who was leading the column, let out a cry of triumph.

"The well is still there!" he shouted.

The Bedouin all cheered and gave thanks to God.

"Where is it?" Augustus asked.

"There," Farouk pointed.

Augustus saw nothing.

"Do not worry," Farouk said. "Living in a city has made you nearsighted. If you lived in the desert you would see it as clearly as you see me."

Augustus continued to stare in the direction they were headed, until after nearly an hour he saw a dark spot near the horizon. After a few more minutes it resolved itself into a cluster of little shrubs. They were half dead, their leaves few and withered, but in the middle of all that sand it looked like the Amazon rainforest.

"Is that the oasis?" Faisal asked.

"It is for today," Augustus said, relieved. He had endangered the entire caravan, and while finding the well did not atone for that, it at least kept matters from becoming worse.

Two of the Bedouin dismounted, got on their knees in the middle of the shrubs, and began to dig in the sand with their hands.

"Where is the well?" Augustus asked.

"It has filled," Farouk replied. "All the small ones fill."

After a minute the Bedouin reached damp sand. They continued to dig until the sand had the consistency of porridge, then thin gruel. This they scooped into a leather bucket and let the sand settle to the bottom. Afterwards they filled the empty water skins.

Everyone drank their fill. The water was gritty, the particles of sand grinding between their teeth, but it was water.

Once they each had a long drink and had topped up every water skin, they headed out again.

Everyone was now in much better spirits, all save Augustus. All his thoughts were for the one thing that could relieve the desolation his body felt, the great hole in his psyche.

Pushing through these thoughts was the realization that he still had an unpleasant task remaining.

He caught up with Moustafa, who rode in front with Farouk. The Bedouin, seeing his approach, urged his camel a little more forward and gave them room.

Nevertheless, Augustus addressed his assistant in English.

"Well, at least we have sufficient water."

"Too sandy," Moustafa grumbled. "It's given me a bellyache."

Augustus coughed. "Hmm, indeed. It isn't exactly champagne at the Savoy."

"I wouldn't know."

"Oh, no. I guess you wouldn't. Look, my dear fellow, I wanted you to know I appreciate you coming all this way. I know you have a family to care for, but you put forth the effort and that speaks good of you. You are quite indispensable to the expedition."

"Are you going to tousle my hair and call me a good boy?" Moustafa snapped.

Augustus paused. "Um, no. More along the lines of an, erm, apology for the things I said the other day. I was quite off my head. The, um, symptoms of well ... you know."

Moustafa gave him a long look.

"Actually say it, Mr. Wall."

Augustus coughed. "I'm ... sorry. I was beastly to you. You deserve better than that."

Moustafa nodded, and Augustus got the distinct impression that he was being dismissed like a naughty schoolboy after a caning. Briefly anger rose in him, but he tamped it down. Moustafa had every right to be angry.

Perhaps I should give him an increase of pay? He thought. *Hmm, he might take it the wrong way. He's a touchy fellow. I'll tell him later when he's cooled down.*

But can anyone cool down in this wretched heat?

They trudged along, Augustus feeling miserable in every way he could imagine. He felt ill, bereft, and his mask itched terribly. The desert began to change. Where once there had been flat, almost featureless sand, now the brown turned to white, and white boulders appeared. These had been scoured by the wind into weird shapes. Boulders as large as a motorcar sat perched on columns so narrow he could have put his arms around them. Others had morphed into recognizable forms. One looked like the Sphinx. Another looked like a rabbit. Some towered over them, while smaller stones stood only waist high, looking like tables with a twisted, single leg. One resembled a giant egg, the effect heightened by the fact that the elements had broken it open to reveal empty space inside.

Faisal did not appear happy, looking all around him with a long face, and every now and then giving a quick glance behind to check that nothing was sneaking up on him.

"The djinn live here," he whispered.

"You have a most efficacious charm," Augustus told him.

Faisal moved his camel closer to Augustus's.

"I hope it works in a place like this."

"Would it do any good to explain that this is white limestone, a perfectly normal type of rock that happens to be prone to erosion from the wind?"

"Thank you for trying to make me feel better, Englishman, but I know djinn country when I see it."

This was said with such authority that Augustus didn't dare contradict him, certainly not so soon after his shabby behavior.

"I'll protect you," Augustus said. "It's only fair after you took care of me."

"Protect yourself, Englishman. The djinn were after you, not me."

"Erm, yes. I did have a rough time of it, didn't I?"

Faisal looked at him, with an expression that was far too serious for such a young face.

"Take care. Once the djinn take an interest in you, they keep coming back."

"I won't let them," Augustus said with sudden determination. He sat straighter in his saddle. "No, the djinn won't get in my head anymore."

He hoped that was true.

CHAPTER TWENTY

Their first sight of Bahariya Oasis was not at all what Moustafa expected. After passing through the strange formations of what the Bedouin called the White Desert, they entered what was called the Black Desert. The change couldn't have been more startling than if they had suddenly come into a forest. Where before the white stone shone brilliant in the day, or turned pink and red with the sunset and sunrise, now the land was as black as iron. Mountains of black stone towered over them, and the desert floor was littered with countless small black pebbles. Jagged black rocks, like giant shards of dark glass, stuck out here and there. The camels tread carefully through the sharp stones, bellowing when they burned their feet. The rock absorbed the sun's heat, radiating it back at the travelers as if they were marching on a frying pan.

Then everything changed.

They had entered another grim stretch of flat land, punctuated now and then by low, rocky hills of the same black stone, when suddenly the ground sloped away before them and they found themselves on the brow of a ridge overlooking a broad valley.

Beneath them lay Bahariya oasis like an emerald in the sand. Palm trees waved in the breeze, and open green fields stretched between them. In the distance—wonder of wonders!—glittered a large lake. The map they had taken from Ainsley Fielding's office showed the valley to be sixty miles long and half as wide, with much of it watered enough to be lush. The valley was green as far as the horizon.

To see such a broad stretch of vegetation after so many days of nothing but sand and stone filled Moustafa's heart with joy, but his attention was distracted by a sight closer to him.

A few yards down the slope, hidden until they had reached the edge, was a European sketching a large boulder.

But this was no ordinary European. Moustafa blinked and looked again to make sure his eyes were not deceiving him.

It was a European woman, quite alone, with a deeply tanned face under her pith helmet. Her brown hair was tucked up beneath the helmet and she wore a khaki shirt of a men's cut and matching trousers.

Trousers!

She sat on a camp chair, one leg crossed over the other, wearing boots like any common soldier. In fact, they indeed looked to be soldier's boots from the British army. Her donkey grazed on some stubble nearby.

When she noticed the approaching caravan, she set aside her sketch pad and pencil and greeted them in perfect Arabic with a Libyan accent.

"Peace be upon you! I didn't expect to see another foreigner. Come to steal my patch, did you?"

For a moment no one spoke. Moustafa couldn't think of what to say and he suspected no one else could either.

Mr. Wall rode a little ahead of the rest, smacked at his camel until it deigned to kneel, and dismounted, almost falling flat on his face as he did so.

"A donkey is a much surer ride, but I suspect you've come from too far away to ride donkeys," the woman said. Moustafa couldn't stop looking at her trousers. They showed … everything.

"Lord preserve me from temptation," he muttered, averting his eyes.

"We come from Cairo," Mr. Wall said, then added quickly. "By the way, do you have a medical kit? I have an acute pain and am in desperate need of a painkiller. I would be most happy to reimburse you."

Abbas snorted.

"It's back in Biwati, the main village here. I'll come back with you. I was just finishing up anyway," she said, gesturing at the boulder.

Mr. Wall and Moustafa looked at the boulder. It was covered with a strange, angular script and a few crude drawings.

"Ancient Libyan," Mr. Wall said.

"And a depiction of the god Bes," Moustafa put in.

The woman cocked her head. "Well, don't you make quite the pair! I am Jocelyn Montjoy."

"I am Sir Augustus Wall, at your service. This is my assistant Moustafa Ghani El Souwaim."

She extended her hand. Mr. Wall took it and was about to bow, when she gave him a handshake. Leaving Mr. Wall to gape, she strode over to Moustafa and gave him a handshake firm enough to give credit to any man.

Mr. Wall clapped his hands. "Right. Best be off. We're losing daylight. Lead us on Biwati."

The woman mounted her donkey, shamelessly riding astride. Mr. Wall mounted his camel as quickly as he was able. His hands trembled.

Faisal leaned over to Moustafa and whispered, "Are the djinn after him again?"

"He'll be fine in a little while. He just needs some … rest. Go to the back of the line."

He didn't want Faisal anywhere near this woman. His morals were bad enough.

"Why?" the child whined.

"Because I said so!" Moustafa snapped.

Faisal grumbled and moved away.

"So, Mrs. Montjoy, are you and your husband excavating here?" Mr. Wall asked as he urged his camel forward.

Moustafa tensed. Professor Harrell was murdered because of his excavations here, and now here was this woman dressed like a man and posing as an archaeologist. She was obviously of loose virtue and probably consorted with the worst dregs of humanity. Could she and her husband— no doubt an equally shifty character—be involved in all this?

What she said in reply to Mr. Wall's question nearly made Moustafa fall off his camel.

"Oh, I'm sad to say he's not here."

"No?" Mr. Wall asked.

"No. Mr. Montjoy is, as Rupert Brooke wrote, 'in a corner of some foreign field that is forever England.'"

Mr. Wall bowed his head. "I am terribly sorry to hear that, madam."

Moustafa couldn't contain his curiosity. "So who did you come with?"

"I came by myself."

"Yourself!"

"Yes, from Cyrenaica."

"Cyrenaica!" Mr. Wall exclaimed. "That's Senussi territory."

"Oh, that tribe has been fully pacified thanks to you chaps," the woman said with a casual air.

"But … but," Moustafa sputtered. "To go through their territory alone, unchaperoned! You could have been—"

"Stuffed with dates and nearly drowned in tea? Oh yes, the hospitality of the Senussi rivals that of the Arabian Bedouin and the merchants of Timbuctoo. And what might your name be?" she asked, turning to Farouk.

Farouk barely managed a reply, which was better than his men, who were struck dumb. Moustafa had to introduce them.

"And I'm Faisal," the boy piped up. He had reappeared, as always. "Do all Englishmen speak Arabic funny?"

Mrs. Montjoy chuckled. "I learned my Arabic in Tripoli. From Sir Augustus's speech, it sounds like he learned his Arabic in Morocco."

"Almost correct," Mr. Wall said. He kicking his camel to such speed that Mrs. Montjoy had trouble keeping up with her donkey. "While convalescing in hospital in France I struck up a friendship with a patient from a Moroccan regiment. He taught me Arabic and I taught him English. It was a way to while away the hours. And months. I've never actually been to Morocco. I say, is this Biwati place nearby?"

"We're almost there," Mrs. Montjoy said, her eyes softening. "I'll take you to my lodgings. I have some tincture that will help your pains."

"Yes, um, thank you. I lost my medical bag in a sandstorm, you see."

"And then he got possessed by djinn," Faisal put in. "But I cured him with a charm."

Moustafa resisted the urge to slap him. The brat would only ask why he got hit and Moustafa wasn't prepared to answer that question.

Mrs. Montjoy smiled at him. "That was very thoughtful of you, Faisal. He's very lucky to have you here to take care of him."

Faisal grinned. "He's going to take me to the moving pictures when we get back!"

"Oh, won't that be fun?"

As they descended the slope, Faisal chattering about their journey and Mr. Wall trying to hurry them on, Moustafa watched this woman's every move. What was her game? Was she some sort of spy? If so, who had sent her, and why had they chosen a spy who stood out so? Surely she must be the talk of the oasis!

They reached the edge of the cultivation, the moist air heavy with the fragrances of life filling their lungs, and Moustafa discovered that she was indeed well known. The farmers tilling their fields waved to her, then stared with frank curiosity at the caravan. Mohammed al-Biwati knew everyone as well. His name showed he had been born here, and he greeted everyone by name and answered all their questions about the Englishman in the strange mask.

We left Cairo with our mission a secret, Moustafa thought with despair, *and now the entire oasis will know of us by sundown.*

They passed through a small, shady village of low mud brick houses, the caravan picking up an escort of little children who waved and called out to them. Women in red and black dresses decorated with glittering coins sewn into the fabric watched them from doorways, their ankles encircled in heavy silver anklets, shy smiles half hidden behind large nose rings of gold.

"Those are funny," Faisal commented. "How do they eat with those on?"

"I'm not sure," Moustafa admitted.

"And when do we eat?" Faisal asked.

"Quiet, I'm thinking."

Thinking about what we're getting ourselves into here. You're no help, and at the moment, all Mr. Wall can think about is getting some of that so-called medication.

They passed through the village and went another half mile before coming to a peaceful glade in the middle of a large stretch of date palms. The area had a small channel of water running through it and plenty of grazing for the camels.

"This is one of the campsites the caravans use," Farouk said.

"I have the house just beyond that row of trees," Mrs. Montjoy told him. "Why don't you and your men pitch camp and I'll take Sir Augustus and his friends to my place."

Farouk looked scandalized. Mrs. Montjoy seemed not to notice, or cared not to notice, and gestured for them to follow. It was all Mr. Wall could do not to whip his camel into a gallop. Sweat poured down his face now, and his body shook so much Moustafa felt sure he would have a heart attack.

They passed through the palm trees and came to a small mud brick house undistinguishable from those of the village except for the windows being open and fitted with fine lace curtains. Several potted flowers stood in a row along the front wall.

"A touch of home always lifts the spirit," Mrs. Montjoy said.

Mr. Wall vaulted from his saddle and stood fidgeting as the others dismounted.

"So what brings you to the Western Desert?" Moustafa couldn't help but ask.

"A whim," she replied cheerily. "I have always been interested in travel, and after my children had grown and Mr. Montjoy was laid to rest, I saw nothing to stop me. I started with a tour through Lapland in the Swedish and Norwegian Arctic, before visiting Iceland and Greenland. Then warmer climes took my fancy. Knowing Italian, I decided the best place to start was Tripoli. I must confess the colonial authorities there were not happy to see me, but I managed. And now I'm here. I'm collecting notes for a book I intend to publish once I return home."

"And when will that be?" Moustafa was amazed that her male relatives would allow such a thing. He didn't think even European men could be that permissive.

Mrs. Montjoy laughed. "Whenever I'm done traveling!"

Before Moustafa could sputter a response, she hurried to the door, where Mr. Wall was already standing, and opened it.

"Stay here with the mounts," Moustafa told Faisal. The less time the child spent around this fallen woman the better. He was corrupt enough.

They entered the house. Mrs. Montjoy had done what she could to transform an oasis home into something a little more European. Besides the lace curtains, the crude wooden table had been covered with a tablecloth, a few prints hung on the walls, and another table was covered with a typewriter and piles of maps and papers.

She turned to Mr. Wall.

"I take it that an opiate would be the most effective cure for your pains?"

Mr. Wall nodded eagerly.

She opened a case sitting against one wall to reveal a large variety of phials and bottles. She pulled out one along with a dropper.

"Only two drops if you want to get some work done this evening," she said, handing it to him. "You can take the bottle. I have a spare. Rest in the bed you'll find through that door."

With shaking hands, Mr. Wall opened the bottle, dipped the dropper in it, and leaned his head back.

He let first one, then two drops fall on his tongue.

Mr. Wall paused for a moment, shaking like a leaf, and then with a visible force of will squeezed the remaining liquid back into the bottle and stoppered it. With a shudder he passed through the doorway and closed the door behind him.

Moustafa squared his shoulders and faced the woman.

"You should not have given that to him," he whispered.

Mrs. Montjoy looked at him with an amused smile.

"Wouldn't the time for objections have been before he took the medicine?"

Moustafa glanced at the closed door.

"He is my employer. It puts me in a difficult position."

"He was in pain. I merely alleviated that pain."

"Don't you realize that vile medicine has its hooks in him? You are like a wine seller giving a bottle to a drunk!"

Mrs. Montjoy inclined her head. "My brother was in the war. He came back without so much as a scratch, at least on the outside. But if he doesn't get a drop of opium at night he wakes up shrieking in terror. I suspect your employer does the same thing, and for far more reason. Which is the worse fate, that or nightly oblivion?"

Before Moustafa could reply, their conversation was interrupted by the sound he least suspected to hear in this remote place—the engine of a motorcar.

CHAPTER TWENTY-ONE

Faisal couldn't believe it. A motorcar—here?

The sound drew closer, and suddenly the motorcar burst through the greenery. It was a beat up, dusty machine, but drove very fast. It was missing a lot of the metal parts and Faisal could see the engine, which was usually hidden beneath metal plates. He also saw that instead of one tire on each corner it had two, stuck one behind the other. A thin English soldier with a deep tan and a blonde moustache sat at the wheel, an Egyptian boy of about fifteen in the seat beside him.

The car screeched to a stop in the front of the house, the camels bellowing in fear. Faisal had tethered them well, though, and they didn't stampede.

The soldier got out.

"Well, hello young man," the soldier said in Arabic. "I don't think I've met you before. You don't look to be of Bedouin stock. How did you get here?"

Faisal blinked. Was this oasis filled with Englishmen who spoke Arabic?

Not being able to find any words, he gestured to the camels.

"Right," the soldier said. "How silly of me. You came with that caravan, of course."

Moustafa and the beardless Englishman emerged from the house.

"Hello Jocelyn. Another newcomer, I see," the soldier strode over to Moustafa. "Captain Claud Williams, Number Five Light Car Patrol. The unholy terror in the Model T is Ahmed Fakhry."

"I am Moustafa Ghani El Souwaim. We have just arrived. My employer, Sir Augustus Wall, has a package for you from Orhan Bey of Cairo. He is most anxious to meet you but he is presently ... indisposed with a slight illness from the journey. He will be with us in a couple of hours."

"Orhan sent me a package? What a fine chap!" Captain Williams pointed to a mountain of black rock that towered over the side of the valley. "My lookout point is up there. I saw you come in and figured you'd head for this spot. It's popular with caravans. You're quite late in the season, though."

Faisal could tell the soldier was curious, but Moustafa didn't tell him why they were here.

"We can talk about that after my employer is feeling better," Moustafa said.

"Would you like some tea, Claud?" the beardless Englishman named Jocelyn asked.

"Would love some, thank you. Ahmed, check the motorcar and then do what you like for a while."

This was said to the boy who had come with him.

Ahmed hopped out of the motorcar and began inspecting the tires. The boy was much taller than Faisal and was beginning to get the broad shoulders and harder features of a man, although it didn't look like he had to shave yet. He wore a green djellaba that was newer and nicer than Faisal's, as well as a pair of good sandals. Faisal went over to him as the adults went inside.

"I'm Faisal. Do you know about motorcars?"

Ahmed grinned. "I sure do. Claud is teaching me everything. First I have to check the tires to make sure the pressure is good, then I have to check that the radiator isn't leaking and check the oil level as well. We filled up with petrol before we left so I know that's all right."

Faisal had no idea what he was saying, but it sure did sound like Ahmed knew what he was talking about. He watched as the older boy fiddled around with the engine.

"So you work for that Englishman?"

"He's from New Zealand."

"Is that next to England?"

"No, it's next to Australia."

"Oh, right," Faisal said, trying to sound like he knew all about it. "I work for an Englishman too. He's in the house resting."

"What's he doing here? Is he an Egyptologist?"

"A what?"

"One of those people who digs up ancient things."

"Yes, that's what he is. I guess. He doesn't dig things up much. Mostly he just buys and sells old things. Does that make him a … whatever you said?"

Ahmed cocked his head. "You don't seem to know much about him."

"He's a bit strange."

Ahmed laughed. "They all are! Hey, have you been to the hot spring yet?"

"The what?" Faisal was beginning to feel like a fool in front of Ahmed. He didn't like that, because if older boys thought you were a fool they beat you up and took your food.

"It's a place where hot water comes out of the earth and makes a big pool. The oasis has plenty of them. Some are cold too. The one here is just right. That's why the caravans like to stop here. I always take a dip if I'm near one. Come on, let's get cleaned up. You're filthy from the desert."

Faisal looked at himself. He didn't look any dirtier than usual.

Ahmed grabbed a piece of soap from a bag in the motorcar and motioned for him to follow.

They passed through a grove of date palms and to an open stretch of cultivated fields. A low farmhouse of mud brick stood not far off. Ahmed led him to a hole in the ground about the size of a doorway. The earth sloped down into the darkness.

Faisal paused. "We're going to bathe in here?"

"No, this isn't the hot spring. I just wanted to show this to you because we don't have them along the Nile. Come on."

Ahmed went down the slope. Faisal trailed along behind. The slope continued down about twenty feet before leveling out. The light grew dim and Faisal stopped, suddenly afraid.

He stood at the entrance to a tunnel running beneath the field. Every hundred feet or so a small opening in the roof allow light in. The tunnel was about as big as a normal hallway, hewn out of the stone. The floor was hidden under flowing water. Ahmed stood a little ahead of him, water up to his knees.

"What is this place?" Faisal asked, trying to keep his voice from trembling.

"It's an aqueduct. There are dozens of them all through the oasis. Some run for miles. The men of the oasis keep them clear of sand and pull water out of them for their fields. There's plenty of water here in the oasis, but it's all underground and they have to channel it everywhere and then pump it out. There are ancient ones too that have filled up with sand. Claud and I explored one once. We couldn't get far."

"We saw a lake when we were coming in. Why don't they just dig irrigation canals from the lake like the fellahin do with the Nile?"

"The lake is salt water. This is fresh water."

"Can we go now?" He didn't like this dark, hidden place with the black water that could have anything swimming beneath the surface.

Ahmed gave him a knowing grin. "Scared of the dark?"

"No. I just ... want to take a bath. I'm dirty from the desert, like you said."

"All right," Ahmed said with a chuckle.

Ahmed led him out of the tunnel and back into the sunlight. They entered another grove of date palms and came to a little glade where the ground sloped down to a small pond. To one side a spring bubbled out of the earth, feeding it. The water ran out the other end and was channeled into the farmland through a network of irrigation canals so narrow that the boys could easily step across them.

Faisal dipped his fingers into the pool.

"It's warm!"

"I told you. Many of them are."

"What kind of magic is this?"

"It's not magic. Claud explained it to me. He says the water comes from deep in the earth, where it's hot. The water in the aqueduct I showed you is cool. It comes from another source. Water comes up all over this oasis. That's because it's in a deep valley and closer to the water underneath the ground. Come on, let's get in."

Faisal looked around to see if they were alone.

"Don't worry," Ahmed said. "The women never come here. There's one of these pools about half an hour's walk away they use."

"They bathe in public?" Faisal asked, shocked. Back in Cairo, not even little girls did that.

"No, silly, they use it for washing. It's the hottest one, too hot to get in. You'd end up looking like a grilled chicken. Come on, let's get in. We can wash our clothes too."

They pulled off their djellabas.

"Wow, you're really skinny," Ahmed said. "I can count all your ribs. You should get your Englishman to feed you more."

"I'm not skinny. You should have seen me before I met him."

They waded in until Faisal was up to his waist and then he eased himself into the water. It felt great!

"Just like a hammam," Ahmed said, ducking his head in the water and then spitting out a long stream.

"I don't go to the hammams."

"Why not?"

"They cost money."

"Doesn't your Englishman pay you?"

"Sure, but I spend it on food."

Faisal went under the water and held his breath for a minute, enjoying the warmth all around him. If hammams felt this good, maybe he should save his money and go sometimes. When he came up for air he saw Ahmed swiping the surface of the pool, forcing a bunch of dirt floating on the surface into the drainage channel.

"Here, take this soap," Ahmed said. "You brought half the desert with you."

As Faisal soaped down, he asked, "So how did you end up working for that soldier?"

"I'm from the Fayoum. He was stationed there. I made money shining boots at the army camp and learned some English. Claud was impressed and hired me as his personal servant. Then he got transferred here and I came. I'm the youngest of four brothers, so there was nothing for me on the farm."

"Wait, you have a family?"

"Of course. Don't you?"

Faisal shook his head.

"So what did you do before you started working for that Englishman?" Ahmed asked.

Faisal shrugged. "I lived on the street."

Ahmed fell silent. Faisal tugged at his hair. The soap had made it really slippery but it wasn't helping him untangle all the knots.

"That's terrible," Ahmed said at last. "Our farm was poor but at least I had a place to sleep."

"I can't believe you left."

"Oh, there was nothing for me there. Like I said, my big brothers were getting all the land. I'd have had to find a job sooner or later."

Faisal shook his head again, the soap suds getting into his eyes and stinging.

"If I had a family, I'd never leave them. Not ever."

"I miss them a lot, but Claud is like family to me now."

"Really?"

"Sure. He's like a big brother or an uncle or something. He's always showing me how to do things like change the oil or play football. I have a lot of work to do around the house and with the car, but I'm learning things too. And he pays me."

Faisal rinsed his hair and thought for a minute. That sounded really great. Ahmed was the luckiest boy ever.

Ahmed grabbed the djellabas and threw them in the water. They scrubbed them down, Ahmed having to show Faisal how to clean his clothes properly, and then they hung them on a nearby bush and luxuriated in the warm pool until their clothing dried and their fingers were all wrinkly from the water.

By the time they returned to the house of the beardless Englishman, the sun had sunk low in the western sky. The others were sitting in the garden under the shade of some palm trees. Faisal's Englishman was there too, although he looked very sleepy, with his eyes only half open. Moustafa was giving him angry looks as if he was mad about the Englishman taking a nap. Moustafa got mad at everything.

"Who are you?" the Englishman asked Faisal as they arrived.

"I'm Faisal, you silly Englishman."

The Englishman smiled. That surprised Faisal even more. The Englishman didn't smile much.

"You must be a different Faisal. The Faisal I know is all dirty. This Faisal is almost presentable."

Ahmed nudged him and winked.

Claud stood. "We only have a couple of more hours of daylight left. I would like to invite you all up to dinner at my house. You can stay the night. I daresay after your journey you'd all appreciate a hot meal and a roof over your heads."

"You gentlemen go without me," the beardless Englishman said. "I have quite a lot of notes to write up."

"You just want to get out of that bumpy ride," Claud said with a laugh. "Never mind. We'll have you up again soon."

Everyone gathered their things and went to the motorcar. Faisal gleefully jumped into the back with the Englishman and Moustafa. He loved riding in motorcars. Claud got behind the wheel and Ahmed got in beside him.

"Let me show them!" Ahmed pleaded.

"We've only just met them," Claud chuckled. "We don't want to frighten them off."

Ahmed pushed on Claud's shoulder, shaking him. "Come on!"

"Oh all right, you little devil." Claud shifted to the other seat while Ahmed let out a whoop and clambered over him to get behind the wheel.

Moustafa gripped the seat. "He's not going to—"

Ahmed revved the engine and the machine shot forward, weaving between the palm trees. Faisal cheered.

Ahmed looked over his shoulder at him and grinned. "And you think I'd stay in the Fayoum when I can to do this?"

"Look where you're going, Ahmed," Claud said. But he was smiling as he said it.

They zipped out of the oasis and into an area of black rock. Little rocks were scattered all over the ground, and large boulders and low hills rose up all around them. Ahmed swerved between them as Faisal bounced in the back seat laughing and clapping.

"You like that, little brother?" Ahmed said. "Claud, we should teach Faisal to drive."

"Can I?" Faisal perked up. "CanIcanIcanIcanIcanIcanI?"

"Certainly not!" Moustafa barked.

But Faisal wasn't asking him, he was asking the Englishman sitting next to him.

"I don't think that would be a good idea," the Englishman said, still smiling his serene smile. Faisal had never seen him in such a good mood. Maybe he'd say yes if Faisal asked enough.

"Oh, please," he asked, shaking his shoulder like Ahmed shoved Claud. "Pleasepleasepleasepleaseplease."

Moustafa slapped him upside the head. "Behave!"

Faisal stuck his tongue out at him, but he couldn't stay in a bad mood for long. The ride was too much fun. After speeding through the hills and boulders, they came to a narrow path climbing up the side of a mountain of black stone. Claud made Ahmed give up the wheel, which he did without too much complaining.

"You know this part is too dangerous for you," Claud said.

It sure did look dangerous. They wound up a narrow path with a steep slope to one side that at times fell off into a sheer drop. The path was covered with lots of loose tiny stones like bits of coal that made the tires swerve and spin, and deep ruts that bounced them the entire way. Even so, Claud handled the motorcar like an expert and they got to the summit of the mountain and drove along a wide ridge. To one side, the oasis lay spread out beneath them, with a glittering lake and empty desert beyond. To the other side lay only desert as far as the eye could see.

"Why do you live all the way up here?" Faisal asked. The palm groves were a lot nicer than all this stone. The sun was strong up here too, even though it had almost set.

"I'm a lookout for the army," Claud explained. "I can watch anyone approaching the oasis from miles away. I spotted your caravan yesterday. During the war the Germans riled up the Senussi from Libya to invade. They took Bahariya and several other oases. Then we pushed them out and I've been here ever since, watching to make sure they don't come back."

"Must be lonely up here."

"I'd go insane if I didn't have Ahmed to talk to. Having visitors is a rare treat."

They trundled along the ridge. At the far end Faisal could see a large house made of the same black stone as the mountain. Claud parked the motorcar beside it.

"Ahmed, get dinner ready," he said.

"I'll help!" Faisal volunteered.

"All right," the Englishman said. He was still sitting in the back seat with a happy smile on the half of his face visible outside his mask. "Just don't eat all the food before we get a chance to get some, eh?"

"And take your time," Claud said, suddenly serious. "The adults have some important things to discuss."

As he said this, he glanced at the letter that the Englishman had brought him all the way from Cairo. Faisal had been wondering about that letter. He'd only seen it once. The Englishman had guarded it closely on the entire trip across the desert.

CHAPTER TWENTY-TWO

Captain Williams' house may have been remote, but it was spacious and reasonably well appointed. There was an entrance hall, a large living room, a bedroom, a kitchen, a dining room, a room with a drafting table where the captain was working on some maps, and a room for a wireless set. A few prints and native blankets had been hung on the wall, and the living room had a decent sized bookshelf. Captain Williams excused himself for a moment and went onto the roof, motioning for Augustus to follow. The roof had an observation platform that gave a splendid view of the surrounding area for many miles in each direction. A heliograph stood at one end, and the antenna for the wireless at the other. Captain Williams took a slow look all around with a powerful set of binoculars.

Augustus watched it all with a serene sense of detachment, as if through a warm, comforting fog. Everything was all right now. That angel in trousers, that Florence Nightingale of the desert, had given him an entire bottle of tincture of opium. A couple of drops had taken all his pains away.

Limiting himself to only a couple had been the most difficult thing he had done in a long time. He had talked himself into it by promising himself that he'd take four more drops tonight to ensure a long, restful sleep. Then three drops every evening would carry him until they got back.

Nothing could bother him now, not even the cross looks Moustafa kept giving him.

After Captain Williams checked that there was no enemy in sight, he went downstairs, entered some notes in a log book, powered up the wireless, and tapped out a signal in Morse code to a station in the Fayoum. After that they settled in the living room. The benches were low and of native manufacture, covered with hard, heavy cushions. Ahmed brought in tea.

"We need to get some sugar," the teenager said.

"We just bought some sugar," Claud replied.

Ahmed glanced in the direction of the kitchen. "There was an … accident."

"Oh all right, we'll get some the next time we go to the village."

"Thanks, Claud."

"Captain Williams," Moustafa corrected. "You should call him Captain Williams, or sir."

Captain Williams laughed. "We're much too far off the beaten track for such formalities."

He smiled at Ahmed as the boy went back in the kitchen. Then he grew serious, turning to Augustus and holding up the letter.

"While you were convalescing, I read this letter Orhan Bey sent. It contains some rather disturbing rumors. As you no doubt know, the Senussi are still giving the Italians trouble in Cyrenaica. Many use Siwa Oasis on our side of the border as a refuge, and the Italian army is left on the border fuming and helpless. Of course we try to help out the dagos when we can. The trouble is the local people shelter them. There's quite a lot of sympathy for the Senussi in all the oases. There's even a Senussi mosque and religious school in the village of Biwati. We didn't have the nerve to shut it down. Would cause more trouble than it would prevent."

"I'm not terribly familiar with the Senussi," Augustus admitted. "It's a Sufi order, is it not?"

Captain Williams nodded. "And not a terribly bad one. It's not as libertine as some of the Sufi sects, and not as dour and strict as the Wahhabis. Sort of a middle path. The only problem with them is they're violently anticolonial. Think they can run the show better than we can. Under that banner they've managed to unite many of the Bedouin tribes, even drawing in Tuareg from as far as Algeria. Orhan Bey has a few connections in the group. Nothing official, mind you, but his grandfather was a bit of a holy man and he gets invited to all the big affairs. It turns out that there are some rumblings in the desert on the Libyan side."

"What sort of rumblings?"

"He wasn't quite clear. All he heard was that their defeat in the last war left the Senussi divided. The previous Sayyid sued for peace, as you know, and got replaced by Sayyid Mohammed Idris, who is now playing ball as the Emir of Cyrenaica. He's no trouble for the Italians or us as long as he's watched. Unfortunately, the stiffer element never surrendered, and have gone off to fight the Italians on their own."

"They haven't made much headway, from what I've heard," Moustafa said.

"No, they're small and disorganized enough that they're not even a match for the Italians, which is saying something. But one of the sheiks has come up with the bright idea of making raids into Egyptian territory, hoping to draw a response from the British that would galvanize the tribes and start the entire show all over again."

"They'd only get another thrashing," Augustus said.

"Yes, but they'd cause no end of trouble in the meantime. So far the raids have been minor. Attacks on caravans, that sort of thing. The reason you haven't heard anything in the press is that we've been calling them bandit raids, and there are so many of those that the papers don't bother reporting on them unless a white man gets killed. Orhan Bey thinks they might be planning something bigger, though, something we can't cover up."

"Did he have any details?" Augustus asked. The seriousness of the situation was beginning to cut through his mental fog.

"No. It's all straw in the wind. He must think it's serious if he trusted a civilian to carry such news to me. I'll have to make a full report once I've investigated."

Augustus took a drag of his cigarette, wondering how much he should reveal of his reason for being here. Upon their first meeting at Mrs. Montjoy's house he had told the captain that he planned to do some excavations. At least that was what he thought he had told him. His mind had been quite hazy from the tincture and now he couldn't entirely recollect what had been said.

"Perhaps I've come at the wrong time to hunt for antiquities?" Augustus asked, fishing.

"Oh, I don't think there's any immediate danger. I'm sort of a last line of defense. There are armored car patrols ranging far out into the desert, plus we have paid informants among the Bedouin on both sides of the line. If there were any large movements of tribals, I suspect we would have heard of it by now. Mostly we're on the lookout for smugglers."

"Is there much smuggling?"

"Yes indeed. The Bedouin smuggle in everything you can imagine— guns, tobacco, hashish … just last month we intercepted a shipment of several barrels of hydrochloric acid. We have a warehouse on base full of confiscated goods."

"What in the world were the Bedouin doing with hydrochloric acid?"

"It's used in the manufacture of cocaine. The drug is quite popular in Cairo, from what I've heard."

"The chief of police tells me the same thing. How many men are stationed here?"

Captain Williams paused for the briefest of moments. "Enough to stave off a raid or civil disturbances."

"But not a major force?"

Another pause. "No."

Augustus decided to change tack. "Ah well, I suspect you are correct. If the Senussi were foolish enough to launch another invasion, you'd have caught wind of it by now. Did you meet an archaeologist named Professor Harrell? He gave a most interesting lecture on his discoveries here upon his return to Cairo."

"Professor Harrell? Is he a friend of yours?"

"No. I never got to meet the man personally."

"Well then I can speak plainly. He has got to be the rudest man I have ever met."

"Really? He seemed gracious enough at the Geographical Association."

"Perhaps because he was playing the crowd, or angling for more funds. He treated me like a squaddie."

"Really?"

"I went to visit him like I went to visit you. He was at the southern edge of the oasis with a small crew. Only half a dozen Egyptians. No foreman, which struck me as unusual. Every archaeologist hires a more advanced native to keep the rest in line. When I went to visit him he brushed me off, saying he was too busy to accept my invitation. When I tried to suggest another date, he told me bluntly to get off his excavation and not to bother him again. The nerve!"

Augustus and Moustafa exchanged a glance.

"That does seem odd," Augustus said.

"Indeed," Captain Williams said, lighting another cigarette. "Anyone this far from civilization is happy for a bit of company, no matter how busy they might be."

"And what about Mrs. Montjoy?" Moustafa asked.

"Mad as a hatter. Good company, though. I've had her up to dinner here on a couple of occasions, and she's returned the hospitality. Ahmed can't make head nor tail of her."

"Faisal thinks she's a man," Moustafa said.

Captain Williams chuckled. "Best not to enlighten him. But what you're really wondering is if she's any sort of security risk. As far as I can tell she is not. The Foreign Office did some checking. She is quite well traveled and the author of two volumes, one on the Arctic regions and another on Central Europe. Coming through the Senussi area does raise a red flag, though. I'm keeping an eye on her by keeping her close."

"I doubt that any hostile powers would send her as a spy. She sticks out too much," Augustus said.

"Or perhaps having her stick out makes her less suspect," Captain Williams replied. "My gut instinct is that she's a good egg, although a cracked one."

"Are there any other foreigners in the oasis?"

"None."

Ahmed and Faisal ran into the room. Ahmed had a football tucked under his arm.

"Can I teach Faisal how to play football?"

"Surely you haven't cooked dinner already?" Captain Williams.

"I've prepared everything. All I need to do is put it on the fire. There's not much daylight left. Please?"

Their host turned to his guests.

"It's still a bit early for dinner," Augustus said.

Captain Williams gave the boys a dismissive wave. "Go on with you."

The boys rushed out of the house.

"You shouldn't be so lax with him," Moustafa chided. "He'll end up slothful and greedy."

"He's all right," Captain Williams said. "It's good to see him have a bit of a childhood. Most of these boys don't get one. When I met Ahmed he was stuck on three feddans of land that were somehow supposed to support a family of eight. He was just skin and bones. Sharp, though. The lads at base would teach him a word in English and quiz him the next day and he'd always remember. Some tried to catch him out with words like 'aorta' or 'tungsten,' but he'd rattle them off as easy as you please."

"He certainly handles that motorcar well enough," Augustus said, getting up. He moved to the window, which overlooked a broad swale on the side of the mountain that created a flat area the size of a couple of football pitches. Little cairns had been set up to mark the goals. In the darkening light, he saw Ahmed and Faisal running down the slope to it, Ahmed kicking the ball ahead of him and Faisal trying to catch up.

"I'd teach him to use the wireless too if I were allowed," Captain Williams said. "Technically I'm not allowed to have a servant at all. The officers' manual says that an adult male is a security risk, which it most certainly is among this population, and it forbids female servants for obvious reasons. It doesn't say you can't have a boy, though. So I'm only going against the spirit of the regulation rather than the letter."

"So how long has he been with you?" Augustus asked. The boys had made it down to the football pitch, and Ahmed was explaining something to Faisal, pointing at the ball and then the goals.

"Three years. Was with me all through the campaign. I'd leave him back at base when I went out on patrol, of course, but I'd give him a ride around in one of the armored cars as a treat. Pretty soon he was pestering me to teach him how to drive the thing. He was only twelve when he first took the wheel of one of His Majesty's armored cars. You can rest assured we did that well out of sight of camp! He learned to cook and clean and shine boots too, got excellent at English, and can hold his own against any soldier on the football pitch."

Augustus lit a cigarette. Ahmed and Faisal were running up and down the pitch now, passing the ball to each other. "He seems happy."

"I like to think so. You see so many of these boys, the youngest sons or the castoffs, begging in the streets or selling trinkets for pennies. Breaks your heart. I thought I had it bad growing up on a sheep farm near Gisborne. I had to get up before dawn to take care of the herds and then walk three miles to school. After my lessons and homework, I had to put in another couple of hours on the farm. I still got a bit of fun, though. Football on weekends. Taking a girl to see the pictures. Fishing and swimming with my friends. But what do these children get?"

"Most don't get anything at all," Augustus said. Ahmed was now acting as goalkeeper as Faisal tried to kick the ball past him.

"Precisely. Childhood disappears quickly enough. It's a shame for them not to have one."

Augustus took a drag from his cigarette, still watching the boys play. "All seems so long ago, doesn't it? When the most important things in the world were who made a goal or who got chosen to be captain of the cricket team. We think it will last forever and then there we are with commissions and responsibilities and …"

A distant part of his mind realized he was rambling, and he had been about to speak of the war, yet the sweet elixir that remarkable woman had given him kept him from going down his usual dark path. He shook off the trace of shadow and went on. "But these little chaps start with all that. In my neighborhood there are shops run by children no older than Faisal. The men are all doing heavy labor, as will the little shopkeepers once they grow up. Twelve hours a day in some tiny market stall. No play, no education." Faisal made a goal and did a cartwheel. "Yet even the ones who have the least seem to have some spirit left in them. It's remarkable how even the littlest things can make them happy."

CHAPTER TWENTY-THREE

Dinner was a friendly affair that Moustafa enjoyed while at the same time feeling slightly uncomfortable. Other than a few quick, casual meals with Mr. Wall in his home, he had never sat at table with Europeans. At least Ahmed turned out to be an adequate cook and Captain Williams was friendly enough.

He had been around a great many Europeans and found they fell into two major categories—the dismissive ones and the earnest ones. Most Europeans looked down on Africans and thought ill of them when they thought of them at all. A much smaller category—missionaries and wealthy young adventurers mostly—were eager to show how much they respected you and were their brother from across the sea, even though they understood almost nothing about you and inevitably regressed back to the first category once they did. Mr. Wall was one of the earnest ones.

No, that wasn't fair. That was Moustafa's lingering anger over the incident with the opium clouding his judgment. Mr. Wall was only partially one of the earnest ones. He fell into a much smaller category, one that included fewer Europeans than Moustafa could count on the fingers of one hand—the truly sympathetic ones.

These Europeans really did want to understand Africans and Africa. They really did want to listen when you spoke about independence. This didn't mean they understood, but at least they were trying. And it didn't guarantee that they'd agree with you once they did understand.

Captain Williams appeared to land at least partially in that category. His adoption of Ahmed and his easy manner when speaking with Moustafa proved it. More to the point, this soldier could prove to be a useful ally while they were here—Moustafa had noted a rifle and pistol in the living room—although stuck up on this mountain he would not be able to be at their side at all times.

After dinner, the boys rushed off to make tea and clean the dishes. Moustafa was surprised to see the Little Infidel volunteering to work, something Moustafa was sure he had never done in his entire useless life. He had quickly attached himself to the older boy. Perhaps Ahmed might have a good effect on him.

As long as Faisal didn't dare call Mr. Wall by his first name. Moustafa would give him a good smacking if he tried.

As the boys clattered around the kitchen, chattering away a mile a minute, Moustafa took the chance to look through Captain Williams's bookshelf. This had become his habit when entering any European home, or at least those where he was allowed to do such a thing.

Most of the volumes were on mechanical engineering, cartography, and the nature of the desert. There was even an entire volume on the formation and movement of sand dunes. These books, while they didn't particularly interest Moustafa, intrigued him. There were so many branches of knowledge. He had always focused on history and archaeology, and yet he hungered to know more about the sciences and arts as well. Between working for Mr. Wall and raising a family, he simply didn't have the time.

A small shelf of antiquities caught his eye. There were various potsherds and some glass beads, most of which dated to the Late Period and the Greco-Roman Period. Next to these sat a few sculpture fragments in the Greek style and a couple of mummified ibises.

Captain Williams and Mr. Wall came over.

"Ah, I see you've found my little museum. I do a few exploratory digs around here when I can spare the time, plus the villagers try to sell me anything they find."

"Are there many sites of interest here?" Moustafa asked.

"Oh yes," Captain Williams said. "I daresay you've already heard of the temple of Alexander. Professor Harrell was digging close to it. Further south there are the remains of a Roman fort and an early Christian church."

"A church?" Moustafa asked, surprised.

"The early Christians liked remote spots," Mr. Wall said. "They wanted to get away from the temptations of the world. Many of the ascetics lived alone in the desert, and small communities would settle in oases or built monasteries."

"There's a monastery at the site too," Captain Williams said, "although all that's left are the foundations. You should visit if you have the time. The church has lost its roof but retains some frescoes on the walls, including a cross and a lovely painting of a man on a horse."

"Saint George?" Mr. Wall asked.

"Quite possibly, although a different saint is attached to the local area. Saint Bartholomew is supposed to have been martyred here, and his headless body is said to be buried in the church grounds. The monastery is still known to the locals as the Monastery of the Head."

"Well, let's hope that we don't lose our own heads during our stay," Mr. Wall said.

Moustafa decided not to comment on that. Working for this fellow, that was always a possibility.

After tea, they bedded down in the living room, Captain Williams providing cushions and blankets. Mr. Wall excused himself to the toilet, taking the bottle of opium with him. Moustafa grumbled and lay down. At least he wouldn't be awoken by his boss screaming in the night.

It proved hard to get to sleep anyway. Faisal and Ahmed stayed up late into the night, giggling and whispering and moving around the house. Then they went into Ahmed's little bedroom off the kitchen, where the whispering and giggling continued. Moustafa wanted to shout at them, but it wasn't his house.

After breakfast the next morning, and once Ahmed and Faisal had gone to wash the dishes, Mr. Wall decided to lay his cards on the table.

"I'm afraid that looking for antiquities is only part of our reason for coming here," he said.

"Really?"

Captain Williams did not look surprised. After all, they hadn't arrived with any equipment or institutional accreditation.

Mr. Wall explained the situation, leaving nothing out. Moustafa felt relieved. If they could trust anyone to help, it would be a member of the British military. Of course there was a small chance that the man was corrupt, but Moustafa didn't think so. And the captain's job was to watch over the oasis. He'd learn what they were up to sooner or later.

Once Mr. Wall finished, Captain Williams thought for a minute.

"I must confess I didn't have any inkling that he was involved in anything more than an archaeological excavation. Looking back now, I can see he was acting suspiciously. But I haven't heard of any newcomers in the oasis besides yourselves, and I know of no other diggings. Whatever I can do to help, I'll be happy to oblige within the constraints of my duty. I'm afraid I'm stuck up on this mountain having to make regular observations for enemy movements. Given what you and Orhan have told me, my post is all the more important now."

"Can you drive us back to our camp?" Mr. Wall asked.

"Of course. I'm not a complete prisoner, although sometimes it feels that way. I have such a good view, and travel by camel is so slow, that I can leave for a few hours without anyone being able to come over the horizon and make it to the oasis. Let me get the motorcar ready."

Captain Williams drove them back down to the caravan camp. Farouk and the others were waiting for them.

The first thing the Bedouin did was to demand payment, with a 20% increase because of the detour to the well. Moustafa angrily pointed out that it only added a day to a ten-day trip, so it should only be a 10% increase. After much haggling they settled for 15%, plus hiring Farouk, Abbas, and Mohammed al-Biwati as guards for their baggage. The other Bedouin had already scattered to their families, taking the remaining food stores with them.

"Some of us might return to Cairo in a little while," Farouk said once the money was handed over. "If you wish to hire us to escort you back, we would be willing."

"We might take you up on that offer," Mr. Wall said.

Once the business dealings were over, Captain Williams said, "I need to get to the mountain. I daren't leave my post for too long. I have just enough time to show you the excavations Professor Harrell was conducting. It's only a couple of miles away."

They got in the motorcar, Ahmed badgering the soldier until he was allowed to drive, and they shot along a narrow, rutted dirt lane. Faisal leaned over his shoulder, watching Ahmed drive while the older boy explained how he did it.

They passed fields of wheat just beginning to ripen, and large groves of date palms where men suspended by ropes were clearing out dead branches and harvesting the dates. Soon they entered the village of Biwati, a collection of low houses of mud brick, many painted with geometric designs in red and yellow, the doors showing white hand marks.

"What are those for?" Mr. Wall asked.

"For averting the evil eye," Captain Williams replied.

"Are there a lot of sorcerers and witches here?" Faisal asked, suddenly worried.

"The villagers think so. I wouldn't worry about it, young man."

They collected a trail of children in the town who ran after them waving. Ahmed rewarded them by honking the horn. Faisal leaned over and honked it again. Moustafa hauled him back into his place.

After a few minutes they passed through an even smaller village and out past the limits of the oasis. The palm grove thinned, the irrigation canals ended, and the grove gave way to sandy scrub for about a quarter of a mile before that, too, disappeared. Ahead, the remains of a small stone temple stood in a barren field littered with potsherds. Beyond that Moustafa spied a few heaps of sand and debris, the spoil from an excavation.

"Stop the car," Captain Williams told Ahmed. "We don't want to fall through the top of a tomb like Professor Harrell's water boy did."

"There are more meticulous ways to find ancient sites," Mr. Wall quipped. He was in fine spirits today.

Of course he is, Moustafa fumed. *He's got that ridiculous drug.*

Moustafa was still angry at his boss for snapping at him back in the desert. Yes, the man had been suffering because he couldn't get his opium, but what he said had been revealing. Moustafa was the help and nothing more.

Ahmed yanked hard on the steering wheel, spinning the motorcar so it ended up on its two left wheels, and screeched to a stop. Both boys laughed hysterically.

"I've created a monster," Captain Williams groaned.

They got out and walked the last two hundred yards to come to a broad pit where the sand had been cleared away to reveal bedrock. A hole about two feet wide was broken through this, leading to darkness.

Mr. Wall pulled an electric torch out of his pocket and got on his belly close to the hole. He crawled forward. Moustafa gritted his teeth as he heard a cracking sound.

"Careful, boss. The tomb's ceiling looks like it's delicate."

Although falling in would serve you right.

"That's why I'm on my belly. It distributes the weight more evenly," Mr. Wall replied. "It would help if the good Professor Harrell had left his ladder."

He shone the torch into the tomb. "Hmm. Interesting. Your turn, Moustafa."

Mr. Wall wriggled back away from the hole and handed the electric torch to him. Moustafa crawled forward, tensing every time the rock crackled beneath him. He was much heavier than his boss.

Nevertheless, he made it to the lip of the hole and shone the torch down into it.

Below was a large, rectangular chamber carved into the stone, measuring about thirty feet by twenty. Several niches were carved in the walls, long enough to hold mummies. All were empty. Even so, Moustafa felt a thrill. Until just a few months ago, this tomb had remained undisturbed for more than two thousand years.

"This is the chamber we saw in Professor Harrell's slideshow," Moustafa said.

"Indeed it is," Mr. Wall said. "I think we should take a closer look."

"We could jump in easily enough, but getting out would be a problem. The floor is a good ten feet down. Captain Williams, do you have any rope in your motorcar?"

"I have a tow chain attached to the Model T, but I daren't drive through here. I'd probably end up breaking through into another tomb, or this one. We have some light cord for securing baggage. I don't think it's strong enough to hold a man."

Moustafa and Mr. Wall looked at Faisal.

The boy gulped.

CHAPTER TWENTY-FOUR

Faisal was not happy. He had agreed to cross a desert and find a man who kills people with a little tube. Wasn't that dangerous enough?

No, now he had to go into an ancient tomb that was probably crawling with djinn.

"Don't worry, little brother," Ahmed said, tying the cord around Faisal's waist. "It's daytime. Djinn don't come out in daytime."

"It's not daytime down there!"

"Don't you have a charm?"

"Yes."

"Then you'll be all right."

"Can't you come down too?"

"The cord won't hold me," Ahmed said, playing out the cord and handing it to Claud and Moustafa.

"I hate being small."

Reluctantly, Faisal moved to the side of the hole and sat down, dangling his feet. He took off his sandals so he could climb better. A weird stink came from below.

"What's that smell?" he asked.

"Smell?" the Englishman said. "I don't smell anything."

He stood a little way off.

"It smells familiar," Faisal said.

"It's nothing. In you go," the Englishman said.

"We have a good hold on the rope," Claud called over.

Then Faisal remembered. "Hey! It's the same smell as those dead people who are all wrapped up. I've smelled that in your house!"

The Englishman looked embarrassed. "Oh, don't worry. Someone took all the mummies out. They can't hurt you."

"That's worse! If the dead people are gone, the djinn don't have anywhere to live. They'll move into my head and live there."

"If you don't get in there right this instant," Moustafa roared, "I'll open up a big hole in your head to make it easier for them to move in!"

Faisal looked at the hole doubtfully. He might be better off taking his chances with Moustafa.

Then Claud spoke up. "If you go in, I'll let you drive the motorcar."

"Really?" Faisal perked up. "Reallyreallyreallyreallyreally?"

"But only to steer," Claud said. "You'll have to sit on Ahmed's lap while he runs the gas, the brake, and the gear shift."

Faisal wasn't quite sure what that meant, but if it meant he got to drive the motorcar, that was fine by him.

It still didn't make him happy about going into this tomb, though.

The Englishman tossed him the electric torch, which he put in his pocket. Then he hung from the lip of the hole by his hands and let go. There was a little jerk as he dropped a few inches before the cord went taut. It was too thin and cut into his waist.

"Ow! Lower me down."

He descended into the darkness, the hole a receding circle of light above him. His eyes began to adjust to the gloom and he made out a room cut from the stone with some darker shadows he didn't like.

As soon as he got his feet on the floor, he pulled out the torch and turned it on.

Trembling, he shone it this way and that, probing every shelf and corner with the light to scare away any djinn. With his free hand he clutched the charm around his neck.

"There's nothing down here," Faisal called up to them.

I hope.

"Take a closer look," the Englishman called down.

"What am I looking for?"

"I don't know. Anything unusual."

"What's unusual in a place like this?"

"Use your head for something other than a home for fleas!" Moustafa bellowed.

Faisal made a crude gesture in Moustafa's direction, then made it with his other hand, then put down the torch and made it with both hands.

He grabbed the torch and glanced around nervously.

"I didn't mean you, djinn," he whispered.

Faisal shone the electric torch around the tomb again, taking a good look this time. The walls were cut with a series of shelves where the mummies had slept. He didn't need the Englishman to have told him this. He could tell from the smell and from a few shreds of old wrappings still lying in the dust.

Summoning his courage, he approached each of the shelves, shining the light along them. He didn't see any of the old things the Englishman was interested in.

"There's nothing down here."

"Keep looking," the Englishman called. His voice sounded very distant.

"I think I've earned two moving pictures for this trip," Faisal grumbled.

Then something caught his eye. In the far corner lay a crumpled up packet of cigarettes. It looked new.

"Did the people who built this tomb smoke cigarettes?" Faisal called up.

"Of course not, you blockhead!" Moustafa shouted.

"Then someone from our times was smoking down here."

He picked up the packet and smoothed it out. The brand wasn't one he recognized. Not that he could read the words written on it, but all the brands had their own pictures or colors and he hadn't seen this one before. He also found the butt of a cigarette someone had crushed out on the ground. It lay next to a little heap of mummy wrappings.

Faisal wrinkled his nose. To pick up the cigarette he'd have to almost touch the old bandages. Yuck.

"Maybe three moving pictures," he grumbled, reaching down to pinch the cigarette butt between two fingernails.

That's when the pile of mummy wrappings moved.

A black scorpion rushed out, straight for his hand.

Faisal screamed and leaped back, but the cord was still taut around his waist and he couldn't get far enough away.

"Pull me up! Pull me up!"

"How many times do I have to tell you there's no such thing as djinn?" the Englishman shouted.

"Not a djinni, a scorpion!" Faisal shouted, leaping onto his right foot as the scorpion tried to sting the left one.

The scorpion rushed at his other foot, bare and vulnerable. Faisal leaped onto his other foot.

He cried out again and the cord bit into his waist as it pulled him into the air. Because he had backed up, he swung forward, right over the scorpion. Faisal yelped and pulled up his legs. He rose, spinning, the bright circle of daylight whirling above him, and then fell hard onto the floor of the tomb.

The cord had snapped. The flashlight rolled away, turning off.

Faisal had fallen onto his back, the wind knocked out of him. He groaned and rolled onto his belly …

… and saw the glistening black scorpion racing for his face.

"Help!" he screamed, scrambling backwards.

Everything went black, and then bright again very quickly. Faisal jerked as something large fell from the ceiling and thumped on the ground.

Ahmed!

"Where is … ah!" Ahmed jumped back as he spotted the scorpion.

The creature paused, then scuttled for Faisal again.

Ahmed tore off his sandal and smacked it down on the scorpion, crushing it with a loud pop. Scorpion juice squirted out in a little puddle.

"Let's get out of here before any more decide to come at us," Ahmed said. "Get on my shoulders."

"Wait." Faisal grabbed the cigarette and the pack, put them in his pocket, and clambered onto Ahmed's back as quickly as he had gone up that palm tree in Cairo.

He stood on Ahmed's shoulders and was just able to reach the lip of the hole. He pulled himself up into the daylight and scrambled away.

"We have to get him out!" Faisal cried. Everyone gathered around.

"I can get myself out, little brother. Hey, you forgot this."

The torch came flying out of the hole.

Faisal heard the sound of running below, and briefly Ahmed's hands grasped the lip of the hole, but a piece of rock snapped away and he disappeared again.

Faisal stood close to the hole, trembling. "Hurry, before another scorpion comes."

He heard Ahmed take another running jump. His hands grasped the edge of the hole once more.

This time the rock held, and he pulled himself up with a grunt. He crawled away from the hole and stood, breathing hard. Faisal gave him a hug. Ahmed was the best!

"Are you two all right?" the Englishman asked.

Faisal and Ahmed both nodded. Ahmed pointed at the Englishman and turned to Faisal.

"He was going to jump in too, but I beat him too it."

"He's kind of clumsy," Faisal said.

"You're welcome," the Englishman said. "What's this about someone smoking down there?"

Faisal pulled the cigarette butt and packet out of his pocket. The Englishman studied them a moment.

"Interesting," he said in a quiet voice. "These are Italian cigarettes."

"Odd to find those here," Claud said. "I doubt Professor Harrell or any of his men were smoking them."

"No. They aren't readily available in Cairo. I suppose some Italian merchants carry them, but I can't recall seeing them at a regular tobacconist's."

"Neither do I," Claud said. "They'd be common enough in Cyrenaica, though."

Mr. Wall and Claud looked at each other as if that was important. Faisal didn't care. He put on his sandals and walked away from the hole before any scorpions or djinn crawled out.

Ahmed followed.

"Are you all right, little brother?"

Faisal put on a brave face. "I've been through worse. I even saw a head without a body once."

"Eeew."

"The Englishman is always finding trouble and I have to get him out of it."

"I help Claud a lot too, even during the war. I got to drive an armored car and everything. He never let me see any fighting, though."

"Stay with us and you will," Faisal grumbled, kicking a dusty old bit of pottery. "So why do Europeans like all this old stuff?"

"Claud is from New Zealand. That's not in Europe."

"He's European, though."

"Yes, pretty much. They all like the old things. They say that studying the past helps them understand how things are now."

"Why not just study what's going on now?"

Ahmed laughed. "Nothing is ever that simple with Europeans. They want to know everything, not just what's going on now but what went on before. They want to know what's at the bottom of the sea and behind the stars. That's why they go everywhere."

"They go to the stars?" Faisal said, his jaw dropping.

"Not yet, but I bet they will."

Faisal looked back at the two Europeans and Moustafa talking next to the hole. Those people were crazy enough to try anything. Moustafa too. Moustafa wanted to be European and often acted more European than the Europeans.

"Going to the stars would be a lot more fun than looking at some dusty tomb with scorpions in it," he said.

"I kind of like it. You get to see things in a different way. Like this."

Ahmed picked up a big piece of broken pottery. It had a long handle on a curved side that ended in a narrow opening. The rest of the pot was gone.

"This is Roman," Ahmed said. "They came after the pharaohs but before the Arabs. It's called an amphora and the Romans used it to hold wine. The Romans drank a lot of wine and if you find one of these, you know the Romans were living here."

"How can you tell all that from a broken jug?" Faisal asked.

"Claud taught me. He likes looking around for old things. He's got some books on it and lets me look at them."

"You can read?"

"Sure. I went to Koranic school back in the Fayoum for a few years. Once I started learning to speak English, Claud taught me how to read English. I'm not too good, though. I need to practice more."

"I'd spend my time practicing with the motorcar, not books."

Ahmed laughed. "Yeah, that's lots more fun. But you know," Ahmed looked around, suddenly serious, "it's good for Egyptians to know about these things. Why should Europeans be the only ones who know about Egyptian history? Maybe one day when I'm older I'll do some digs of my own."

CHAPTER TWENTY-FIVE

Augustus strolled with the others across the sandy waste, wondering how many tombs lay hidden beneath their feet. Tombs were rarely found in isolation. They tended to come in vast necropoli, like those at Giza and Saqqara. Claud had told him that in the bluffs overlooking the depression in which the oasis sat, there were rows of tombs cut into the rock. There was archaeological potential to this remote place, something that had attracted Ainsley Fielding, Carl Riding, and the other plotters—mostly still unknown—at the Geographical Association of Egypt.

They headed for the temple of Alexander, a jumble of ruins standing only waist high. It looked like it had once been a compact stone rectangle with little exterior decoration. Augustus figured that it wouldn't have taken too many sandstorms like they had endured to scour off any paint and bas-reliefs. Perhaps the ancients hadn't even bothered putting any embellishments on the outside.

He walked in a wide line with Moustafa to one side and Claud to the other, scanning the ground for any other evidence of unusual activity. Other than a large number of potsherds and a few minor artifacts such as beads and sculpture fragments, they saw nothing of note.

"We've attracted attention," Claud said, indicating the edge of the palm grove half a mile away. A few local men stood there, watching.

"We do stand out," Augustus said.

"Mark my word, the locals know our every move, and you can rest assured those Bedouin you hired will have told everyone they met everything they know about you."

Augustus turned back to the boys, who were lagging behind.

"Stay close," he called to them.

Faisal ran up to him, holding a piece of an amphora.

"The Romans were drinking wine here," he said.

"They most certainly were. I didn't know you were interested in archaeology."

"Egyptians should know about Egyptian history," he said in a serious voice.

Augustus glanced at Ahmed, then back at Faisal.

"That's quite correct."

"Do you think the Romans were smoking those cigarettes?" Faisal asked.

"Um, no. The Romans didn't smoke. They preferred wine."

Faisal nodded. "That's true. They were bad Muslims."

"You might even say they weren't Muslims at all. Since you have a new-found interest in the past, do you know what this building is?"

"It's not another tomb, is it?" Faisal said, clearly worried.

"No. It's a temple."

"That's worse! Sorcerers go to temples to make magic."

"No they don't, Faisal."

"Yes they do," Ahmed chimed in, finally catching up. "We had a temple near our village. The local sorcerer went there all the time. Once a woman went there to pray to the old gods for a son. All her sons had died as babies. She got a son, all right, but it was born all twisted and lame. God punished her for acting like a pagan."

"It's not uncommon, boss," Moustafa said. "It happens with ignorant villagers in the Soudan too."

"I see. Well, no one try casting any spells and no one will give birth to twisted babies."

"All right, Englishman," Faisal said in all seriousness.

While they could have entered the crumbled building from any side, Augustus led them to the old entrance. As he suspected, he saw none of the decoration that temple exteriors usually had, only blank rock polished to a fine sheen by the desert wind. They entered, Faisal drawing close to him and clutching his charm.

Rubble lay everywhere, and they had to step over or on large blocks of stone. Portions of the wall still stood in many places, and the sand had obviously been recently cleared away from the interior, no doubt by the late Professor Harrell. The sand, which had lain undisturbed for centuries, had helped preserve the interior decoration. Bas-reliefs showed lines of gods, and at the far end of the temple, a pharaoh stood offering libations to them. Next to the ruler was a cartouche.

Moustafa took in a sharp breath.

"The cartouche of Alexander the Great!" he cried. "It was in one of the books Herr Schäfer lent me."

"What's a cartouche?" Faisal asked.

"See this oval with the pictures inside?" Augustus said.

"Those pictures are writing," Faisal said. Augustus remembered explaining that to him once before. He hadn't thought the boy had paid any attention.

"Yes they are, and when they are in an oval like this they are the name of a king or queen, in this case Alexander the Great."

"So he drank wine here?"

The Englishman chuckled. "Perhaps he did. But Alexander was Macedonian, not Roman."

"Yes," Faisal nodded.

"You know what Macedonians were?"

"Um, like Romans but different."

"True as far as it goes. They are more like Greeks."

"Oh, like the tailors and the people who own the grocery stores in the nice parts of town?"

"Yes, but warriors. Alexander the Great was one of the greatest warriors in history."

They studied the artwork for a time. Moustafa began to decipher the inscriptions, writing them down in a small notebook he always carried with him. The boys got bored and began to play tag around the ruins. Claud looked at them and grinned.

"He loves having Faisal here," he told Augustus. "I suspect he misses having other children around, and he still is half a child. Sometimes I leave him down here to play with the other boys but he's an outsider and they make sure he knows it. These servant boys deserve a bit of fun."

"Faisal isn't really my servant. He's a local street urchin with a talent for making himself useful."

"Then you should hire him full time."

"Oh, I don't think—"

"And what are you gentleman doing?" a female voice said behind them.

They spun around to see Jocelyn Montjoy standing at the temple entrance, wearing her trousers, army boots, and pith helmet.

She glanced at Augustus' hand, which had instinctively gone to his pocket to grab his automatic. He let go of his gun and pulled his hand out. He hoped she hadn't realized what he had in there.

"Is everything all right?" she asked, arching an eyebrow.

"Um, yes. Perfectly. We've come to see the sights."

"This is where the Romans came to drink wine," Faisal said, holding up the amphora fragment. "They had to come to a temple because they weren't allowed to drink wine in the mosque."

"That's a very interesting interpretation of history, young man," Jocelyn said.

"So what brings you here?" Moustafa asked. Augustus heard a note of suspicion and accusation creep into the Nubian's voice.

"I heard you had driven through Biwati and decided to see how you were getting on. The local people pointed me in the right direction. I followed on Bucephalus."

"Bucephalus?" Augustus asked.

"My trusty donkey."

"You named your donkey after Alexander the Great's warhorse?"

"He is a noble animal and deserves a noble name," she said with a smile.

Augustus laughed. How charming this woman was!

She approached. "And how are you feeling, Augustus? May I call you Augustus?"

"Only if I can call you Jocelyn," he said with a bow.

"I wouldn't dream of having you call me anything else."

Augustus flushed. Compared with Zehra, Jocelyn was not a beauty, but she was kind and interesting and available.

And something about those trousers … who would have thought trousers could be fetching on a woman?

"How are things in Biwati?" Claud asked.

"Quite festive. There's a *zikr* at the Senussi mosque. There must be a large crowd inside. You can hear them chanting the ninety-nine names of God across the entire village. I've been invited to a *zikr* among the women tonight. They don't get theirs until after they feed the men, of course. All the ladies are busy with cooking at the moment, so I might as well spend time with interesting men."

That was music to Augustus's ears.

"Are there any newcomers in the village?" Claud asked.

"Not that I am aware, but as you know I am much more acquainted with the women than the men. Have you seen any caravans from your mountaintop?"

"No, but I can't keep track of all the individual travelers and small groups. Those come and go all the time."

Jocelyn laughed. "The war is over, dear boy. Not every religious rite is the forefront of an invasion."

Augustus had his doubts about that.

Claud turned to Augustus.

"I had best get back up the mountain. I can drop you off at your camp."

"I'll drive us there!" Faisal said, rushing up.

"I haven't forgotten my promise," Claud said.

"Oh dear," Jocelyn said, eyeing Faisal. "I do believe I'll ride Bucephalus."

"Nonsense," Augustus said. "We wouldn't dream of leaving you. We'll all walk."

"But I want to drive the motorcar!" Faisal whined.

"Don't worry, Augustus. You go ahead and I'll join you at your campground," Jocelyn said.

His heart leapt. She was actually making a point of spending time with him!

Moustafa turned to him.

"Boss, Herr Schäfer wanted me to make some sketches of Greco-Roman art while I was here, for possible inclusion in his book. If you don't mind, I'd like to stay. I can walk back to the camp later. It's not too far."

"Very well. I didn't know Heinrich had poached you from my service. Draw to your heart's content."

Normally Augustus would have been irritated at having his assistant leave for a side project, especially just as everything was getting interesting, but the relief at having a steady supply of medicine, combined with the proximity of such a fascinating member of the fairer sex, made him indulgent.

In a lower voice, he added, "Keep a pistol with you."

"I will. And I'll stay until well after dark. I want to see what happens here at night."

"Take care not to be seen."

Moustafa nodded and went to the motorcar to fetch his things.

When he came back, Faisal held up the amphora fragment.

"Maybe you should draw this."

Augustus could tell by the look on Moustafa's face that he was about to give his usual angry reply, but then he hesitated and said, "Oh, I think Herr Schäfer has plenty of drawings of amphorae. Why don't you keep it?"

Moustafa headed for the temple. The rest of the group strolled to Claud's stripped-down Model T, Faisal and Ahmed running ahead. Augustus wondered how much of Moustafa's interest in sketching the temple was inspired by the fear of being in a motorcar with Faisal at the wheel. Augustus felt tempted to stay and help with the sketches. If Jocelyn hadn't been mounting her donkey and urging it in the direction of their campsite, he would have.

Ahmed sat in the driver's seat with his hand on the gear shift. Faisal sat on his lap, gripping the wheel, grinning from ear to ear.

"Perhaps we should just wait here," Augustus said as they approached the motorcar.

"Trust me, we'll be safer in than out," Claud replied.

They got in, Ahmed gave some final instructions and started the engine.

Faisal shouted with glee as the motorcar moved forward, thankfully slowly, and Faisal turned the wheel this way and that. Soon they were zigzagging all around the field.

"Try to keep close to the tree line to avoid any tombs," Claud said.

"But not too close," Augustus added, gripping the side of the motorcar. He'd been in artillery barrages less frightening than this.

"Let's go faster!" Faisal shouted.

"I don't think—" Claud started.

Too late. With an excited whoop, Ahmed slammed on the gas and they shot forward.

Straight for the tree line.

"Watch out!" Augustus shouted.

Faisal yanked the wheel to the right, the car swerved onto two wheels and nearly tossed everyone overboard before righting itself.

"I thought you said we'd be safer in than out!" Augustus shouted.

"We're alive, aren't we?" Claud replied. "At least we're not heading for the trees anymore."

"Good job, little brother!" Ahmed said. "Now turn the wheel hard to the left and keep turning."

"That's not—"

Augustus didn't get to finish, because he was too busy hanging on for dear life.

The car spun in a circle, sending up waves of sand in all directions. Both boys were laughing maniacally. Then Faisal straightened out and shot forward again.

"All right, slow down," Claud said.

"Which way to camp?" Faisal asked. "I'll drive us there."

"No you will not!" Augustus said. It came out more as a plea than an order.

Ahmed pointed to a narrow gap in the trees. "It's that way. Let's see if you can make it."

Faisal zigzagged toward the path. Augustus prepared to jump out.

"That's all for now," Claud said. "Perhaps you can drive again some other time. Come now, Ahmed. Apply the brake."

Ahmed slowed down and stopped before they hit anything. It took some coaxing to get Faisal in the back seat. Once he was, Claud took the wheel and headed into the village of Biwati. The boys couldn't stop laughing.

"We should take a look at what's happening," Claud said, growing serious again. "We won't get too close. The Senussi don't like foreigners."

"I should have brought Moustafa along to act as intermediary," Augustus said.

"By now they all know that he's with you. If there's anyone they like less than foreigners, it's natives who work for foreigners."

"Some local religious boys tried to beat me up a month ago," Ahmed said.

"I bet you beat them until they were black and blue," Faisal said.

"I sure did, little brother."

A glance from Claud told Augustus that the fight hadn't been so one-sided as the youth let on.

They parked the motorcar at the edge of the village, immediately attracting a curious crowd of children. There were no men on the streets, and the women disappeared into the houses as soon as they arrived.

Claud led them up what passed for the main street—a narrow, dusty lane flanked by low houses of mud brick. The houses were made of the same stuff as the ground, and looked as if they had grown out of it. The only splash of color came from the muted browns and greens of the geometric designs painted along many of the walls and windowsills. All doors and shutters were shut tight.

A gaggle of small children followed them, pestering Faisal and Ahmed with questions about what they were doing.

"Is there any way we can get rid of these little mites?" Augustus asked.

"Surely you've been in Egypt long enough to know the answer to that," Claud said with a laugh.

"We can hardly be unobtrusive with this lot following us."

"We can't be unobtrusive at all. Have you noted how so many of the windows open a crack after we pass? The womenfolk are watching us, and will report everything we do to the men. Many of the men will be at the *zikr*, while others are in the fields. Even those who chose to work and not pray are often swayed by the Senussi, so we must tread carefully."

Over the sounds of the children, they could hear chanting, a rhythmic droning that grew in volume as they went up the street.

Soon they came to a small plaza lined with larger houses, some even two stories high. An entire side of the plaza was taken up by the mosque. Enclosed by a mud brick wall ten feet high, there was little to see except a crude minaret made of the same material that didn't stand more than twenty feet tall. Next to it was a heavy wooden gate, as shut tight as the doors to the houses. Two burly men stood in front of it. They scowled as the foreigners came into view.

"Well, that's that, I suppose," Augustus said.

"Indeed," Claud replied. They spoke in English now, worried about what the village children might overhear. "It's good for me to show my face so they know we're watching."

"What about the garrison?"

"It's a mile outside of town. We'll drop by and talk with them. These gatherings are not unusual and we tend to steer clear so as to not stir things up, but given the letter that Orhan sent and the clues you've discovered, I'm worried. Something's going on here."

They walked back to the motorcar ...

... and found someone had slashed the tires and dumped camel dung on all the seats.

CHAPTER TWENTY-SIX

Moustafa felt at ease as he sat on a fallen block of the temple wall and sketched the bas-relief of Alexander offering to the gods. Herr Schäfer was sure to love this. Moustafa swelled with pride to think his drawings would go into such a great work of analysis. The scholar had allowed him to read some of the chapters in manuscript and they were brilliant. Drawings of these remote sites would add even more value to the work. Indeed, they may be the first modern sketches ever to be published. Some of the early explorers must have passed this way, but those drawings would be crude and difficult to find. Professor Harrell had no doubt drawn this scene as well, but who knows what happened to those drawings or if they would ever see the light of day?

He sat, sketch pad on his knee, a fine pen in his hand, and lost himself to the work.

Moustafa took his time. It was already past noon and he planned on staying until after sunset. He had a hunch there might be something interesting to see around here once it got dark. He had wanted to communicate that to Mr. Wall, but he certainly wasn't going to take the chance while that woman was within earshot. He didn't trust her one bit.

Mr. Wall was obviously besotted with her. Why did a man of such intelligence become such a fool in the presence of women?

Moustafa remained seated while sketching, and when he had to move to sketch another portion of the wall, he crawled there. There had been a group of peasants watching them from a distance. He hoped they hadn't noticed that he had remained behind.

One by one, he sketched each of the remaining bas-reliefs. These were mostly standard processions of deities that could be found on the walls of countless temples and tombs all along the Nile. Their conformity was what made them interesting. Herr Schäfer had pointed out the fusion of styles in the gilded mummies that had been found here. In this temple, however, Alexander had adhered closely to traditional Egyptian styles. He had obviously wanted to prove the prophecy of the oracle of Amun-Re to be true, that he was the living embodiment of the sun god and thus the pharaoh of all Egypt.

Moustafa sketched it all with care, the ancient invocations resonating in his head as he drew the corresponding hieroglyphs.

As he did so, the words of the Bedouin came back to him.

Muslims shouldn't concern themselves with such things.

That stung. He was a better Muslim than most. He didn't touch alcohol, avoided looking at women, did his five prayers. One day, God willing, he would go on the Hajj. It wasn't like he believed in any of these pagan idols. He wasn't some superstitious villager sneaking off to cast spells in old temples. That was the worst sin possible, to put another being before God …

… and yet he couldn't help feel a small kernel of doubt. When Egypt had been pagan, it had been the greatest civilization in the world. Now it was Muslim and what was it? A colony. A colony that relied upon Christians for its technology, its sciences, even its appreciation of its own past. How could such a thing be possible?

It's a test of our faith, Moustafa thought. *It has to be. God is punishing us for being weak Muslims. Look how many Egyptians skip their prayers or drink alcohol. And those belly dancing bars!*

Moustafa shuddered. He had to go to one of those dens of iniquity once on a case. The things he had seen there …

"God help me avoid temptation," he whispered.

Yes, it was all a test. He began to see the pattern now. God had allowed

Egypt to groan under the iron fist of the Mamluks and Ottomans—fellow Muslims—because the Egyptians had strayed from the narrow path. Then God had swept them away and brought in Christians—first the French, then the English—to test the Egyptians' faith. Would all that wealth, all those amazing inventions, pull the Egyptians away from the true path?

It hadn't. There were still many bad Muslims in Egypt, but it was no worse than before. No one was renouncing Islam. And there was a new, educated class of Muslims, people like Moustafa himself, who were taking the best from Western civilization while remaining true to their own. It would be these Muslims, and a few Copts too, who would bring Egypt back to its former glory.

One Copt, Marcus Simaika, had even offered him a job. The Christian was a wealthy man who scoured the land for Coptic artifacts, getting permission from the pope in Alexandria to enter the oldest monasteries and churches to collect neglected manuscripts and works of art to put in the Coptic Museum he had founded.

Moustafa had met him on a case, and Simaika had offered him a job.

"Wouldn't you rather work for an Egyptian? I could teach you Coptic, and teach you all about our art. You could come on my collection trips. Wouldn't you like to explore the storage rooms of monasteries that date back a thousand years, uncovering old manuscripts that haven't been read in centuries? Once we have our freedom we will need trained men like you to manage our heritage. There could be a place for you in the new order."

Months later, those words still sang in his ears. He still had Simaika's business card tucked away at home. Many times after a long day of work at Mr. Wall's house he would pull it out and study it. He especially did this on days when Mr. Wall was rude or took him for granted.

Wouldn't it be better to work for an Egyptian?

"Maybe so," he whispered to himself, "but right now you're working for a European and he is giving you some great opportunities. Be content with what God has written for you. Only He knows what comes next."

The light was fading and his sketches were complete. Moustafa put away his drawing materials, used a bit of water from his water skin to wash, and unrolled his prayer rug in the direction of Mecca. Faintly in the distance he could hear a muezzin in the village making the call to prayer. All up and down the Nile, and in many other countries besides, that same call was being heard. He and millions of other Muslims around the world made their submission to God. It was something they did together, and it made Moustafa fell better. All would come out as was written.

After he was done praying, he waited.

The moon rose and the stars came out. Other than the breeze blowing through the shattered stones of Alexander's temple, and the occasional far-off caw of a bird, the edge of the desert was shrouded in silence.

He lay in the sand as the last warmth seeped out of it. Tired after the long afternoon's work in the sun, Moustafa fell asleep.

When he jerked awake, the moon's thin crescent was high in the sky and the stars shone bright and clear.

He lay where he was, listening. His sleep-fogged mind had the impression that a noise had awoken him.

Then he heard it again—the sound of hushed conversation.

It came from the direction of the tomb excavated by Professor Harrell.

Moustafa peeked from behind the remains of the temple wall and spotted a small group of dark figures moving across the sand, which glowed softly in the moonlight and put them in stark relief.

There were six or seven of them, and he could see some carried picks and shovels.

They stopped at a bare stretch of sand about a hundred yards from him, a little to the left of the excavated tomb. The one in front moved his hands through the sand and pulled a rope out from beneath it. A trapdoor opened with a creak.

One by one the figures disappeared into the ground. As the last went through the trapdoor, he closed it behind him with a soft thud.

Moustafa checked his revolver was fully loaded and peered around. He saw no one else in the desert. To his left, the edge of the oasis was a dark wall of trees and shadow. He heard no sound there but the rustle of the palm fronds in the breeze.

He did not trust that tree line. A sentry could easily stand there, completely still, and remain invisible.

He waited a full minute studying every part of the tree line, and not seeing anything, tiptoed out of the ruins.

After a few steps from the temple he hesitated, ready to bolt back to its cover if anyone fired, but the oasis remained still and silent but for the waving fronds of the palms. He moved toward the trap door.

He barely made it halfway there before two silent figures burst out of the shadows of the tree line and sprinted for him. They wore the loose, dark robes of the Bedouin, the bottom half of their faces covered with the edge of their *keffiyehs*. Moonlight glinted off the metal of their scimitars.

Moustafa smiled. They had spotted him from the start, but waited until he had nowhere to run before showing themselves. Now they rushed him like they had the advantage. The fools had obviously not seen his gun.

He waited until they were twenty yards away before he held his pistol high and said in loud, clear voice, "If you don't want to get shot, you'll drop your weapons."

Their response was not what he anticipated.

Like trained fighters, they split up, angling in different directions while still advancing. Both pulled guns from their pockets.

Moustafa fired at the one on the left. The man spun and fell. Moustafa dropped to one knee a split second before the man on the right fired, and his bullet hummed over Moustafa's head.

Moustafa fired a second time, but his aim was off and instead of hitting the man's body, he hit the man's pistol, making it fly from his gun.

Good enough.

Moustafa stood, leveling his pistol.

"All right. Now you drop your sword and we'll—"

"God is great!" the man shouted, rushing for him.

Moustafa couldn't believe it. The fellow was still several paces from him. This was suicide.

Moustafa aimed for his head and fired.

The trigger stuck, the cylinder moving only slightly, the hammer pulling back a little and stopping.

Moustafa backpedaled, slapped the cylinder, and tried to fire again.

Nothing.

What a time for his pistol to jam!

Then the man was upon him.

Moustafa ducked to the side as the scimitar slashed down, flashing in the moonlight. He backed away, grabbing his pistol by the barrel and holding it like a club.

He had to back away even further as the man slashed again, nearly opening up Moustafa's chest.

Moustafa kept backpedaling, angling to the left to try to grab the gun of the Bedouin he had shot.

The remaining Bedouin anticipated this move and positioned himself to block him. To do so required him to stop his charge and that gave Moustafa the chance to do the smartest thing he could think of—run.

He bolted for the temple, the only bit of cover close by. He heard the soft patter of bare feet on the sand behind him.

Moustafa glanced over his shoulder. The man was gaining on him. In his bloodlust, the fool hadn't thought to pick up his friend's gun.

It didn't matter. He was armed with a scimitar and Moustafa only had a useless revolver.

Moustafa vaulted over the low wall of the temple just as the Bedouin slashed at him, cutting the tail end of Moustafa's robe.

Moustafa spun around, ready to club him if the man tried to jump over the wall, but the Bedouin was too smart for that. He ran a few paces to the right and through a gap in the masonry.

That gave time for Moustafa to try and unjam the revolver. No luck. He thought he had cleaned it thoroughly after the sandstorm. More sand must have gotten into the works after that.

The man was upon him again. Moustafa blocked his blade with the pistol, the clang of metal on metal loud in the night.

Moustafa ducked behind a pillar tall enough to block the Bedouin's next swing, but the lithe man stepped around it quickly enough to make

Moustafa back away and lose the shelter.

Moustafa knew he had to think of something quick. It was only a matter of moments before this fellow gutted him like a fish.

He backpedaled again, then stumbled and fell.

The Bedouin let out a triumphant cry and stepped forward, raising his scimitar high …

… and giving Moustafa enough time to grab a handful of sand and throw it in his face.

Then he threw the pistol.

The gun hit the Bedouin in the cheekbone, causing him to stagger back.

Moustafa scrambled to his feet, grabbed his opponent's sword arm, and gave him three hard punches to the stomach. Then he slammed the Bedouin's head against a block of stone, leaving a spatter of blood as the man's face split open.

The scimitar fell to the ground. Moustafa lifted the man up and was about to break his back on a nearby stone when the cocking of a rifle made him freeze.

Five dark figures stood in a semicircle. All had rifles trained on him. Beyond, he could see the trapdoor in the desert had reopened. More men issued from it.

"Let him go," one of the figures ordered.

Moustafa lifted the man higher and shook him. "Back off or I'll kill him."

"Kill him and we'll kill you," came the response. "Let him go and you will live to see dawn."

"And the sunset after that?" Moustafa asked.

"That depends on you."

Moustafa hesitated, then let out a sigh and put the man back on his feet. The Bedouin staggered away and Moustafa raised his hands in the air.

He was their prisoner.

CHAPTER TWENTY-SEVEN

How could anyone do such a thing to that wonderful motorcar? The motorcar was a mess. Claud stomped around and shouted a bunch of bad words—Faisal didn't need to know English to know they were bad—and they headed off to the army base a couple of miles away. Claud told them his fellow soldiers would come with another motorcar and help him fix everything.

They wouldn't be able to fix Faisal's Roman jug. He had left it on the back seat and the vandals had thrown it against a stone, smashing it into a thousand pieces.

Why would they do that?

As they passed through Biwati, they saw the streets were deserted. Even the children had disappeared. Faisal could still hear the men chanting in the mosque. He kept close to the Englishman, who had his hand in the pocket where he kept his gun. That wasn't a good sign.

"Are they going to attack us?" Faisal asked.

"They very well might. Once we get to the soldiers we should go straight to the temple and pick up Moustafa."

"They won't attack him," Claud replied. "This sort of thing never escalates into violence."

"Are you quite certain?" the Englishman asked.

"Don't worry. Petty vandalism is quite common. I was a fool to leave the motorcar for even a moment. When the army puts up notices, they get pulled down. If we order food from the market, half the time it's spoiled. And the troops aren't allowed to come into town alone. I only get free reign because I'm a scout."

"Still, perhaps we should check on Moustafa."

"That would give away his position. The peasants had moved off before we left him there, so they will assume he is with us, or back at camp. Leave him alone to scout and then he can come back under cover of darkness."

The Englishman nodded. "Yes, I suppose he'll be all right."

"Why does everyone here hate the English?" Faisal asked.

"They don't all hate the English," Claud replied. "That mosque is part of a religious order called the Senussi. They want to kick out all the foreigners from North Africa. But they're a hard lot, and many of the locals don't like them. The Senussi try to stop them making date palm wine and smoking and praying at saint's tombs."

Faisal thought about this. Many of the fellahin along the Nile drank date palm wine. It was alcohol and bad, but what was wrong with smoking and praying at the tombs of holy men? Everyone did that.

As they passed through the palm groves, heading for the base, a few men tending the palm trees stopped their work and came over to greet them.

"Why are you walking, Mr. Claud?" one of them asked.

"Oh, hello Mohammed. Someone wrecked my Model T."

"Bah! The village has gone mad with religion. Come, we will escort you to the base so there will be no trouble."

"That's quite all right," the Englishman said. They all turned and stared at his mask. "We wouldn't want to cause trouble between you and your neighbors."

"They are the ones who cause trouble," another farmer said. "During the war, when the Senussi took over the oasis, they stole all the food. We nearly starved! And they took away many young men to join their army."

"I'm sorry to hear that," the Englishman said.

The men walked to either side of them, holding their sickles. The groves seemed to have no limit. Faisal had never been to an oasis before, and he had always imagined a little place, like an island in the Nile surrounded not by water but by sand. Maybe twenty palm trees and a little well at most. This place was so much bigger. The date palms gave cool shade, and every now and then the groves open up into cultivated fields. Everywhere there were little channels of water. They passed another hot spring where some men were bathing. Faisal felt like stripping off and taking a dip, but Claud and the Englishman obviously wanted to get to the base as fast as possible so he didn't ask.

One of the farmers smiled down at him.

"So, Mr. Claud has another servant!" he said.

"Oh no, I work for the other Englishman," Faisal told him.

The man bent closer. "Why does he wear that thing on his face?"

"A German cannon tore his face apart."

"God protect him," the farmer said, shaking his head. "The war was a scourge upon this land. The soldiers tell me it was even worse in Europe."

"You know the soldiers?"

"We trade with them. Many farmers won't, or will try to cheat them, but we are at peace with the English. And they give us a good price."

"Foreigners don't know the prices of things," Faisal agreed. "You can make good money off them."

The man laughed and patted him on the shoulder. "You are a clever boy, I see."

Faisal grinned.

The army base was a lot smaller than Faisal imagined. He had imagined a place like the Citadel in Cairo, an old fort on a hill with cannons and machine guns poking out everywhere.

Instead it was only a few buildings surrounded by barbed wire and one wooden tower next to the gate. A soldier stood in the tower and two more at the gate. The buildings included one long building like the barracks in the Citadel, plus a couple of smaller ones that looked like houses, a big garage where Faisal could see some men working on motorcars, and another building from which cooking smells came out.

Faisal's stomach grumbled. They hadn't eaten in a while. Maybe the soldiers would invite them for lunch.

The peasants went back to their fields and groves and the rest of the group approached the gate. The guards talked with Claud for a minute in English and let them through.

Once they were inside, Claud turned to Ahmed and switched to Arabic.

"You boys amuse yourselves for a minute. We have to speak with the commander."

Once Claud and the Englishman had entered one of the smaller buildings, Ahmed tugged on Faisal's sleeve.

"Want to see the garage?"

Faisal forgot all about his empty stomach.

They ran for the garage. In front were two motorcars like the one Claud had, all stripped down so they weighed less and wouldn't sink into the sand. The two soldiers working on them raised their greasy hands in greeting as they spotted Ahmed.

"They know you?" Faisal asked.

"Sure! I come here all the time."

Ahmed started speaking to them in English. He spoke a bit slowly and had to repeat things sometimes so the soldiers understood, but Faisal was still impressed.

One of the motorcars had the hood up. Faisal peered inside. He had never seen an engine before. It looked really complicated with all sorts of strange metal things that connected to one another, plus some hoses and a fan. How could anyone make sense out of all this?

"You like it?" Ahmed asked.

"It's amazing."

Ahmed started explaining the engine to him, pointing out the different parts and saying lots of unfamiliar words. Faisal didn't understand much of it. He got the idea that all of these pieces moved at the same time, some pieces moving other pieces and that's how they made the wheels turn.

"You sure know a lot," Faisal told the older boy.

"Claud is teaching me everything. So are Mark and Terrence."

"Who?"

"Them," he pointed at the two soldiers.

One of the soldiers looked at Faisal and then said something to Ahmed in English, gesturing toward the inside of the garage. Ahmed nodded eagerly.

"Mark is going to show you something even better than an engine," Ahmed said.

The soldier named Mark went over to a large door that took up the entire side of the building and opened it. As the door creaked open, Faisal peered inside.

He gasped.

A motorcar stood inside, unlike any motorcar he had ever seen.

It was all covered in metal plates that looked a lot thicker and stronger than the usual sides of a motorcar. There was a metal roof too, so you couldn't see where the driver or passengers sat. Little slits on the front and sides were the only way to see in or out.

And on top of the car was the strangest thing of all.

It was a big metal thing shaped like a barrel. A machine gun poked out of the front, with another slit on top of it.

"What is this?" Faisal said, his voice hushed with awe.

"It's an armored car," Ahmed said. "Bullets can't do anything to it. Claud used one in the war against the Senussi."

"No wonder the British rule everything!"

The soldier named Mark went inside the garage and gestured for the boys to follow. Faisal hesitated at the entrance.

"It's all right, little brother."

Faisal went up to the armored car and peeked inside. It looked a lot like a regular motorcar on the inside except there were metal plates all around and some strange things he didn't recognize.

Mark rapped his knuckles on the metal.

"*Zehn*," he said in Arabic, smiling at Faisal. "Good."

"You speak Arabic?"

Mark just shook his head, laughed, and said something in English.

He pointed to Faisal and then to the metal barrel with the machine gun.

Faisal looked at it uncertainly. Mark picked him up and set him on top of the hood of the car. From there he could see that on top of the barrel was a hatch for getting inside.

Mark clambered onto the hood as well while Ahmed stood by, smiling. The soldier pointed at the machine gun, pointed at Faisal, and shook his head while saying something in English.

Faisal nodded. He didn't want to touch the machine gun anyway. He'd been in a few gunfights and knew how dangerous those things were. Plus, they made the Englishman go away in his head and Faisal didn't like that.

Mark opened the hatch and gestured for Faisal to get in. Faisal hesitated, but his excitement was stronger than his nervousness and he climbed onto the barrel. Inside were a couple of rungs like a ladder so you had something to hold. There was a seat for the person using the machine gun. It was awful cramped in there, even for someone his size, but he was used to crawling through tight spots. It came in handy when breaking into houses.

He squeezed inside and sat on the seat. He was too short to reach the slit above the machine gun and had to lift himself up to see out.

Mark's head appeared in the hatch.

"*Zehn?*"

Faisal laughed. It was the only word Mark the soldier knew, but it was the only word he needed for this. "*Zehn! Zehn!*"

Mark pointed down. Faisal got the message. He could explore more.

He got out of the machine gunner's seat and climbed down into the lower part of the armored car. It was darker in here, but less cramped. In front were two seats and the steering wheel and all the usual things you saw in a motorcar. There were also two seats in back. Strapped to the wall were pistols and a short shovel and a couple of boxes Faisal didn't dare open.

He climbed all around, looking at everything.

"Isn't it something?" Ahmed said from outside.

"It sure is," Faisal whispered.

At last he climbed out and sat at the edge of the hatch, his legs dangling inside the big barrel with the machine gun. Mark stood on the hood next to him, saying something in English that sounded friendly. He tousled Faisal's hair and pulled a small packet of paper from his pocket. He opened it up to show a piece of chocolate. This he broke into three pieces, tossing one to Ahmed, putting one in his own mouth, and offering the last to Faisal.

It was the biggest piece.

Faisal smiled at him and took it.

Mark the soldier tousled his hair again and said something in a kind voice.

As the sweet, wonderful chocolate melted in Faisal's mouth and he looked around at the armored car and the smiling soldier, he suddenly felt very strange, like he was two people, the one he was and another one standing back a bit looking at the first one.

He thought about what it was like on Ibn al-Nafis Street, and how Karim the watchman tried to beat him if he came close to the motorcar of the Englishman's friend. He thought about how everyone ignored him when he begged for food, and how the merchants in the bazaar kept a close eye on him anytime he passed by. He thought about how everyone said "Go away" or "Don't touch that."

The Englishmen did that sometimes too, but not all of them, and not all the time. What Egyptian had ever let him ride in a motorcar? Or climb inside an armored car? Or tousle his hair and give him chocolate? Mark the soldier only spoke one word of Arabic and treated him better than Egyptians who had known him for years.

Claud treated him nicely too, and Claud was from another foreign country.

Why did foreigners treat him better than Egyptians?

The feeling of being two people got stronger. When he was with the Englishman, he was useful, even trusted. The Englishman relied on him. Sure, he told him to go away sometimes, and got impatient with him a lot, but he treated him better than any Egyptian adult he knew. Even Mina's parents didn't treat him so well.

Why was it that most of his good times were with foreigners? Was he a foreigner too somehow?

He sure didn't fit in back in Cairo, none of the street kids did. They were ignored or slapped around and never made to feel part of anything. The foreigners were treated better, of course, but they weren't part of anything either. They had their own place, a separate place like the street kids.

Did this make Faisal more like the foreigners than like an Egyptian?

CHAPTER TWENTY-EIGHT

The commandant was an older officer named Major Belgrave. At sixty, with his gray hair and sizeable paunch, he looked well past his prime. But he had fought the Dervishes, the Boers, the Aro tribe, and the Turks, so was certainly sharp enough to keep the peace in this far corner of the globe. Major Belgrave was quick to give them everything they needed. They set out with two motorcars, one for them and another full of soldiers.

"A show of force is in order. The Senussi are getting too bold," Major Belgrave pronounced. "We daren't shut down the mosque and madrasa, but we can't stand by and let government property be vandalized."

Once they got to the wrecked Model T, a mechanic from base helped Claud change the tires. The boys tried to help too, but only succeeded in getting underfoot. The soldiers set out to make a slow patrol around town. They made a point of marching past the mosque more than once.

Faisal remained uncharacteristically quiet this entire time. Augustus looked at him askance once or twice. The boy stood by the side of the lane, watching the mechanic at work before looking out across the oasis and then looking back at the mechanic again. He seemed pensive, a rare state for him.

Just as the car got fitted with new tires and cleaned of camel dung, a most welcome sight came down the road.

Jocelyn.

She had left Bucephalus behind and was strolling down the dirt lane between the mud brick houses as calmly as if she was window shopping in Mayfair.

Augustus hurried up to her.

"Are you all right?"

Jocelyn looked at him curiously. "Shouldn't I be?"

"There's been a spot of trouble with the locals. They vandalized Captain Williams' motorcar."

"Oh dear. Well, it wasn't the women. We've been sipping tea and gossiping about the men. The women here are quite secluded and are thankful for some new company."

"And what are they saying about the big meeting in the mosque?"

Jocelyn glanced uncertainly in the direction of the mosque and madrasa. "They say it's just a religious meeting. It sounds larger than the others I've heard, and I got the impression that they were keeping something from me. Of course they probably know little themselves. The women here are kept in a state of ignorance. Whatever they do manage to wheedle out of their husbands isn't going to be shared with a foreigner."

"Would you care to join us for some tea back at our camp?" Augustus asked, his heart beating faster.

"Oh, that would be lovely."

"I'm afraid we must be off," Captain Williams said. "I need to get back to my post. You should be all right. As I said before, these things never escalate into violence. Keep a sharp lookout in your camp in any case. I'll come down tomorrow and check on you."

"Bring Ahmed back too!" Faisal said, jumping up and down.

"Of course," the soldier said with a grin. "I'll drive you to your camp. It's on the way."

When they got there, Farouk came up to them, his face grim.

"I have bad news, Mr. Wall. A group of farmers we didn't recognize came with some chickens to sell us, and while we were distracted, one of them got into your luggage. I think they might have stolen something."

Irritated by the interruption, Augustus apologized to Jocelyn and told Farouk to go make some tea for their guest. Jocelyn went with them, chattering away in Arabic, and Augustus searched through the baggage. His binoculars, some tinned food, and a few packets of Woodbines were gone.

"The Bedouin took the things, Englishman," Faisal whispered.

Augustus hadn't realized he was still there. "How do you know?"

"I could tell by the look on your face each time you found something gone. Things were taken from three different bags. Would the farmers have been able to distract the Bedouin for so long?"

"Hmm, I see your point."

"And they said they came selling chickens. So where are the feathers? The farmers would have held them up to show them off, and even if the Bedouin didn't buy any, there should be a few feathers around."

Augustus smiled. "You're quite the little detective."

Faisal jumped up and spun around. "You wouldn't have solved any of those murders without me. You said so."

"You're quite the little thief too. How about while I talk with Jocelyn you sneak around and try to find out where my things are. Steal them back for me."

Augustus gave a description of what was missing. Faisal nodded.

"All right. I'll wait until it's dark so they don't see me. The sun will set soon. Right now I'm going to the hot spring. Do you have any soap?"

Augustus nearly had a heart attack.

"Did you just ask me for ... soap?"

"Sure. Bathing in the hot spring feels good. It's like a hammam. After I'm done maybe you and the other Englishman would like to go."

"Oh! Um ... I don't think, she—I mean he—would want to. Anyway, here's your soap. Keep it."

Faisal ran off.

When Augustus joined Jocelyn at the small campfire the Bedouin always kept lit, he found her comfortably settled on a crate covered in blankets. Another was set nearby for him, with a third crate in between to serve as a table. Farouk and Abbas busied themselves making tea. He looked wryly at the Bedouin, so eager to show hospitality after robbing him.

"I apologize for the rather crude surroundings," he said as he sat down.

"Oh, pay it no mind. I've been living rough for many months now, and I find the desert, especially this oasis, far more comfortable than Lapland or Svalbard."

"Your Arctic journeys sound interesting. Whatever made you decide to go all the way up there?"

The woman shrugged, crossing her legs in a most fetching manner. Augustus had to admit that while he had at first been rather shocked at seeing a woman in trousers, now he saw the advantages and hoped they would one day become the fashion.

"Because it was remote, I suppose. I had traveled some with my late husband. All the usual places—France and Italy. Germany before the war. And while it was all very interesting and improving, I found myself looking at the edges of the maps, at the far north and the far south, and the blank spots in Africa and the Middle East. There's nothing that excites me more than a white area on a map. After I became widowed, I had savings and a modest pension, and so I decided to indulge myself."

"Claud tells me you've written some books."

She laughed. "They provide the excuse for my travels."

"I should like to read one."

"I don't have any at hand. My last copies went to a darling little Franciscan running an orphanage in Benghazi."

"I shall have to hunt them up in Cairo then. I know an excellent bookseller who can order anything."

"You must give me his address. I shall be in Cairo before long."

"Really?" Augustus winced at the boyish tone of glee with which he said this.

"Yes, in the autumn. I shall probably spend the summer in Bahariya. It will be too hot to travel the desert by the time my work is finished here."

"Another book?"

"I am writing about the women of the Libyan Desert. So little is known about them. Most explorers are men, you see, and don't meet the local women."

"You are the only woman I've spoken with since I left Cairo."

"How are your explorations going?" Jocelyn asked.

Augustus remembered they were posing as Egyptologists. That disguise had worn pretty thin.

"Moustafa is drawing the temple of Alexander as we speak. Today we were looking at an area I suspect is a Greco-Roman necropolis. This has been the first day of any sort of real work. Starting a bit slow, I'm afraid."

"You look much better."

"Yes, thanks to you," Augustus said, embarrassed. "The, um, pain is much relieved."

To his shock, Jocelyn put a hand on his knee. "There's no need to be embarrassed, Augustus. My brother went through the war and cannot sleep at night without his dose of opium."

Augustus looked away. He almost said that it was unmanly to wake up at night screaming, or to need a nightly dose just to keep away the nightmares like some fragile child. But to say such things would be to insult her brother too, and many other good men besides, so he said nothing.

"You mustn't feel I think ill of you," Jocelyn said. "On the contrary, I admire you. Despite all you went through here you are, making archaeological explorations and running your own business. You even found a native woman to marry."

"Married a native woman? Whatever do you mean?"

"Faisal is your son, isn't he?"

"Good Lord, no! He's a waif who has attached himself to me like a limpet."

Jocelyn smiled. "Attached to you he most certainly is. He watches you like a hawk."

"No doubt looking for the next handout. I've become a ready source of falafel and piastres."

"For such an intelligent man, Augustus, you can be extraordinarily stupid."

Augustus wasn't quite sure what she meant by that. "Well, he can be useful at times, I must admit. I'm not faulting the boy, you know. But no, I don't have a wife, native or otherwise. Have you never thought to remarry?"

Jocelyn clucked her tongue. "Heavens no. I'm not looking for a knight in shining armor. Mine fell on the field of battle and while I miss him dearly, I do not miss the state of matrimony. Now I am as free as the wind."

"But don't you get lonely?"

"Don't you?"

Augustus paused. This conversation had gone too far. If he answered with a lie, Jocelyn would see it. If he answered with the truth, he might follow up by making a fool of himself.

He turned to the Bedouin. "Farouk, is there more tea?"

They drank more tea and soon the conversation got back on a lighter vein. Jocelyn recounted her adventures among the Senussi. Augustus, remembering his purpose for being here, tried to tease out any information about the religious group's intentions.

"I didn't get to speak to many of the men, except for the boys and a few men I hired as guides. They were mostly regretful of the war. Proud, of course, with all sorts of boasts about their valor in battle, but most saw attacking Egypt as a major mistake."

"Most?"

Jocelyn took a sip of her tea and looked askance at the Bedouin. She had been speaking in English, but the automatic movement told Augustus that what she had to say was important.

"I met a few of the more ardent followers of the sect, who still clung to the idea that all foreigners needed to be kicked out of North Africa."

"I'm surprised they talked to you at all."

"'Lectured' would be the better term. Strictly speaking, the more devout Senussi will not interact with an unbeliever. This comes up against their natural curiosity and sense of hospitality. What you must remember is that these people were desert dwellers long before they were Muslims, and Muslims long before they joined the Senussi order. Old habits die hard. Whenever I met a lone Senussi in the desert, they always invited me to tea whether they wanted to or not. If I met a group, someone, willing or unwilling, would make sure I was taken care of and most of the others would pretend I didn't exist."

"You're lucky you didn't get attacked. I would never travel through that region."

Jocelyn smiled. "I wouldn't recommend that you do. As a man, you'd probably be killed. As a woman, the natives aren't sure what to think of me. It didn't always save me. In one village I was denounced as a spy. The local sheik had to spirit me away in the dead of night. He's the one who gave me Bucephalus."

"What did the Senussi think of your being English?"

Jocelyn laughed. "I told them I was Danish!"

Augustus smiled. This woman was a clever one. "Did they even know where Denmark is?"

"No, but I assured them Denmark took no part in the last war."

"You mentioned that this meeting is bigger than earlier ones. Are there newcomers in town?"

"Just today I heard some talk among the women that there are. The farmers often have a shed next to their fields if the fields are far away from their house. This allows them to stay overnight if they must rise earlier than usual or if they need to guard their crops during one of the many feuds that happen here. Several women mentioned that travelers have rented out those sheds."

"Travelers?"

"They said nothing more."

"Did they say how many of these travelers had come?"

"No. Why? You seem concerned."

"Oh, it is nothing," Augustus said.

Having already started with the lie that they were conducting excavations, he didn't want to admit the truth. Plus, he didn't want to involve her. He was aware that he had a habit of putting his associates in danger, and a woman had no place in a murder investigation. The killer with the blowgun was around here somewhere.

He realized the most chivalrous thing to do was to distance himself from her. It would keep her safer. But he found that impossible. Her company was too welcome.

They talked until sunset. The Bedouin made dinner, which did not include chicken, and they ate, Faisal sitting a bit apart. After they finished, Faisal came over and tugged on his arm.

"What is it?" Augustus asked, irritated at the interruption.

Faisal jerked his head toward the other side of camp.

"I need to speak with you," he whispered.

"Speak to me then."

Faisal glanced at Jocelyn and jerked his head toward the other side of camp again.

"Alone."

"Oh go with him, Augustus," Jocelyn said. "At his age whatever he is thinking at the moment is the most important thing in the world."

Grumbling, Augustus stood and walked with Faisal through the darkening camp.

"What is it?" he demanded.

"Moustafa isn't back yet." Faisal looked worried.

"He wanted to wait until dark and see if anything was happening around the tombs at night."

"We should be with him in case there's trouble."

Augustus was about to object, and then realized the boy was right. He had been so enthralled by that fascinating woman that he had forgotten his mission.

"Very well then. We'll wait until it's fully dark so we can go there undetected."

"Oh, I found your binoculars in Abbas's bag. I slipped them out without him seeing and put them back in yours."

"Good boy, did you find the other things?"

Faisal smiled proudly. "A pack of your cigarettes. They were already open and half were gone. I guess they smoked them. I didn't find any of the other cigarettes or the tinned food. I bet they sold them."

"And here we are stuck with them all night."

"Maybe we could go up to the mountain once we find Moustafa?" the boy asked hopefully.

"It's too far, and I have the feeling we'll be quite busy tonight. You can see your friend tomorrow. Tonight we have work to do."

Jocelyn soon left to write up her notes. Augustus and Faisal waited another hour before telling the Bedouin they were going to visit Jocelyn.

As soon as they got out of sight of camp, they left the path and sneaked through palm groves, avoiding the scattered farms. Once they got to the edge of the oasis, the low bulk of Alexander's temple a shadow in the middle distance, they watched and waited for a time. No one was about.

"I'll go fetch him," Faisal whispered.

"All right. Be careful."

Faisal moved off, his bare feet silent as they padded on the sand. The boy stuck to every shadow, every dark spot in the lighter stretch of the desert's edge. Augustus watched, impressed, as he flitted from the shadow of a rock to the shelter of a log, before crawling along behind a low rill in the sand and then scurrying to the darkness of a shrub. Anything that reflected less of the pale moonlight than the sand, Faisal stuck to, pausing and looking around before daring to expose himself as he bolted to the next bit of shelter.

Augustus nodded in approval. The boy would have done credit to any trench raiding party in No Man's Land.

He disappeared in the distance.

Augustus waited, eyes and ears alert. He saw and heard nothing but the rustle of the wind in the palm trees and the occasional cry of a night bird. He remained patient. If the war had taught him anything, it taught him to remain patient and let the specialist do his job.

"He's not there."

Augustus had turned around and half raised his pistol before he recognized Faisal's voice.

The boy was just visible as a darker shadow in the gloom of the palm grove behind him.

"How did you get back there?"

"By being quiet. You be quiet too. He's not there. I think he's been kidnapped."

"Why do you say that?"

"Something I touched. Come." His voice came out strained. Augustus followed without a word.

The boy led him further into the grove, then squatted on the sloping bank of an irrigation canal deep enough to hide them from view of the surrounding area.

Faisal stuck his hand out.

"Turn on that electric torch you have," he said.

Augustus did as he asked. The light shone on the boy's hand and he saw a dark stain on the palm and fingers.

Blood.

CHAPTER TWENTY-NINE

Moustafa half expected his captors to kill him on the spot. Instead they searched him for weapons and hustled him off into the palm groves. There they bound his hands behind his back and blindfolded him.

They remained silent. All he heard was their footsteps and the labored breathing of the two men carrying the Bedouin he had killed.

They led him along a path and then cut through some fields. He soon lost all sense of direction. All he knew was that they walked far, for at least half an hour. At last they slowed and he heard whispered voices. He was pushed forward and a door closed behind him, the dull clatter of wood on wood telling him they had barred the door from the outside.

He stood for a minute, listening. No one seemed to be with him. The voices outside sounded distant and he could not make out their words.

Squatting, he was able to rub his face against his knees until he freed himself of the blindfold.

That didn't help much. He was inside a hut of palm branches, a peaked roof just visible above. The hut was a few paces to a side and completely empty. The structure was common in villages all over Egypt and Sudan, a cheap and easily built shelter to store tools or other items. It would be easy enough to smash through a wall, but he had no doubt there were guards waiting to kill him if he did. Even if he could get out of the ropes it would be suicide to try.

And the ropes were tied securely. They had made sure of that.

So he leaned against the central column holding up the roof and waited.

About an hour later they came for him.

The beam rattled, the door opened, and a lantern shone in his face. He blinked at the sudden light and waited for his eyes to adjust.

Three men, the bottom of their faces covered by headscarves, came through the door. The one in the center held the lantern and a pistol. The two flanking him held rifles.

"Who are you?" the man holding the lantern demanded.

"A good Muslim who was attacked in the night and defended himself," Moustafa replied.

"Good Muslims do not copy ancient pictures. I looked through your things and found your drawings. I had the pleasure of using them to wipe my ass in the privy just now, and then I used water to wash myself for I realized I had only made myself dirtier."

Moustafa ground his teeth. A day's work gone because of this ignorant peasant!

"If I am found dead, things will go very badly for you," Moustafa warned.

The man with the lantern chuckled. "Oh, you mean they will try and kill us? They are trying to do that already. Now who are you and why were you spying on us?"

"I wasn't spying. I was sketching the temples and fell asleep. When I awoke I—"

The cocking of his interrogator's revolver told him that his story was not going to be accepted.

"You are a spy in the pay of the English. Just this afternoon your master went to the army base."

"He is not my master," Moustafa growled.

All three of his captors laughed.

"He is as much your master as if he bought you in the slave market in

Dongola," the man with the lantern said. "You speak to him in English and say 'Yes sir' and 'No sir' and take his pay to draw these filthy pagan pictures. You gave up your heritage and your religion in order to drive in motorcars and eat pork in European restaurants."

"You wouldn't speak to me like that if we were alone," Moustafa seethed.

"And you will not listen no matter what I say. Now tell me what you are doing here. Who told you we were here?"

Then Moustafa understood. He had suspected before but now he was certain. He had fallen into the hands of the Senussi. They were obviously here trying to foment an insurrection against the British, but how did that fit in with Professor Harrell's discoveries? And what was that hidden underground chamber near the tomb?

His interrogator raised his pistol.

"Speak."

"We are here on an archaeological excavation. I was—"

"Lie again and you're a dead man."

Silence hung in the air between them.

"You won't shoot me. Others will hear," Moustafa said with a confidence that he didn't feel.

His captor nodded.

"You are right, Nubian. We are close to a village where they have rejected the true path. So we will gag you and gut you like a lamb. And we will do it slowly until you tell us all we want to know. Hold him!"

This last was said to the two men with rifles. They slung their weapons and approached. Moustafa waited until the last moment and then lashed out with his foot, planting a hard kick in one man's stomach. He grunted and doubled over. The second man dodged back before Moustafa could regain his balance and kick again, so Moustafa charged him.

The plan was to ram into him with his shoulder, knock him over, and make a break for the open door.

That was not how it worked out.

The man with the lantern swung his pistol down, the end of the barrel striking Moustafa in the temple. Moustafa saw a flare of light, then hit the ground.

He struggled to rise, but a kick to the ribs stopped him.

Cursing, the two men with the rifles picked him up, gave him another couple of punches, and slammed him so hard into the central pillar that several palm fronds fell from the roof. They pinioned his bound arms behind him, making him hiss in pain as his arms were almost wrenched from their sockets.

The man with the lantern holstered his revolver, placed the lantern on the dirt floor, and gave him a wicked grin as he drew a curved Bedouin dagger.

"Now then, let's find out what you have to say."

Moustafa sent up a quick prayer to God to protect his wife and children.

A barked command from outside made the interrogator stop. He turned toward the door, then glanced back at Moustafa with obvious disappointment.

They let him go. One of the riflemen gave him a final punch in the stomach and they all left, barring the door behind them. Moustafa sank to the ground, his whole body aching.

There was a hushed conversation outside followed by receding footsteps. As the sound of their talk faded, Moustafa could pick up another conversation, one that sounded further away.

He perked up his ears. The language was not Arabic.

The words were so faint that it took him some time to figure out what he was hearing.

Turkish.

Moustafa struggled to his feet, walked over to the wall, and placed his ear against the thin barrier of palm fronds. He could hear more clearly now. It was definitely two men speaking to each other in Turkish. He had heard enough Turkish on the streets of Cairo to recognize the language.

Unfortunately, he didn't speak it.

Ainsley Fielding had a coded message written in Turkish. Since the war, it was doubtful any Turks would be allowed to remain in a sensitive border area such as this one. So what were they doing here? And how did that fit into Fielding's criminal operations? How did that fit into Harrell's murder?

After a while the conversation stopped. He heard nothing else except the occasional sound of movement or a cough outside his hut, no doubt from the guards. Moustafa tried to squirm out of his bonds and got nowhere. Sighing with resignation, he lay down on the floor and tried to sleep.

He did not know how long he lay there, the night growing cold around him and keeping him awake, but a muffled cry outside made him sit up. A moment later it was followed by another.

Moustafa had just managed to get to his feet when the door opened.

"Shh," whispered a dark figure, barely visible in the gloom. "Are you tied up?"

The man spoke in Arabic.

"My hands are tied behind my back," Moustafa whispered in reply.

Unseen hands fumbled around until they found his wrists, then a knife cut away the ropes. Moustafa gasped in relief and flexed his fingers.

"Come, Nubian," whispered his savior. "And be quiet about it."

He stepped outside. The crescent moon was behind a palm tree and there was not much more light outside the hut than inside. All he could see was a few dark figures clustered near the hut, and two bodies stretched out in the dirt.

Without a word, the newcomers led him along a path.

They had not gotten more than a hundred yards when there was a shout from their right, followed by a gunshot.

Everyone hit the ground. Moustafa peered through the almost pitch black undergrowth and could not see who had fired.

"Anyone hurt?" the man who had freed him asked. He sounded like the leader.

Several people replied in the negative.

It didn't matter. The sentry had done his duty.

There were shouts behind them. Several lights bobbed in the distance.

"Let's go," the leader said.

The sentry fired again. The shot went wide. Moustafa guessed the man had heard them but didn't know their exact location.

They crept along the path, keeping low and trying to keep silent.

Their pursuers didn't have to and moved faster. The lights began to draw closer.

"How are you with a gun, Nubian?" someone whispered.

"A good shot."

The man put a rifle in his hands.

"A spare from one of your guards," the shadowy figure explained. "We will hang back a little and fire on them to allow our friends to escape."

"Fair enough, considering you helped me escape," Moustafa whispered back.

His companion gave him a handful of cartridges, which Moustafa put in his pocket. He felt around the rifle, which he could barely see, and could tell it was a single-shot bolt action. He couldn't tell what make. Mr. Wall probably could. There was nothing about weapons that lunatic didn't know.

The man who had given him the rifle whispered something to the others and they departed. Then he tapped Moustafa on the shoulder and moved to the side of the path. As quietly as they could, they found a good position to lie down in the brush, rifles trained on the path. Moustafa nodded, impressed. This man was more than just a farmer. He knew how to fight. He supposed all the oasis people did. They were of Bedouin stock, after all, and for millennia had to ward off raids from their cousins who had remained in the desert.

Moustafa didn't have long to wait. The Senussi, thinking the men who had freed him were in headlong flight, rushed down the path to catch up.

He and his companion saw the flitting shadows at the same time. Both fired. In the brief flash of light Moustafa saw a man twist and fall.

Moustafa racked the bolt and placed another cartridge in the chamber. When he aimed again he didn't see anything. The Senussi had gone to ground.

He lowered his aim and fired in the general direction where they had been. He had no idea if he hit anything or not.

For a moment there was no response, and then it came from all over.

The Senussi had spread out to their front and flank and poured a steady fire of rifle and pistol shots at them. Moustafa and his companion pressed themselves flat against the earth.

"Come, Nubian," the man screamed in his ear. "We have delayed them as much as we can."

When the fire slackened, they crawled in the direction their friends had fled. Stray shots snapped through the palm grove, searching for them. Moustafa wished he had one of those flash grenades his boss had made. That would even things up a bit.

They made it about fifty yards without being hit. From the sound of the guns and the muzzle flashes, he could tell the Senussi were slowly following. Moustafa and his companion got behind a log and fired several more times in rapid succession.

"Let's go before they flank us again," the man said.

They sprang up and ran hunched over, barely seeing the palm trees in time to avoid running into them. After a moment the Senussi started firing again, but they aimed at the log and none of their bullets came close.

Within a minute Moustafa and his companion caught up to the others and together they ran down the path, across some fields, and through another palm grove. At last, after another couple of miles of running, they felt safe enough to stop.

They stood at the edge of a hamlet, perhaps ten or twelve buildings within sight of each other, their walls pale in the faint moonlight.

"This is a friendly settlement," the leader said, barely winded from the long run. "It will be safe to rest here for a while."

"Who are you?" Moustafa asked. "What's going on?"

The man approached him, pulling the keffiyeh away to reveal his face. Moustafa couldn't see him clearly, but he looked Bedouin, although all the people he had seen in the oasis appeared to be of Bedouin stock.

"Nubian, you have stepped into a fight you do not understand," the man said. "And your friends are in far greater danger than what we saved you from."

CHAPTER THIRTY

Faisal hated having to get up to pee in the middle of the night. The hours of darkness were when the djinn flitted around the countryside, seeking lone travelers to curse or possess. In Cairo, you also had to watch out for the human jackals that prowled the streets at night.

There was that danger here as well. Moustafa was still missing, and earlier in the evening they had heard the distant crackle of gunfire.

The Englishman had grown worried and moved all their animals and things to the beardless Englishman's house. Jocelyn didn't think there was any danger, but they had a talk in English and finally the three of them bunked down in the little house, barring the door and all the windows. The animals they left hobbled outside. The Bedouin left. Faisal didn't think they'd see them again. They sure wouldn't be any help if people started shooting at each other around here.

The beardless Englishman slept in the bedroom, while Faisal and his Englishman lay down on the floor with their blankets.

That had gone fine until Faisal had woken up in the dead of night. He had drunk too much of that wonderfully sweet Bedouin tea after dinner and now he had to go.

But where? He couldn't do it inside, and he didn't want to do it outside.

The hearth? No, that would stink. Out the window? The table and chairs weren't tall enough to stand on. Maybe there was an empty bottle or something that he could go in and then pour it out the window? He didn't see any.

He had no choice. He had to go outside.

The Englishman was sleeping soundly. He had left his mask on, which he never did when sleeping. Faisal guessed he was embarrassed to show his face in front of that other Englishman.

Faisal tiptoed across the room and, quietly as he could, eased the bar off the door. He spat on the hinges so they wouldn't creak when he opened it.

All this caution was to keep the beardless Englishman from waking up. His Englishman could sleep through anything.

Everything was quiet outside. The crescent moon hung low in the west and only gave a hint of light. The dark shadows of the palm trees towered over the house like huge monsters. The camels stood nearby, not looking worried at all. But of course camels wouldn't be worried. Djinn didn't go after camels and neither did bullies or bandits or those Senussi people the Englishman had been talking about. The only time camels had to worry was when there was a rich man's wedding and one got cooked on a spit.

Faisal hesitated at the door, peering into the night. He was tempted to do his business right there and hurry back inside, but one of the Englishmen might notice in the morning and get mad.

Plucking up his courage, he tiptoed away from the house to where some bushes grew not far off.

"Ahh, that's better," he whispered, trying to hurry.

"Psst. Faisal."

"GAH!"

"Quiet, you lice-ridden little fool!"

"Moustafa!" Faisal said, too loudly. He dropped to a whisper. "Moustafa. You're alive. Wait, don't look. I'm peeing."

"I know. You almost hit me."

"Sorry, but you shouldn't hide in the closest bush to the house. Where else am I supposed to go? OK, now I'm done."

Moustafa came around the bush, followed by several other figures.

"What happened? I found blood at that temple place and later we heard shooting."

"The Senussi captured me. These men live here and are against them. It looks like we have stepped into the middle of a tribal feud, Little Infidel. Where's Mr. Wall?"

"Asleep inside. When we heard the shooting we decided to move in with the other Englishman."

"That's what I figured. We went to the camp first but found it abandoned."

"The Bedouin left?"

"Yes, and that makes me nervous. They must know something is about to happen. Let's get inside and wake Mr. Wall, if we can."

"He sure does sleep soundly," Faisal agreed.

"Too soundly," Moustafa grumbled.

They left the farmers outside and entered the house. Faisal lit a lamp and knocked on the door of the beardless Englishman's bedroom to wake him up while Moustafa shook his Englishman.

To Faisal's surprise, Moustafa was actually successful.

"Ugh, what's going on?" the Englishman said groggily.

Moustafa repeated to him what had happened.

The Englishman sat up and checked his pistol. "We heard the firing and I feared something like this. Good thing I only took one tonight."

"One what?" Faisal asked.

"Um, nothing."

Jocelyn came out of the bedroom and Moustafa called in one of the farmers.

"This is Waheeb," Moustafa said. "He's the leader of a group of farmers and Bedouin merchants resisting the Senussi."

"Some of our men accompanied you to the base yesterday," Waheeb said. "We have spies among the Senussi and we got word that they had captured a Nubian. Immediately we knew he was one of your group. The village where he was kept is only four miles away. If they're going to strike, they'll be coming soon."

"I'll put the kettle on," Jocelyn said.

"We need to leave," Moustafa said.

The beardless Englishman stopped. "Leave my home? I think not. If we go out into the open, we'll get cut down. They know the land better than we do."

"We can offer you shelter," Waheeb said.

"And endanger your wives and children? No. We'll make a stand here. These walls are thick and will stop bullets." Jocelyn went back into the bedroom and emerged with a hunting rifle and a pistol. "I've never killed anything more than a gazelle, but I won't hesitate to use these."

The other men looked shocked. Faisal was confused. Why would they be so surprised that Jocelyn would be willing to fight?

The two Englishmen got into a long argument in English, waving their arms and stamping their feet. The beardless Englishman won. The conversation switched back to Arabic.

"Here's what we'll do," Jocelyn said while preparing tea. "We'll put out the lamp and lie in wait. They'll try to creep up to the house and we'll get the drop on them. Waheeb, you hide your men nearby, and once the firing starts, come at them from the rear."

Waheeb, for some reason, stared at him in wonder. Faisal scratched his head. It sounded like a good plan. Why was Waheeb so surprised that the beardless Englishman had come up with it? Sure, he was too young to grow a beard, but Faisal was even younger and he came up with good plans all the time.

After a bit more of the pointless talking adults like to do, Waheeb and his men disappeared into the night. Moustafa and the Englishman got their guns ready, loading them all and setting them where they could reach them quickly. Faisal saw enough guns that each could have three or four. The Englishman also pulled out some food tins and set them near one of the windows.

"Are we going to have a meal too?" Faisal asked, picking one up.

"Don't touch that!" the Englishman cried.

He grabbed both of Faisal's hands, then gently took the tin from him.

"What's the matter?" Faisal asked.

"This is a bomb."

"The food blows up? If you eat at Omar's roast chicken stand your stomach will feel like it's blowing up. Don't go there."

"Keep quiet and stay out of the way, Little Infidel!" Moustafa shouted.

"Quiet, we're supposed to surprise them," the Englishman said. "But do keep your hands off everything, Faisal."

Faisal went and sat in a corner. They would need him sooner or later.

They doused the lamp and sipped tea in the dark, the three adults each at a window with the shutters open a crack. The moon had set. Faisal could only see them because the starlight made the outside just a little bit brighter than the inside and he could see their silhouettes against the night.

"I heard something," Moustafa said in a faint whisper.

The Englishman crept over to Moustafa's window and looked out for a moment.

Suddenly he opened the window and tossed something out of it. He slammed the shutter closed an instant later. There was a loud bang outside and a bright flare around the edges of the shutter, so bright they left thin lines of light in Faisal's eyes.

Then Moustafa and the other two opened their shutters again and started firing out.

Faisal hid under the table.

It had happened again. Another fight. Why did the Englishman bring violence wherever he went?

The gunshots jabbed at his ears. He covered them with his hands but that didn't keep all the sound out. He could hear the thump of the bullets hitting the mud brick walls.

But not against the wall where the Englishman and Moustafa were firing out of. Had they killed all those Senussi?

The bullets hammered on the front wall, one punching a hole through the front door and making Faisal yelp. The wall where Jocelyn stood was taking a lot of hits too, but he stood his ground, taking care with each shot.

Faisal's Englishman ran over to help, while Moustafa ran to the front door.

The firing increased. The Englishman shouted something and Faisal closed his eyes, afraid of another one of those bombs. He still had lights flashing in front of his eyes from the last one.

A boom and a flash of red light through his eyelids told him he had guessed right.

Faisal opened his eyes to see both Englishmen standing side by side and pouring fire out the window. His Englishman was shouting something in English. It sounded strange, different than his normal speech, and Faisal knew he had gone away in his head again.

That was all right. He fought better when he was away in his head.

Moustafa tossed aside a rifle and grabbed a pair of pistols he had left on the table. He ran back to the window and fired both at the same time, not even flinching as a Senussi bullet tore a chunk out of the windowsill. Another two holes appeared in the door. One of the bullets smacked into the tabletop.

Faisal crawled out from under the table and headed for the bedroom on his hands and knees. The front room wasn't safe anymore.

The bedroom was dark, which normally would scare him but there was so much racket in the front room that any djinn hiding in the shadows would have flown away with their fingers in their ears.

But all that noise wasn't so loud that he couldn't hear someone smashing through the bedroom window.

CHAPTER THIRTY-ONE

The Germans had headquarters surrounded. How they got so far behind the lines was a mystery. It must be a platoon of *Sturmtruppen*. Strange they didn't attack with grenades or flamethrowers. Maybe they used up all their heavy weaponry getting here. There was enough small arms fire to keep the defenders occupied, though.

The subaltern, a lad too young to grow a beard, was holding well, taking his time and aiming his shots. Damn the generals for sending someone so young out here. The native was doing well too. Why he was here was a mystery as well. Perhaps he was from one of the labor battalions.

No time to think. Fight or die. The only two options now.

He could only see the enemy by their muzzle flares, and damn there were enough of them.

The subaltern crouched down to reload his rifle and a pistol he had laid on the floor. He himself had only a few shots left in the captured German submachine gun. He had already sent a few bursts through the brush the enemy was hiding in.

A cluster of three muzzle flares to his right caught his eye. He ignored the bullets as they flaked off chunks of the wall and directed a burst in their direction. The next time they fired he was happy to see only two muzzle flares.

Some shouting behind him made him duck and turn.

A child poked his head around the corner and said something in a foreign language, pointing into the next room.

What the Devil was a child doing in HQ? None of this made any sense.

A crash and the flare of livid yellow light was clear enough. The Germans had found a back way and were trying to smoke them out.

He ran to the doorway, almost stumbling over the boy, and sprang into the room, leading with his gun, its muzzle already spitting bullets.

But there was nothing to shoot at.

The room looked strange. The flames took up one corner under a small window. The walls looked like they were made of some sort of mud brick. No, it must be a dugout and that was soil. So why was there a window?

And what of these furnishings? A crude bed, now aflame, plus various steamer trunks, pictures on the walls, a vase with flowers. The place looked almost feminine. No maps, no kit, no weapons. This didn't look like a military base at all.

What was happening?

A lungful of smoke made him cough through his confusion and take action.

"We have to make a break through the front door!"

The subaltern and the native had already realized that. They stood side by side at the front window, pouring fire at the Germans outside.

Just as he ran for the door, the native let out a cheer and turned to him.

"Boss, the farmers have driven them off!"

Farmers?

He noticed he had a spare magazine for the submachine gun stuck in his belt. He snapped it in place. His belt didn't look regulation. Neither did his clothes. Why was his dressed as a civilian?

No, he was in uniform and the battle was still on.

As the native rushed to the back room, announcing he'd put out the fire, he strode to the door, submachine gun at the ready.

The boy stopped him, shouting something in a foreign language.

"Stay out of the line of fire!" he told the child, pushing him to one side.

The boy would not be moved. He got in front of him again and grabbed him by the ears, actually grabbed him by both ears, pulled his head down, and shouted at him in that same foreign language.

Arabic.

Arabic?

"The fight is over, you silly Englishman! We won!"

"Who are you? What is this place?"

"You're in …"

Faisal's voice trailed off as Augustus staggered back, hitting his legs against the low table and ending up sitting down hard on it. An empty magazine clattered to the floor.

Reality came crashing in on him.

They were all staring—Faisal, Moustafa, and (oh God!) Jocelyn.

"I … I am quite all right," he said, rubbing his eyes. His face was drenched in sweat. The skin around his mask itched horribly, but he didn't dare lift it to scratch the irritated skin.

Jocelyn approached him.

"Augustus, what's the matter?"

Faisal got between them and started pushing Jocelyn toward the door.

"He's fine now. Leave him alone. He's embarrassed."

"But—"

"Go make sure the Senussi are gone."

Jocelyn hesitated, then walked out the door with a final concerned glance over her shoulder.

Augustus coughed. Smoke hung in the room as a thick haze. Faisal picked up one of the blankets and flapped it, trying to get the smoke out the door. Without rising, Augustus turned to look into the bedroom. Moustafa had emptied several water jars on the bed, dousing the flames, but the smoke remained heavy in there and he came out, coughing and wiping his eyes.

"Let's get out of here, boss."

"You … go ahead. Check on the others."

Moustafa reloaded a pistol and hurried out.

"Come on, Englishman," Faisal said, coughing as he continued to flap the blanket. "It stinks in here."

"You go out too, Faisal," Augustus said, still sitting on the table.

Faisal came over and put a hand on his shoulder. "It's all right, Englishman."

Augustus looked at the floor and shook his head. "She must think I'm a complete nutter."

Faisal looked confused. "Who?"

"Um, Jocelyn. He. He must think I'm a complete nutter."

He coughed, waving his hand in front of his face. The smoke was still thick. Faisal tugged at him.

"Come on."

Reluctantly Augustus put a fresh magazine in his submachine gun and headed out the door.

He couldn't see anything. The glare of the fire and the flash of so many gunshots had left him all but blind. He ducked back inside, grabbed an electric torch, and flicked it on.

A quick check of the surroundings revealed corpses all around the house. He estimated at least a score of them, more than half clustered in the area where he had blinded them with a flash bomb and slaughtered them while they staggered around out in the open. The camels were gone, either stolen by the Senussi or taken as payment by the farmers for services rendered, he was not sure.

A cry from behind a palm tree made him spin around, leveling his submachine gun. Faisal yelped and hit the dirt. He hadn't realized the boy had followed him.

A man came out from behind the palm, his hands raised. One of them held a bloody knife.

"Don't shoot. I'm with you," the man said.

Augustus recognized him as one of the farmers.

"What happened?" Augustus asked.

"A Senussi lay wounded behind that tree," the farmer said. "I finished him off."

"You killed a wounded man?"

The farmer wiped his knife in the sand. "Of course. He might have been able to identify us."

"Don't do that again."

The farmer looked up, confused. "They are a danger."

"I want to question them."

"Too late. That was the last."

"Boss! Over here," Moustafa called from the other side of the house.

Augustus passed through a collection of corpses, from which two farmers were gathering weapons and checking pockets, and found Waheeb, Moustafa, and Jocelyn crouched near a thicket. They were speaking in low tones.

He tried not to look at Jocelyn as he came up to them.

Luckily it was Waheeb who addressed him.

"Most of my men are pursuing the remaining Senussi. The soldiers will be here soon. We will gather the Senussi weapons and go. I will come tomorrow and we will talk."

Augustus nodded. "How many did you lose?"

"Three killed. Five more injured but not badly. God willing, they will recover."

"I'll treat them," Jocelyn said, standing up. "Let me get my medical kit."

"No. We have already taken them away. We must not be here when the soldiers come or there will be questions. Now I must go."

"Send for me tomorrow and I will treat your wounded," Jocelyn said. "In this darkness the soldiers might not know where to go. I'll get their attention."

She hurried back into the house and a minute later emerged with a flare gun. The farmers were already leaving, heading in the opposite direction of the military base. Snapping a cartridge into the breach, she waited a couple of minutes to give the farmers a head start then raised it to the sky and fired. A long sputtering arc lit up the night, and the flare burst into a brilliant red star. Augustus looked away and shuddered, an image of mud flickering briefly over the sand.

By the time the soldiers arrived, with two lorries full of troops being led by an armored car, the Senussi and the farmers were long gone. Major Belgrave had come out personally. The portly man, a gun strapped to his belt and a scowl on his face, surveyed the scene in the headlights of the lorries as his men spread out to search the surrounding area.

Augustus gave him a brief account of the fight, leaving out Moustafa's capture.

"And then some other natives came out of the bushes and attacked these chaps," he concluded. "They saved us."

The major looked around again.

"Where are all their guns?"

"The other chaps took them."

Major Belgrave frowned. "And you let them?"

"It hardly seemed polite to stop them after what they did for us. Besides, we barely survived the first siege. I was in no haste to start another."

The major studied him for a moment, brow furrowed. Then looked away and said in an off-manner tone, "This oasis is awash in illegal arms. It would have been nice to get those out of circulation."

With that, he walked over to where the flash grenade had left a burn mark on the ground. A few fragments of the jam tin lay about. The major bent over and studied them. Giving Augustus a sharp look, he said, "You had better gather your things and come to the base."

"Very well." While Augustus wasn't pleased with this turn of events, he saw no way to avoid it.

Jocelyn was given a ride in the front of the lorry with the major. The rest of them got in back with the soldiers. Faisal tried to speak to them in Arabic, but none of them spoke the language and Augustus was in no mood to translate. At last the boy fell quiet, giving him and Moustafa a moment to confer.

"The good major recognized the flash bomb," Augustus told his assistant in Arabic. "He's not going to be terribly accepting of our archaeologist story anymore."

"Surely he can be relied upon to help in a murder investigation."

Moustafa kept his tone neutral, as if they were talking about routine matters. Good man.

"Except we have no authority and this is now a warzone. He might see us as pests and send us packing."

Moustafa thought for a moment.

"Did he see that German machine gun of yours, boss?"

"I think so, yes."

"Then here is what we do. Stick to the archaeology story. After he finishes questioning you I will find a good moment to take him aside and tell him that because of the war you always go about heavily armed. I will say you made those flash bombs. He knows you did anyway, and an admission from me might smooth things over."

"Won't an admission from me smooth things over more?"

"I will say the war affected you badly, boss. That you have become obsessed with weapons but are harmless enough if unprovoked."

"Well, that's hardly flattering."

"And yet true. And it is only an eccentricity. The English are very accepting of eccentricities. Tomorrow, if we are allowed to leave camp, I suggest another look around the temple area to find that trapdoor I saw."

"Won't that arouse suspicion? These oasis people are all eyes."

"I won't go during the daylight," Moustafa said. "As far as the Senussi know, I have disappeared. In the darkness of the gun battle I doubt anyone could have recognized me. If you find anything interesting I can join you at night."

"All right. I was showing interest in the temple anyway. I'll go back and see what I can see."

To his surprise, the interview with Major Belgrave was a short one. The officer questioned him again about the attack on the camp, and asked about the remains of the flash bomb. Augustus explained that he had been in the trenches and so of course knew how to make one. Major Belgrave did not ask why he would be toting one around the Western Desert.

Just as he was drifting off the sleep in an unused corner of the barracks, Moustafa tiptoed up to him.

"Boss, I spoke to the major."

"And?"

Moustafa glanced over his shoulder at the sleeping men in their orderly row of cots.

"He said he suspected as much and asked that I keep an eye on you."

"Wonderful," Augustus grumbled, turning over and putting his back to Moustafa.

Now everyone thought he was mad—his assistant, the major, and worst of all Jocelyn.

Plus, he was stuck in a barracks, a place he had sworn he would never sleep again in his life. Everything—the uniforms hanging on pegs, the pieces of kit stowed away on the shelves, the smell of boot polish and gun oil—it all reminded him of the war.

And yet none of that bothered him too much. The three drops of opium he had taken before going to bed were beginning to work their magic.

The next morning, Major Belgrave sent out a large force to scour the oasis. One squad escorted Augustus and Faisal to their old camp and to Jocelyn's house so they could gather anything they had left behind. Jocelyn was on strict instructions not to leave base.

"I cannot be responsible for a woman's safety in such conditions," the major told her.

Her response had not been pleasant.

Augustus and Faisal found the house had not been looted as they feared.

"People probably thought some soldiers stayed here last night as a trap," Faisal said.

"Hm, good luck for us," Augustus said, loading the back of a lorry with their baggage. "Now we need to give these chaps the slip. But how?"

"Give me a match and some bullets," Faisal said.

"Boys shouldn't play with matches and bullets."

"The boys who spend time with you should."

"Good Lord. Here you go."

"Wait here, and be ready to run for the temple."

Faisal disappeared, unnoticed by the soldiers standing guard. Once again Augustus was struck at how invisible the little tyke could be. Everyone overlooked him, even soldiers on duty. Augustus pretended to be looking for something in his baggage, telling the driver they would leave shortly.

Just as his excuse was wearing thin, several shots snapped though the palm grove to the east.

"Everyone down!" the sergeant in command barked. His troops didn't need to be told. Veterans to a man, they had dropped at the first shot, eyes roving the tree line, searching for the attackers.

Augustus ducked around Jocelyn's cottage and was gone.

He hadn't made it half a mile before Faisal popped out of a bush and joined him.

"What did you do?" Augustus asked.

The boy jumped into the air and spun around. "I made a little fire out of some dried palm fronds, and then threw the bullets into it."

"That's very dangerous."

"Well, I didn't stand by and watch, you silly Englishman."

An hour later they were crouching behind the remains of a pylon in the temple of Alexander. Augustus took out his binoculars.

"Good thing you got these back for me," he said. Faisal grinned.

He scanned the desert in the direction Moustafa had told him. Back in the trenches he had done this every day, with either binoculars from the support trenches or a periscope at the front line. For hours, months, he had scanned the enemy line, looking for the slightest change.

Once, in the winter of 1916, he had shivered in a freezing Flanders drizzle as he studied the enemy positions from an observation post set between the front trench and the support trench. It was a miserable heap of bricks that had once been a house. Sappers had burrowed into it, shored it up, and made a space inside just big enough for a man to lie down, with a space between two bricks no bigger than the palm of his hand to look out.

The sappers had done all this without disturbing the profile of the brick pile. As far as the Germans could see, no one had touched it.

They hadn't managed to make it waterproof, however, and the rain percolated through the pile to run down his neck and create a chilly pool in which he lay.

For hours he'd lie there—shivering, watching.

Like in peacetime, in war patience is rewarded.

About twenty yards in front of the German line stood the shattered remains of a tree, stripped long ago of its leaves and branches. Now all that remained was a stump about two feet tall.

It had been there for as long as he could remember, except that it was different now.

It took him two hours to notice the change. The trunk was pockmarked with bullet holes. Three of them made an almost straight line at a diagonal a little to the right of center.

Now the center one was a bit off from the other two.

He stared, trying to convince himself he was wrong, then he reported it to his commanding officer.

A trench mortar revealed the truth. His officer gave the crew the coordinates and they hit it on the first try. Instead of splintering, the tree trunk cracked open. Blood spurted everywhere as the man inside was torn apart.

It was a hollow steel observation point, no doubt connected to the German trench by a tunnel. Some clever German artist had studied the tree trunk and then under cover of darkness switched it with an exact duplicate.

Or almost an exact duplicate.

An eye for detail often meant the difference between life and death.

And it might now.

There.

In the middle distance, perhaps a hundred yards from the temple, he spotted a scattering of small objects shining white in the sun, brighter and paler than the surrounding desert sand.

He focused in. The sources of the reflection were too small to make out at first, but after a minute he realized what they were.

Chips of white limestone.

There were no outcroppings of limestone within sight. Why would they be there?

He scanned further with the binoculars, seeing no footprints or obvious marks where they had been wiped clean, and he saw no trapdoor.

"They cover their tracks well," he muttered.

"It was windy last night," Faisal said.

Augustus nodded.

"Now why do you think there would be chips of stone near the trapdoor Moustafa told us about?" he asked the boy.

"They are digging underground, looking for tombs so they can sell the treasure?"

"Perhaps," Augustus said, putting away the binoculars. "Or perhaps they are digging for something else."

Faisal peered around. "There's no way we can check until after dark."

"No there isn't. Let's go back."

Faisal looked concerned. "You're going to make me go down there, aren't you?"

"It won't be as dangerous as throwing bullets into a campfire."

"That's what you think."

CHAPTER THIRTY-TWO

That night Moustafa could finally rejoin the others at Mrs. Montjoy's house, which still bore numerous pockmarks from bullets and scorching around the bedroom. At least the bodies and blood had all been cleared away. Mr. Wall had decided to stay there since it was a "defensible position." Of course, the military base was much more defensible, but was too safe for Mr. Wall's taste.

Now instead of worrying about the Senussi, they had to avoid the British sentries that had been set up in a cordon around Biwati. While the soldiers could not stand at every path, they did cover every road and major lane, the one to the temple included.

The distant sound of a motor gave them a possible solution. Faisal perked up, bouncing from one foot to the other and then jumping into the air and spinning around as Captain Williams and Ahmed came into view riding in the Model T. They drove up to the cottage and screeched to a halt, sending a cloud of dust into their faces.

Captain Williams got out and shook Mr. Wall's hand. The boys ran off.

"I'm glad to see you," Mr. Wall said in a low voice. "I was wondering if you could give us a lift through the cordon."

The soldier laughed. "Want to take another look at that temple, eh? Have you gotten any leads?"

Mr. Wall told them all that had happened the previous night.

Claud grew serious. "The wireless operator at the base sent me a message. The major is requesting that I send an enquiry to the Cairo police about you."

"When was this?" Mr. Wall asked.

"Never fear. My transmitter suddenly developed some trouble."

"How very thoughtful of it," Mr. Wall commented, lighting a cigarette and offering one to the captain.

"Thank you," Captain Williams said, taking it. "I'll have to send the request soon, however, or it will be my head."

Mr. Wall lit the captain's cigarette for him.

"Are you certain he didn't send the message himself from the station at the base?"

"That wireless would have trouble reaching. Mine is more powerful and is on top of a mountain, so it's mine that we use to speak with Cairo."

What a wonderful invention, Moustafa thought. *I must ask him to suggest a book on this.*

Claud went on. "You've been having quite the adventure. This is certainly a more complete story than what I heard on the wireless. Yes, I'll keep mum about your farmer friends, and not just because they helped you. I have reason to suspect there's a turncoat at base."

"A turncoat? One of the soldiers?" Moustafa couldn't believe it.

Claud nodded, his face stony. "It must be one of Belgrave's men. None of the natives are allowed to enter. Ahmed comes and goes, of course, and your servant, but whoever is giving out information knows far more than they could ever learn."

"Such as?"

"Information about our patrols and supply convoys. There were a few attacks over the winter. A prisoner we captured told us they were the Senussi. We questioned him about who gave them information about our movements, but he either wouldn't tell or didn't know. He was just a common fighter, so more likely the latter."

"I've read nothing in the papers about this," Moustafa said.

"Actually you have. We reported them as bandit attacks. We didn't want to give the Senussi any free publicity. Might stir things up, which is what they want."

"Do you have any suspects?" Mr. Wall asked.

Captain Williams shook his head. "None, I'm afraid. And it's not for lack of trying."

"Does Major Belgrave have any suspects?"

"I haven't spoken to him about it, because I didn't want the culprit to catch wind of it and know I'm looking for him. I'm sure the major has his suspicions. The old warhorse isn't stupid. As far as I can tell, whatever investigation he's conducting is being done on the sly."

"We shouldn't go back to the base," Moustafa said.

"The major will insist, but no you should not," Captain Williams said.

"Do you think Jocelyn is safe?" Mr. Wall asked, a note of worry creeping into his voice.

"She's not a threat to the Senussi as long as she's at the base, so I think she'll be safe enough. Whoever is leaking information wouldn't want to show his hand so obviously."

"We need an excuse not to stay there," Moustafa said. "Could you invite us to stay at your house again?"

"Certainly, and I'll tell them you stayed at my house last night too. 'Very sorry, sir, I should have mentioned it. Unforgiveable oversight,'" the officer said with a smile. "But I suspect you'll be creeping around the desert and oasis all night."

"That we will," Mr. Wall said.

"We should set out, then. I'll loop around near the temple and drop you off, and then drive back to the mountain. I can't stay away from my post for too long, not with things as unsettled as this."

Moustafa looked around. "Where is the Little Infidel?"

"Perhaps he is bathing in the spring," Mr. Wall said.

"Bathing?" Moustafa had never associated that word with the gutter rat.

"He asked me for soap."

Moustafa blinked. Could that little thief be taking the first cautious steps toward civilization?

"Oh, there they are," Claud said, pointing.

Faisal and Ahmed were almost out of sight on the other side of the grove and just beyond the tree line. They were sitting on a log, with their feet on a smaller log. Ahmed was going through motions with his hands and feet while Faisal imitated them.

"What the devil are they doing?" Mr. Wall asked.

"Up to no good, I'm sure," Moustafa said. "You two, get over here!"

The boys came running up.

"Ahmed was teaching me how to drive," Faisal said.

"A log is the only thing you'll ever drive," Moustafa growled. "Stay close. We have work to do."

Faisal gulped. "You're going to make me go into a tomb again, aren't you?"

Ahmed put a hand on his shoulder. "Don't worry, I'll come along too."

Claud looked concerned. "I don't think it would be safe for you to stay down here tonight."

"But I want to be with Faisal," Ahmed whined, suddenly sounding a lot younger.

"And I want you out of the line of fire."

Ahmed groaned. "You never let me go on patrol either!"

"Of course not, I—"

Moustafa cut off what sounded to him like a longstanding argument. "We should get going."

They spent the next hour driving around the desert, looking for signs of the Senussi and finding none.

"They're a tricky lot," Captain Williams told them. "Good at hiding their tracks. I'll drop you off in the desert just out of sight of the oasis and away from any caravan route. You can stay hidden until nightfall and then creep back in and reconnoiter the area."

They did that, spending a dull, hot afternoon in the desert under the shade of a tarpaulin the captain lent them. Faisal whined about Ahmed being made to return to the mountain, adding to the dreariness of the day. Why did his boss have to bring the Little Infidel along on every case?

When the sun finally set, they returned to the temple and lay in wait for two hours. No one came into sight. It appeared that whatever the Senussi had been doing beneath that trapdoor, they had decided to suspend their activities after the fight.

Moustafa didn't try to fool himself. They may have taken heavy losses, but they were not the kind of men who would give up just because of that. They were like the Dervishes who fought the British down in the Soudan. Fired up with the righteousness of Allah, they had been convinced their cause was just.

Their cause had been just, but they had not been righteous. The leaders of the Dervishes didn't care for the common people like the Koran says good leaders should. When famine in the Soudan left entire villages starving, did the Khalifa distribute *zakat*? No, he scoured every farm for the smallest crumb to feed his armies. From what that farmer said, the Senussi had done something similar in Bahariya.

He had never had a proper conversation with any Senussi, but he had met many veterans from the army of the Mahdi and Khalifa. The rank and file were good enough men, but they believed too much in their leaders and when their blood ran hot they were utterly fearless. He remembered how his uncle's eyes lit up as he recalled the battles of twenty years before.

It did not take long to find the trapdoor. Moustafa still had a general idea where it was, and Mr. Wall had spotted those stones he thought had come from beneath the ground. After only a few minutes of feeling around the sand, Moustafa's fingers curled around a length of buried rope.

He pulled, and the trapdoor came up with a loud creak, revealing a square opening and a ladder leading down into Stygian darkness.

"Shh," Faisal said. "You'll wake every Senussi from here to Libya."

Moustafa cuffed him, making sure to do it quietly, and took an electric torch out of his pocket. He cupped his hand around it to reduce the light as he flicked it on.

Beneath they saw a tomb much like the one that Professor Harrell had discovered. It was stripped bare, the shelves containing only a few scraps of linen. This one had paintings on the walls, but it was another detail that caught his eye—heaps of rock spoil on the floor.

Poking his head further in, he shone the light around. At the far corner was a crudely hacked tunnel leading into darkness.

Moustafa handed the torch to Faisal, drew his revolver, and went down the ladder. After some coaxing from Mr. Wall, the boy followed. His boss took up the rear.

"Savages!" Moustafa growled. They had dug the tunnel right through a beautiful painting of the journey of the boat of the sun god through the sky. Now all that was visible was the tip of the prow and a few inches of the stern.

The paintings on the other walls were destroyed too. The Senussi had hacked away the faces of every figure—the gods and goddesses, the pharaoh and the *ka* of the dead people who had been laid to rest here. A perfectly preserved example of Late Period tomb art had been wrecked.

They hadn't even been digging any tunnels into the other walls. This had been simple vandalism.

He spotted more vandalism in the mummy niches. Several mummies lay there, smashed and defaced, the gilding that had once covered them having been ripped away.

Faisal shone the light down the tunnel. It ran about thirty yards before ending in a rough wall. Several picks and shovels leaned against it.

"There's not enough spoil here," Mr. Wall said, indicating the heaps of stone. "They must be disposing of it somewhere in the desert at night. I wonder what they're doing?"

"Searching for other tombs, I suppose," Moustafa said.

"Can we go now?" Faisal asked, studying the mummies like they were going to rise up and grab him.

"Quiet, Faisal," Mr. Wall said before turning back to Moustafa. "Wouldn't it be easier to check from the top? Professor Harrell said the roof was very thin. And we saw that ourselves. I would think it easier to drive a rod into the ground at various spots, hoping to break through into a tomb."

"That's true, boss, but maybe they wanted to do it in secret."

"Oh! Oh! I know what they're doing!" Faisal said.

"The troops hardly patrol this area," Mr. Wall said.

"I think they are doing it to avoid competition from other robbers," Moustafa said.

"I know what they're doing," Faisal repeated.

"I thought these affairs were all worked out among the fellahin. Isn't it usually that one or two families run the show and have to give the headman and the ulema their bit?"

"That's true along the Nile, sir, but who knows way out here?"

"I KNOW WHAT THEY'RE DOING!"

Mr. Wall and Moustafa turned to him.

"They're trying to get into the aqueducts," Faisal said like he was explaining it to a pair of halfwits.

"What aqueducts?" Moustafa asked.

"The ones that feed the water everywhere."

"Those little channels? Why would they do that? Be quiet and let us figure this out."

"No, the old tunnels! They were what the Romans and all those people used. Ahmed showed me. They go all over. Most got lost under bushes and dirt and things."

Mr. Wall rubbed his jaw. "Interesting, but why would there be one of those at the edge of the desert?"

He and Moustafa got the answer at the same time. They turned to each other.

"The temple!" they said in unison.

"Notice how this tunnel is at an angle, like it's meant to intersect a line between the oasis and the temple," Moustafa said.

Mr. Wall smacked his fist into his palm. "Yes, and once they find the tunnel, they can find the entrance into the temple. It provides enough cover to get in and out for someone approaching from the desert. They need never go into the oasis and chance being spotted."

Moustafa turned to Faisal. "Did Ahmed say they are all connected?"

"Um, I think so. They go for miles."

"A perfect way to get troops to key positions within the oasis," Mr.

Wall said.

"But they can't get large numbers of troops to the oasis, not with Captain Williams watching. He said there are patrols out in the desert too."

"No, but remember he told us they can't check all lone travelers or small parties? I bet they've been filtering in for some time."

"They can't bring enough in to attack the base. We stood them off and there were only two of us."

"Three," Faisal said.

"I didn't see you helping!" Moustafa growled. "At least you kept out of the way for once."

"The other Englishman helped."

Moustafa and his boss exchanged glances.

"How silly of me," Mr. Wall said to please the child. "Of course there were three. But even so, the Senussi put in a pretty poor showing."

"We knew they were coming, boss. With this tunnel, the men at the base won't have it so easy."

"We still have the manpower problem. They can't get the numbers anywhere near the oasis without Claud seeing them. And of those already here, we must have bled them dry."

"Perhaps they will send a group to take over the mountain and then a large force hiding out in the desert will come rushing in."

Mr. Wall shook his head. "This bunch are too savvy for that. They'll know about the wireless at base, and they'll know that if Claud doesn't check in, the soldiers will know something's wrong. No, I think they're not waiting for a large force, but a small one. Maybe only one or two men."

"What could one or two men do?" Faisal asked.

"If you had been in the war you wouldn't ask that," Mr. Wall said.

Faisal shuddered. "I don't want to go to one of those European wars."

"Um, no. What I mean is that a couple of men with three or four camels could bring in all sorts of hardware that would balance the scales—a trench mortar, or a case of grenades. Maybe even a disassembled field gun wrapped up to look like sacks of cloth."

"The Senussi smashed an Italian army in the last war. They took everything from machine guns to trucks," Moustafa said, wondering at the odd sense of pride he felt at that.

"Much was taken back by our lads, but you're right, there still must be a lot of it about." He turned to Faisal. "You say Ahmed knows about these tunnels?"

"Sure. He showed me the entrance to one. It's not far from our camp."

"Right where a bunch of British soldiers are on guard. That won't do."

Moustafa suppressed a groan. Once again, Mr. Wall wanted to solve everything himself. He didn't want to bring in the army, even though this was an army matter.

"Ahmed knows about other tunnels. He knows everything about Bahariya," Faisal said.

Moustafa nodded. At least the other boy was good for something. "The captain said he would come down the mountain tomorrow morning to see us, and keep up the sham that we went up with him."

"I hope he brings Ahmed," Mr. Wall said.

"Of course he will, you silly Englishman, they go everywhere together."

"He better," Moustafa said, eyeing the tunnel. "Because if I'm estimating the distance correctly, this tunnel is almost finished."

CHAPTER THIRTY-THREE

Faisal did not like the look of this tunnel.

Ahmed had led them to a palm grove a couple of miles from the base, where a few farms stood out of sight behind a thick screen of trees. A couple of farmers had spotted them, but Claud's uniform had scared them off. He hoped they were the good Bahariyans and not the Senussi.

But he was more worried about this tunnel than a whole army of Senussi.

It was set into a small rise of ground and surrounded by date palms. The entrance was mostly filled in and just big enough to fit Ahmed, and so overgrown that Faisal hadn't seen it until they were standing right in front of it.

The adults couldn't fit through at all. Just his luck.

"Careful, there might be scorpions or snakes here," Ahmed said.

"I'm more worried about djinn."

"Stop speaking nonsense!" Moustafa barked. "But be careful of scorpions and snakes."

They grabbed a couple of fallen palm fronds, stripped the dried greenery off them, and used the hard wooden spines with their sharp edges to beat back the bushes in front of the entrance. Lots of bugs scuttled out. Faisal and Ahmed jumped away.

"Just bugs, nothing dangerous," Ahmed said.

Faisal didn't reply. He knew the older boy was trying to make him feel better. Nothing was going to make him feel better about this.

The Englishman handed Faisal his electric torch. Faisal fiddled with it. All you had to do was push a little knob on the side forward and light came out. The Europeans had so many nice things.

"Be careful in there," the Englishman said.

If the Englishman wanted them to be careful, he wouldn't be sending them in there at all. Faisal didn't bother to say that. Moustafa would only shout at him and the Englishman would say something silly like there were no djinn to worry about.

They moved past the brush and into the shadowy tunnel, the air becoming moist and cool. Faisal turned on the electric torch.

"Is Augustus going to allow you to keep that?" Ahmed asked.

"You shouldn't call them by their first name. Not even Moustafa does that with foreigners."

"Why not?"

Faisal shrugged. He wasn't quite sure. He called lots of Egyptian adults by their first name. Somehow he knew the foreign adults wouldn't like it, though.

"Did he give it to you?" Ahmed asked again.

"No. Just lent it," Faisal said. They had only stepped a few paces inside. He shone the torch down the aqueduct. They stood on a slope of sand that had partially filled in the tunnel. Further down, he could see it was clear and unblocked. The electric torch reached pretty far, shining off the stone walls and dark water, but beyond lay only shadows. That worried him.

"I'd like one of those," Ahmed said.

"So would I, but how could I afford the batteries? Keep quiet, we don't know what's in here."

Ahmed had obviously never broken into a house or anything. He didn't know when he needed to be quiet.

They moved forward. The aqueduct was cut into the rock to make a tunnel just wide enough for him and Ahmed to walk side by side and a bit taller than a grown man. Within a couple of paces from the entrance it sloped down into water, which was cool and came up to his knees. The tunnel ran straight as an arrow as far as the light could reach.

"This is heading in the direction of the temple, just like Augustus thought it would," Ahmed said, his voice echoing down the tunnel.

"Shh."

Ahmed nodded, realizing his mistake.

They waded into the water, Faisal gritting his teeth at the noise they made. There was no way they could walk quietly through this much water. It splashed with every step. He might be able to sneak through it alone, maybe, but not with Ahmed, and there was no way he was going any further without Ahmed.

They continued, Faisal shivering a bit from fear and the cold air and water. The bottom of the tunnel was sand, unlike the stone walls and ceiling. Faisal and Ahmed kept stumbling over rocks and other objects lying on the bottom. He didn't even want to think what else might be hiding in the inky water. Good thing he had kept his sandals on.

After the heat of day outside, this felt like a Cairo alley in wintertime. He clutched his charm, hoping it would protect him against water djinn like it had against desert djinn. But what would protect him against the Senussi? Sure, they couldn't have come in the way he and Ahmed had, but there must be plenty of other ways inside.

That's what the adults were hoping. Of course they hadn't wanted to spend the time looking for an entrance they could fit in. Instead they had insisted Faisal explore the one entrance Ahmed knew about near the temple.

Every few steps, Faisal glanced over his shoulder at the dwindling light of the entrance. He really didn't want to be doing this.

Then a thought came to him.

"If this was cut out of stone, why are we walking on sand?" he asked in a whisper.

"There's stone underneath the sand. A lot of these tunnels have filled up," Ahmed explained. "That's why they've been forgotten. I've found entrances to aqueducts that were totally full of sand."

"How could the people here forget they built something like this? It looks like it took a lot of work."

The tunnel continued straight and empty. Faisal had more confidence now that no Senussi were down here to hear them. The djinn would spot them whether they spoke or not. Still, he kept his voice down.

"Because the people alive today didn't build them," Ahmed said. "Not even their great-grandparents did. Claud says that some of the aqueducts were built by the Persians, or even earlier, maybe in the New Kingdom."

Faisal nodded like he knew what the older boy was talking about. He had heard of the Persians. They had invaded Egypt a long time ago from somewhere. Maybe Europe. He didn't know what the New Kingdom was. Moustafa and the Englishman talked about it sometimes but Faisal had never asked them what they meant.

Ahmed looked around at the tunnel.

"You know, people who have lived all their lives here don't know about this place, and we do."

"And the Senussi," Faisal said, watching all the shadows.

Ahmed didn't look worried.

"It's like when Claud and I go out to the ruins and kick around in the sand. We always find old things people haven't seen in thousands of years. I like these old places. Back in the Fayoum I went to the pyramids."

"The Fayoum is near Cairo?" That would be good. Once Ahmed moved back they could visit each other.

"No, it's pretty far. A couple of days by steamboat."

"But the pyramids are near Cairo. I've seen them."

"The Fayoum pyramids are different pyramids."

"Oh, right. Those."

Ahmed laughed. "It's all right, little brother. Lots of Egyptians don't know their country. They're stuck in Cairo or a village and never get to go anywhere."

"We get to go lots of places," Faisal grumbled, looking around. "Dark places full of snakes and djinn and people with guns."

They came to a heap of sand that almost blocked their path. A small hole in the ceiling let in some feeble light. Faisal could see the hole was choked with dried palm fronds and leaves and other things.

"This is one of the access holes," Ahmed said. "In the old times they'd lower buckets down to get the water. And they could climb down with a ladder to clear out the tunnel."

"Just that one little hole to water all the fields above?"

"Oh no, we've passed plenty but we couldn't see them because they're all blocked up."

"And so is this tunnel. I guess we have to go back," Faisal said, turning around and glancing hopefully at Ahmed.

"We can dig out the sand a bit and crawl through. We need to see what's on the other side."

Faisal slumped.

"I knew you were going to say that."

They got to work. There was already a small space between the mound of sand and the ceiling, which they cleared enough to crawl through. Then, out of curiosity, they cleared away some of the brush and sticks to peek out to the surface. They found themselves in a dry field with only a few scrawny palm trees and withered bushes scattered about, one of the patches of desert that Faisal had seen in parts of the oasis where the water didn't reach.

But it had been watered once. The aqueduct proved it. How could someone forget to water their field? Maybe there was a war or something.

"Hey, look," Ahmed said.

Ahmed had already slid down the far side of the mound of sand. He was pointing at some shape on the wall.

"Shine your torch on this," he said.

Faisal slid down the sand and did what he asked. It was some of the old picture writing, carved into the wall. Faisal saw an ibis and a little squiggly thing and what looked like an eye.

"What does it say?" Faisal asked.

"I don't know," Ahmed said with a shrug. "When I'm a man I'm going to be an Egyptologist, but not like your Englishman. I'm going to be one of the ones who does the digs and shows off what they find in Cairo. They get in the newspaper even. Imagine that, 'Dr. Fakhry makes amazing discovery.'"

"Wow."

Faisal had never thought he could be in a newspaper, unless he was caught stealing something really valuable. Newspapers were good for lighting fires or stuffing inside your djellaba on cold nights so you could sleep better. He couldn't even read the newspaper. Ahmed could. Ahmed could do everything. He could drive and cook good food and play football. That got Ahmed a good job and a nice place to live.

And that got Faisal to thinking, and thinking about anything was better than thinking about this dark tunnel with its water and its shadows and its drippy noises. As they continued down the tunnel, Faisal thought about how the Englishman only wanted him around when there was trouble. Sometimes he'd beg from the Englishman on his evening walks. He was usually good for a piastre or two, but he soon got impatient if Faisal stuck around too long. And if the Englishman knew he was living on the roof, there would be a lot of shouting, that was for sure. And that shouting would end with Faisal living in an alley again.

But Ahmed got to live with Claud and had his own room and everything. Why did Ahmed get these things and Faisal didn't?

It must be because Ahmed was useful all of the time and Faisal was only useful part of the time.

But that wasn't true! He guarded the Englishman's house from robbers and djinn. The Englishman didn't know that. He only saw the things he asked him to do.

Like now.

So he needed to prove to the Englishman he was useful all of the time.

But how was he supposed to do that? The Englishman didn't want him around to cook or check the engine of the motorcar. He only wanted him around for the dangerous things.

Suddenly Faisal stopped thinking about the Englishman. They had come to an intersection. The underground aqueduct ran off in three directions.

To the right, the tunnel was filled in with sand just beyond the intersection. The tunnel to the left was mostly filled in too and looked like it got worse further on, while the one that went straight ahead was clear as far as they could see.

"Which way?" Faisal asked.

Ahmed shrugged. "I guess straight. That's the easiest. I think it's still leading toward the temple. It's hard to tell, though. The tunnel could be turning a little bit and we wouldn't notice."

"What if there are more tunnels? What if we get lost down here?" Faisal said. He wasn't sure how long they had been underground already, and he didn't know how long the batteries in the electric torch would last. If the thing went out while they were so far from the entrance, they would die for sure.

"Let's keep going straight no matter what happens," Ahmed suggested. "That way we can't get lost."

That sounded like a good idea. It was the clearest route anyway.

They were just moving past the intersection when a noise down the right-hand tunnel made them stop cold.

Muffled voices came from that way.

At least he thought they were voices. The noises were so faint, so blunted by the mound of sand, that it was more a hint of sound than an actual noise. But his gut reaction was that they were voices. It was like hearing conversation inside a house while you were trying to sleep in the alley outside. The noise was more felt than heard.

Faisal felt his skin prickle. Was it djinn or Senussi? He couldn't decide which would be worse.

But how could they be hearing the sounds at all?

They peered at the heap of sand and debris blocking the path, but couldn't see an opening.

"Turn off the torch," Ahmed whispered.

"Are you crazy?"

Ahmed nudged him. "Just for a minute."

Faisal gulped, but he had a good idea why Ahmed wanted him to do it, so he did it.

He clicked the button and the aqueduct was plunged into darkness.

For a moment there was silence. Faisal saw nothing but black.

Then his eyes began to adjust. The faintest wisp of light, a reflection of a reflection, came to him from the direction they had been headed. A bit of light filtering through one of those blocked holes in the ceiling? He hoped so. He hoped it wasn't something dangerous.

In the direction of the blocked tunnel, he heard the sound again. Yes, it was definitely voices, but they had changed in tone. Closer, and yet softer, as if they were hushed and whispering.

A crunch of sand. A twig snapped, a little sound that sounded like a pistol shot in the general silence of the dark. Faisal jumped.

Then came a sound that weakened Faisal's knees and almost sent him screaming blindly back the way they had come.

The regular scraping of a shovel on sand.

It came from the heap of debris blocking the tunnel. There could be no mistake. Some people were on the other side digging in Faisal and Ahmed's direction.

Faisal reached out and gripped Ahmed. The bigger boy hadn't moved. That reassured Faisal a bit. He wasn't alone.

Then Ahmed started to tremble just as much as Faisal was. That made Faisal even more scared.

The scraping continued. The voices had stopped.

Faisal tugged on Ahmed's arm, pulling him to the left and into the tunnel they had been about to go down. He felt Ahmed tense, then relax, a silent agreement to follow.

Although it terrified him to continue into the unknown, he figured it would be safer than going back the way they had come. This tunnel led somewhere. He was sure of it. All the other ways were blocked but the tunnel hadn't filled with water. That meant the way ahead was clear. They wouldn't be trapped. And the way back was long and straight. If the Senussi or whoever was on the other side of that pile of sand chased them down there, they'd catch them for sure. There might be some shelter the other way.

Or more danger.

Then he had another thought. What if the aqueduct was like a well, where the water came up to only a certain level and stayed there? The tunnel ahead could be blocked and still the rest of the aqueduct wouldn't fill. Were aqueducts the same as wells? The only aqueduct he had ever seen was the old Ottoman one that ran through Cairo, and that was above ground.

He wished he was back in Cairo now. There he knew everything. He knew how to take care of himself. Here everything was unfamiliar.

Faisal raised his feet only a little above the floor, sliding his legs forward instead of walking normally. He didn't want to make the smallest splash, nothing that the diggers could hear. He still gripped Ahmed's djellaba. Reaching out with his other hand, he touched his fingertips to the wall and used that to guide him.

For a moment he thought they'd be able to creep away. Ahmed was being just as silent as he was even though he was bigger and never had to sneak like Faisal had to every day. Yes, maybe they'd make it.

And then, disaster.

Faisal raised his foot, slid it forward, and jabbed his toe against a sharp stone.

He did not cry out, but he jerked his foot back from the pain and got off balance for a moment. Ahmed grabbed him to steady him, which only made it worse. His body twisted, and his legs made a ripple in the water that splashed against the wall.

In the silent tunnel, even that little splash and the ripple that followed it sounded as loud as one of the Englishman's gunfights.

He heard a whisper from behind them, less muffled than before. The scraping of a shovel on sand grew louder, quicker.

Faisal and Ahmed moved forward, less cautious about making sound now but still taking care. Faisal hoped the diggers wouldn't hear them because of the sound of their own shovel.

Then a faint light appeared behind them. Faisal's heart clenched.

The diggers had broken through.

Faisal turned, eyes wide. The scraping continued and the light grew brighter, bright enough to see the outline of the intersection and to reflect off the black water, still rippling from Faisal's clumsy movement.

They're seeing that, he thought. *They know which way we went.*

Faisal tugged on Ahmed's arm and they hurried down the aqueduct and into the unknown.

The light behind them grew bright enough that it illuminated their way. The tunnel continued straight, with the water knee deep and no obstructions ahead.

A shout behind them. The boys didn't bother trying to be quiet now. They splashed through the water as fast as they could, the noise echoing down the dank tunnel.

Suddenly they were caught in a bright light. Faisal glanced over his shoulder and saw not one, but two electric torches shining on them. They bobbed back and forth as the men holding them pursued.

"Come on!" Ahmed said.

"Where?" Faisal asked, his legs pumping, struggling against the water that pulled on his legs and slowed him down. This tunnel just kept going straight.

"Don't!" a man shouted from behind.

Faisal looked over his shoulder, confused as to what the man meant, and saw a third man had broken ahead of the two torches. In perfect silhouette, he could clearly see he held a pistol.

A pistol aimed at them.

One of the men carrying a torch put a hand on the man's pistol arm and stopped him from firing.

Faisal was too scared to wonder much at this good luck. They kept running. Their pursuers had stopped. After a few steps, Faisal glanced over his shoulder again, eyes blinking at the bright glow of the electric torches.

Now a new figure stood in front, backlit by the torches about forty feet behind Faisal and Ahmed. Faisal stumbled because he wasn't looking where he was going, and paused. Something about that man looked familiar. He could only see his shape, but he thought he had seen him before.

The man pulled what looked like a flute from beneath his robes and raised it to his lips.

"Little brother, come on!" Ahmed stood a few paces further down the tunnel.

Faisal leapt at his friend, hit him hard in the belly, and brought him down into the water with a splash.

Faisal didn't hear the poison dart fly over them. He didn't need to.

"Come on, and keep low!" Faisal cried.

They splashed through the water. By some miracle, the electric torch didn't turn off when it got dunked. It was one of the Englishman's war things. Maybe it was designed to get wet.

No time to think about that. The man with the blowgun was loading again.

"Those darts are poisonous, Ahmed. Careful you don't step on the one he already shot."

"How am I supposed to see it?"

Faisal didn't have an answer to that. It was underwater somewhere along their path, a little spike of death lying in wait.

More death was behind them, though. They ran.

There was a whoosh of air as a dart shot right between them.

Another intersection came into view up ahead and Faisal got an idea. He grabbed Ahmed by the sleeve and turned off the electric torch. There was still enough light to see from the Senussi's torches, but they were pretty far away and the boys were in shadow. They'd make a harder target.

Except that the two of them running side by side took up almost the whole tunnel.

When they got to the intersection, Faisal pulled Ahmed to the right just before a dart shot past.

They paused for a moment, trying to catch their breath. The sound of splashing footsteps growing closer spurred them into action.

Faisal glanced around. He could barely see anything, but he could see that the tunnel they had ducked into was nearly full of sand not ten paces from where they stood.

Almost, but not quite. There was just enough space between the sand and the ceiling for them to squeeze through, and there would be a hole to the surface on top of that big pile. It must have been totally blocked, because he could not see it, but it had to be there. Maybe they could dig their way out.

He tugged on Ahmed's sleeve again and they ran to the heap of sand and clambered up.

Once they got to the top, Faisal groaned with disappointment. The hole to the surface was blocked with a fallen palm tree.

Just then, the Senussi came around the corner.

"There they are!" one shouted, pointing.

The boys scrambled down the far side of the sand pile before another poison dart came their way.

Faisal was about to switch the torch back on when he noticed a faint glimmer up ahead.

"Look!" he said.

"Let's go, little brother. It's our only chance."

They splashed through the water, stumbling over bits of stone and sunken debris, and made it to the next heap of sand just as the Senussi torch poked over the top of the last pile and shone right on them.

At least it lit their way. Faisal could now make out the hole in the ceiling. It was blocked with palm fronds and dried sticks from bushes, the gnarled wood poking down from the surface like old fingers. They clambered up the pile of sand, cursing as it gave way beneath them and slowed their progress, and got to the top.

Faisal grabbed some sticks and hauled them down, bringing a cascade of sand down onto the two of them. Ahmed grabbed another armful and yanked it out of place. Suddenly harsh sunlight glared through the hole.

A whoosh of air and a soft *thunk* made Ahmed cry out.

"Are you hit?" Faisal said, going cold.

Ahmed held up one of the sticks he had just removed from the hole. A dart was stuck in it. The older boy tossed it aside with a shudder and hauled himself out of the hole. The upper part of his body appeared a moment later and he grabbed Faisal's arm.

Just as Ahmed lifted him up, Faisal screamed as something tugged on his djellaba.

CHAPTER THIRTY-FOUR

Augustus surveyed the two bedraggled, terrified, exhausted boys and felt a strange emotion. It took some time for him to identify it as guilt.

He hadn't felt guilt much since the war. That emotion had been burnt out of him with all the killing. He hadn't felt much fear either, death having precious little to take from him.

But these two—a child and a half-child—were afraid, and that made guilt rise up in him like a cold fist.

He may not have anything to lose, but they had everything to lose. They were at the start of their lives and he had put them in danger, not once but several times.

And he knew he would have to do it again.

They had appeared more than three hours after they had entered the tunnel, staggering up to Jocelyn's house, tired and filthy, their faces drawn and eyes wide from what they had experienced. They had babbled out an incoherent tale of being chased through the aqueduct, with Faisal adding some djinn laughing at them as poison darts flew through the air.

The part about the poison darts was true at least. As they had crawled out of the access hole, the man with the blowgun had taken a final shot at Faisal and the dart caught in the hem of the boy's djellaba. He was lucky he hadn't pricked himself before he noticed it was there. Faisal and Ahmed had then fled through the palm groves, losing their pursuers and making their way back. As they arrived, Faisal had presented Augustus and Moustafa with the dart.

They sat the boys down and took the liberty of using Jocelyn's kitchen to brew them some tea. The woman was still confined to barracks on base, Major Belgrave not wishing to risk the life of one of the King's female subjects in the current situation.

Their own absence would be missed soon enough as well. Claud had had to return to the mountaintop. Hopefully he had left an excuse on their behalf with the soldiers at the nearby road.

Once the boys had drunk some tea, eaten a large heap of dates, and calmed down enough to form coherent sentences, he got a more sensible story out of them.

It was just as he had suspected. The Senussi were exploring the old aqueducts to find a way to surprise the troops. The base stood right in the middle of Bahariya Oasis. There was a high probability that an aqueduct passed close to it, or even beneath it.

A good thing Ahmed had alerted them to that possibility. These little mites came in handy sometimes.

That still didn't explain Dr. Harrell's involvement, or the involvement of the secret group in the Geographical Association.

"So tell me more about this tunnel."

"It kept going straight," Faisal said. "We think it goes to the temple but we had to take another way to escape from the Senussi. We came out near our old camp and the hot spring."

"Then the Senussi could be on us at any moment," Moustafa said, grabbing a gun and going to the window.

"There's a patrol between that place and this house," Ahmed said.

Moustafa shrugged. "So? You got around them."

Augustus scratched his chin. Yes, the soldiers stuck to the town and the main paths. They didn't have the numbers to patrol the palm groves, and venturing into them would put them at greater risk of ambush.

"We saw some old picture writing," Faisal said. "Egyptians built the tunnel."

"Are you reading hieroglyphs now?" Augustus said, amused.

"What are hieroglyphs?"

Ahmed nudged him. "Ancient Egyptian writing, dummy."

"Oh right," Faisal said, nodding. "Those. Yes, we found that."

Augustus had his doubts. "Are you sure? What did it look like? A bunch of triangles all clumped together and carved in rows?"

"No, picture writing like I said."

So not Persian, then. And the boy would have recognized Latin letters even if he couldn't read them.

So that meant that particular aqueduct really was Egyptian.

And that meant that it no doubt connected the temple to the oasis interior.

"You boys have done well."

Faisal grinned from ear to ear. Ahmed only nodded and sipped his tea.

"We need to explore that tunnel further," Augustus told them.

Faisal's grin vanished.

"Don't worry, we're coming with you this time."

"That makes me worry more, Englishman. Danger follows you."

Again that feeling of guilt. The boy had already suffered a sandstorm, a gunfight, nearly getting stung by a scorpion, and being chased by the Senussi.

Maybe I should leave him behind. I could have Claud drive him to the base and leave him there.

The moment after he thought about it, he realized he wouldn't do it. Faisal was too useful.

This isn't your choice, he reminded himself. *It's his.*

"Yes, we will be going into more danger," he said. "Perhaps it would be better if you stayed at the military base?"

Faisal looked at him like he had just been insulted.

"Who will take care of you?" the boy asked.

Augustus blinked. He glanced at Ahmed, who nodded.

"I'm coming too," the older boy said.

Augustus sighed. Their consent didn't make him feel much better about what he was leading them into.

"Very well, then. We will wait until sundown and then get started."

"But what do we do?" Faisal asked.

"We'll catch them by surprise. First, we go scout the—"

The sound of someone clearing his throat in the open doorway made them all turn.

Major Belgrave stood there, backed by a squad of men. He did not look happy.

"Sir Augustus, I'm afraid you and your ... employees will have to come with us."

Augustus tried to put on an innocent face, acutely aware that it was about as convincing as the innocent faces Faisal tried to put on after being caught pinching something.

"What's the matter, major?" he asked in a pleasant voice.

All he got was a frown in return.

"The matter is that you've ignored my instructions and given my soldiers the slip twice now. You've lied about where you were and what you've been doing. Now you're coming with us so we can find out what exactly you've been up to. And once Captain Williams comes down I'll be having some strong words with him."

Oh dear. Augustus hoped he hadn't gotten the chap into any serious trouble.

So once again Augustus and his companions had to load their things into the back of a truck under the escort of several soldiers. This time, however, they suffered the indignity of being disarmed. The men, under Major Belgrave's increasingly disapproving eye, rummaged through the baggage, pulling out one weapon after another.

Moustafa's giant Soudanese sword got the most comment until they found Augustus' flash grenades. The German submachine gun was much admired, as well as the sheer size of the rest of the collection—rifles and pistols, and knives of all varieties. Augustus thought for a minute that at least his sword cane would be spared scrutiny until Major Belgrave, surveying the arsenal laid out on a tarp next to one of the trucks, took Augustus' cane from his hands, fiddled with it a bit, and found how to twist it open and withdraw the blade.

"I must say, Sir Augustus," the major muttered, shaking his head, "I can't decide if you're a mercenary or madman."

"Isn't a private citizen allowed to defend himself?"

"Not to this extent while in a warzone and lying to an officer in the King's service. Let's go."

They headed out, Augustus and rest sitting glumly in the back of one of the trucks. The soldiers hemmed them in to keep them from jumping out the back.

Ahmed looked the most downcast of them all.

"I hope Claud doesn't get in trouble. They might make him let me go," was all he said.

"Don't worry," Faisal whispered to him. "If that happens I'll my make Englishman hire you."

Good Lord, two of them? That was a terrifying prospect.

But he had more immediate problems. How could he solve this case now that he was essentially under arrest?

The column passed through the camp's front gate. Augustus noticed the number of sentries had doubled. The trucks parked, and the two boys were instructed to go to a barracks room. A pair of soldiers went with them.

"Your servants will be kept under guard. We've been a bit too lax with Ahmed, letting him have the run of the base," Major Belgrave said. He turned to Moustafa. "You are of greater interest. I'll need to speak with you, along with your employer."

They were marched under heavy guard through the center of the camp to Major Belgrave's office. As they passed a small private officer's hut, Jocelyn stepped out and watched them with concern. Augustus felt too embarrassed to greet her with more than an abashed nod.

Soon they found themselves seated in front of the major's desk, the major studying them from across a heap of paperwork, four soldiers arrayed behind them.

"Now how about the two of you tell me what you're really doing here."

Augustus leaned forward a little and asked in a low voice. "Would it be possible to speak without the enlisted men present?"

"No."

Augustus lowered his voice further. "It's just that we have reason to believe that one of them might be passing information to—"

"To the Senussi? I arrested the culprit last night."

Augustus felt a bit disappointed. He had been looking forward to investigating the leak in the base's security and revealing the guilty part to the major with some dramatic flourish.

"Well," Augustus cleared his throat. "That's good news."

"How did you know there was a breach in our security? And what are you doing here?"

Augustus decided to counter these two questions with one of his own. "Why was the man giving information to the Senussi?"

"How about you answer my questions first."

"Oh, um," he glanced at Moustafa, who provided no succor. "Well, it's rather odd really. We came to investigate the antiquities of the area and—"

Major Belgrave's frown deepened. "If you're an Egyptologist, I'm the governor General of India."

Moustafa looked scandalized. "Mr. Wall is the most respected antiquities dealer in Cairo!"

The major barely glanced at him. "That may be so, but that doesn't explain why you suddenly show up in a remote oasis at the very moment the Senussi are planning an attack."

Augustus paused. The game was up. If he answered the major's questions, he would be confined to barracks for the rest of the action.

But if he didn't, he'd still be confined to barracks, and the base would be left vulnerable.

The skin around his mask was itching terribly again. The ride here had been a hot one, making his sensitive skin sweat under the muffling heat of the metal mask. The major hadn't even offered them a drink of water.

What to do? He yearned to solve all this himself, but he didn't see a way to do that now. The Senussi could attack at any moment, perhaps this very evening. He needed to act now.

"Major, you and your men are in more danger than you realize."

"And how is that?"

Augustus paused again, torn between impulse and honesty. He looked around the room—at the maps, the uniforms, at the young men guarding them, barely out of their teens, and let out a sigh.

"Allow me to explain."

CHAPTER THIRTY-FIVE

Mr. Wall squirmed in his seat like an uncomfortable schoolchild being brought before the teacher as he told all he knew about Dr. Harrell's murder and their subsequent findings. The major listened without interruption, then without saying a word to Moustafa's boss, called in an orderly.

"Have the wireless station tell Captain Williams to come down before nightfall. And bring those two Arab boys in here."

The two boys were led into the office, looking guiltier than ever. The major commanded Mr. Wall and Moustafa to be silent and asked for their version of events, Ahmed having to translate for Faisal.

To Moustafa's relief, the boys' version of events tallied with their own. He was even more relieved to hear Ahmed mistranslating some of Faisal's more elaborate claims.

Like not telling a major of the British Army that the Senussi had hired an army of djinn to creep out of the ground beneath the base so they could kidnap all the soldiers and take them to the City of Brass. Ahmed didn't translate that at all.

Captain Williams was having a good effect on that lad. Faisal could learn a thing or two from him.

Once they were done, Major Belgrave leaned back in his chair, folded his hands over his belly, and surveyed them.

"The most fantastic thing about your story is that I believe it."

Mr. Wall perked up. "You do? Um, I mean, of course you do."

"At first I thought you might be an arms merchant, but you were too obvious in your movements for that, and your personal arsenal was too varied. The Senussi have knives aplenty, and don't want pistols or, ahem, sword canes and broadswords. They want rifles and you only have three of those. Then there was the fight at Mrs. Montjoy's cottage, and your defense of the anti-Senussi faction. Yes, I know about them. Not as much as I'd like to, but enough. Also, you showed up well after the trouble had already started."

Mr. Wall let out a relieved sigh. "Thank you for seeing things clearly, major. I—"

"You may have come after the trouble has already started, but you've only added to it!" Major Belgrave snapped. "Not only have you brought the shooting war into the oasis itself, but you've alerted the Senussi to the fact that we know about the aqueducts. You've inflamed the natives without getting any closer to knowing who killed Dr. Harrell or why."

Mr. Wall fell silent. Moustafa didn't feel like speaking up either. It was true that they had made a mess of the investigation. Why would Dr. Harrell be killed for investigating a tomb? He had made no mention of the aqueducts in his speech, nor was there any evidence that had he found the second tomb where the Senussi were digging a tunnel. If he knew nothing about the Senussi plans, why kill him at all? Wouldn't that just attract attention?

Before Moustafa could think further along these lines, Major Belgrave continued.

"Take care, Sir Augustus. You are confined to this camp until we put down the rebellion. Do not attempt an escape. We will be watching you. As for you, Ahmed, we've been watching you for some time."

"I didn't do anything!"

The major smiled. "No you did not. At first I worried about a key officer having a native servant, but I tested you about a month ago to check your loyalty."

"You did?"

"Remember when Private Powell let slip that a patrol was going out?"

"You mean Mark? I was surprised he would tell me something he wasn't supposed to."

"Yes. We knew you were going into Biwati later for a swim. That would give you sufficient time away from our sight to relay that information to the Senussi. We sent the patrol out on the same route as we told you, with a surprise force watching the best ambush point. The Senussi never showed, proving you weren't one of them."

"Of course not! I'd never betray Claud or the British." Ahmed seemed hurt that the major had even suspected him.

"You did very well, Ahmed. You should join one of the native regiments when you're older. I'd put in a good word for you."

"Oh no, I'm going to be an Egyptologist."

Major Belgrave gestured at Mr. Wall. "Don't take any inspiration from this chap. He's nothing but trouble."

His tone was more amused than angry. Moustafa felt like telling him a thing or two about Mr. Wall. He wouldn't be so amused then.

"So who is this man you arrested, major?" Moustafa asked.

The major's lips pursed as if he had tasted something sour. "A Corporal Righton. Thoroughly bad character. He was never liked in barracks and I've had him up on minor charges on numerous occasions. He's also suspected of the theft of an army pay box."

"Really?" Moustafa had trouble believing such a thing was possible.

"Indeed. He's a mechanic and has been shuffled around a bit between regiments. His previous posting was with a regiment down in Farafra Oasis about 120 miles south of here. Their pay box was stolen last year. A suspect was arrested, Private Righton's sole friend on the base. Both were on a day's leave when the theft occurred. Two masked men ambushed the Model T bringing the pay box and overwhelmed the driver and guard. In the struggle, the driver managed to identify one of the men by a distinctive mole on his hand, and we arrested Private Righton's friend. The man has never confessed or named his accomplice, and the strongbox has never been found."

"No doubt it's buried in the desert somewhere," Moustafa said.

"Indeed. It is our belief that Corporal Righton was feeding information to the Senussi in exchange for safe passage through the desert back to Farafra, where he could retrieve the strongbox and disappear."

"But how did you identify him as the man feeding information to the Senussi?" Mr. Wall asked.

"The same way I found out about the anti-Senussi faction here. One of the farmers came to me and told me that Righton was meeting in secret with key people from the Senussi mosque. I had him tailed and found it was true."

"Has the corporal confessed?" Moustafa asked.

"No. He's been as mum as his accomplice. We know it's him, but we don't have any definitive proof. He's keeping quiet and insisting on an attorney."

Mr. Wall scratched his jaw. "This still doesn't explain the Turkish notes we found in Ainsley Fielding's office, or the Turkish conversation Moustafa heard while he was in captivity."

"I suspect some pan-Turkish elements from Constantinople are behind it," the major said. "The Ottomans were the one of the factions arming the Senussi during the last war, after all."

"But they failed last time, why try again?" Ahmed asked.

Moustafa knew the answer to that. The Mahdi's men failed time and again against the British, but they kept charging the guns.

"I can't say I know," the major said. "But they certainly are trying and that's the thing we have to worry about. I'll send out some patrols around the base to look for openings to those aqueducts you alerted me to."

"An excellent idea," Mr. Wall said. "But take care not to disturb the entrances or venture in. I have an idea of how we can turn the tables on our fundamentalist friends."

Moustafa glanced at Faisal and saw a look of despair on the boy's face.

Moustafa sympathized. Mr. Wall's "idea" no doubt involved more gunfire and more than their fair share of mortal danger.

"Would it be possible to question to prisoner?" Moustafa asked.

Major Belgrave shrugged. "I suppose. I doubt you'll get much out of him. He's keeping quiet, hoping silence will save him."

Or hoping the Senussi will save him, Moustafa thought.

The major led them to a small hut to one side of the parade ground. A sentry stood in front. The hut was barely big enough for a man to lay down and had a heavy bolt on the outside of the door.

"Open the door and have the prisoner come out," Major Belgrave ordered.

The sentry did as he was told, bringing out a thin, cunning looking man in his early twenties. His eyes shifted between the newcomers, sizing them up.

"Stand at attention, you slouch!" Major Belgrave thundered.

Corporal Righton shot him a contemptuous look. The sentry booted him in the rear and the corporal made a semblance of military posture.

"How you got through basic training I'll never know," the major grumbled.

"We know about your Ottoman friends," Moustafa said, taking a chance.

Instead of guilt or worry, all Righton's face betrayed was a momentary confusion before getting back on guard.

"The Ottomans are helping the Senussi, aren't they?" Moustafa continued. "You've been feeding them information so they can attack the base."

"I've never met an Ottoman in my whole bloody life. During the war I was stuck here the entire time, drying up in the desert and not getting a single chance to do something useful."

"A perfect posting for a useless man," Major Belgrave grumbled.

"They killed Professor Harrell," Mr. Wall said.

Righton's head jerked in the direction of the speaker, his eyes going wide before he got control of himself.

"Don't know who you mean," he muttered.

"Yes you do," Moustafa said.

"Wait, now I remember," the major said, pointing a finger at Righton. "You used to lounge about his excavation on your off hours. I thought it odd for someone as uneducated as you, but the professor never complained so I didn't think much of it. And one time I sent you into town on an errand and you came back late. I wrote you up for it."

Righton glowered at his interrogators but said nothing.

"Speak, or you will most certainly hang," Mr. Wall said.

"I have the right to legal representation," Righton mumbled, not looking at any of them.

"A big word for you, Righton," the major said. He turned to the sentry. "Private Towton, take a walk around the base and come back in five minutes."

Private Towton grinned. "Yes, sir. Gladly, sir."

The private walked away, turning the corner of the nearest building.

Then Major Belgrave did something more suitable to the Mamluk or Ottoman army than the British one.

He shoved Righton back into his cell with a strength surprising for one of his years, strode in after him, and pulled out his revolver. Righton cringed as the cold steel muzzle pressed against his temple.

"The base is in danger. My men are in danger. If the Senussi attack and you haven't told us all you know, I swear to God I will kill you and write in the report you were caught in crossfire."

Righton trembled, but got a hold of himself after a few moments. "And if I talk, will you promise not to give me the ultimate penalty?"

Major Belgrave studied him. "Very well."

Righton's eyes shifted from the major to Mr. Wall and back to the major. He paused for a moment, then came to a decision.

"I was already working for the Senussi when Dr. Harrell showed up. They told me he had been sent to help them, but that he didn't know that himself, that he was a tool in their hands."

"To do what?" Moustafa asked. "Sent by whom?"

Righton shook his head. "I don't know who sent him. The Senussi said that they had big friends in Cairo who had been bribed to help them."

"Bribed by whom?" Moustafa pressed.

Righton glared at him. "They didn't tell me because I didn't need to know."

Moustafa glared back. A traitor to his own army talking to him like that? He'd like to teach him a lesson. But the rogue had a point. There was no reason for him to know such details. Obviously it was Carl Riding, Ainsley Fielding, and the other conspirators at the Geographical Association of Egypt. And who had given them the money? The Turks? This was getting stranger and stranger.

"Go on," Major Belgrave ordered.

"The Senussi told me to keep an eye on Harrell and gain his confidence. I was to pose as a soldier doing some smuggling on the side."

The major snorted. "An easy part for you to play."

"Harrell was told that he was supposed to make contact with smugglers in the region and help them learn of a better way to get contraband in and out of the oasis."

"The tunnels," Mr. Wall said.

Righton nodded. "Harrell was a greedy bloke, a toff with a respectable job but that wasn't enough for him. Not sure what he wanted money for but he wanted it. So these people in Cairo paid him a pretty penny to help the Senussi."

"But he didn't know they were Senussi, is that right?" Moustafa asked.

"We weren't supposed to let him know. He came looking for tombs, but also to trace the underground aqueducts. The Senussi had heard of them when they had control of this place during the Great War, but they never learned their secrets. The locals wouldn't tell them. So whoever sent him from Cairo figured an English archaeologist would have better luck."

"And did he find them?"

"Some. Not the ones we needed. The Senussi wanted one that passed close to this base. He didn't like the sound of that, so I had to convince him that the army was involved in the smuggling. He let slip that he thought one aqueduct might lead from the temple of Alexander into a network that would take you here to the base, but if he found it he never told us."

"Why not?" Moustafa asked.

Righton grimaced. "Because he figured it all out. He figured out that it wasn't smugglers he was working for, but the Senussi. So he scarpered in the middle of the night. There were fewer Senussi at the oasis then than there are now, and they couldn't gather a force in time to follow him. He got away."

"Pity his patriotism didn't extend to informing us," Major Belgrave grumbled.

"Not until he learned the Ottomans were involved, and guessed just what the Senussi were up to," Mr. Wall said.

Everyone turned to him.

"Sir Thomas Russell Pasha told me Harrell made an appointment to see him. Sadly, his colleagues at the Geographical Association killed him off before he could make that appointment. I suspect that when Harrell got back, he made some inquiries and learned the extent of the conspiracy. Harrell thought he was just doing a bit of dark trading with some smugglers for extra cash. When he learned those so-called smugglers were former enemies of the empire, he panicked and left. Then back in Cairo he learned that they, and the conspirators, were being funded by radical elements among the Turks who want to strike back at the enemies who humiliated them in the last war. He had learned too much, and had to be done away with in a manner that would keep anyone else from talking."

Righton's eyes had been widening throughout Mr. Wall's speech. He started to tremble.

"I didn't know the Turks were involved," the private said. "And I didn't know they planned on attacking the base. I swear!"

"You must have suspected they'd attack," Mr. Wall said in a cool voice. "Not even one as dim as you could have failed to grasp that. As for not knowing about the Turks being involved, I believe you. You're hardly the sort to be trusted with that information."

Mr. Wall moved apart from them with the major.

"I have an idea how we can foil the attack ..." Moustafa heard him saying before they moved out of earshot.

Faisal stared at them. "Is the Englishman going to make us go in those aqueducts again?"

"Almost certainly," Moustafa replied, feeling sorry for the boy.

"The Senussi were lucky to find those aqueducts. Ahmed says hardly anyone in Bahariya knows where they are, and absolutely no one knows where they all go. We peeked out one of the holes in the ceiling and only found dry sand. They had forgotten it was even there and let their field dry up!"

Moustafa sighed. "The Egyptians were great once and have lost so much."

"The Nubians too?"

Moustafa shook his head. "The Nubians even more."

"Why?"

Moustafa clucked his tongue but didn't answer.

"Why did the Egyptians and Nubians forget so much?" Faisal persisted.

"Stop asking silly questions!"

A minute later, the boy's worst fears were confirmed.

Mr. Wall came up to them.

"The major and I have hit on a plan. We are going to pretend we suspect nothing, but the troops in the base will be on high alert. We believe the Senussi and their Turkish advisors will come through the aqueducts tonight with whatever surprise they have in store for us. There are still a couple of hours of daylight left, time enough to find the entrance and scout the tunnels to find a good spot for an ambush."

"And you want me to go and look," Faisal groaned.

"I'll come too, little brother," Ahmed said, although he didn't say it with much gusto.

"Don't worry," Mr. Wall said. "We're sending Moustafa with you."

"But he's big and clumsy. All of Bahariya will hear him!" Faisal complained.

"Quiet!" Moustafa barked, cuffing him.

Mr. Wall smiled. "Now all we need is for the soldiers to find the entrance to the aqueduct."

Within an hour they had, hidden behind a low dune about one hundred yards from the western perimeter. The entrance was completely filled in and the soldiers would have never found it if they hadn't moved across the ground in a long line, each man pressing a stiff wire into the sand to look for cavities. Another half hour of shoveling and they had revealed an opening into one of the tunnels.

Once they were done, Moustafa shone an electric torch down the subterranean aqueduct. As far as the eye could see, the tunnel was about half full of damp sand.

"Look," Faisal said.

Several footprints were impressed onto the sand, coming right up to where the blockage had been. Most were of people in sandals. One set of footprints, however, had been made by someone in boots.

"That must be one of the Turkish soldiers the Englishman was talking about," Faisal said.

"It could have been made by the British soldiers while they were clearing the sand," Moustafa replied.

"No, those over there are British tracks. The boots there are different."

Moustafa compared the two sets.

"I guess you're right," he conceded.

"I'm glad you finally believe me about something. Do you also believe me that going down here is a really bad idea?"

"Yes," Moustafa said with a sigh. "Sadly, I do believe you about that."

CHAPTER THIRTY-SIX

O nce again, Faisal found himself doing something for the Englishman that he really, really didn't want to do.

Why did that always happen? Ahmed got to do fun things, like take care of the motorcar. Why did Faisal always have to break into houses full of scary masks and servants with guns, or walk down tunnels full of djinn and Senussi?

It wasn't fair.

He felt a bit better having Moustafa along, although he'd never tell the Nubian that because he'd start thinking he was more important than he was. Moustafa walked in front, gripping a rifle and with a pistol hanging from his belt. He also had that big Nubian sword strapped to his back. Faisal came right behind holding an electric torch, and Ahmed took up the rear with another electric torch.

Faisal would have felt even better if some of the soldiers had come with them, like Claud or Mark. When he had suggested it, the Englishman only shook his head.

"The fewer the better. That way you can move more silently."

Silently? Ha! Moustafa made more noise than a herd of camels.

He wasn't too bad while they were walking on the sand that filled the tunnel for the first few minutes, but then that disappeared and they walked through water like in the other tunnels. Faisal tried to show Moustafa how to move his legs to make the least amount of splashing and noise, but the big Nubian was too clumsy.

The aqueduct carried on straight for a long way. They passed an intersection but kept going straight because that was in the direction of the old temple the Englishman thought the Senussi would come from. Once Faisal had Moustafa stop, not to try and get him to be quieter—he had already done that several times—but because he thought he heard something behind them. They shone their torches in that direction and stood silently for a minute. The sound didn't repeat. Probably a djinn and not a Senussi. Faisal clutched his charm and they kept on going.

Not long after that, they came to a break in the wall. A little above Faisal's head was a hole big enough for a large man to pass through, roughly hacked out. Standing on his tiptoes, Faisal could just see that it led to some sort of chamber.

Moustafa peered inside and took in a sharp breath of air. Ahmed did as well.

"What is it?" Faisal asked.

"It's amazing," Moustafa said.

"What?"

"I wish Claud could see this," Ahmed said.

"What? What?"

"Let's go explore," Moustafa said.

Before either of them could do anything, Faisal hopped up and gripped the bottom edge of the hole. He was the explorer in this group.

He hauled himself up, and paused.

It was a tomb. It looked a bit bigger than the others they had been in, and in better condition. The walls were painted with pictures of djinn that had human bodies and animal heads. Faisal spotted the djinn with the crocodile head from the Englishman's house, the very same djinn Faisal had turned to stone with one of Khadija umm Mohammed's charms.

Faisal yelped and dropped back into the tunnel with a splash.

"I'm not going in there!"

"Keep quiet," Moustafa said. "I want to have a look."

"Me too," Ahmed said.

They started climbing in. Faisal stood there uncertainly. A moment later he jerked his head in the direction of the way they had come. Had that been a splash he had heard? He peered in that direction as far as the light of his torch would allow. The sound did not come again.

The others had already climbed inside. Ahmed poked his head out of the hole.

"Coming?"

Faisal looked from the hole to the tunnel to the hole again. Should he face djinn with Moustafa and Ahmed or face djinn alone?

"I'm coming," he grumbled. "And I deserve a lot of moving picture shows for this."

He hopped up to the lip of the hole and crawled through.

The hole was right at the level of the floor. Faisal stood up and made a slow turn, his eyes wide.

This tomb was a bit different than the others. It was a large room with four round pillars holding up the ceiling. All the walls and even the pillars were painted with pictures of djinn and people and birds and thrones and baboons. On two walls there were little portals to small side chambers that didn't have any paintings but had some old stinky mummy wrappings.

"This tomb is older than the aqueduct," Moustafa said. "See how the aqueduct clips the very edge of it? The workmen must have discovered it and looted it centuries ago."

"Yes, this is ancient Egyptian, not Persian or Roman," Faisal said.

Moustafa cocked his head and looked at him.

"You can tell because there's picture writing on the walls," Faisal explained.

"Well, yes. That's correct." Moustafa entered one of the side chambers and looked around.

Faisal wrinkled his nose and followed. At his feet he saw some bits of old pottery and picked them up.

"Do you think the Englishman could sell these in his shop?"

"Um, no."

"The Senussi broke that Roman wine thing," Faisal said, feeling glum.

Moustafa shook his head. "Idiots."

"Why would they do that?"

"Some people have no respect for the past."

"It didn't have any wine in it."

"It's not about that. Some people are so uneducated they hate anything that's different, especially different ideas. They see ancient things and all they think is 'Paganism! We must destroy it!' But really they're destroying their own heritage."

"We're Roman?"

"No, you're Egyptian, and don't forget it. But the Romans were part of our past too, just like the Greeks and the ancient Egyptians. I've seen temples where the villagers have hacked the faces off all the depictions of the gods just because they are afraid of them. As if some fake god could hurt them! They say they do this in the name of Islam but if they truly had faith they wouldn't have anything to fear from some faded old paintings."

"I wish they hadn't broken the jug. I kind of liked carrying around something two hundred years old."

Moustafa laughed. "More like two thousand!"

Faisal gaped. "Two thousand?"

"Oh yes. Many of the things I handle in the shop are twice as old as that."

"Aren't you afraid you'll break them?"

"No, because I'm careful and attentive to my work. You should learn that and stop being so lazy."

"What's the oldest thing you've touched?"

Moustafa smiled, his eyes going dreamy. For the moment he seemed to have forgotten all about the danger they were in. "A little alabaster statue from the Pre-dynastic period. At least five thousand years old. Maybe even six thousand. No one really knows much about that time."

"Wow."

Moustafa picked up a small lamp sitting in the corner and showed it to him. It was ceramic, with a design of a pair of palm fronds on the triangular top around the hole into which the oil was poured. The tip of the spout still carried the black of many fires that had gone out long ago.

It was all in one piece. Not even a crack.

"That's a funny lamp," Faisal said.

"It's from what we call the Late Period. About 2,500 years ago."

"That's … a long time." Faisal said, trying to grasp the idea.

"That 250 of your lifetimes."

Faisal's jaw dropped. "That's even older than the jug!"

"Yes it is," Moustafa said. "I'm surprised you remember. Here."

He handed the boy the lamp.

Faisal held it gingerly, glancing at Moustafa for reassurance.

"They're sturdy," Moustafa told him. "Just keep it out of the hands of the Senussi."

"Oh yes. They smash everything."

"They do bad things but for good reasons."

"Like when I break into a house for the Englishman?"

"Um, I suppose. The Senussi believe some silly things, like smashing ancient artifacts, but they have pride too. They want to rule themselves, not have an Englishman or an Italian ruling over them."

"What's so wrong with that? They have motorcars and aeroplanes and all sorts of good things."

Moustafa looked like he about to snap at him again, but controlled himself. Taking a deep breath, he explained, "Yes, the Europeans are very clever, but they are not Egyptian or Nubian. Only Egyptians and Nubians understand our problems, so they would make better rulers."

"But the Europeans treat me better than the Egyptians."

"What are you talking about, boy, they gunned us down in the streets!"

"That was the chief of police's fault. He's a bad European. Most Europeans are good."

Moustafa groaned. He glared at Faisal, who cringed back thinking he was going to get hit. After a moment Moustafa took a breath and said,

"You're right that most Europeans are good, at least good to one another. But they see us as inferior."

"The Englishman doesn't think that way, and neither does Claud."

"Stop calling him that. He's Captain Williams to you. And you're right, a few don't think that way, but most do. And the colonial government is set up on that belief. As long as the English are in charge we will be servants in our own country."

"But if the English leave, we'll just be servants to rich Egyptians."

Moustafa smacked him upside the head.

"Don't talk nonsense!"

"Oh, what a lovely tomb!" Jocelyn's voice came from the front room. "And do stop giving the child anti-colonial lectures. He is quite correct that for someone of his station it makes absolutely no difference who is in charge."

Moustafa sputtered and looked too embarrassed to speak. Faisal went to the main room, where Ahmed was helping the beardless Englishman crawl through the hole. Jocelyn stood and looked around.

"Yes, this is quite impressive. But I don't think there are any Senussi here."

Moustafa finally got his mouth working. "W-what are you doing here? This is no place for you."

Jocelyn looked at him for a moment.

"My *place* is wherever I am."

Moustafa looked away.

"Did the Englishman send you down?" Faisal asked.

Jocelyn smiled. "Not exactly. The soldiers are busy preparing for the Senussi attack."

"There was a sentry at the entrance to the aqueduct," Moustafa said. "How did you get past him?"

Jocelyn's smile widened. "I sent him on an errand and slipped inside. The men of the garrison, while showing an aching formality, are yet still quite attentive."

"We're taking you back to the surface," Moustafa said, heading for the hole.

"There's no time," the beardless Englishman said.

"We'll make time."

"We have to scout out the tunnels before sundown. That leaves us little more than an hour. You'll waste half of that taking me to the surface and getting back here."

Moustafa balled his fists and for a moment Faisal thought he was going to hit something. Faisal backed off in case that something turned out to be him. Finally, the Soudanese got himself under control.

"All right, but at the first sign of trouble you run back to the base."

They all continued along the aqueduct toward the temple.

"It might be best if you give me your revolver," Jocelyn said.

"Absolutely not," Moustafa grumbled.

"Two guns are better than one."

"No."

Faisal got up behind Moustafa and eased the revolver out of his holster without the Nubian noticing. He handed it to Jocelyn, putting a finger to his lips. Jocelyn winked at him.

Faisal didn't understand why Moustafa was so angry. Why shouldn't the beardless Englishman join them?

"Thank you for the lamp," Faisal said to cheer Moustafa up.

"Don't mention it," Moustafa grumbled.

"I really like it. Late Period, right?"

"That's right."

"Is that before or after the Old Kingdom?"

"Long after. Now be quiet and look out for Senussi."

Faisal wasn't kidding. He loved the lamp. He didn't have one at home. It would be good to have.

Oh, but won't the neighbors see the light and wonder who was up on the Englishman's roof? Well, he would use it only inside his shed, and with the doorway covered with a mat. And even if they did see the light, it wasn't like the Englishman ever talked to his neighbors anyway.

A European fork, spoon, and knife, and now an ancient Egyptian lamp. The shed on the Englishman's roof was the best place he ever had.

He hoped he would live long enough to get back to it.

"Hey, look," Ahmed said.

He pointed to some picture writing on the wall.

"It's the same that we saw before," Faisal said. "We're almost there."

Faisal had thought the tunnels had begun to look familiar. It was hard to tell, though, because all these tunnels looked more or less the same.

Suddenly his heart leapt. He switched off his electric torch and made Ahmed turn off his too.

"What are you doing, Little Infidel?" Moustafa demanded.

"Shhh," Faisal said.

In as quiet a voice as he could use and still be heard, he explained why he and Ahmed hadn't recognized the tunnel until they saw the picture writing. The heaps of sand had been cleared away, and the hole they had crawled out of had been blocked up again.

The Senussi had been here, preparing the tunnel for their attack.

They were probably close.

Moustafa and Jocelyn must have realized that too, because they fell quiet. For several minutes they listened.

And then they heard a noise that made Faisal want to run screaming down the underground aqueduct all the way back to the army base.

CHAPTER THIRTY-SEVEN

Everything was prepared. The majority of the troops were positioned in hidden spots along the perimeter. A few stayed inside one of the barracks with all the lights on and making a great deal of noise as if the bulk of the soldiers were inside having a party. A pair of scouts hid near the temple of Alexander watching to see when the Senussi would enter. Once they did, the scouts would send up a flare.

Augustus worried that the main Senussi force, the one he presumed would attack the base from the surface, would spot the flare and warn their fellows, but Major Belgrave put him at ease.

"Even if they do see it, it's not so simple calling off an attack. This will be their one chance, and they think Allah will watch over them. I just hope your party down in the aqueduct is successful. We need to know what sort of surprise the Senussi are bringing us."

"I have faith in Moustafa. Besides, we have our own surprise."

Major Belgrave's men had set up a trench mortar ranged on the opening of the aqueduct. Anyone coming out of there would enter a deadly field of shrapnel. Its arcing fire could lob shells right behind the mound that hid the tunnel from view of the base.

Unfortunately, there was no way to get rid of the mound itself. Just below the sand was an outcropping of limestone and would take days to remove with picks.

They had an additional worry. Other than the trench mortar and a Lewis gun, they had no other heavy weaponry except for the armored car, and Major Belgrave let Augustus in on a secret.

"The motor isn't working and there's no way to repair it with the facilities we have at hand. We radioed for a spare part from Cairo a month ago, but they still haven't sent it to us. Red tape at the Quartermaster's Office. Once it's fully dark and there are no prying eyes to see, we'll push it out onto the parade ground. It will have a partial field of fire between the buildings at all four sides of the base."

Augustus nodded, "And that will funnel any attackers to the spaces in front of the buildings where the armored car can't shoot, and the men at the windows can fire on them as the Senussi bunch up. Good thinking."

Major Belgrave may have been a bit long in the tooth, Augustus thought with admiration, but he knew a thing or two about fighting.

Augustus felt in surprisingly good spirits. Why did the threat of battle make him so chipper?

He checked his watch. Shouldn't Moustafa and the others be back by now? It was nearly dark, and they had promised to be back well before then. Faisal had been quite clear on the issue and Augustus felt confident that the urchin would pester Moustafa until the Nubian either returned or went mad.

To take his mind off things, he went to the small cabin reserved for Jocelyn's use.

She didn't answer his knock.

"Oh dear," he muttered. "You didn't."

He found the door unlocked and opened it, something he would normally never do to a lady, but he fully expected this particular lady to have absconded.

And he was right.

A quick search through the base confirmed it. She was gone.

Damn that woman! Of all the times to be wilful!

What to do? Go hunt for her? But he had no idea where she had gone. Back to her cottage? Somewhere else in the oasis? Surely not down into the aqueduct?

Then a horrible, uncharitable thought crept into his mind.

What if Jocelyn was a spy for the Senussi? She had come through their territory unmolested, drank tea with their women, and walked through their villages without trouble and seemingly without fear.

No, he would not believe it! Firstly and secondly, she was a foreigner and a woman. The Senussi would never trust someone like her.

Unless she had been sent as an emissary by a foreign power …

… the Turkish letter. The snippets of Turkish conversation Moustafa had heard during his captivity. Could the Turks have sent her, thinking her very outlandishness would act as a cover?

No, it couldn't be!

But it made sense. She knew Arabic, and she seemed to get along well with the natives. Plus, she had a remarkable ability to appear when least expected.

And he had told her everything.

But wait, she had fought at the cottage. The Senussi might have assumed she had departed. Could she have been shamming when firing out the window? He had been too out of his own head to really notice whether she had been actually aiming at anything. And she wouldn't have dared turn her gun on them. She might have gotten one of them, but not the other. Perhaps life was too dear to gamble it.

Or had she even fought at all? Perhaps she had hidden in a dark corner as the gunfire went all around her, much as Faisal had done. He had been too far gone to be sure. She had certainly pretended that she had fought afterwards, and Faisal had intimated that she had, but the boy had been ducking bullets so much he couldn't be counted on to know what happened. And Moustafa had not said anything.

Could it all be a lie?

A twisting nausea gripped his stomach.

Please don't be true, he thought. *Please don't be yet another enemy.*

Augustus felt at a loss. He left Jocelyn's quarters, passing by the guardhouse and the storage room where they kept the goods confiscated from Bedouin smugglers. He went to the perimeter, where the last glimmerings of the sunset shone in his eyes. A couple of men were hunkered down behind an emplacement of sandbags, sharing a smoke and waiting for the battle to come.

The wind blew in his face, coming off the great Western Desert all the way from Libya. The wind always came from the west here. He studied the low rock outcropping to his front right behind which hid the entrance to the aqueduct, and tried to imagine the line it made as it ran along the edge of the camp before heading for the temple of Alexander.

Augustus felt a slow, familiar sensation creeping up on him. His troubled thoughts began to drop away, replaced by nothing.

At least no conscious thought. Beneath the surface something was building, like a volcano at the bottom of the sea.

He knew this sensation, knew it was important, and let it take its time.

"Sir," one of the soldiers said. "Best to get out of sight. The Senussi might decide to make an early start of it."

Augustus barely heard him, and did not move at the squaddie's good advice. Something was falling into place. The aqueduct. The line it made across the western perimeter. Upwind.

It was upwind, along nearly the entire length of the base.

Upwind. The prevailing wind came from the west, blowing over the subterranean aqueduct and into the faces of him and the soldiers.

Why did he feel that was significant? The aqueduct was underground. The wind did not touch it.

But it blew over the entrance, and it blew over the access holes Faisal had told him connected the aqueducts to the surface every twenty paces or so.

The wind blowing over the access holes. Claud Williams joking, "just last month we intercepted a shipment of several barrels of hydrochloric acid."

Hydrochloric acid. Wind. The access holes.

Mustard gas!

"He had the air of a student learning from two respected teachers."

They're making mustard gas.

Ainsley Fielding was an expert in botany and chemistry. The Amazonian native an expert in poisons. They taught the man who killed Dr. Harrell how to make mustard gas. Hydrochloric acid mixed with sulfur. Sulfur is easy enough to find in the desert, and the Senussi were smuggling in the acid from Cyrenaica.

They needed to silence him. When Harrell guessed at its true nature he came to Cairo, under the guise of giving a lecture, but really to make an appointment to see Sir Thomas. He was going to tell all, and got killed for it.

Mustard gas.

Augustus staggered back. One of the soldiers called out to him, but he didn't hear.

He was already going away.

Augustus remembered the first time he saw mustard gas. The Germans had used it on several sectors already, and news of it had spread like wildfire through the British army. It was a terrible death, those who had witnessed it said. Your eyes burned and blood came out your nostrils and mouth. It ripped apart your lungs with every breath, leaving you hacking up great gobs of blood and flesh. But you couldn't bring it up quickly enough, they said, and you ended up drowning in your own blood. And even if you didn't, even if you only got a whiff, it tore apart the surface of your eyes, leaving you blind.

The regiment was issued gas masks, but men in the know said they were poorly made, and one in ten would leak. One in ten would let in the gas to tear your eyes and fill your lungs with blood.

Augustus and everyone in his regiment lived in mortal fear of a gas attack. You could keep your head down and reduce your chances of catching a bullet. You could dive for a dugout and be reasonably safe from artillery shells. There was nothing you could do if the gas came. It crept into every foxhole, filled every dugout.

And then it came.

Augustus was in his dugout early one morning filling out a report on the previous night's observations. He had noticed some unusual activity along the line. At first he had taken it for a wire laying party. Each side spent much time in No Man's Land replacing barbed wire the other side had cut. They had sent up a few flares, but the Germans had gone to ground and the snipers only got one or two of them. Augustus hadn't given it too much thought, until the day dawned cold and overcast, and looking out over the lip of the trench he could clearly see that none of the German wire had been replaced, and none of their own had been cut.

He had been pulled out of writing his report by the loud, persistent clonking of a metal bar on an empty shell casing. The alert.

"Gas! Gas!" someone shouted.

"Everyone get your masks on!" he ordered as he stormed out of the dugout, putting on his own.

The men didn't need to be told. Every one of them had grabbed their mask at the first utterance of the feared word.

Augustus rushed to the nearest periscope and looked at the eyepiece.

Then he understood the previous night's activity.

From shell holes all along the line, great plumes of dirty yellow gas billowed out.

The prevailing wind in Flanders was from the east in the mornings, and the gas blew toward them, each cloud spreading out to merge with the others into a wall of toxins.

Augustus would never forget that sight, and never forget how he saw with his own eyes that the rumor that one gas mask in ten didn't work was true. Dimly through the dirty eyepieces of his mask, and the yellowish haze that settled on the trench, he saw men go down, writhing in the mud, trying to take a breath of air but every inhalation quickening their doom.

And now it was happening again, long after the war was over.

He staggered over sand that was quickly turning to mud. He blinked, trying to see the palm trees that were shrouded by shattered poplars. He needed to focus. He needed to stay here, in Egypt, and not go back to Flanders.

It didn't help to have a man in a British army uniform standing in front of him talking.

What was he saying?

"Are you all right, sir?"

"Gas," Augustus managed to force out. "They've made mustard gas and they're going to force it out the access holes of the aqueduct."

"What's that, sir?"

Augustus shook his head to clear it, forcing his eyes to focus on what was in front of him instead of what he should have put behind him.

"I need to see Major Belgrave," he said. "It's not enough to guard the entrance. We need men in the tunnel."

And I need to get to get down there and save Moustafa and the boys.

He strode for Major Belgrave's quarters, his vision finally cleared. Now he knew the Senussi's strategy. The surface attack would only be to pen them in, so that the gas could blow over them and choke them all to death. Augustus felt sure there wasn't a single gas mask on base. In the Western Desert campaigns, there had been no need. Neither the Senussi nor the Ottomans had used gas.

Which is why they were surprising the British with it now.

He had to warn the major and get a strong force down in the aqueduct before the attack happened. Twenty men and a machine gun should do it. The aqueduct was narrow, and they could hold off any number of Senussi. If the Bedouin and their Turkish advisors tried to use the gas within the confines of the tunnel, they'd die too.

A small, strong force in the tunnel, and the battle against the Senussi would be half won.

The sound of an approaching engine made Augustus turn. Through the barbed wire, Augustus could see Captain Williams' familiar stripped-down Model T Ford speeding along the track toward the base, just visible in the fading light.

Just as Williams came to the straightaway that formed the final stretch of track leading to the base, a volley of rifle fire raked the motorcar. Williams swerved and hit a palm tree, coming to a dead halt.

Another volley followed the first, and then suddenly from all four sides, hidden Bedouin poured fire at the base.

The attack was on, and there was no way to get a troop of men to the aqueduct now.

They were trapped.

CHAPTER THIRTY-EIGHT

Moustafa's first thought when the Senussi came charging down the tunnel was that his boss was going to fire him for putting that idiot woman in danger. Soon he had more important things to worry about.

Like the poison dart that shot an inch over his head.

And the several spears that followed it.

The Senussi, from what he could see of them in the wavering light of the electric torches, carried guns too, mostly rifles strapped across their backs, but they did not use them. Obviously they didn't want to make too much noise and alert the soldiers on the surface.

Moustafa had no such compunction. He leveled his rifle and took out a man in front who was about the throw a spear.

Racking the bolt, he shot the next man who raised a spear at him. In the confusion he couldn't see the man with the blowgun. He feared one of those poison darts far more than a dozen spears.

"Get back to the tomb!" Moustafa shouted. "We need the cover."

The boys took his advice. That fallen woman did not.

Moustafa blinked to see she had his pistol in his hand, which she proceeded to empty down the narrow tunnel to great effect.

The Senussi fell back, a trail of groaning men lying half submerged behind them. Moustafa fired a third shot to cover their own retreat. The tomb was fifty yards behind them. He could just see the lights of the boys' electric torches disappear as they hopped into the hole in the tunnel wall.

Moustafa and Mrs. Montjoy sprinted for the relative safety of the tomb. For once Moustafa was grateful she was wearing trousers. The water would have pulled on her skirts and slowed her down.

They were almost to the hole when the Senussi got reorganized. A bullet panged off the tunnel wall inches from Moustafa's head. Another splashed in the water just behind Mrs. Montjoy. Now that Moustafa had made so much noise, they felt free to use their guns.

"Get in! I'll hold them off," he ordered, turning and going to one knee.

To his surprise, the woman actually obeyed him. Most likely because she was out of bullets.

Moustafa fired, but in the glare of the electric torches shining his way he could not see if he hit anyone. A bullet struck the water close to him, splashing his face. Moustafa fired another shot, then leaped for the hole, struggling to get through as quickly as possible.

Mrs. Montjoy grabbed him under the shoulders and hauled him in like an oversized fish.

"Do you have any more cartridges for the pistol?" she asked.

Moustafa reached into his pocket and poured a handful on the floor as the gods and goddess looked on. Faisal had pulled Ahmed further in and away from the hole. The Little Infidel had been in enough gunfights to know how to take cover.

Moustafa reloaded and glanced out the hole. The Senussi had advanced a few yards. He gave them another shot and ducked back out of sight before they had time to reply.

"Now what?" Faisal asked, peeking from around a painted column.

Good question. They were stuck here. The tunnel ran straight for several hundred more yards before they could get to the surface. There was no way they could make it. Although they were safe for the moment, they were trapped.

He could hear the Senussi advancing, the splashing of their countless feet echoing down the tunnel, loud even to Moustafa's ringing ears. This fight had obviously upset their timing, and they wanted to get rid of Moustafa and his companions as quickly as possible.

Mrs. Montjoy pushed past him to fire out of the hole but flinched back as a rain of bullets chased her.

"We seem to be in a spot of difficulty," she said.

Moustafa thought for a moment, then gestured for the boys to come closer.

"They'll be on us any second," he told them. He stood, his head almost brushing the ceiling of the tomb, and drew his sword, a sword not used since the days of the Mahdi. "Just as they come up to the hole I will jump out and fight them hand to hand with this. That will keep them occupied while you run away. Get out as fast as you can. I will not be able to hold them for long."

Mrs. Montjoy stood. "But—"

"Do as I say, woman! Take care of the children."

The footsteps grew near. Slowed. The shouts fell to whispers. Moustafa faced the hole, repeating the *shahada* to himself, the Muslim declaration of faith. There was no way he could live through this, but if he timed his attack well, he at least could save the boys, and perhaps his example would make that low woman reform her life.

There is no god but God. Muhammad is the messenger of God, he said in his mind, over and over again. May God forgive him for not saying it out loud. God could hear his thoughts, and he did not want the Senussi to hear his words. Then they would know where he was.

The Senussi tried to move silently, but they were too many. Every step, every shift of weight, rippled the water.

How to know when they were close enough for him to strike down, but far enough away for him to get out of the hole without getting struck down himself?

Mrs. Montjoy solved that problem for him. Without exposing her head, she hooked her arm around the edge of the hole and fired blindly down the tunnel.

Moustafa leapt legs first through the hole. By some miracle, he didn't smack his head against the sides of the breach and he managed to land on his feet.

Right in front of a disorganized mob of Senussi.

A man barely three feet in front of him struggled to hold up another man who had fallen into his arms, his chest streaming with blood. Moustafa let out a bellow, raised his sword high, and brought it down on him, the blade cleaving deep into his shoulder.

The man shrieked in pain and horror and fell, taking his friend with him.

Wrenching the sword free, Moustafa swung again, hitting the next man just as he raised his rifle.

Shots rang out, and two more Senussi fell. He hoped Mrs. Montjoy would stop firing now and take the boys out of here. The tunnel was swarming with Bedouin warriors. He could not hold them long.

But he could hold them for a while.

He felt the blood pulse in his veins, and finally knew the thrill his uncle had felt at facing guns with only a sword.

His uncle's words came back to him, told to him during one of his many war stories when Moustafa was a boy back in his village so many years ago.

Once you close with the enemy, keep pressing them. Don't give them a chance to use their guns. As long as you do that, you will have the advantage.

Moustafa took a couple of steps forward, swinging his large sword and cutting a swath through the Senussi ranks. Once or twice he misjudged the distance and the tip of the sword clanged against the side of the tunnel. He winced when this happened, but the sword was well forged and it did not break.

The Senussi gave ground. A few of the braver ones tried to face him with their spears or scimitars, but they had less reach and far less strength. Moustafa kept pressing them, not giving them time or room to bring their rifles to bear.

They began to move back more quickly, the riflemen trying to duck and weave around the spearmen in order to get a good shot. He didn't let them.

Then all at once the last man with a scimitar fell, Moustafa cut down the rifleman behind him, and the entire crowd moved back. He roared, barreling into them, cutting down three more in rapid succession. And then there were no more Senussi within reach.

They were retreating! Moustafa let out a bellow that echoed off the tunnel walls. The Bedouin were famous fighters, but they had never faced a Nubian!

He laughed and taunted them, waving the bloody sword over his head.

Then sense returned. He was acting like a madman. Good God, he was acting like Mr. Wall!

The Senussi wouldn't remain broken for long. He had to get out of here while he could. God had granted him a chance to escape and see his family again, and it would be impious to waste it.

He sprinted down the tunnel. Somewhere in the confusion he had forgotten his rifle. He wondered if one of the others had grabbed it. They had disappeared up ahead. Had they made it out?

There was little light in the tunnel, just the far flickering of the Senussi torches. That suited him fine. That meant they were in light and he was running into darkness. They wouldn't be able to see him.

But they didn't need to see him. All they had to do was keep firing down the narrow, straight aqueduct and they were bound to hit him sooner or later.

Moustafa stumbled as his shoulder hit the wall. He slowed, moving through almost pitch darkness. Why couldn't he see the electric torches his companions had carried? Had they made it out of the tunnel already, or had some trouble befallen them?

Reluctantly, he sheathed his sword, and reached out with both hands so that his fingertips brushed both walls. He felt terribly exposed walking like this in the dark, but it was the only way to move forward.

Now that the ringing in his ears had subsided, he could hear other sounds. From above and ahead he heard gunshots, although he could not see the access holes or entrance. Moustafa realized it must be fully night outside, for no light shone in from anywhere.

Except from behind. The distant torchlight grew stronger. The Senussi were advancing again.

He tried to move faster, hoping not to trip in his near blindness. Something strange stuck him about the fight. The men in the front, those he had been fighting, had carried spears and swords and guns, as was to be expected. When they retreated, however, he had seen those who took up the rear of the column. Some of them had been carrying ladders, while others carried steel cylinders with wide metal bases on them. He couldn't be sure in the confusion, but he thought he had seen wires coming off of them with some sort of switch.

Bombs? And what were the ladders for? They didn't need them to get out of the entrance.

Then it hit him. They weren't going to go out the entrance at all, they were going to come up through the access holes. Maybe they would set off those bombs or whatever they were all along the line.

But he hadn't seen any trench mortar or other device. How would they launch the bombs at the base? The aqueduct ran along the entire western perimeter, but it was still a good hundred yards away.

They must have had some sort of mortar or grenade launcher he hadn't seen. They were going to bombard the entire base from the safety of those access holes. The soldiers wouldn't even be able to see them.

He had to warn the others.

Another thing struck him as strange. A couple of the men carrying those devices hadn't been Bedouin. Their features were different—darker and broader, and they had worn shirts and trousers. He had the impression that they might have been Turks.

The light behind him grew brighter, gleaming faintly off the water at his feet. He could see himself again, and pretty soon they would be able to see him too.

When would this accursed tunnel end?

The sound of firing grew louder. Moustafa stumbled forward, hurrying as fast as he dared. The water lowered, and then disappeared. He walked along a stretch of sand and saw the entrance ahead, an oval of starlit sky and the faint silhouettes of a few palm trees.

The firing was loud and continuous. Where were the others?

Getting on his belly, Moustafa crawled forward and poked his head out of the entrance. A low rock outcropping hid the nearest portion of the base from him, but further on he could see the line of barbed wire. From two different spots he saw the flare of rifles and the steady tonguing flame of a machine gun.

To his left he could see the staccato shots of the Senussi coming from the palm grove. They were spread out, each man having found his own cover and taking care with his shots.

Moustafa squinted as a series of flares shot up high into the sky above the base, illuminating a large area with a wavering light and descending gradually on little parachutes.

In the baleful red glare, he saw Captain Williams' Model T Ford had crashed into a palm tree about two hundred yards away, the engine still running. He did not see the captain.

Then suddenly he saw a sight that made his blood run cold.

Faisal leaped into the driver's seat and started fiddling with controls. A bullet panged off the side off the motorcar, setting off sparks. The boy flinched but did not run off.

Then with, a great grinding of gears, the motorcar lurched to life and Faisal zoomed away.

In reverse.

CHAPTER THIRTY-NINE

A motorcar was a lot harder to drive than it looked. How did you get this thing to go forwards? Ahmed had told him, but practicing with logs and sticks was very different than doing the real thing.

Especially with Senussi shooting at him.

And it was hard to see where he was going when everything had turned bright and red from those lights in the sky and he was going backwards and the motorcar kept bouncing over bumps.

The worst part was trying to dodge the trees. He had ended up in the palm grove and the Senussi were all around him trying to shoot at him. Bullets whizzed by right next to his head and hit the motorcar. He hoped they didn't wreck it.

He hoped they didn't wreck him.

He had to get moving forward or he would never get back and save Claud and the others. When he, Jocelyn, and Ahmed had gotten out of the tunnel, the fight had already begun. Knowing the Senussi in the aqueduct would catch them soon, they had crawled on their bellies to where they saw the motorcar and found Claud hidden in a little ditch in the sand. He had banged his head but wasn't too hurt. Then the fire had increased and they got stuck there.

That's when Faisal had snuck off to get the motorcar to save everyone.

Now he needed to save himself.

He took his foot off the gas pedal and stepped on the brake. At least he got that right. The motorcar came to a stop.

Now how to get it to move forwards?

The gearshift! Right. Why wouldn't it move? Oh right, that other pedal. Whatever it was called. You had to step on that before you could move the gears.

"Silly foreigners! Why do you have to make everything so complicated?"

Just as he stepped on the third pedal, he heard a shout behind him. A Senussi with a scimitar leaped onto the back of the motorcar, looking like he was about to cut off Faisal's head.

Faisal slammed on the gas pedal and the motorcar shot backwards, still in reverse. The man fell from the sudden speed and ended up lying on the back seat.

The motorcar flew through the palm grove, Faisal desperately trying to avoid trees. Senussi leaped up from their hiding places and ran off to avoid getting run over.

Then the man in the back seat rose up with a snarl. The red light from the flares gleamed off the keen blade of his scimitar.

The motorcar slammed into a palm tree, and the Senussi fell forward, banging his forehead against the back seat. The impact of the motorcar shook several palm fronds from the tree that landed on the Senussi with a thump, leaving him buried.

A groan told Faisal that the man was not dead. Faisal threw the scimitar out of the motorcar, then the palm fronds, and then the Senussi. The man was heavy and it took a few moments to heave him over. He landed on the sand with a thud and a curse.

Faisal got back into the driver's seat. Now where was he? Oh right, that pedal thing, and the gear stick.

He stepped on the pedal and moved the stick around. There came a terrible grinding from the engine but at last it lurched forward.

That was better. He was getting to understand this motorcar much better. Maybe when the Englishman saw how well he drove he would buy them a motorcar in Cairo.

But he had to live first. The Senussi had regrouped and were starting to fire at him again.

He steered toward where Ahmed and the others lay hidden. Or at least tried to. The steering wheel wasn't doing what it was told. It would either turn the car too much or turn it too little. Faisal ended up zigzagging across the sand right past the entrance to the aqueduct.

He screamed as a big, dark figure leaped out of the entrance and right into the back of the motorcar.

Faisal zigzagged even harder, trying to shake this new attacker.

"Stop driving like a maniac and let me drive!" Moustafa shouted.

"Oh, it's you. Hold on, I have to save the others."

"Let me drive!"

Moustafa gripped the back of the seat, his eyes bugged out and sweat pouring off his face. He sure looked scared. Faisal had never seen Moustafa looked scared before. The Senussi must have scared him.

They zigzagged right over to the ditch and Faisal slammed on the breaks, making Moustafa tumble into the front seat, his sword flying from its sheath and nearly cutting Faisal's head off. The others piled into the back seat.

Faisal hit the gas but for some reason they went backwards. He must have stepped on the third pedal when he ducked the sword and Moustafa must have hit the gear shift when he landed in front.

It didn't matter. You could go pretty fast backwards. Steering was harder, though.

"Let me out! I'll take my chances with the Senussi!" Moustafa shouted. At least that's what Faisal thought he said. It was hard to hear him because Moustafa was upside down.

"Little brother! Stop before you kill us all."

"Don't worry."

Faisal didn't want to stop because the Senussi were shooting again. So he backed up all the way to the gate of the base and right through it. It was just a weak wooden gate and smashed all to splinters when he drove through.

At last he put on the brakes and Ahmed showed him how to turn off the engine. Moustafa leaped out of the motorcar, followed by Jocelyn, who helped Claud. Several soldiers ran up, looking confused as to whether they should shoot him or not.

Then the Englishman appeared, carrying several artillery shells strapped together.

"Did I do a good job?" Faisal asked him.

He didn't reply. He shouted something in English to the soldiers. Faisal and Ahmed jumped in the back seat while the men set the artillery shells in the passenger's side seat in the front.

Shouting again in English, the Englishman got in and drove right out of the shattered gate.

"Where are we going?" Faisal asked.

The Englishman glanced over his shoulder and jerked.

"What are you two doing back there? I told you to get out."

"Did you? Well, you said it in English."

"I can't be expected to remember … oh never mind. Stay down. There's no time to drop you off. When I say jump, jump out of the motorcar, do you understand?"

"Sure."

They sped right for the entrance to the aqueduct. The Senussi started firing again and the motorcar swerved as one of the tires made a loud bang. The motorcar skidded, but somehow the Englishman managed to keep control.

"Jump!"

Faisal and Ahmed jumped.

They hit hard, but luckily it was soft sand. Faisal rolled for several feet before ending up with his face in the dust. He looked up, spitting sand out of his mouth.

Just in time to see the Englishman leap out of the motorcar, which shot right at the entrance to the aqueduct.

It was too big to fit through. As it slammed into the stone sides, it lit up in a great explosion that threw Faisal backwards. From all along the line of the aqueduct, smoke and sand and debris shot out of the access holes.

Then there was a low rumble and the sand buckled and crumpled.

Then Faisal could see no more as a great cloud of sand obscured his vision.

Waving his hand in front of his face, the first thing he saw was Ahmed. He was smiling.

"Wow, little brother. Your foreigner is almost as fun as mine."

Faisal got to his feet.

"Englishman?" he shouted, barely able to hear his own words over the ringing in his ears. "Are you all right, Englishman?"

A figure stumbled out of the haze. It was the Englishman, adjusting his mask and limping badly. Faisal ran up to him.

"Did they shoot you?"

"No. I fell wrong as I jumped out," the Englishman said, coughing out a lungful of sand. "I've twisted my ankle."

"Lean on me."

The Englishman put his arm around Faisal's shoulders.

"It seems I've been leaning on you quite a bit lately."

"You've never twisted your ankle before, you silly Englishman."

CHAPTER FORTY

Five days later ...

It was going to be a hot trip back. The summer was almost upon them and they had to pay an exorbitant price to get some Bedouin to guide them to Cairo. Augustus could have gotten Farouk and his crew to do the job for less, but not after those petty thefts. Of course, this group of Bedouin might try the same thing, but it was the principle of the matter.

Augustus had made sure the camels were loaded with plenty of water, and carefully counted out the drops of opium remaining in the bottle Jocelyn had given him. He had more than enough to see him home to a city full of understanding chemists.

Major Belgrave had arranged for them to have a military escort as well. The prisoner Righton had to be taken back to Cairo, and so five soldiers would be going with them.

"The Senussi have scattered," the Major told him two days after the battle. "Those we didn't shoot, the locals have taken care of. I don't think we will be having trouble from them anytime soon. Pity we didn't capture any of those Turks alive. It would have been interesting to question them. I suppose you've found all you need for your murder investigation, at any rate."

At Claud's insistence, they were spending a final evening at his house on the mountain. Other than a bad bump on his head, the captain had survived the battle unscathed. Moustafa was hard at work putting some finishing touches on his sketches, while Augustus rechecked the saddlebags he had piled in the spare room to make sure everything was in its place. He kept tincture in his pocket. He would not risk it being lost in another sandstorm.

Faisal came up to him.

"These look like nice saddlebags. The Bedouin are right that the people in Bahariya make the best."

"Fine works of art, to be sure," Augustus said. Actually rather crude, but attractive enough in a barbaric way. He doubted he would be able to sell any in his shop.

"Can I have one when we get home?" the boy asked.

"I suppose. Whatever would you want one for?"

"It's for my friend."

"Oh, all right."

"Would filling it with sand ruin it?"

"What an incredible question. Why would you want to put sand in it?"

Faisal giggled. "For fun. Would it?"

"No, it would just make it sandy. I'm not going to give you one of these saddlebags if you're going to act foolishly with it."

"I won't fill it with sand, then." Faisal walked over to a saddlebag leaning against the wall. The bag was stuffed with a bag of flour so they could bake loaves in the sand. The bag was all puffed out from the flour and he could see all the detailed stitching in green and blue.

"I'll take this one."

"Why that one?"

"Because it's the best, you silly Englishman."

"You have a fine eye for art."

Faisal reached into his pocket and pulled out a Late Period lamp. "This is ancient Egyptian."

"Indeed it is. Where did you get that?"

"Moustafa gave it to me. We found it in a tomb." Faisal looked around sadly. "I'm sure going to miss Ahmed. Claud too. This place is fun."

"Yes." Augustus cleared his throat. "I wanted to talk with you about that. I've been speaking with Captain Williams and—"

"Who's Captain Williams?" Faisal asked.

"Whose house do you think we've been sleeping in?"

"Oh! You mean Claud."

"You should call him Captain Williams. In any case, I've been speaking with him about you. I know you've made good friends with his servant boy, and you certainly show a unique talent for driving, and I was wondering if you wanted to stay here."

Faisal's jaw dropped. "Stay here? You mean not go back to Cairo?"

The boy stared around the house and through the window at the motorcar parked nearby and the football pitch in the little valley beyond.

"Yes, you could stay here," Augustus went on. "Captain Williams said he'd be happy to take you on as a servant. He said you'd be good company for Ahmed. He couldn't pay you much but—"

Faisal looked back at him. "No."

Augustus and Faisal stared at each other for a moment.

"Are you quite certain? I would have thought you would have—"

"No."

The answer came out surprisingly firm.

"Now listen, Faisal. You should think this thing through."

"My place is in Cairo."

"Well, there could be a place for you here too."

Faisal had been looking at him steadily this entire time. "Then who would help you in your adventures?"

"Um, well, Moustafa certainly … I mean, you have been helpful too, but …"

"Thank you for asking, Englishman, but my place is in Cairo."

On the day of their departure, Jocelyn came to meet them. It was early morning and she and Augustus went for a walk alone together in the palm groves. It took some time before they made it far enough away from the camels that they could no longer hear Faisal. The boy had been clutching

Ahmed and bawling his eyes out all morning.

"Poor Faisal," Jocelyn said. "He really grew attached to Claud's servant."

"I arranged for him to stay," Augustus replied. "I don't know why he refused."

"Silly man."

Augustus didn't know what to say to that and so changed the subject.

"Are you sure you want to spend the summer here? It seems a beastly place to suffer through the hot months."

"All the better for my book. The women will be even more confined to home than usual, and I will have more time to interview them. I'm learning so much already."

"I'm surprised Major Belgrave doesn't force you to go."

In fact, Augustus had tried to get the officer to do that very thing, calculating that she would be forced to join their caravan.

"Oh, with the Senussi defeated there isn't much danger. I've moved to a village that is staunchly anti-Senussi, the same one that rescued Moustafa. I'll be safer there than anywhere in Egypt."

"But in the autumn you'll come to Cairo."

"Yes, Augustus," Jocelyn said with a chuckle. He had asked several times already. Somehow he couldn't stop asking.

"It's a wonderful city. We can go to the Egyptian Museum. And there's a fine opera house. Some good dining too, which after your long desert journey I'm sure you'll appreciate, and ..."

Augustus realized he was babbling and forced himself to stop.

Jocelyn smiled. "High culture and society have never much interested me. If it did, I would have stayed in Europe. I do want to peruse your dear little shop, and spend time with a most interesting gentleman."

Jocelyn stopped. Augustus turned to face her.

"The hour is getting late," she said softly. "The Bedouin will want to get started."

"Are you quite sure you don't want to come with us?"

Jocelyn smiled, put a hand on his mask, and planted a kiss on his lips. Augustus almost pulled away, but checked himself at the last moment.

"I'll see you in Cairo," she said, "and you better arrange another adventure at least as diverting as this one."

***

Mr. Wall had gone fully insane. Moustafa's boss was singing, actually singing, as their camels passed through the volcanic wasteland of the Black Desert and passed into the eerie formations of the White Desert. It was some scandalous song not befitting Mr. Wall's station. It was a good thing he sang in English so the Little Infidel and the Bedouin couldn't understand. The soldiers found it amusing, though, and once he had sung it once, they took up the chorus when he started a second time. Their voices echoed off the strange limestone sculptures to come back at them from all sides.

At least that made the Little Infidel stop crying. Now he was looking all about him and clutching his charm, thinking an entire army of djinn was mocking them.

Such superstition. If Egypt and the Soudan were ever to be free, that sort of thinking needed to be stamped out. How could they ever win their freedom when the people thought like Faisal, or the Senussi?

What fools those Senussi had been! Did they think they could kick out the British and Italians through armed force? The Senussi had no armored cars, no aeroplanes, no artillery. Did they think simply shouting "God is Great!" would lead them to victory? The Mahdi's army had thought the same thing and the British slaughtered them. Even if the Senussi had gassed the entire base, they would have never been able to march on Cairo.

As much as he wanted Egypt and the Soudan to become independent and fuse together as one great nation, he did not want it if fools such as the Senussi and the Mahdi got in charge. They would be ten times worse than the British. He had not felt any great guilt in fighting the Senussi. They would have only oppressed the farmers of Bahariya and drawn them into a conflict they would have inevitably lost.

It was the same with the hotheads he occasionally met in the cafes of

Cairo who called for violent revolution. He understood their anger and their frustration, but turned a deaf ear to their plans.

No, an uprising would only lead to bloodshed, most of it Egyptian. The Soudan would be even worse because the tribes would start fighting each other as much as the British. Egypt and the Soudan had to become free one day, and the only way to do that was to build a popular movement of such widespread support that the British would have no choice but to leave.

And that movement had to be led by educated men, men who knew about economics and engineering and law. And yes, there would be a place for scholars among them. There was no point in crying for independence if you didn't have the tools to build a nation once you attained it.

A bright vision appeared before him, a vision of an independent Egypt and Soudan, led by those who brought together the best of Western learning with the true faith of Islam. He could be one of those people. Perhaps if he built upon his journal articles and developed a reputation, when independence day came he could rise to an important position at a university, or in the Ministry of Education. It wouldn't matter if those arrogant foreign Egyptologists never accepted him, he could be a leading scholar in his own country, revered by his own countrymen.

But when? When? He had no idea. Years, mostly likely. Decades, even. There was still much ignorance and superstition. That would have to be eradicated through education and proper leadership. That would never come from a colonial power; he saw that now. The British only educated enough Egyptians and Soudanese to help them run the colony. They had no interest in the rest of the population. Only a native government would care enough to make any real change in society. Only people like him cared enough.

Perhaps he would make a good teacher. Hadn't he gotten that flea-bitten beggar boy interested in his own past? On their last night in Captain Williams' house, Faisal had poured some oil in the lamp and lit it. He and Ahmed had stayed up all night chattering away by its light. Yes, perhaps his future in the new order would be as an educator.

And the best way to have a bright future was to start building it up today.

His hand rested on his saddlebags, where a sheaf of drawings was carefully packed next to Herr Schäfer's books. After the Senussi had been defeated, Moustafa had asked that they could stay for a few extra days so he could sketch the antiquities of the oasis. Mr. Wall had readily agreed. He wanted to spend more time with that fallen woman. Faisal, of course, hadn't complained either. One day, while he was making a new sketch of the temple of Alexander to replace the one the Senussi had destroyed, he heard a shriek of laughter and was terrified to see Captain William's Model T tearing around the desert nearby with Faisal at the wheel. Ahmed sat in the passenger's seat and the captain, grinning from ear to ear, sat in the back.

Captain Williams was far too indulgent. Mr. Wall was becoming the same way. The Little Infidel could get away with almost anything these days. At least he had learned to drive forwards instead of backwards.

Moustafa shrugged. The important thing was that he got to make the sketches, not only of the temple, but of the tombs as well, and of a Roman fort and crumbling Coptic church to the south of the oasis. One day those sketches would grace Herr Schäfer's book, and in the meantime he had enough information for another scholarly article for the *Journal of Egyptian Archaeology*.

Moustafa smiled as they passed through the last of the strange limestone formations of the White Desert and entered the vast stretch of pale brown sand that would lead him home. Nur and the children waited for him there. After a few well-earned days of rest with his family, he would get to work, building up his scholarly reputation.

And the work was not just for himself, it was for his children's future, a future where Egyptians and Soudanese scholars would interpret their own past, and where his children would be taught their history by professors of their own race.

He would see that day. He was sure of it.

***

Faisal felt much better when they left the Desert of the Djinn behind and got into the open sand. There were djinn here too, of course, but not as many of them. They sure were lucky to get through that place a second time without being possessed.

"Hey, Englishman. What were you singing?"

For some reason the Englishman looked embarrassed.

"Just an old song," he said.

"Was it a spell to protect us from djinn?"

"I've told you time and again that djinn don't exist."

"One possessed you."

The Englishman coughed. "I have that one under control."

Moustafa muttered something under his breath.

Faisal looked out over the vast stretch of the desert. It sure was hot, hotter even than when they had come out here. At least the *khamseen*, the fifty days of baking winds that blew up from the Soudan, wasn't due for another month. He sure didn't want to be in the desert then.

It was hot enough already. He wished he could take a dip in one of those pools back at Bahariya.

Maybe Ahmed was having a swim right now. Or working on the motorcar or talking to Mark at the army base. He sure had a fun life. Too bad Ahmed and Claud didn't live in Cairo. He'd miss them.

But their place was in Bahariya, and his place was in Cairo, in his little shed on the Englishman's roof. If he had stayed in the oasis, who would give Mina a saddlebag, or give the Englishman's spare food to the street boys? Who would protect the Englishman's house, or prove Moustafa wrong? He had responsibilities. Nobody knew or appreciated that he had responsibilities, but that didn't mean he could just ignore them.

It would have been nice to have spent more time with Ahmed, though. Even just a few more days. Faisal had learned a lot from him, like about ancient things and how to get along with foreigners.

"Hey, Englishman!"

"What is it now, Faisal?"

"How do you say camel in English?"

"Camel."

"Gamel."

"No, camel. *Gamel* is the Arabic word. There are no camels in England so when we came here we took your word for them."

"Then why not just say *gamel,* you silly Englishman?"

"I'm not sure. I think because camel is easier to say for us."

"Caaamel."

"Close."

"How do you say oasis?"

"Oasis."

"We say *wuasis.*"

"We got that from you too. England is very wet. There are no deserts so we took your word."

"How many words did you take from us? Am I speaking English already?"

"Not quite. We say desert, not *sahara*, but we call this desert *sahara* because that's what you call it and it's the biggest desert in the world."

"Dayseeert. It sure is big, Englishman. How many more days do we have until we get home?"

"Ten or eleven, I believe. We're heading on the same route as before."

"How do you say *shay?*"

"Tea."

"Teee. How do you say *masjid?*"

"Mosque. Are you going to do this all the way to Cairo?"

"Mussk. What else are we going to do? Go to the moving pictures?"

"I'm not sure there's a program planned for the next few sand dunes."

"Of course there isn't, you silly Englishman. How do you say *mtarrba?*"

And for ten days, as their camels passed over one sand dune after another, Faisal asked word after word. He asked so many he didn't realize he was asking the same words twice, or ten times. And after a while he didn't have to ask for certain words. It was a great game and he never tired of it. The game helped pass the time in this dead place and it made him feel less sad about leaving Ahmed. And it helped keep the djinn away, because all djinn are scared of European voices.

The best part was that the Englishman never tired of the game either.

HISTORICAL NOTE

While the main characters and story in this novel are fictional, the historical background is as accurate as I could make it. The Geographical Association of Egypt, Bahariya Oasis, and Birqash Camel Market are all real places and all well worth seeing if you come to Egypt.

Bahariya Oasis is no longer as remote as it was in 1919. The caravan route Augustus, Moustafa, and Faisal took is now a paved highway. There is electricity and all the modern conveniences for those in the oasis who can afford them. Still, at night when the stars glimmer in the desert sky, and quiet settles on the palm groves, it can feel much as it did a century ago.

Take care in Birqash Camel Market. I know this from personal experience. It wasn't Moustafa who got run over by a donkey, it was me!

A couple of the minor characters are also real, such as Sir Thomas Russell Pasha, Commandant of the Cairo Police.

Captain Claud Williams (1876-1970) served as commander of the No. 5 Light Car patrol in the Senussi Campaign during World War One and also helped map the Western Desert. His wartime memoirs were posthumously published as *Light Car Patrols 1916-19: War and Exploration in Egypt and Libya with the Model T Ford*, edited by Russell McGuirk.

Atop a mountain overlooking Bahariya Oasis stands the ruins of an extensive stone house. Local legend has it that Claud Williams lived up here acting as a lookout during the time in which this novel takes place. In fact, he was already demobilized and on his way back to New Zealand. McGuirk suggests that the house dates to the Second World War, when a unit of Allied soldiers driving more advanced cars called the Long Range Desert Group fought against the Italians and the Germans. That famous outfit owed much to the pioneering work of Captain Williams and the Light Car Patrols.

The spot is still known as English Mountain and the ruins of the house can still be seen. I chose legend over fact because the story of Captain Williams was too good to leave out.

Faisal's friend Ahmed Fakhry grew up to be one of Egypt's leading archaeologists, excavating in Bahariya Oasis in the late 1930s and early 1940s. Professor Fakhry (1905-1973) excavated the temple of Alexander as well as many other sites in the oases of Bahariya, Siwa, Farafra, Kharga, and Dakhla. He found some Roman-era tombs at Bahariya in 1947, but a revolution was brewing in Egypt at that time and he was unable to excavate them fully. In reality, Professor Fakhry grew up in the Fayoum and didn't get to the oases of the Western Desert until later in life. As far as I know he never met Captain Williams, but I couldn't resist the temptation to give him an early start to his career. Faisal needed an Egyptian boy to explain to him the importance of learning English and why the silly Englishman was so interested in dusty old things buried in the desert.

I also played with geography a bit. While the White Desert, Black Desert, and the Libyan engravings at Qasr al-Zahw all exist, none of them lie on the caravan route between Cairo and Bahariya. I didn't want to miss the chance to put the region's most interesting landmarks in their path.

Another real figure is Heinrich Schäfer. I am glad to say he finally did finish his *Principles of Egyptian Art* which, while a weighty academic tome, is still one of the most thorough introductions to understanding the art of ancient Egypt almost a hundred years after it was written.

Besides Schäfer's *Principles of Egyptian Art,* two other excellent books that helped with researching this novel are *Bahriyah and Farafra* by Ahmed Fakhry and *The Western Desert of Egypt* by Cassandra Vivian, both of which are published by the American University in Cairo Press. Their bookshop just off Tahrir Square is a treasure trove of learning on all aspects of Egyptian history and culture. I also relied on William Edward Lane's classic study, *Manners and Customs of the Modern Egyptians* and the 1929 edition of the *Baedeker's Guide to Egypt and the Sudan.* A more modern guide to the country is the *Blue Guide to Egypt,* now sadly out of print. The 1993 edition has an extra long section on Cairo and proved an invaluable companion on my many rambles through the medieval districts where much of the Cairo action takes place.

The "Golden Mummies" in Bahariya Oasis are real, but they weren't discovered by the fictitious Professor Harrell in 1919. In fact, they were discovered in 1996 when an Antiquities Guard working at the temple of Alexander the Great was walking his donkey in the desert near the temple. Suddenly the donkey's leg disappeared down a hole. After the guard extricated his braying animal, he peeked inside the hole and saw that it was a tomb. The ensuing excavation revealed hundreds of mummies in the styles described in the novel, and the famous Egyptologist Dr. Zahi Hawass estimates the necropolis encompasses four square miles and there may be as many as 10,000 mummies hidden under the desert sands. Excavations are continuing.

The Egyptologists should be careful. They might uncover an ancient underground aqueduct and some canisters of mustard gas.

About the Author

Sean McLachlan worked for ten years as an archaeologist in Israel, Cyprus, Bulgaria, and the United States before becoming a full-time writer. He is the author of numerous fiction and nonfiction books, which are listed on the following pages. When he's not writing, he enjoys hiking, reading, traveling, and, most of all, teaching his son about the world. He divides his time between Madrid, Oxford, and Cairo.

To find out more about Sean's work and travels, visit him at his Amazon page or his blog, and feel free to friend him on Goodreads, Twitter, and Facebook.

You might also enjoy his newsletter, *Sean's Travels and Tales*, which comes out every one or two months. Each issue features a short story, a travel article, a coupon for a free or discounted book, and updates on future projects. You can subscribe using the link below. Your email will not be shared with anyone else.

Amazon: http://www.amazon.com/Sean-McLachlan/e/B001H6MUQI
Goodreads: http://www.goodreads.com/author/show/623273.Sean_McLachlan
Blog: http://midlistwriter.blogspot.com
Twitter: https://twitter.com/@writersean
Facebook: https://www.facebook.com/writersean
Newsletter: http://eepurl.com/bJfiDn

Fiction by Sean McLachlan

Tangier Bank Heist: An Interzone Mystery

Right after the war, Tangier was the craziest town in North Africa. Everything was for sale and the price was cheap. The perverts came for the flesh. The addicts came for the drugs. A whole army of hustlers and grifters came for the loose laws and free flow of cash and contraband.

So why was I here? Because it was the only place that would have me. Besides, it was a great place to be a detective. You got cases like in no other place I'd ever been, and I'd been all over. Cases you couldn't believe ever happened. Like when I had to track down the guy who stole the bank.

No, he didn't rob the bank, he stole it.

Here's how it happened . . .

Available in electronic edition. Print edition coming soon!

Three Passports to Trouble (Interzone Mystery Book 2)

Back in the days when Tangier was an International Zone, the city was full of refugees. People fleeing Stalin. People fleeing Franco. People fleeing the Nuremburg Trials. Tangier offered a safe haven from the chaos of Europe.

The International Council had to keep a delicate balance, tolerating everything from anti-capitalist agitators to Germans with murky pasts. It was the only way to keep the peace, and it worked.

Until an anarchist was found dead with a fascist dagger in his chest.

And I got stuck with the case just when I had to smuggle a couple of Party operatives out of town.

Available in electronic edition. Print edition coming soon!

The Case of the Purloined Pyramid (The Masked Man of Cairo Book One)

An ancient mystery. A modern murder.

Sir Augustus Wall, a horribly mutilated veteran of the Great War, has left Europe behind to open an antiquities shop in Cairo. But Europe's troubles follow him as a priceless inscription is stolen and those who know its secrets start turning up dead. Teaming up with Egyptology expert Moustafa Ghani, and Faisal, an irritating street urchin he just can't shake, Sir Wall must unravel an ancient secret and face his own dark past.

Available in electronic edition and Print edition!

The Case of the Shifting Sarcophagus (The Masked Man of Cairo Book Two)
An Old Kingdom coffin. A body from yesterday.
Sir Augustus Wall had seen a lot of death. From the fields of Flanders to the alleys of Cairo, he'd solved several murders and sent many men to their grave. But he's never had a body delivered to his antiquities shop encased in a 5,000 year-old coffin. Soon he finds himself fighting a vicious street gang bent on causing national mayhem while his assistant, Moustafa Ghani, faces his own enemies in the form of colonial powers determined to ruin him. Throughout all this runs the street urchin Faisal. Ignored as usual, dismissed as usual, he has the most important fight of all.
Available in electronic edition. Print edition coming soon!

Radio Hope (Toxic World Book One)
In a world shattered by war, pollution, and disease...
A gunslinging mother longs to find a safe refuge for her son.
A frustrated revolutionary delivers water to villagers living on a toxic waste dump.
The assistant mayor of humanity's last city hopes he will never have to take command.
One thing gives them the promise of a better future—Radio Hope, a mysterious station that broadcasts vital information about surviving in a blighted world. But when a mad prophet and his army of fanatics march out of the wildlands on a crusade to purify the land with blood and fire, all three will find their lives intertwining, and changing forever.
Available in electronic edition and Print edition!

Refugees from the Righteous Horde (Toxic World Book Two)
When you only have one shot, you better aim true.
In a ravaged world, civilization's last outpost is reeling after fighting off the fanatical warriors of the Righteous Horde. Sheriff Annette Cruz becomes New City's long arm of vengeance as she sets off across the wildlands to take out the cult's leader. All she has is a sniper's rifle with one bullet and a former cultist with his own agenda. Meanwhile, one of the cult's escaped slaves makes a discovery that could tear New City apart...
Refugees from the Righteous Horde continues the Toxic World series started in Radio Hope, an ongoing narrative of humanity's struggle to rebuild the world it ruined.
Available in electronic edition.

We Had Flags (Toxic World Book Three)

A law doesn't work if everyone breaks it.

For forty years, New City has been a bastion of order in a fallen world. One crucial law has maintained the peace: it is illegal to place responsibility for the collapse of civilization on any one group. Anyone found guilty of Blaming is branded and stripped of citizenship.

But when some unwelcome visitors arrive from across the sea, old wounds break open, and no one is safe from Blame.

Available in electronic edition.

Emergency Transmission (Toxic World Book Four)

Trust is the only thing that can save the world.

The problem is, everyone has their own agenda.

When an offshore platform starts emitting toxic fumes that threaten to destroy the last outposts of civilization, the residents of New City have to team up with a foreign freighter to fix it. But a lingering mistrust remains, and neither side has the resources to stop the leak.

That is, until help comes from the least reliable source.

Can old enemies finally set aside their differences for the greater good?

Available in electronic edition.

The Scavenger (A Toxic World Novelette)

In a world shattered by war, pollution, and disease, a lone scavenger discovers a priceless relic from the Old Times.

The problem is, it's stuck in the middle of the worst wasteland he knows—a contaminated city inhabited by insane chem addicts and vengeful villagers. Only his wits, his gun, and an unlikely ally can get him out alive.

Set in the Toxic World series introduced in the novel *Radio Hope*, this 10,000-word story explores more of the dangers and personalities that make up a post-apocalyptic world that's all too possible.

Available in electronic edition.

Trench Raiders (Trench Raiders Book One)

September 1914: The British Expeditionary Force has the Germans on the run, or so they think.

After a month of bitter fighting, the British are battered, exhausted, and down to half their strength, yet they've helped save Paris and are pushing towards Berlin. Then the retreating Germans decide to make a stand. Holding a steep slope beside the River Aisne, the entrenched Germans mow down the advancing British with machine gun fire. Soon the British dig in too, and it looks like the war might grind down into deadly stalemate.

Searching through No-Man's Land in the darkness, Private Timothy Crawford of the Oxfordshire and Buckinghamshire Light Infantry finds a chink in the German armor. But can this lowly private, who spends as much time in the battalion guardhouse as he does on the parade ground, convince his commanding officer to risk everything for a chance to break through?

Available in electronic edition.

Digging In (Trench Raiders Book Two)

October 1914: The British line is about to break.

After two months of hard fighting, the British Expeditionary Force is short of men, ammunition, and ideas. With their line stretched to the breaking point, aerial reconnaissance spots German reinforcements massing for the big push. As their trenches are hammered by a German artillery battery, the men of the Oxfordshire and Buckinghamshire Light Infantry come up with a desperate plan—a daring raid behind enemy lines to destroy the enemy guns and give the British a chance to stop the German army from breaking through.

Available in electronic edition.

No Man's Land (Trench Raiders Book Three)

No Man's Land—a hellscape of shell craters and dead bodies. Soldiers have fought over it, charged across it, and bled on it for a year of grueling war, but neither side has dominated it.

Until now.

An elite German raiding party is passing through No Man's Land every night, attacking the British trenches at will. The Oxfordshire and Buckinghamshire Light Infantry need to reassert control over their front lines.

So the exhausted men of Company E decide to set a trap, a nighttime ambush in the middle of No Man's Land, where any mistake can be fatal. But the few surviving veterans are leading recruits who have only been in the trenches for two weeks. Mistakes are inevitable.

Available in electronic edition.

Christmas Truce

Christmas 1914

In the cold, muddy trenches of the Western Front, there is a strange silence. As the members of a crack English trench raiding team enjoy their first day of peace in months, they call out holiday greetings to the men on the German line. Soon both sides are fraternizing in No Man's Land.

But when the English recognize some enemy raiders who only a few days before launched a deadly attack on their position, can they keep the peace through the Christmas truce?

Available in electronic edition.

Warpath into Sonora

Arizona 1846

Nantan, a young Apache warrior, is building a name for himself by leading raids against Mexican ranches to impress his war chief, and the chief's lovely daughter. But there is one thing he and all other Apaches fear—a ruthless band of Mexican scalp hunters who slaughter entire villages.

Nantan and his friends have sworn to fight back, but they are inexperienced, and led by a war chief driven mad with a thirst for revenge. Can they track their tribe's worst enemy into unknown territory and defeat them?

Available in electronic edition.

A Fine Likeness (House Divided Book One)

A Confederate guerrilla and a Union captain discover there's something more dangerous in the woods than each other.

Jimmy Rawlins is a teenage bushwhacker who leads his friends on ambushes of Union patrols. They join infamous guerrilla leader Bloody Bill Anderson on a raid through Missouri, but Jimmy questions his commitment to the cause when he discovers this madman plans to sacrifice a Union prisoner in a hellish ritual to raise the Confederate dead.

Richard Addison is an aging captain of a lackluster Union militia. Depressed over his son's death in battle, a glimpse of Jimmy changes his life. Jimmy and his son look so much alike that Addison becomes obsessed with saving him from Bloody Bill. Captain Addison must wreck his reputation to win this war within a war, while Jimmy must decide whether to betray the Confederacy to stop the evil arising in the woods of Missouri.

Available in electronic edition and Print edition!

The River of Desperation (House Divided Book Two)

In the waning days of the Civil War, a secret conflict still rages…

Lieutenant Allen Addison of the *USS Essex* is looking forward to the South's defeat so he can build the life he's always wanted. Love and a promising business await him in St. Louis, but he is swept up in a primeval war between the forces of Order and Chaos, a struggle he doesn't understand and can barely believe in. Soon he is fighting to keep a grip on his sanity as he tries to save St. Louis from destruction. The long-awaited sequel to *A Fine Likeness* continues the story of two opposing forces that threaten to tear the world apart.

Available in electronic edition.

The Last Hotel Room

He came to Tangier to die, but life isn't done with him yet.

Tom Miller has lost his job, his wife, and his dreams. Broke and alone, he ends up in a flophouse in Morocco, ready to end it all. But soon he finds himself tangled in a web of danger and duty as he's pulled into scamming tourists for a crooked cop while trying to help a Syrian refugee boy survive life on the streets. Can a lifelong loser do something good for a change?

A portion of my royalties will go to a charity for Syrian refugees.

Available in electronic edition and Print edition!

The Night the Nazis Came to Dinner and Other Dark Tales

A spectral dinner party goes horribly wrong...

An immortal warrior hopes a final battle will set him free...

A big-game hunter preys on endangered species to supply an illicit restaurant...

A new technology soothes First World guilt...

Here are four dark tales that straddle the boundary between reality and speculation. You better hope they don't come true.

Available in electronic edition.

The Quintessence of Absence

Can a drug-addicted sorcerer sober up long enough to save a kidnapped girl and his own duchy?

In an alternate eighteenth-century Germany where magic is real and paganism never died, Lothar is in the bonds of nepenthe, a powerful drug that gives him ecstatic visions. It has also taken his job, his friends, and his self-respect. Now his old employer has rehired Lothar to find the man's daughter, who is in the grip of her own addiction to nepenthe.

As Lothar digs deeper into the girl's disappearance, he uncovers a plot that threatens the entire Duchy of Anhalt, and finds that the only way to stop it is to face his own weakness.

Available in electronic edition.

Writing Books by Sean McLachlan

Writing Secrets of the World's Most Prolific Authors

What does it take to write 100 books? What about 500? Or 1,000?

That may sound like an impossibly high number, but it isn't. Some of the world's most successful authors wrote hundreds of books over the course of highly lucrative careers. Isaac Asimov wrote more than 300 books. Enid Blyton wrote more than 800. Legendary Western writer Lauren Bosworth Paine wrote close to 1,000.

Some wrote even more.

This book examines the techniques and daily habits of more than a dozen of these remarkable writers to show how anyone with the right mindset can massively increase their word count without sacrificing quality. Learn the secrets of working on several projects simultaneously, of reducing the time needed for each book, and how to build the work ethic you need to become more prolific than you ever thought possible.

Available in electronic edition and Print edition!

History Books by Sean McLachlan

Wild West History

Apache Warrior vs. US Cavalryman: 1846-86 (Osprey: 2016)

Tombstone—Wyatt Earp, the O.K. Corral, and the Vendetta Ride (Osprey: 2013)

The Last Ride of the James-Younger Gang (Osprey: 2012)

Civil War History

Ride Around Missouri: Shelby's Great Raid 1863 (Osprey: 2011)

American Civil War Guerrilla Tactics (Osprey: 2009)

Missouri History

Outlaw Tales of Missouri (Globe Pequot: 2009)

Missouri: An Illustrated History (Hippocrene: 2008)

It Happened in Missouri (Globe Pequot: 2007)

Medieval History

Medieval Handgonnes: The First Black Powder Infantry Weapons (Osprey: 2010)

Byzantium: An Illustrated History (Hippocrene: 2004)

African History

Armies of the Adowa Campaign 1896: The Italian Disaster in Ethiopia (Osprey: 2011)

Purchase copies of any of these titles here:

http://www.amazon.com/Sean-McLachlan/e/B001H6MUQI

Made in the USA
Middletown, DE
09 August 2023